HER MAJESTY'S ROYAL COVEN

Also by Juno Dawson

FICTION
Margot & Me
All of the Above
Under My Skin
Say Her Name
Cruel Summer
Hollow Pike
Clean
Meat Market
Wonderland
Stay Another Day
Grave Matter

NON-FICTION
The Gender Games
Mind Your Head
This Book is Gay
Being a Boy
What is Gender? How Does it Define Us?
What's the T?

HER MAJESTY'S ROYAL COVEN

JUNO DAWSON

HARPER
Voyager

Harper*Voyager*
An imprint of HarperCollins*Publishers* Ltd
1 London Bridge Street
London SE1 9GF

www.harpercollins.co.uk

HarperCollins*Publishers*
1st Floor, Watermarque Building, Ringsend Road
Dublin 4, Ireland

First published by HarperCollins*Publishers* Ltd 2022
1

A catalogue record for this book is available from the British Library

ISBN: 978-0-00-847850-6 (HB)
ISBN: 978-0-00-847851-3 (TPB)

Typeset in Sabon LT Std by
Palimpsest Book Production Ltd, Falkirk, Stirlingshire

Printed and bound in the UK using 100% Renewable Electricity
at CPI Group (UK) Ltd

MIX
Paper from
responsible sources
FSC
www.fsc.org   FSC C007454

This book is produced from independently certified FSC™ paper
to ensure responsible forest management.

For more information visit: www.harpercollins.co.uk/green

Dedicated to *my* coven,
the 'Adult Lady Helpline'

Evil spirits observe silly young girls who are more given to curiosity, and so more easily led astray by elderly workers of harmful magic.

The Malleus Maleficarum, 1486

I agree with whoever said [the Spice Girls] are soft porn. They're the antichrist.

Thom Yorke of Radiohead, 1997

Places of
Supernormal Interest

Callanish Stones

St. Magnus Cathedral

The Spirits of Glencoe

Iona Abbey

The Devil's Pulpit

Fife

EDINBURGH

The Wigtown Martyrs

Islandmagee Trials

Carrickfergus Trials

The Pendle Trials

Malham Cove

HEBDEN BRIDGE

MANCHESTER

Druid's Circle

Stonehenge

Hampton Court, Home to Boleyn

LONDON

Wookey Hole

The Witchfinder General

Boscastle

WELCOME TO
HEBDEN BRIDGE

Hardcastle Craggs National Trust Estate

Niamh's Cottage

HEPTONSTALL

Very Steep Hill!

Old Packhorse Bridge

HEBDEN BRIDGE

The Picture House & Baptist Church

The Tea Cozy

25 YEARS EARLIER . . .

The night before the summer solstice, five girls hid in a treehouse. The shack, much too nice to call a shack, was sturdy enough, cradled in the arthritic branches of a three-hundred-year-old oak. Below, in Vance Hall, preparations for tomorrow's festivities were finalised. It was more an excuse for the grown-ups to fetch up the dustier wines from the cellar two days in a row than it was a planning meeting. Their elders, quite some way past tipsy, truthfully hadn't noticed the girls were absent.

Up in the tree, the youngest of the girls, Leonie, was upset because the eldest, Helena, said she couldn't marry Stephen Gately from Boyzone. 'I'm not playing,' Leonie said.

A congregation of candles burned in the treehouse window, wax trickling off the ledge into lumpy stalactites. Skittish amber light danced up the walls, casting campfire shadows across Leonie's face. 'Why does Elle always get to pick first?'

Elle's bottom lip quivered, her baby blue eyes filling with tears. Again. *That* was why Elle always got to pick first.

She really could turn the waterworks off and on at will.

'I think they can both marry Stephen,' Niamh Kelly said, ever the peacemaker.

'No they can't!' her twin sister said at the top of her voice. 'How's that going to work?'

Niamh scowled at her. 'I don't think we're actually going to marry Boyzone, do you, Ciara? We're ten!'

Helena said with authority, 'When Elle is twenty, he'll be thirty, so that's OK.'

Leonie stood as if to leave the treehouse, her fists balled tight.

'Oh, if you're going to storm off like a kid, fine!' said Helena. 'You can both have Stephen. Poor Keith.'

Leonie nudged the trapdoor with her toe. 'It's not even that, Helena. It's just a game. It's stupid. Anyway, I said I'm gonna marry the Fresh Prince, so it don't even matter.'

There was a moment of hush because they all knew what was really troubling her, for it troubled them all. The candles sputtered and there was a drunken hoot of adult laughter from inside the house. 'I don't wanna do tomorrow.' Leonie said what she meant at last. She returned to the carpet and sat cross-legged. 'My dad don't want me to do it. He says it's *evil.*'

'Your dad is an eejit,' Ciara bellowed.

Niamh, the elder of the Kelly twins by three-and-a-half minutes said, 'In Ireland, we're considered lucky.'

'Is he saying my grandma is evil?' Elle added. 'She's, like, the nicest person in the whole world!'

It was harder for Leonie; the first in her line, at least in living memory, to exhibit the traits. How could Helena hope to understand? Her mother, her mother's mother and all the Vance mothers before that had been blessed too. 'Leonie,' Helena said with the absolute certainty only a bossy thirteen-year-old could possess. 'Tomorrow is easy peasy, just like an assembly at school. We'll line up, swear the oath, Julia Collins will bless you, and that's all. Nothing *actually* changes.'

She really emphasised the *ak-shully*, but they all knew, in the honesty of their hearts, that it was a lie. There were so few of them left now, fewer with every generation. This life, this oath, wasn't like when Ciara cut her fringe with a pair of nail scissors. That soon grew out, but there was no turning back from tomorrow. The bell had sounded, and playtime was over. Leonie was only nine.

'I'm nervous too,' Elle offered, taking Leonie's hand.

'Me too,' said Niamh who then turned to her sister.

'I suppose,' Ciara agreed reluctantly.

Helena brought one of the candles into the centre of the filthy old rug. 'Here, form a circle,' she said. 'Let's practise the oath.'

'Ach, do we have to?' Ciara groaned but Helena shushed her. She wasn't intimidated by the twins, no matter how much the elders swooned over their potential.

'If we know it off by heart, there's nothing to be nervous about, is there?'

Niamh understood this would help Leonie and chastised her sister. The girls gathered around the candle and joined hands. It's hard to say how much was in their minds, but the girls would all later swear they felt a current flowing through their human circuit, sharing and amplifying their own latent gifts.

'All together,' Helena said, and they launched into it.

> *To the mother I swear*
> *To solemnly uphold the sacred sisterhood*
> *Her power is mine to wield*

> *The secret ours to keep*
> *The earth ours to protect*
> *An enemy of my sister is mine*
> *The strength is divine*
> *Our bond everlasting*
> *Let no man tear us asunder*
> *The coven is sovereign*
> *Until my dying breath.*

And they all knew it off by heart. Every single word.

The following night, they were allowed to wear their midnight-black velvet capes for the first time. They smelled brand new, of the plastic they came wrapped in. Too long (*you'll grow into them*), they lifted them up to stop the hems trailing along the undergrowth as they climbed Pendle Hill.

The procession snaked uphill into the heart of the thick forest that smothered the valley like a fur. They each carried a lantern jar to light the way, but the uneven path was a real ankle-snapper by night. Eventually, charcoal trees parted to reveal a moonlit clearing, a flat boulder at its centre. There was power in this place, any fool could feel it.

It was scary for the girls, of course, to be surrounded by all the elders. A hundred of them, faces half-hidden by their hoods. Scarier still to watch each of them, in turn, approach the stone slab to leave their offering. They pricked their thumbs with a silver blade and deposited a tiny red pearl of blood into the yew tree cauldron. Julia Collins, her matronly face peering out from under her cowl, summoned the girls one at a time. They drank from the chalice until their eyes turned black and, when that happened, she dipped her finger into the yew bowl and drew the mark of the pentagram on their young foreheads.

And as the clock dolefully struck one in the village far in the distance, they stopped being girls, and finally became witches.

HER MAJESTY'S ROYAL COVEN
COV.UK

Hello, and thank you for expressing an interest in HER
MAJESTY'S ROYAL COVEN. This is our online home on
the Darker Web™.

My name is Helena Vance, and I'm the serving High Priestess of
HMRC. It is my great honour to lead the United Kingdom's largest,
and only, coven affiliated with the global One Coven Alliance™.

Through joining HMRC, you can become a part of an illustrious
witching legacy stretching back to our founding sister, Anne Boleyn.
We serve Gaia through service to the planet, the country, the
monarch, and the people. We work as a team to support the UK
Government in the handling of supernormal events and incidences,
to uphold the tradition of witchcraft in the United Kingdom, and
to safeguard our continued legacy.

HMRC is a place for women and girls to reach their full potential,
develop their gifts, and enjoy the protection and sisterhood that only
an official coven can provide.

Click here to launch your application. Under 16s require parental
permission.

Helena Vance,
High Priestess

Chapter One

HIGHER SCIENCE

Niamh

In her dreams, Conrad was still alive.

They were banal, domestic little scenes: she could still smell whatever dinner he'd cooked, and she'd be washing the dishes when he'd slide his arms around her waist. She'd feel the brush of his lips against the nape of her neck, *The Archers* low in the background. The oddest fragments returned to her: Sunday morning toast crumbs in bed coming back to haunt them on Sunday night; leaning over him to look out of the plane window as they were coming in to land at Dublin; walking the dog through Hardcastle Crags on a lazy Saturday afternoon – *that* smell of damp mulch and wild garlic.

Other times she'd simply dream she was listening to him breathe. He always fell asleep the second his head touched the pillow, like he had narcolepsy or something, and so Niamh, a fitful sleeper at best, would often fixate on his peaceful tide to quiet her chatty brain.

Awaking now, she reached for him, only to feel the cold side of the bed.

It was like pressing a thumb on a bruise every single time.

Why am I awake?

Her phone. Her phone was ringing. She remembered she was on call. Shite.

She kicked off the duvet and pushed a nest of auburn hair out of her face. Her phone vibrated on the nightstand, the display reading BARKER FARM. It was 00.53. Still the Witching Hour, she thought ruefully. A common misconception; any hour's grand for witching.

Niamh cleared her throat. She always thought it seemed unprofessional to sound like she'd been sleeping while on call, although it was rare for someone to phone this late.

'Hello? Mrs Barker?'

'Oh hello, Dr Kelly,' Joan said in her best telephone voice. 'I do hope I didn't wake you?'

'Not at all,' Niamh lied. 'Are you OK out there?'

'It's Pepper again . . .' No further explanation was necessary. The horse was old. Old and tired.

'I'll be right over in ten,' Niamh said.

She threw on whatever mismatched clothes were piled on the back of her dresser chair, and pulled her hair into a ponytail. Tiger barely stirred from his basket as she tiptoed through the kitchen, offering only a nasal *huff* to express his irritation at being awakened. The Border Terrier was quite used to her nocturnal comings and goings.

It was a cold night for late March, not quite cold enough for a frost, but not far off either. A shame, she'd hoped to file winter away for another year. She wrapped a scarf – a gift knitted for her by one of her clients – around her neck as she walked. Niamh reached her Land Rover and, checking in the rear-view mirror, pressed her eyes with the pads of her thumbs, trying to look less bleary. It didn't entirely work, needless to say.

The Barker farm was only a short drive away, on the other side of Hebden Bridge. Niamh knew the route in her sleep, but thought it best to play the radio real loudly, just in case. The road from Heptonstall village towards Hebden Bridge town, in the gutter of the valley, was winding and perilously steep, slick with earlier rain. She drove carefully, windows open wide to wake herself up.

Normally bustling, Hebden Bridge was almost eerily quiet. The pubs, bars and restaurants had kicked out hours ago and Market Street was dark. Niamh drove until the cottages and old mills opened out into the dark sprawl of Cragg Vale. On the horizon, the farmhouse was the last light for miles.

The gates were open, ready, and she swung the Land Rover down the bumpy dirt track towards the riding school. Joan Barker was waiting, a wax jacket over her flannel pyjamas, tartan legs tucked into her wellies. Niamh turned off the engine and stepped out of the car, dragging her kit bag off the passenger seat as she went. 'How's she doing, Joan?'

'Oh, Dr Kelly, she's not in a good way.'

A familiar dread in her stomach. 'Let's go take a look shall we?'

As soon as they were in the stable, Niamh didn't need to use any arcane skills to see Pepper was in a bad way. 'Oh dear,' Niamh said, kneeling alongside the old Cleveland that rested in the hay, her breathing shallow.

'Do you need anything, doctor?' Joan asked.

It might be best if Joan was out of the way for a moment or two. If she saw what was about to happen, Niamh would find it very difficult to explain. 'I've everything I need for Pepper, but you've not got a black coffee for me have you? It's some ways past my bedtime.'

'Of course. I'll be back in two shakes.' Joan turned on her heel to head back to the farmhouse. It's true what they say about Yorkshire folks: they'd do anything for you and the kettle is never cold.

When the coast was clear, Niamh placed her hands on Pepper's flank. 'Oh, my poor sweet girl.'

With animals, it wasn't that she could *hear* whole thoughts in the way she could with humans. Thoughts, like light and sound, travel in waves, and she was able to tune in to a frequency if the mood took her fancy, but animals communicate on a pure emotional level. Right now, Niamh could feel mournful weariness, sheer exhaustion, coming from Pepper. In short, she'd had enough. It was like looking in a mirror and recognising it on your face, rather than hearing it.

Niamh was a far better sentient than she was a healer. She could locate a problem, feel the angry reds in an animal's body, but wasn't gifted enough to make it go away entirely by herself the way a healer would. She could absorb *some* of the pain though, soothe the poor thing.

Niamh sent her thoughts clear into the horse's mind. *You're hanging on so hard, aren't you? Just let go, my girl, you can go now. Rest. You've done ever so well, and been ever so good.*

From Pepper, there was a last stubborn push, and a twitch of her hind legs. She whinnied softly. Niamh understood. Pepper didn't want to let her mistress down.

Oh, you aren't. Joan loves you and doesn't want you suffering, now, does she? Lean back into it and drift away, old girl. There's nothing left to do here, and Joan is made of stern stuff. She'll be overcome at first, but then there'll only be love.

And with that, from Pepper, she felt blessed relief. Like she'd been given permission. 'I can help you go,' Niamh said aloud. She reached into her kit and produced a vial of *Eternal Repose*: a tincture of valerian and hemlock Annie had taught her to make not long after she graduated. Pepper was in pain, this would ease her off. It'd be like falling asleep with the heating on. She unscrewed the cap of the little brown bottle. *Open wide*, she told Pepper and the horse obliged. Niamh placed a couple of drops on her tongue. 'There you go, sweet girl.' Niamh rested her head against Pepper's and almost heard her gratitude, so strong it was.

Joan came back into the stables carrying a steaming mug of coffee. 'How is she, doctor?'

Niamh stood and took the drink from her. The worst part. 'She's dying, Mrs Barker. I'm so sorry. This'll be her last night.'

Her lip wobbled. 'There's nothing you can do?'

'I've made her comfortable, she won't feel any pain.' Niamh wrapped an arm around her and steered her into Pepper's bay. 'Here, let's be with her as she falls asleep. She knows we're here.'

Niamh and the farmer knelt at Pepper's side as her breath ebbed out like low tide was coming.

Chapter Two

THE STING

Helena

The ceiling had more holes in it than a colander. Their vantage point, a derelict warehouse, was bitterly cold, and Helena had been standing on a crust of pigeon shit since dawn. She didn't complain. That wouldn't do at all in front of the others. She had to lead by example, and didn't tolerate whiners.

She had to be so mindful, in an organisation made up almost entirely of women, to snuff out little fires of dissent before they sent smoke signals to the warlocks or, worse, the government. That meant no gossip; no bitching and definitely no whining. Her Majesty's Royal Coven was strong, impenetrable and united.

Helena frequently referred back to Eva Kovacic's keynote speech at CovCon 18: she spoke so eloquently of how the patriarchy, above all else, fears women coming together, so internal female division only succeeds in greasing that machine. Helena had adopted it as a personal mantra since.

She raised the binoculars to her face. The street outside was quiet, rush hour petering out. The odd straggler, now late for the office, hurried past the redbrick safehouse, latte in hand, but that was about it. Helena turned to Sandhya and – following her own credo – kept her irritation at bay. 'Do we have *anything*?'

Sandhya lifted her fingers to her temple and wordlessly spoke to the sentients waiting outside in the van. 'Nothing yet, ma'am.'

Bird shit landed about a centimetre in front of Helena's Prada loafers. She felt it whizz past her nose and took a step back. The pigeons in the rafters cooed, mocking her. 'For Gaia's sake,' she snapped, turning on Emma, the young oracle on her team. Emma, has the intelligence changed?'

'No ma'am. He will come today. We have seen it.' Like many of the younger oracles, she made no attempt to hide her baldness with a wig, wearing it as a badge of pride. All well and good, but where was he?

'Did you happen to see a *time* at all? Could I bob out for a croissant?'

'Ma'am,' Sandhya interrupted. 'We might have something. Someone on the street is using a glamour.'

Peasant magic, thought Helena. Had he stooped so low? That meant he knew he was being surveilled too, if he went to the effort to disguise himself. 'Can the sentients tell who?' She looked again into her binoculars. On the street opposite the old chocolate factory, it was a perfectly normal day in Manchester. Helena saw a woman with a pram, a couple of older women with overflowing grocery bags, a man who wore the tell-tale salmon-pink tie and shiny suit of a letting agent, and some Chinese students most likely on their way to their first lecture of the day. They were only a few streets away from Manchester Met.

'They're working on it,' Sandhya said, touching her temple again. Helena wished she wouldn't do that, it was most annoying, and sentients didn't need to poke their faces to relay messages. She was only doing it to signal to *her* that she was working, but it only succeeded in making her assistant look like she had an oncoming migraine.

Helena looked down to the street again. One of the students – a young man with bleached hair – hung back a little from his group, playing on his phone. He looked like tween fodder from the K-Pop bands her daughter liked. Was he with the group? Or trying to get lost in a crowd?

The boy dallied, looking directly at the nondescript townhouse they were guarding that morning. After a moment, he looked over his shoulder and then back at the safehouse. He was *not* with the others.

'That's him,' Helena said, throwing the binoculars to one of her aides. Sometimes you don't need to be psychic, you just need to be observant. 'The kid with bleached hair. Mobilise and cloak the whole street.'

Flexing her fingers, Helena surged the air in the room forwards, blasting the final remaining shards of glass out of the skeletal window frames. She swelled an air cushion underfoot, letting it lift her up and carry her out of the exit she'd created. She was *not* letting Travis Smythe get away again. She'd waited a long time for this little reckoning.

Her heart raced, almost giddy.

No. She had to put personal vendettas aside. Unprofessional.

As she plummeted towards street level, her overcoat billowing, she saw her team leap out of their fake DPD van and sprint towards the mark. She was right. As soon as Smythe saw what was happening, he let the glamour go, reverting to his usual appearance: lithe and lanky, with dreadlocks almost to his waist.

He clocked the intercept team first and, with a flick of

his wrist, tossed a parked car at three of her witches. It barrelled through the air towards them. He'd grown more powerful since the war. Luckily, Jen Yamato's telekinesis was *more* powerful, and she caught the vehicle mid-air with her mind before it hit them. She held the car, a Fiesta, aloft, so that Robyn and Clare could duck and roll under it. Again using his powers, Smythe knocked Clare clean off her feet, slamming her against the steps of the safe-house. She landed with a pained cry.

Behind him, a little further down the road, Helena landed gracefully. Stray pedestrians strolled by, blind to what was happening. Sandhya's cloaking spell was evidently working. They weren't technically *invisible*, but mundanes wouldn't see them either. Sandhya, high above them, was implanting a very simple instruction in their minds over and over: *nothing to see here.* 'Give it up, Smythe,' she barked. 'We have you surrounded. You're done.'

At the same time, she channelled as much wind as she could. Soon, an icy gale tore down Bombay Street. 'Fuck you, Vance!' Smythe screamed against the wind, staggering backwards.

'Why would you come here? Right under our noses?' Helena expertly manipulated her field, charging the ions in the air. A storm brewed at her fingertips.

Smythe snatched the car out of Jen's grasp and hurled it overhead in an arc towards Helena. She discharged her self-made lightning, a hundred million volts streaming from her hands into the sad little Fiesta. It exploded around her, but she felt nothing. She cooled the air around her to freezing, creating a safe cocoon for herself. Stepping through the fire as if it were nothing, she saw Smythe wince. She'd grown more powerful since the war too.

He went to make a run for it, but Robyn intervened.

'Stay where you are,' she stated calmly, and he froze like his feet were superglued to the tarmac. She was a Level 4 sentient and he was only a man.

'Get out of my head, you cunt,' Smythe snarled.

'I don't like that word,' Helena said, reaching his side. She charged the air around her again, just in case. Robyn couldn't hold another sentient for very long, even a male one. 'Why *did* you come back, Travis? You could have laid low in Italy for the rest of your pathetic life.' Bologna was getting quite the reputation as a hotbed of dissidence, a focal point for the growing unrest across Europe.

Every decade or so, a witch or – as was more likely the case – a warlock had the bright idea of rising up against their mundane oppressors as if they were the first to conceive the notion. Helena checked herself. Was she still meant to call mundanes HOLA? *Humans of Limited Ability*. She recalled Snow telling her that acronym was now distinctly un-PC. Mundanes have lots of abilities, after all, albeit not very interesting ones.

The coven was aware of pockets of simmering discontent in Eastern Europe, Russia, but no one was in a hurry to repeat Dabney Hale's civil war. And now she had Hale's most vicious accomplice in custody. Let that send a message to anyone who thought about rocking the boat. Smythe had so much witch blood on his hands. He deserved the Pipes for what he did.

'I'm waiting,' Helena hissed, blue electric cracking between her fingers.

'You know why I came . . .'

She cast a pointed glance towards the safehouse. 'Her?'

'Her.'

Helena laughed. She couldn't help herself. 'Fool. Do you think she'd have done the same?'

18

Smythe's amber eyes seethed, burning with hatred. He was about to reply, but Helena reached into her coat pocket and blew some *Sandman* into his face. On reflection, there wasn't anything he could say that she wanted to hear. He breathed the pink powder in and, a second later, his eyes rolled back into his head. Robyn released him and he slumped to the ground.

She was quietly impressed with her restraint. It would be fair and just to set him alight for what he'd done. Hale had given the orders, but Smythe – and others like him – had willingly carried them out.

Instead, Helena checked on poor Clare, who'd taken quite the hit. Her colleague picked herself up out of the gutter, dignity dented more than her body. Satisfied she was fine, Helena issued the sub-team instructions: 'Secure him, get clean-up in, and trace the owner of the vehicle for reimbursement.' She nodded at the townhouse. 'I'm going to check in on Sleeping Beauty, and then I think I'm overdue a visit to Hebden Bridge . . .'

With a flick of her fingers, Jen lifted Smythe's limp fish of a body, floating it towards the van. Helena covered her face against the thick smoke billowing from the wreckage. She held both her hands over the fire and it was extinguished in a heartbeat.

Travis Smythe in chains before 10 a.m. Any other week and this would be cause for great celebration, but alas, that rodent was the least of her troubles.

As High Priestess there had never been a problem she couldn't fix. If her job mostly consisted of spinning plates, she'd kept hundreds of them aloft for years, but this was something new and worrying and she hated, truly loathed, to admit it but she needed help. She needed Niamh.

Chapter Three

THE OTHER COVEN

Leonie

Rise and shine, my love.

Chinara's words found their way into the deepest strata of Leonie's slumber. She'd been having the most wonderful dream too: a girls' holiday to Jamaica with Rihanna. The absolute contentment of a solid eight hours but, on waking, it slipped through her fingers. Gone, dust on a dry wind. How frustrating.

Coming to with a groan, Leonie stretched out diagonally across the big bed and reluctantly joined the morning. Heavenly white light filtered through the Venetian blinds, the day full of spring promise. Stylistically, they were trying the whole minimal thing: white bed linen, stripped white floors, white orchids, white everything. So far, it was really fucking hard to keep clean and tidy.

Chinara knelt atop the duvet and leaned in for a kiss. 'Wakey, wakey, sleepyhead.'

'What time is it?'

'Late. I've already been to the gym.'

'Of course you have.' Leonie sat up and pulled off her

bonnet, freeing her hair. She can't have been *that* drunk last night if she'd remembered to stick it on. She looked at the clock; it was only nine thirty. *Late?* Aren't witches supposed to be nocturnal? Her tongue felt like carpet.

'Good night?' Chinara asked, wriggling effortlessly out of her sports bra – a feat Leonie could never pull off. Her girlfriend's body was *fit*, tight as a drum, her skin glistened with sweat beads. Something growled in Leonie's tummy and she honestly couldn't say if she was horny or hungry or nauseous.

'Drag-queen bingo and then tequila shots in Brixton.' She felt that was all the explanation necessary. There was definitely going to be a headache situation any minute now. Chinara subscribed to the kale smoothie, paleo, *my body is a temple* school of thought, and rarely drank, but didn't care (much) that Leonie did.

'Coffee, babe?'

'Yes.' And then she remembered her date. 'Oh no, wait. I'm meeting my brother. Shit. In like an hour. Fuck.'

Chinara frowned. 'Radley's in London?'

Leonie consciously tried to sweep the fog from her brain. Booze massively dulled her gift, she ought to rein it in a bit. 'Yeah. Some boring warlock shit. Babe, do you think you could bring the shower to me?' She was kidding, but didn't doubt she probably *could* divert the water from the bathroom if motivated.

With a gentle wave, Chinara manipulated the air around her, lifting Leonie clean off the mattress. 'There, you're up. Better?'

Leonie laughed, feeling wholly safe in her hold. 'That's cheating.'

Chinara floated her, light as a feather, across the bedroom and into her arms. They kissed tenderly, although

Leonie dreaded to think what her breath was like: shitty cat litter or something. That reminded her – the cat needed her fucking worming pills. She needed to hire a new assistant badly. Her last one had 'gone travelling', the selfish cunt.

'Get that sexy ass in the shower.' Chinara slapped her on the bum. Leonie was out the bedroom door when her girlfriend called back. 'Oh Lee – you might wanna check the Diaspora group chat.'

She looked back. 'What is it?'

'Bri says there's something going down in HMRC.'

Bri's visions were flawless. Leonie's hangover, a little fucking sleep paralysis goblin squatting on her brain, didn't need that shit. 'What?'

Chinara shook her head. 'Something big.'

FUCK HMRC.

Chinara chuckled, hearing her loud and clear.

Sabrina – Bri – wasn't forthcoming. Leonie messaged her from the 68 bus, all the while covering her nose to block out some commuter's rancid B.O. Or maybe the bus itself just honked of bin juice. Hard to say with London buses. She rolled a ciggie in her lap, willing the traffic to hurry up.

Bri, it turned out, sensed the oracles up at HMRC in Manchester getting their knickers in a twist. That was nothing new. That was why Leonie liked working with a lone oracle here in London. The girls at HMRC, they riled each other up, battery hens clucking at nothing. There was a prophecy every other week. Leonie was inclined to think that yes – the world is blatantly fucked – you don't need twenty oracles to tell you that, Sugar Tits.

Radley was waiting outside Brockwell Park Lido when

her bus pulled up. The pool had just reopened for the season and a few swimmers were brave enough to take a dip. 'Sorry I'm late,' she said, making a show of running the last few metres to greet him.

'It's OK,' he said, almost smiling. 'I always tell you to arrive fifteen minutes before I want you to.'

'Shade,' Leonie said, hugging her little brother, which was a joke given he towered over her. 'Radley . . . are you going grey?' She poked at a few silver wires in his neat beard.

He slapped her hand away. 'Thank you for pointing that out. Nice to see you too.'

She laughed, the cigarette pinched between her lips. Gods, he was so square, so stiff, like he'd left all the cardboard in his shirt before he put it on. How were they from the same gene pool, honestly? 'Come on, I need a coffee or I'm gonna be that messy bitch puking over a bin on the street.'

They strolled through the park – peak bluebell season, which was a banging coincidence – to the Brockwell Hall café, got coffees and then carried on down to the pond to feed the ducks. A baggy of birdfeed for 50p. Bargain.

They dawdled on mundane family gossip: their Auntie Louisa was now in full remission, which was good (although she did treat their mum like a doormat), and their Cousin Nick was looking at jail time for insurance fraud. Riveting stuff. Their mother was one of five Bajan siblings, so there was always plenty of material to work with. All the news, of course, came via their mum, happily ensconced in her flat in Leeds. Chapel Allerton – the 'Notting Hill of the North' according to estate agents – was all cute coffee shops and organic grocers, a far cry from the estate they'd grown up on.

Both of the Jackman children had inherited their work ethic from their mother. To get off that estate she'd cleaned offices, taken on sewing, and been a childminder until she'd landed on her feet with a nine-to-five admin job at the Yorkshire Bank. She worked there still, waiting for retirement or redundancy, whichever came first.

Esther Jackman didn't pretend to understand their *lifestyle*, as she called it, but always asked after their respective covens.

As they walked, neither of them mentioned their dad. Why would they? He was barely even a memory any more. He'd be lucky if he got a fucking footnote in her memoir, frankly.

Leonie watched a mallard dive to the bottom of the pond, its rear flashing white. She found it hysterically funny. Gods, she really must be hungover. Vanilla sun filtered through the leaves, making the algae-thick water the colour of mushy peas somehow. She and Rad sat side by side on a bench, comfortably silent as he checked his emails. 'Sorry,' he said. 'Work stuff.'

She decided to take the bait. 'Go on then. How's the cabal?'

'Officially, all cabal matters are classified, but informally, very well thank you.'

Leonie pulled a face. 'Gods, you sound like a proper Tory, man.'

'On the contrary, the Warlocks' Cabal is fully bipartisan.'

'Oh lighten up!' she laughed. 'It's me. And I'm not wearing a fucking wire.'

Somehow, he managed to sit up even straighter. 'Would you be at liberty to tell me about your little coven?'

Why couldn't he just be a brother? Didn't he ever take a day off? 'Yes! I will literally tell you anything you want to know! You know what, this is why people are done with your bullshit, Rad. You *and* HMRC. It's all so cloak and dagger all the time. Literally! Like why? What's the point? Also, baby brother, kindly fucking refrain from calling my life's work a *little coven*. Misogynoir; look it up.'

He grinned, sly. 'Well that touched a nerve.'

She took a moment to sulk. A coven should be a community, not a haughty members club. There was no need for all the bells and whistles, those cloaks and daggers.

'I'm sorry.' He backed down. 'What you've done with Diaspora is hugely impressive. Everyone thinks so.'

'Oh, I know,' Leonie returned with a mischievous smile. 'You could join, you know? Unlike *some* organisations I don't care to name, we are fully inclusive of both witches *and* warlocks of colour.'

'Leonie . . .'

She swivelled so they sat knee to knee. She meant it, too. Before they'd been sent to different homes to be trained, they'd been thick as thieves. He'd been a proper limpet when they were kids. Maybe it was their dad's disappearing act, or maybe it's because there weren't many mixed kids on the Belle Isle estate at that time, but they were closer than most. Leonie once dropped a paving stone on Gavin Lee's head because he'd called Radley a poofter. Gavin needed three stitches in his scalp and it was Leonie who turned out to be queer. 'No, listen! It'd be sick. I could be, like, the face of the revolution and you could do all the boring paperwork and meetings and shit. We'd be such a boss team!'

He laughed properly this time. 'Well as tempting as *that* sounds, I've finally got the cabal back in shape. It's something we can be proud of again.' There was such shame in his voice. Dabney Hale, in his guise as High Priest, had used the cabal as a Trojan horse for his uprising. After the war, Helena had wanted to disband the whole outfit.

It wasn't your fault, Rad.

'I know.' He immediately blocked her from his thoughts. He filled his head with memories of their dad. A hostile, not to mention dick, move.

'Radley . . .'

'Please stay out of my head, it isn't fair.' Technically, her brother was a Level 2 healer, but his real strength rested in his fastidiousness and endless patience – traits she sorely lacked. He continued to check his messages, ignoring the blossoms and the ducks and the bees. 'Honestly, I'm very settled at the cabal. And some support would be appreciated, Leonie. First Black leader, youngest ever leader . . .'

'I am proud,' Leonie said quietly. And she was. Of both of them. They'd done all right for a pair of mixed-race, broken-home babies from Leeds. She reached into her bag for her tin of tobacco. Her lungs felt swampy from last night. She'd caved and bought a packet of Marlboros and always felt it the next day.

'I can effect more change from within the cabal than I can do from . . . oh, for crying out loud!' he exploded midsentence, sending a family of ducklings running for cover.

'You scared the ducks, you wanker!' Leonie snapped. 'What is it? You wanna try putting that thing on aeroplane mode, you know? You'll get finger cancer or some shit.'

'Unbelievable!' He slammed his phone down on the bench. 'I'm going to have to go.'

Her interest was piqued. Her brother was hard to ruffle. She tried often enough. 'What's up?'

He clenched his jaw so hard, the vein in his neck pulsed. He must give himself the worst cluster headaches, Leonie thought. For a moment she thought he was going to tell her it was classified, but he was sufficiently annoyed to spill. 'Bloody Helena Vance is what's up.'

'Uh-oh. What now?'

'We just got word. They've detained Travis Smythe.'

Now Leonie was shook. The last cobwebs of her hang-over were blasted away. Was that the trouble Bri had sensed? This was a big deal, especially for Helena. Leonie had been at the Somerset Floods, seen the limp bodies floating on the water. She'd been right alongside her when Helena had realised one of those bodies was Stefan. She would never ever forget her pained howl; her twisted face; the way she'd folded up, for as long as she lived. 'Oh wow . . . OK. Well that's a good thing, right?'

Radley's nostrils flared. 'He betrayed his oath to the Warlocks' Cabal, he was *our* jurisdiction.' He raised his phone to his ear and told her, 'I need to get to Manchester. I should be on this.'

Leonie stood too. 'Radley, wait. It doesn't matter. Think about it. He's like the last traitor to be caught . . . it's *over.*'

Radley spoke into his phone. 'This is Jackman. Can I get an urgent teleport back to the office immediately please? Thanks.'

Leonie tugged on his sleeve. 'Rad. The war is over.'

He looked at her, stern. 'But the fight goes on.'

Before he could say another word, her brother dissolved into specks of dust, scattered on the breeze. Leonie was left alone with the ducks.

Chapter Four

UNEXPECTED GUESTS

Niamh

Elle looked flustered: pink-cheeked and fanning herself with the menu. Niamh, running her customary ten minutes late, hurried into the Tea Cosy and apologised, taking her place at the table.

'It's fine,' Elle said. 'It's been a *day*, and it isn't even eleven o'clock yet.' She didn't look her usual immaculate self this morning, her hair twisted into an uncharacteristically messy bun.

Niamh felt out of sorts too. She hadn't arrived back from the Barker farm until almost three in the end. One of those gauzy, gluey mornings where you couldn't be quite certain you'd ever woken up.

'I'm definitely having the full English and no one can judge me for it,' Elle said.

'Fair play,' Niamh said, scanning the menu, although she always had the same thing: avocado on sourdough. Basic, yes, but she managed to convince herself it was good for her because it was green.

Hebden Bridge had wholeheartedly embraced 'foodie'

culture. For herself, Niamh bristled at the label but sure liked all the snacks. Twice a week there was a bustling farmer's market on St George's Square, and it was worth coming down for the churros alone. When it wasn't a market day, the plaza housed enough cafés to allow visiting a different one every day of the week: greasy spoons, hipster Edison bulb bakeries and twee gingham-bunting tearooms. Just over the bridge on Market Street, the Tea Cosy was Niamh's personal favourite: decked out with tie-dye wall hangings; shelves of well-thumbed paperbacks; and a vinyl collection which featured plenty of Kate Bush, Fleetwood Mac and Blondie. The food was knowingly 'rustic', just the right side of pretentious.

'So what's wrong? You left me on a cliffhanger, doll.' Elle had messaged yesterday evening to ask if she was free for brunch today. They tried to meet up every couple of weeks when life didn't shit in their path, but this time Niamh strongly sensed her old friend's distress. She'd felt it halfway down the street, pulsing off her in murky waves.

Elle sighed deeply and sipped her water. 'I don't want to bombard you,' she said meekly. 'Get a coffee first. You might need it.'

Niamh reached over the table and took Elle's hand. 'Darl, what is it?'

'What's the worst thing that could happen?'

Niamh felt her heart plummet. '*Demons?*' she breathed.

Elle's blue eyes widened. 'Oh no! Not that! It's Holly . . .'

Niamh recalibrated her internal catastrophe-o-meter. 'Ah, I see . . .' The waitress came to the table and they halted conversation a moment to give her their order. 'Go on, then . . .'

Elle shook her head despondently, and Niamh clicked. This was the day Elle had been dreading for almost fifteen years. 'It's started.'

Niamh didn't need to ask what. She leaned further in and lowered her voice. Too soon for tourist season, the café was almost full with the post-Pilates, yummy-mummy crew . . . and they were all mundane as far as Niamh could tell with a quick skim. 'Well, we always knew this might be a possibility . . .' A fifty-fifty one, to be precise, if a witch has a baby with a mundane.

'I know,' sighed Elle. 'But when Milo *didn't*, I assumed Holly would be the same. I thought I'd dodged a bullet.'

Niamh chose not to launch into a critique of that standpoint. Internalised witchphobia if ever she heard it. She didn't regard her heritage as a bullet worth dodging. Sure, life was complicated sometimes . . . but she wouldn't choose to be without her powers if there was a magic cure. 'How do you know? What can she do?'

The coffees arrived and they fell artificially silent again. Heaven only knows what the waitress thought they were discussing. 'I think she might be a sentient,' Elle admitted. 'Sometimes she knows what one of us is thinking, even when we've said nothing and . . .' she trailed off.

'And what?'

'Oh Niamh, this is so embarrassing. Do you promise not to judge me?'

Niamh smiled. 'Not for your sausages or anything else.'

'She can . . .' Elle paused, 'see through my glamour.'

Niamh fixed her in a puzzled expression. 'And what glamour would that be?'

Elle couldn't look her in the eye. 'The usual . . . just a little enchantment so Jez sees me as a little thinner . . . a little younger . . . a little blonder . . .'

Niamh's jaw hung open. 'Elle Pearson!'

'You said you wouldn't judge!'

'I lied, consider yourself judged! That is an outrageous use of your talents, as you are well aware.'

'Oh, everyone does it.'

'I wouldn't.'

'You look like a supermodel.'

Niamh tutted loudly. 'Hardly!' Their volume had crept up, and they reined themselves in. 'I cannot believe you are *casting spells* on your husband,' she whispered. As it happened, Niamh wasn't Jez Pearson's biggest fan. That was an understatement. But he was mundane, and Elle using her powers on him was a definite no-no.

'Can we stick to the point?' Elle said. 'My daughter can see through it.'

Niamh bit her tongue. There was plenty she could say to Elle regarding her husband, but now wasn't the time. Niamh could feel quite well how tense Elle was. 'OK, start at the beginning. How do you know?'

'The other day, I mentioned, in passing, I was a size ten. She looked me up and down and said, *Mum, you are not a size ten*. Little cow. She's right, I'm not, but she's not meant to see that.'

Niamh wanted to grasp Elle by the shoulders and shake sense into her. Elle Pearson was *gorgeous*, so she was, gorgeous enough to be a *weathergirl* or an *air hostess*. How dare she think so little of herself. 'If we weren't in a café, I'd slap some sense into you, Pearson. You're stunning at any size, you loon.' Elle didn't look convinced. 'Does Holly know what she is?'

'No,' Elle said, the weight of the world squashing her onto her chair. 'I need to do it, rip the plaster off.'

'Elle, you must tell her who she is. And fast. It's so scary

31

if you don't know.' In girls, so it's said, powers *usually* start manifesting around the first menstruation – although she herself had started long before that. Niamh hadn't seen Holly in a while, but the last time she did, she'd thought she'd noticed that subtle shift towards womanliness.

'I know, I know. That's why I wanted to see you – if I tell someone, I can't back out of it. I needed a kick up the bum. I'll do it tonight,' she said. 'Well that's put me right off my fry-up.'

Niamh loved Elle Pearson née Device with all four chambers of her heart. Of the old group she was the easiest to understand: a simple woman who wanted simple things. And she'd mostly got them: handsome husband; angel babies; a part-time community nursing job. Unusually, she'd never done a stint at HMRC; only helping out briefly during the war. To all intents and purposes, she was a witch in name only. And what a name. Device women were killed at the trials. And now that legacy would live on in Holly.

Perhaps it was the cachet of her family that meant something about Elle's choices never quite sat right with Niamh – the secrecy, the shame at who she was – and for that, she did judge her a little. And she judged herself for judging.

She decided to ask a sticky question. 'Will you tell Jez and Milo too?'

Elle looked back at her as if she were mad. 'What? No. Why?'

Niamh tilted her head, not needing to say anything.

'What? Just tell my husband of almost eighteen years, *guess what, I'm a witch and I've been lying about it the whole time?'*

'Well now you're asking Holly to lie about it too.'

'Niamh, don't. I already feel wretched.'

'Would you rather I only ever told you what you wanted to hear?'

Elle smiled a little, but pouted. 'If I wanted tough love, I'd have invited Helena.'

Niamh laughed heartily. 'True. You should put a little more faith in Jez. Conrad understood.' At the mention of his name, her heart deflated like a week-old balloon. She'd been twenty, at University College Dublin to study, and they'd met at a bar on Grafton Street. After a full-on month of intense, studenty dating, she'd 'come out' to him. He was surprisingly chill about the whole thing, although it later transpired that by 'witch' he thought she'd meant she was into candles and crystals. Which, to be fair, she was.

Now Elle took her hand. At once, Niamh felt some of the sadness drain into her healer friend. 'You don't have to do that,' Niamh said.

'I want to,' Elle stated simply, all the while absorbing the melancholy like a sponge. 'Conrad was a very special man. I love Jez to bits, but – let's be honest – he's a Yorkshire mechanic. If he knew the things we knew I think his head might explode.'

Niamh laughed again. To fall in love with a mundane was truly a curse, yet still probably preferable to falling in love with a warlock. On the darkest winter nights, she had considered enchanting herself to desire women, but that seemed like a lot of hard work to avoid men. 'I think you should be the one to tell Holly,' she said. 'But I'm more than happy to do some craftwork with her after school.'

'Would you really?' Elle perked up.

'Sure! Glad to!' During what she considered her HMRC 'service' after college, that had been her role – working with developing witches and the occasional warlock. An untrained witch is a grenade, just waiting to go off. The oracles would foresee them, then send them to be mentored by older witches like her.

If there were more of them, some sort of school or academy might be in order, but – over the last hundred years or so – numbers just continued to dwindle. A lot of witches didn't want kids; some fell for mundanes; and *no one*, aside from a few demented right-wing 'Trad Witches', mostly in the States, wanted to police who witches could and couldn't make babies with. There were, of course, witches like Leonie, where the gift re-emerges after generations of dormancy, but girls like her were few and far between.

'You are a lifesaver, thank you,' Elle said as their brunch arrived. They tucked in and conversation moved on to more standard topics. 'What have you got planned for your day off?'

'A lot of nothing. Bit of cleaning, food delivery is due at one . . .'

'Is that right?' Elle said, a mischievous twinkle in her eye. 'And would Luke be dropping that off?'

'Maybe,' Niamh said. 'What of it?'

'Nothing. Just how much fresh fruit and veg does one woman need?'

Niamh felt her cheeks blush. 'Fibre. It's good for you.'

Elle laughed so hard the table rocked.

After brunch, and as it was her only day off from the surgery this week, Niamh returned home and did her daily (well, daily was the *aim*) meditation in the cottage garden.

As ever, she did so naked. She didn't like having anything between her skin and the earth and the air; she wanted to feel their sameness.

A dry-stone wall and trees and shrubs shielded her from the gaze of any ramblers who might stray close to the house, although – of course – she could always cloak the garden if need be. The eighteenth-century weaver's cottage, her inheritance from her nan, was half-hidden by ivy and sat at the top of Heptonstall village, on the border of Midgehole.

People from outside Yorkshire refer to this part of the world as 'Brontë Country', although in reality they mean 'windy, hilly and exposed'. At the very peak of the valley, the sturdy cottage had somehow weathered the centuries, still shouldering the brunt of everything the moors had to throw at her. Although this wasn't at all where she'd pictured herself winding up at twenty-four, thirty-four-year-old Niamh greatly enjoyed the privacy and quiet, not to mention the plunging vista. Heptonstall almost seemed to lean vertiginously over the valley below.

She was content up here, observing life below, the way she imagined Gaia to. It's a life skill, finding the sweet-spot between solitude and loneliness.

She felt the breeze on her bare skin, plugged herself into the source. It's all one great circuit: the power in her blood was borrowed from the roots, which borrowed from the soil, which borrowed from the rain, which borrowed from the air. All a witch ever does is bend that flow to her will. Right now, she felt ions swarm around her, pulsate through her bones and ebb harmlessly back into the earth. She felt renewed, recharged.

She missed the doorbell, but heard Tiger barking inside. *Mistress. Come. Urgency. Now.* Dogs, honestly. Everything is always so sodding earnest. 'Fuck,' she said aloud, grabbing her t-shirt and scrabbling to get it over her head. She ran towards the back door, stepping into elasticated yoga pants. As she feared, Luke was already heading down the side of the house. 'Niamh?' his deep voice boomed. 'Are you there? I'm a bit early.'

She hoisted the pants up, checking for camel toe. 'It's fine! I'm in the garden, Luke!'

Luke's broad frame appeared over the gate, arms full with his produce. Niamh opened the gate to let him in. 'Kitchen?' he said, and she led him inside.

He plonked the wooden crate on the countertop and dusted off his bear-paw hands on his apron. 'Some nice fresh stuff in there today: chicory hearts, radishes, chard . . . oh and first rhubarb of the year too.'

'Great, thanks Luke.' Niamh didn't have the heart to tell him she wasn't much of a cook, and never knew what to do with half the things he brought her. She totally relied on recipes from Elle. 'How you going?'

'Same old, can't complain . . . looks like sun's trying to get out.' His Yorkshire accent was as broad as his chest. Niamh was fond of both. He shoved his hands in his pockets, awkward. Niamh felt bad: his unease was, at least partly, her doing. Their conversation, once a merry jig, had two left feet all of a sudden.

'Busy week?' she said, trying to keep him in the kitchen a moment or two longer.

'Manic, yeah.' His eyes were blue, blue like the sea in a travel brochure. No one wouldn't notice. 'It's barmy, but again . . . I shouldn't moan, should I? A lot of people aren't so well off.' The way Luke told it, he started Green & Good almost three years ago after losing a decent job at Manchester Airport in the recession. It started out small: he bought a van and drove around all the different farm shops and butchers, delivering organic food right to folk's doors. At a place like Hebden Bridge, where everyone wanted to do their bit, and to be *seen* doing their bit, business was thriving.

She'd once tried to explain the unique charms of Hebden Bridge to some of the Irish side of her family because it didn't, honestly, make a whole lot of sense. Formerly a gritty, salt-of-the-earth Yorkshire textile mill town like any other, most of the houses were tightly-packed factory workers' terraces – dinky two-up-two-downs fashioned in grim sandstone. Not obviously aspirational for mundanes, although witches had lived in and around the Dales, brimming with power, for centuries.

During the seventies, the town somehow transformed, with a little help from Ted Hughes, into a liberal safe haven for artists, musicians, lesbians and even more witches. Hughes's old house, mere metres from Niamh's cottage, was now a writer's retreat, while Sylvia Plath's final resting place was five minutes in the other direction in the St Thomas à Becket churchyard. People came from all over the world, leaving pens and pencils at her grave.

As is the way with such things, the area gradually gentrified, attracting burned-out Londoners who wanted a slice of the bohemian pie. Nowadays, no mill worker could afford one of those terraces, and tourists flocked to the cobbled streets, searching for a taste of a bygone era that had mostly gone by. It was however, ideally sandwiched between the Yorkshire Dales to the north and the Peak District to the south.

Luke now employed a team of drivers, and had a fleet of vans, but always seemed to find the time to drop off Niamh's veg box.

He slouched in her doorway, some sort of masculine

question mark. 'Can I . . . um . . . get you a cup of tea or something? Or . . . ?'

'You're good,' he said, eyes to the floor. 'I'd best be off, still got a few runs to do today.' She sensed his prickling desire to get away, it almost felt like sunburn inside her skin, and that made her sad.

He started towards the door, but Niamh stopped him, tentatively resting her hand on a meaty bicep. 'Luke, wait,' she said. 'We're hunky-dory, aren't we?'

He sighed. 'Yeah. Yeah, of course we are.' Then he admitted, his face turning pink, 'I just feel so stupid . . .'

She smiled up at him. 'That's some crazy talk, that is. You've no need to. You asked me out! So what? Where's the drama?'

She wasn't a teenager, so she wasn't going to kid herself. Of *course* she was attracted to him. He was so handsome, about as different from Conrad Chen as you could get, and maybe that was part of the appeal. Conrad was athletic and lean with poetically intense and dark eyes which betrayed just how daft he was, whereas Luke was a burly, hunky St Bernard of a man. He looked back at her now expectantly, face wide open. 'I'm embarrassed. I misread some signals . . .'

Niamh never misread signals. That was very much her forte. 'You didn't, Luke.' She busied herself, unpacking the fruit and veg into the fridge, trying to tease some normality back into the room, but she admitted, 'There were signals.'

He said nothing for a second. 'I don't know if that's worse . . .' He faked a wry laugh.

Niamh shook her head. 'I think you're quality, I do, but . . .'

'But Conrad?'

She shut the fridge and leaned on it. Over the years, she'd read plenty of minds thinking *but they weren't actually married*, but that made no difference to Niamh. 'I still wear his ring.' Some sort of reflex from back in the day, her left hand shot up like a flag, proudly displaying her engagement ring. She lowered it at once, not meaning to rub Luke's face in it. 'You know what, I'm going to put the kettle on, because I need tea even if you don't. I've every herbal tea known to man, so take your pick.' She lifted the kettle off the stove and filled it with fresh water.

Luke pulled out a chair and sat at her kitchen table. He hesitated. 'I shouldn't say what I'm about to say. This is the dickest move, probably, but it's been eight years and . . .'

Ah, the *it's time to move on* aria. She was familiar. She'd heard all the remixes. 'I know but . . .'

'Not for me, for you,' he said sincerely. It washed across her like bathwater, the strength of his affection. How was she meant to ignore that, never mind resist it? Lust is a mighty intoxicating thing, especially when it's coming from someone as tasty as Luke Watts. 'I'm not saying it for me – OK I am – but it should be *someone*, Niamh. You're so . . . and you . . . and you deserve love. Doesn't everyone? If I'm speaking out of turn, I'm sorry, but I don't think Conrad would want you to be alone.'

It was hard to know what Conrad would want, and that was sort of the whole problem. It would be only too easy to let Luke envelop her in his big arms and make new memories to replace the painful ones, but she couldn't. Forgetting wasn't right. 'I'm not alone,' she said truthfully. 'I've got my friends, and I've got Tiger, of course.' The Border Terrier sat beside her, scratching his ear with a hind leg. 'And I've got you.'

That only succeeded in making him sadder. She wished she hadn't said it at once. For a while now, she'd been aware that Luke was in a holding pattern, hoping she'd give him clearance to land.

'You do,' he said, faking brightness for her benefit. 'If we're just gonna be friends, I'll make it work. I will. I wish I hadn't said owt.'

'I don't,' Niamh said, very aware she'd known how he felt for months before he plucked up the courage to ask her out. There are specific drawbacks to telepathy.

'I've made things weird.'

'You haven't, I promise.'

He rubbed his rough jaw. 'But now if I suggest going to the cinema or something, you'll think I'm asking you out *out* not just to see a horror film.' That was how this had all started. Elle hated horror films and Niamh had wanted to see *Rosemary's Baby* at the Picture House and had asked Luke to be her sidekick for the night.

'Well then, how about I do the asking?' she said. '*The Exorcist* is showing next week. Why don't we go? As two adult friends who love brutal films?'

The disappointment rolled off him noisily, but he hid it well physically. 'Love that film. I'm in.'

'Great!' Marigold yellow sunshine beamed in through the kitchen windows and warmed the side of his face. What if this was her life? It looked right, somehow, him hunched over her kitchen table.

At first, Niamh thought she was imagining things, but she sniffed the air and there was a definite twinge of sulphur on the wind. The hairs on her arms bristled. The kitchen felt charged with static, and it was nothing to do with Luke's arms this time. Someone was about to teleport.

'OK,' she said suddenly, 'I'd better . . . um . . . I've got some things to do. Can we rain check on the tea? But I'll text you about the film and we'll sort times?'

Luke's brow furrowed. It wasn't like her to hurry him out. 'Yeah, sure. You OK?'

On the stove, the kettle started to whistle and she lifted it off. 'I didn't realise how late it was. I'm so sorry to hustle you out.'

'It's fine,' he said, although he did look a little puzzled, if not hurt. 'See you later, Niamh.' They crossed paths under the wooden beam and he gave her a brief kiss on the cheek. A very safe kiss for very safe friends.

She followed him out to the garden and braced herself. She held her breath until he was in the van and he rolled down the drive. She gave him a jolly wave and willed him to get out of sight. How the fuck would she explain someone appearing out of thin air? She'd have had to wipe his memory, and she wouldn't feel right about that. His van vanished on the horizon and she breathed a sigh of relief.

There were enough charms and enchantments on the cottage to prevent an intruder from teleporting directly into her home, suggesting it was someone she knew . . . but still better to be prepared. She readied herself, her mind tight like a spring. If she wanted to, she could split their molecules apart before they fully materialised.

Niamh felt ions and energies shift and pulse. The air felt close, charged like after a thunderstorm. A sudden wind whipped across the lawn, shaking leaves from the apple tree and petals from her daffs. The hens clucked and flustered, hurrying back into the coop. A tornado of silver and gold particles whirled into the centre of the garden, rapidly taking human shape. In no more than a couple of seconds, Helena appeared from the ether. She was soon solid, and the winds died down. Niamh relaxed.

'Ginger!' Helena – dressed in a chic trouser suit – strode forward and pulled Niamh into a tight hug. She looked like money; nails done, makeup subtle, not a centimetre of regrowth in sight. Helena had had a haircut since she saw her last, her chocolate hair now skimming her collar.

'Well this can't be good. What brings Posh to Hebden Bridge?'

Helena swept past her into the kitchen and pouted. 'Can't I spontaneously visit one of my dearest friends? Must we endlessly plan every gathering for months? Have you got a coffee, love? I'm running on fumes.'

Niamh followed her inside, aghast. 'Helena!'

'What?'

'Don't you *what* me, madame.' Niamh lifted the kettle back onto the stove. Helena made herself right at home, draping her overcoat over the back of a chair and kicking off her shoes. 'You're not telling me you teleported here on a Monday afternoon for a coffee.'

Teleportation is fucking hard work. It takes a small army of elementals, healers and sentients to make sure you don't end up molecular salad all over the floor. Taking someone apart and putting them back together again in a different place is advanced stuff. If it was child's play, Niamh wouldn't need the car. As it was, she loathed teleportation. It was somehow even less natural than flying on aeroplanes, and she wasn't keen on those, either.

'You can't fool a telepath can you? Yes, I'm here on HMRC business.' Niamh reached for two mugs in the cupboard and found the cafetière under the sink. 'But we can have a coffee break as well, can't we? It's been months. I miss your face.'

Niamh scooped coffee into the pot. 'Helena . . . before you even start, I don't work for HMRC any more.'

'I am fully aware of that. I just want to pick your brain about something.'

Niamh gave the coffee a quick stir and carried it to the table to brew. 'I doubt that somehow, but go on.' She sat opposite Helena and awaited her command. This was the way it was: Helena was the eldest, therefore she was in charge. It had been true when they were tweens, and it remained so. The only difference now was that Helena was the most powerful witch in the *country*, not just the treehouse.

Helena exhaled before launching into it. 'Good news first. We arrested Travis Smythe this morning in Manchester.' She spoke with cautious victory.

Niamh let that sink in for a second. 'Was he . . . ?'

'On his way to your sister? Yes. I confess we somewhat used her as bait. We leaked her location to Bologna to smoke him out. It worked like a charm.' A pause. 'Niamh?'

'Good. It's good,' she said finally. 'Good you've caught him at last.'

She stiffened. 'It wasn't for lack of trying . . .'

'I know. Helena, I *know*. I didn't mean it like that.' Travis Smythe may not have killed Helena's husband with his own hands, but it *was* him who gave the order.

'I thought you should know. Ciara is safe and sound.'

Every time she heard her sister's name it was another lash of the cane. The elapsing years didn't make it any less raw or painful. 'Any change?'

'None.'

Niamh nodded and poured the coffee.

'It's been a while since you visited her,' Helena said.

Niamh looked her oldest friend in the eye. 'I know. I . . . after all these years, I don't know what to say to her any more.'

Helena took a sip from her mug. 'She's in there, Niamh. She knows when you visit, I really believe that. You could guide her back . . .'

Niamh stood abruptly to fetch the biscuit tin because Niamh knew, and Helena knew, that it might be safer for the whole world that Ciara remained in that hospital bed. She changed the subject. 'You're not telling me you teleported in just to give me an update on my sister. Could have been an email.'

'In the name of Gaia, you are suspicious.'

'Darl, I'm also psychic.' As an experienced witch, Helena was mature enough to keep her precise thoughts occluded, but Niamh could sense quite well that there was something on the tip of her tongue. With time, a witch could become expert at hiding their intentions from a sentient – they trained them for it at HMRC in case of hostage situations.

Helena stared into her mug. 'You're right. I didn't just come here to tell you about Smythe.'

Niamh felt it. There was something wrong. Something haunted Helena. It was steely, heavy, driving the air from the room. 'Hels . . . what is it? You're scaring me now.'

'There's been a prophecy . . .'

'Oh here we go . . .' Niamh groaned. The oracles were always full of doom. That's why they never got invited to parties.

Helena shook her head. 'There's never been one like this, Niamh. You don't understand. Not even before the war.'

Helena's steady gaze was loaded with the sort of resolution Niamh hadn't seen in almost a decade. Like a scorched forest, it had taken time, years even, for silliness and absurdity and glib playfulness to return to the coven, or even to life, full stop. Conrad, Stef, and so many more had died, and neither Helena nor Niamh would truly heal, not ever. Some bore scars on their skin and others – like they had – bore scars within. Niamh didn't have to look very hard to see Helena's, however much she tried to cover them.

Niamh had learned, with time, to keep her grief in the shoebox under the bed with all the photos and mixtapes and old love letters. It was present, always, but she could work around it, knowing it was there.

Only now Helena wore her war face once more. Niamh blinked back the sting of tears. She could not, *would not*, go through those days again. She was still broken from last time, held together with sellotape and staples. 'Fuck,' she said, her voice hoarse. 'Please tell me you're kidding?'

'I wish I was.'

'You're serious?'

She nodded.

'Worse than the *war*?'

Another nod.

Neither said anything for a moment. The kitchen was silent aside from the hum of the fridge. Niamh wondered if these were the last good seconds before bad times returned.

I need you, Niamh.

Helena Vance was not the type woman to ask for help.

How can I help?

Relief washed over her face, and she was just Hels, not the High Priestess, for a second. Her lips tightened and she was business once more. She said simply, 'I need you to come back to the coven.'

Chapter Five

THE SULLIED CHILD

Niamh

They materialised in the lobby and, as she did every time, Niamh checked they'd put her back together in the correct fashion. It didn't *hurt* so much as feel like pins and needles all the way to the bone. Cellular colonic. Unsettling to say the very least.

The foyer to the HMRC offices had lost none of its Victorian splendour over the decades. Niamh felt dwarfed by the towering marble pillars. The intricate, spiral mosaic tiles on the floor were hypnotic if you stared too long and vast potted palms spilled out of the corners all the way to the stained-glass ceiling.

Niamh couldn't precisely pinpoint the last time she'd set foot in this building, it had been so long, but she vividly remembered the Nicole-Kidman-walking-away-from-her-Cruise-marriage energy she'd felt that day. The *freedom*.

As far as the mundanes of Manchester knew, this was a tax office, so naturally they avoided it like the plague. Niamh, even now, felt like a pigeon-toed little spod when she came here. She always had been a bad fit, not nearly polished enough to belong in a building like this. Before they'd teleported, she had changed into jeans and a t-shirt – that's all she owned these days – but it was a statement also. She was *not* HMRC.

Her personal ick factor aside, she was proud Helena had resisted numerous government attempts to get them to relocate to London. The largest and oldest covens had always been in the north and Scotland, because – simply put – the north is more magical. It was only right they should remain in their spiritual home, and no High Priestess needs the mundane authorities watching over their shoulder at any case.

Quite used to such sudden arrivals, an aloof receptionist barely flinched behind the imposing mahogany desk, but Sandhya Kaur rushed over to greet them. Why, the last time Niamh had seen Sandhya, she'd been a keen pupil in her introductory lessons before the war, and now here she was: a grown adult woman wielding an iPad with purpose. Niamh gawped at her. 'Sandhya! Look at you all grown up!'

Sandhya beamed and the two embraced. Their energies briefly combined and Niamh felt the familiar jade haze of a reunion. Helena, however, had no time for a catch-up. 'Are the oracles ready?'

'Yes, ma'am. In the Dome.'

Sandhya handed Niamh a lanyard with a visitor pass. Too fucking right. She'd made it very clear to Helena before the teleport, she was here for consultancy purposes only. She was a *vet,* both a veterinarian and a veteran. This wasn't her life any more.

Helena led the way. They took the lift to the fifth floor, home to the single largest division of HMRC: Supernormal Security. They navigated the open plan office where officious witches went about their business. On Helena's arrival, the kitchen area quickly emptied out. Niamh favoured the types of careers you saw in children's picture books: teachers and bakers and the like. She never really understood half of what the people in HMRC did. What even *is* a project manager? Tucked away in gentle RED Team (Recruitment, Education and Development), Niamh had always felt like a tiny cog in a vast machine. And she hadn't enjoyed it.

Sandhya continued to pass memos to her boss. 'The Home Office wants to talk about the involvement of the Russian coven in a recent poisoning . . .'

'Not our jurisdiction.'

'Moira Roberts wants to discuss Scottish funding . . .'

'Ha! I'm sure she does. That can wait.'

Sandhya then added, 'And when you have a minute, Radley Jackman would like to circle back on the raid this morning.'

Helena grimaced. 'He's not seriously going to whine about the capture of one of the most wanted men in the world is he?'

'He's asking why he wasn't informed,' Sandhya replied sheepishly.

Helena guffawed and said no more. Niamh was almost relieved that the Warlocks' Rights movement hadn't died down. It was pleasingly consistent to know that some things never change.

At the very top of the building was the beautiful domed oratorium, installed when HMRC first opened its doors – formally – in 1870. The design had been perfected some hundred years earlier by the hugely talented witch Lady Elizabeth Wilbraham. The domes, designed to amplify time, helped oracles better see the past and future. The structure had since been copied the whole world over. There were Wilbraham oratoriums in all the major witching capitals: Salem, Port au Prince, Moscow, Kinshasa, Jaipur, New Orleans, Osaka.

Outside the double doors, Helena pressed a buzzer and waited. One didn't disturb oracles while they were immersed in the timelines. To break them out of a deep trance might kill them. There was a click almost right away and the doors were opened from the inside. A wave of icy air billowed into the hallway and a young oracle stood aside to let them in.

The cavernous room was dimly lit to emulate moonlight, cool silver-grey lights running under the tiered seating. Quartz crystals on delicate chains hung in clusters from the central dome, each one calibrated precisely to filter interference from the air. They were like the stars at night. Twenty or so bald skulls were like moons as Helena and Niamh descended the stairs. The oracles were dotted across the tiers in silence, deep in contemplation.

Niamh didn't want to find oracles unnerving, but she did, always had. To her, being a witch was like being in a big friendly sorority, and there was something about the oracles' monastic detachment from the rest of them that had always creeped her out. They seemed to exist in their own dimension, living and socialising together, almost like a convent. Oh, except for Annie, Elle's grandmother, of course. She was a cool oracle.

In the centre of the room, cross-legged, was Irina Konvalinka, the Head Oracle since Annie retired after the war. Irina was a pale, stern woman with flint eyes. A shapeless black dress hung off her skeletal collarbones. Niamh shivered. True, the dome was refrigerated to slow the oracles' heart rates into a trance, but it was more than that. There was something specific about Irina's manner that unsettled Niamh.

Then again, her team had spectacularly failed to foresee the death of her husband-to-be, so there was that too.

'Niamh Maryanne, daughter of Miranda and Brendan,' Irina said, eyes fixed in her direction, but seeing nothing in this world. Like so many oracles, she was now blind from staring too long into time.

'You knew I'd come?' Niamh asked Helena as much as the oracle.

Helena said nothing but Irina went on. 'We always knew your time in the coven was not at an end. We told you as much when you left.'

'I just thought you were being foreboding, like.'

'They often are,' Helena said wryly. 'But not on this occasion. We've seen something highly concerning. Take a seat.'

Niamh pulled up a cushion and sat opposite Irina, mirroring her posture. Niamh knew the drill. 'OK, fire away.'

An expectant hush settled over the oratorium. The room was fully soundproofed. Silence here meant silence. Irina settled herself. 'See as I see,' the older woman said, reaching a bony finger towards Niamh's third eye: the powerful chakra between her physical eyes. Those, she now closed and bridged the oracle's mind.

A sensation she could only call a 'brain-freeze' reverberated from her skull all the way down her spine, and suddenly she was transported away from the dome and to a snow-covered street.

This was what the oracles foresaw.

A mournful wind howled through what was left of the ruins, and it took her a moment to realise she was not in some distant warzone, but the Northern Quarter in Manchester's city centre, or rather, what was left of it. Only the ragged bones of buildings were left standing and rubble was strewn into the road.

It felt all too real, and Niamh reminded herself it was not. At least not *yet*. The air was acrid, tinged with smoke, gritty dust and burning flesh. Covering her mouth, Niamh realised with horror that this wasn't snow. It was ash.

Oh gods, no.

She couldn't fight the urge to get away, far away. She almost tripped over her feet, breaking into a run. Bodies with charred skin were half buried in debris, rotting where they lay. Blood ran through the gutters. Her first thought was that this was the aftermath of a bomb, a nuclear weapon. Was it just this street? She turned the corner and saw yet more horror. A pram lay on its side in the middle of the road. An ambulance burned, smashed into the front of a bakery. However far she ran, and wherever she looked, Manchester was devastated.

And then she saw why.

Through smoke and fog, a formidable silhouette loomed overhead, taller than the rooftops. She screwed her eyes shut because she never wanted to see its face. Niamh felt its malignancy in the pit of her stomach, and she dared not reach out with her mind, for, instinctively, she already knew its name.

Leviathan.

And that was quite enough of that, thank you very much. She withdrew from Irina's mind the way you can consciously remove yourself from a nightmare.

Her eyes snapped open, irrationally furious. 'Leviathan? Come on now . . .' You don't throw that name around for shock value. It wasn't fucking clickbait.

A young plump oracle stood and hurried down from the second tier. 'It's true, Dr Kelly. The clearest vision I've ever seen. I was the first to see it after he arrived.'

Niamh looked to Helena, confused. 'Who? Travis Smythe?'

'The Sullied Child,' Irina rasped before Helena could answer.

'That's a fairy tale to scare little witches!'

The oracle continued unabated. 'For generations, we've beheld a child in our reverie. The symbol recurred hundreds of times in a hundred different forms. A boychild who would bring untold ruination on a scale never before witnessed. We didn't know where he would come from, or when, but we knew he would herald the beginning. The beginning of the end times. A point of no return. The end of witchkind and men alike.'

Niamh rolled her eyes and looked to Helena. Oracles were pure exhausting. Because their visions were often . . . *vague* at best, they were prone to talking up their importance. Funding was tight and the government was always looking to scale back somewhere. Niamh wasn't an oracle at *all*, not one drop, but Annie had once told her it was like watching movie trailers. Some portents gave away the whole plot, while others were highly misleading. That's why they needed so many oracles: together, they wove some sort of cohesive tapestry but, like all witches, they were in decline.

Right now, Helena's face was as grave as Irina's. 'Helena?'

'We think we've found him. The child.' She turned to Sandhya, who handed her the iPad. 'Look at this.'

Niamh took the tablet from Helena and saw a series of photographs; the shell of what was once a school from the looks of thing. It was now a blackened husk. 'What's this?'

'That *used* to be a referral unit for students with special educational needs near Edinburgh.'

'And this kid . . . burned it down?'

Helena took a deep breath. 'Not exactly. He destroyed it with lightning bolts.'

'Oh. He's an elemental?'

'An adept.' Helena's throat sounded tight.

'What?'

Adepts, witches in possession of more than a single gift, were as rare as hen's teeth, and she should know, she *was* one. As children she and Ciara had been treated like rare and precious orchids, which was flattering and stifling in equal measure. Male adepts were rarer still. She'd only ever known one: Dabney Hale, and look how that turned out. There had been a time, in the years leading up to the war, when some had questioned if Hale was the legendary Sullied Child. Nope, just a run-of-the-mill megalomaniac, it transpired.

In the sparse light, Helena looked gaunt, worried sick. It was unsettling; Helena was the go-to in a crisis. Rock solid.

'That happened last month and we were sent to Scotland to retrieve him. He's powerful, Niamh. More powerful than any warlock I've ever seen. More powerful than most witches his age.'

Really, girl?

Yes, really.

Impossible. Warlocks are simply not as gifted as witches. *Gaia favours her daughters.* Fact. Everyone knew that, it was a fundamental principal. The boffins at Psyence UK had speculated for years about a genetic component on

53

the X chromosome that made women more receptive to Gaia; more able to channel and harness her power. Niamh sighed.

'What does Annie have to say on all this?' Annie Device was the best oracle she'd ever known, and had always been able to make the scariest visions, the worst bogeymen under the bed, seem tolerable.

'I haven't told her. She's old now, Niamh. I don't want to worry her.'

'But—'

'But nothing. You saw what we saw.'

'Fair enough, I'll bite, but what does a wee Scottish arsonist have to do with the Beast destroying Manchester? That's quite a stretch.'

'Leviathan will rise,' one of the oracles in the back row suddenly blurted out. Niamh jolted off her cushion.

'It's not just Manchester,' Irina said coolly, ignoring the outburst. 'It's everywhere, the whole world over.'

'It's the first domino to fall,' Helena added. 'The oracles believe the Sullied Child will, in time, invoke the Beast and allow Him to cross into our reality.'

'Leviathan will rise!' an elderly oracle shrieked. Niamh's skin bristled.

Helena put her hand over Niamh's. 'Will you come see him? He . . . he doesn't speak.'

'At all?'

'No. He hasn't said a single word since we found him. None of my sentients can read him, Niamh. I've never seen anything like it.' And then she added, just for her, *I'm scared.* Never did she think she'd ever hear Helena Vance admit that.

Another oracle on the front row writhed like she'd been shocked. 'Leviathan will rise!'

Where is he?

Grierlings.

Fucking hell. All right. But I can't promise—

'Leviathan will rise!'

Another oracle spasmed, like electricity was passing through her elderly frame. 'Leviathan will rise!'

'Leviathan will rise!'

Soon every oracle in the room joined in the chant. Niamh's head pounded. It was dizzying: the collective fear, the panic.

Posh, you need to get me the fuck out of this room.

Leviathan will rise.

Chapter Six

GRIERLINGS

Niamh

For obvious reasons, no one was teleporting in or out of the coven's highest security prison, so they travelled the mundane way: by people carrier. Sandhya sat up front, busily tapping away on her phone, while Niamh and Helena rode in the back. The driver was a young warlock. Niamh sensed some latent sentiency in him, but not much. An S1 at most.

They were stuck in traffic. Ongoing works at Salford Quays meant getting out of the city centre was arduous, even off-peak. 'So,' Helena said, a slight curve in the corner of her lips. 'How's things with the farmer?'

'The farmer?'

She took a sip from her venti latte. 'What's his name? Luke, was it?'

Niamh pouted slightly. Helena couldn't be *that* concerned about this kid if she had time to tease her. 'He's not a farmer! He runs a very successful start-up, thank you very much.'

Helena grinned.

'Ah, there's nothing to tell. We're just friends, that's all.'

And then Stefan filled Helena's head. The memories were so potent, she couldn't hope to hide them from Niamh. She even caught the phantom of his cologne. A handsome man was her Stef: tall, blond and broad shouldered. Proud Norwegian warlock stock. Niamh knew what the sudden recollection meant, because she felt it too. Any thought of moving on, of being with another man, was met by a wrecking ball of guilt.

When your lover dies, time stops still. In eight years all manner of fates might have befallen them had they lived, but, as it was, Conrad and Stefan remained perfect in both youth and reputation, sealed in amber forever more. To even think about it was a great betrayal.

'I'm just not quite there yet,' Niamh said softly.

Helena's gaze fell. 'Me either. Sorry, I shouldn't have pushed. Maybe one day, eh?'

'Sure.'

Helena squeaked on the leather seats. 'You know, I've gotten used to it just being me and Snow now. We're a watertight unit. I'm not sure how a man would get in.'

Niamh seized on the chance to change the subject as the warlock honked his horn at a taxi who cut him up on a roundabout. 'How is Snow?' Niamh hadn't seen Helena's daughter since last Samhain, and even then it was in passing.

'Good, really good. You wouldn't recognise her, she's so grown up now.'

'Is it this year she takes her exams?'

'Next year! Don't! I feel a hundred years old. I probably look a hundred years old.'

'You don't, and, anyway, you can always "do an Elle" and start casting a glamour on yourself.'

'She doesn't!' Helena said, rightly horrified.

'I know! I told her! She wouldn't hear it!' Niamh shook her head. 'Will Snow join HMRC?' Any daughter of Helena Vance was *definitely* joining HMRC, but Niamh thought it polite to ask.

'I don't want to push her either way but I hope so. She'll take the oath at solstice.' Taking the oath is like getting a driving licence. It was controversial, but any young witch legally *has* to register with HMRC, even if she doesn't end up *working* there.

The car finally wriggled free of the roadworks and they sped outside the city. Grierlings was about five miles down the motorway, in the midst of the industrial wastes.

It was flattering, in a way, that Helena had brought this puzzle to her. A reminder that she was, at least on paper, one of the more powerful witches in the country, even if she seldom used her powers these days. She'd be lying if she said she didn't take a certain pride in her Level 5 status, but she didn't feel the need to compete any more. If she was honest, what had pushed her was wanting to be just that bit more powerful than her twin. Now, it didn't matter. She'd won, and Ciara wouldn't use her powers ever again.

Niamh knew she *shouldn't* pull the following thread but it was like an especially itchy scab, demanding to be picked at.

'Why come to me, Helena?' she asked, her voice low so Sandhya wouldn't earwig. 'Leonie could have . . .'

Helena cut her dead with her trademark iron glare. 'You are the most powerful *adept* I know.' She inhaled. 'Anyway, Leonie and I aren't exactly on good terms, are we. I'm hardly in a position to be asking her for favours.'

Niamh trod carefully. 'You didn't call her Scary Spice again, did you? You know she doesn't like it.'

At that, Helena chuckled. 'No. No I didn't.'

'She's still your friend, Helena.'

'Is that so?'

'Yes.' And Niamh meant it. 'Business is business, friendship is friendship. I left the coven and we're still friends.'

Helena's tone struggled to remain neutral. The bitterness cut through, lime sharp. 'She started a rival coven, Niamh, and stole some of my most powerful witches in the process.'

'Helena,' Niamh said with finality. 'They were women, not Barbie dolls. They weren't *yours* to steal.' Helena went to argue, but Niamh cut her off. 'And it's not a *rival* coven, it's just *another* coven. They have very different aims.' From what Niamh could tell, Diaspora was a community for a minority within a minority, whereas HMRC would always have its mission.

'Let's agree to disagree,' Helena said tersely, sliding down shutters on the conversation.

Niamh missed when it was easy. When the biggest strife in the world was who was going to have to begrudgingly accept the role of Sporty Spice. As the redheads, she and Ciara had fought tooth and nail to be Geri, but one of them – usually Ciara to be fair – had to shove their hair in a ponytail and grab a tracksuit. They used to play dress-up in Helena's bedroom – which was twice the size of Niamh's mum and dad's bedroom back in Galway, *and* she had a double bed – and learn the choreography. If she tried, she could still remember the plastic strawberry twang of Helena's Juicy Tube lip gloss and how it glued her hair to her face.

It was hard to pinpoint exactly when it got hard, when adult life set in like plaque. The war certainly didn't help. It forced them all to grow up real fast, grow prematurely thick hides. She sometimes wondered how they did it back then – a bunch of twenty-something upstarts taking on the world – and if she'd have the energy now. She hoped she wouldn't have to find out.

The car turned off the motorway and down the anonymous, unmarked road towards Grierlings. To mundanes, the prison was a disused, derelict ironworks. A powerful glamour was continually cast over the whole building. A guard saw the car approach and the gates slid open. Even *without* the glamour it was a drab structure. It was a brutal-looking site, with three brickwork cubes, and not a curved line in sight. It had been years since Niamh visited, but it all came back to her now. There were three blocks: one low security, one high security and then the third block with chimneys for the Pipes.

That whole period, the sorry weeks and months right after they quashed the insurgence, was so dark. So many conversations she'd wished they'd never had to have, or even entertain. *What to do with the ones who survived.* If you betray your coven, and break that very simple oath, the sentence is fire. But this was not the seventeenth century, and what would they be if their laws lagged behind those of mundanes? The answer, it seemed, was this dumping ground.

She felt it in her gut. Grierlings was a terrible place devoid of hope. She'd sworn never to return, and yet here she was again. Already she felt the sluggish, nauseous sensation of being in the containment field.

The cement foundations of Grierlings were mixed with mercury to truncate the gifts of any witch or warlock above. Mistletoe, a magical sedative, was woven through the wooden window frames and bannisters. Air laced with *Sister's Malady* was pumped through the air conditioning.

Niamh shivered as the flu-like feeling kicked in, and wondered if it eased off if you had a permanent stay.

Sue Porter, the Chief Warden, greeted them at the car. She'd had the same Lego bob haircut since Niamh could remember. She looked like a mole and always smelled of the Polo mint she'd tried to cover her cigarette with. 'Good afternoon, Ms Vance,' she said.

Helena stood tall, emerging from the back of the car elegantly. 'Any change?'

'None, ma'am. We've tried everything to get him to calm down but . . .' The woman grovelled like a dog anticipating a kick.

'Never mind. Let's take a look, shall we? Can you get them to turn off the air conditioning?'

Sue's eyes widened. 'Is that a good idea?'

'I need Niamh to be able to read him.'

The warden looked far from certain, but radioed in the request. With Sue and Helena leading the way, Niamh followed them into the highest security wing. It smelled strongly of bleach. Reflexively, Niamh let her mind reach out, but found only muffled signals. Muffled, but sad. Thoughts of resentment and petty retribution, of the pecking order. There was no one happy here.

Honestly, she thought, what was the point of this place?

A klaxon sounded and the first doors opened onto an antechamber. Their bodies – and minds – were scanned for weapons. Jewellery was removed and placed in a security box to stop enchanted items being smuggled in; the right stone can hold immense power. When the guards were satisfied, they proceeded to the main body of the prison.

'Dare I ask about Hale?' Niamh asked quietly, the name leaving a bad taste on her tongue.

'What about him?' Helena replied.

A good question. 'Is he dead yet?'

'Not as yet. Would you care to pay him a visit? He's in the east wing.'

Niamh gritted her teeth together. 'I would not care for that.' She believed it was called cognitive dissonance: being philosophically and morally against capital punishment but wanting Dabney Hale dead for all the suffering he caused. It didn't sit right with her that Hale was getting special treatment here, as bleak as it was, while Conrad was six feet under.

Helena's heels clicked on the tiled floor as they made their way down the entrance hall. Through chain-link fencing, Niamh saw the central mess hall. This wing housed warlocks. Nearly all had been part of the rebellion. Before the war, there hadn't been much need for a prison, now it was almost at capacity.

One muscular youth, arms like hams, caught sight of them as they passed by on their way to the elevator. He'd have barely been legal when the war broke out – all the easier for Hale to manipulate. He played well with young warlocks who sometimes struggled to reconcile how women could be the more powerful sex if they'd grown up in the mundane world, where quite the opposite was true. Keeping Hale away from other inmates was the official reason as to why he was in a suite by himself. The unofficial reason was that Lady Hale was a major HMRC donor.

'Look who it is, lads!' the muscular inmate called. 'It's the High fuckin' Priestess! You awight darlin?'

'She finally come to chop our cocks off?' an older inmate yelled, which drew a huge laugh.

Helena just kept on walking, head high.

'As long as she sucks it before she cuts it off, I don't care.'

'Dyke bitches.'

'Ignore them,' Niamh told her.

Helena looked nonchalantly over her shoulder at Niamh. 'Do you think there's anything a man could say to derail me?'

No, Niamh couldn't think of a single thing.

The old freight elevator creaked and wheezed downwards into the basement. It was operated by a stocky warlock with an earring and a bat tattoo on his neck. They arrived and he hoisted the concertina door aside for them.

'You're keeping this kid in the cellar?' Niamh asked.

Sue answered before Helena could. 'It was the only way we could dampen his powers . . . put him nearer the foundations.' There was an unmistakeably defensive edge to her voice.

Niamh threw Helena a pointed look. 'And how old did you say he was?'

'We were hoping you could tell us.' Helena marched down the basement corridor. It was colder down here, damp, and Niamh felt the nausea even more acutely. She swallowed back bile. 'We can't find a birth certificate at the mundane social services and he was never registered at HMRC or the cabal, which begs an awful lot of questions.'

Sue swiped her security pass at a set of imposing red double doors.

'Is it safe?' Helena asked.

Sue didn't look at all sure. 'Just be careful.'

Niamh was determined to keep a poker face, but why anyone would warn Helena, a Level 5 elemental, to be careful was concerning. Sue opened the door for them.

The basement was signposted as storage, but inside the dark vault, Niamh could make out what looked like a zoo enclosure. It was hexagonal – a powerful shape in witchcraft lore – with metal grille running around all six sides and overhead. The strip lights hummed, offering only anaemic light in the windowless room.

'Oh my goddess . . .' Niamh muttered under her breath. This couldn't be real.

It was as if the cage were underwater, an aquarium. Inside the structure, a metal bedframe, a thin mattress, bedding, a dinner tray and a plastic beaker hovered, rolling and bouncing off the sides like they were caught up in a gentle tornado. Instinctively Niamh knew she wouldn't be able to levitate such large objects under the containment measures, so how was . . .

'Where is he?' she asked. Other than the spiralling furniture, there didn't look to be anyone in the cage.

Helena shifted her weight on her hip. 'Top right corner . . .'

Niamh gasped. In the darkest corner, a skinny teenage boy was pressed against the roof, the way a spider hides in its web. His skin looked pasty, clammy almost, and there were dark circles like bruises under his eyes. Greasy, raven-black hair hung over his face. Niamh wouldn't like to put an exact age on him – puberty is a fucker. He could be anywhere from thirteen to sixteen. He shrunk further into his hideaway, like some cornered creature.

'What the fuck?' Niamh exclaimed a lot more loudly than she intended.

'I'm so sorry, Ms Vance,' Sue said. 'We did try to sedate him as much as possible but . . .'

'It's all right,' Helena said before turning to Niamh. 'Niamh? Can you hear him?'

Niamh was furious. She hadn't been at all prepared for this and felt hijacked. If Helena had been aiming for shock value, job well done.

Nonetheless, she reached out with her mind, through the bars and towards the boy. She didn't do it for Helena, but because this whole situation felt very wrong. His eyes widened and he retreated further, hiding his face. A horrible jarring noise filled her head, a full-throated scream, really. She withdrew at once. She felt Helena's eyes on her and tried again, more tentatively this time.

It was akin to reading her animals at the surgery. She wasn't getting any words, thoughts or memories, just pure feeling: anger and rage, certainly, but mostly fear. More than fear, abject terror. Niamh felt her heart rate quicken, her palms sweating. Her healer abilities kicked in, absorbing some of his anguish.

'He's scared,' she told the others sharply. 'Terrified. But I don't think you needed me to tell you that. Look at him.'

'Tell that to the other kids in his school,' Helena said. 'It's a miracle no one was killed. Can you get inside his head? Does he have a name?'

Niamh tried once more, but heard only the same ear-splitting cry. It was worse than nails down a chalkboard. 'No!' she yelped, reeling. 'I can't! He's apoplectic . . . and there's a million things down here messing with my powers. I can't do this here and, honestly, I wish you hadn't dragged me into it.'

Helena blinked slowly. 'Niamh, be reasonable. We can't let him out because he might destroy half of Manchester . . .'

'He's a kid! Look at him!'

'He's feral.'

'Did you stop to think he's acting up because you have him in a *cage* like a dog? Actually, Helena, I have a dog and I wouldn't put him in a cage.'

Sue cleared her throat and backed off slightly. Helena shot Niamh a clear warning, but Niamh wasn't scared of her. It's hard to be scared of a woman you've seen piss her pants while off her tits on Jägerbombs. That aside, Niamh didn't want to embarrass Helena while she was in work mode.

'What do you suggest?' Helena asked tersely.

Niamh looked up at the hunched figure pressed against the ceiling of the cage. 'Will you give me a minute alone with him?'

'Oh I don't think that's safe . . .' Sue snivelled back to her.

'He's in a cage and I'm a Level 5 adept. I think I'll cope.'

Helena huffed. 'Fine. Just don't touch the cage. Yesterday he managed to electrify it.' Niamh wished someone had mentioned that before she touched it a minute ago. 'I'll be right outside.'

Helena, Sue and the warlock guard backed off, leaving Niamh and the boy alone in the vault. She took a step closer and craned her neck to get a better look. She took several deep breaths. If she was going to open her mind to him, she wanted it as calm, and as non-threatening, as possible. She conjured the same soothing, ocean-blue mental stance she used on scared cats and dogs in the practice.

Hello up there. I know you can hear me.

Nothing.

They tell me you're an adept. So am I. Do you even know what that means? Do you know where you are?

66

The boy finally peeked out from under the sleeve of his hoodie to look at her.

My name is Niamh Kelly. What am I to call you?

She reached out again. Mercifully, the howl inside his head was more of a whimper. He was listening. He wasn't giving anything away either. Where she ought to be able to see a reflection of what he was thinking, there was a thick oily blackness.

Let's start at the beginning, then. I'm a witch. You're one too. About 0.5% of the population has some magical ability in them, even if they don't know it. We call male witches warlocks if you didn't already know. That's why you can do all this mad stuff. Have you always been able to do things like this?

The bedframe fell to the floor with a mighty crash and Niamh recoiled slightly. It was working. One by one, the items circling his cage crashed down to earth with a clang. By focusing on her, he couldn't expend thoughtwaves on telekinesis.

I'm so sorry they've locked you up down here. I know you're scared, I can feel it real strongly in your head. They're scared of you too. Understand that. You're so young to be this powerful.

He looked down at her, his big brown eyes inscrutable.

You are, you know. Incredibly powerful. When I was your age, I could barely float the remote control to the sofa. You shouldn't be scared though. You're not the first kid to go through this, and you won't be the last. We all turn out OK in the end.

That was a lie, and she wondered if he could read her. He said nothing.

You've been to school, so you know how this works. I want to help you out here, but you're gonna need to give me something. If you can stay calm and . . . come down from the ceiling, I'll get you out of this shitty cellar. How does that sound?

There was nothing for a moment.

And then, scarcely a whisper: *I don't know how to get down.*

His voice was so small, so timid, Niamh almost laughed. Almost.

Oh, you poor thing.

You can hear me?

Yes, I can, and I can get you down gently. Just let go with your mind. Picture coming down. Let go.

He slipped off the ceiling and Niamh raised a hand to catch him. He was so light. She'd worried with the dampeners she might struggle, but there was nothing to him. She lowered him slowly to the earth where he landed on two feet before pressing himself into the corner and drawing his knees up to his chest.

There! That wasn't so hard was it?

He said no more.

Wait here. I need to go talk to the posh one about getting you out. You . . . sit tight.

Niamh backed slowly out of the cellar, not wanting to set him off again. Outside, Helena was politely ignoring Sue in the dank corridor by pretending to reply to emails on her phone, but there was no way she had a signal down here.

'OK,' Niamh said quietly. 'I think I'm making progress.'

'You got a name?'

'No, but he's off the ceiling and so is all the furniture. So let's call that a minor win.'

'So what now?'

'Why don't you let him out?'

Helena shook her head. 'You know I can't . . .'

'You can! He's cooperating. You've got Dabney Hale on his own fucking wing for crying out loud and he killed half the witches in HMRC.'

Niamh stopped. She'd gone too far. Helena's nostrils flared, her lips grew tighter.

'I'm sorry,' Niamh said. 'Look, here's an idea. Why don't you let him come to Hebden Bridge with me?' She wasn't quite sure why she offered that, but it was out now and there was no taking it back.

'What?'

She was going to regret this. 'Well . . . think about it. I'm out in the middle of nowhere. It's safe. It's what my job used to be. I think he trusts me. I'm not getting a grain of malice; if he destroyed that school it's because he can't control his powers, which isn't a crime. I can read him while he's asleep, but more importantly I don't think we should be keeping kids in cages, Helena. It's not a great look.'

Helena considered this, chewing her lip thoughtfully. 'Very well. Take him to Hebden Bridge. I'm going to send a small security team with you though. Do you know Robyn Jones? Very powerful sentient. I'll have her put a squad together.'

Niamh glanced back through the porthole window in the door and saw the slight boy still squatting in the shadows. 'I think that's overkill, but whatever makes you happy.'

'Niamh,' Helena said, very serious. 'Please stop. You saw what the oracles saw.'

She had, and the vision of that shape towering over the city did scare her. It scared her more than anything had in many years. But demons are tricksters. They manifest in the way that affects *you* most. Leviathan was the demon king of fear, and she was duly scared.

'Oracles see a lot of things,' she said, although she came up short in conviction. 'They don't all come to pass.'

Helena lowered her voice and dragged her by the arm away from Sue, like a child in a supermarket getting a dressing down. 'If this child continues to . . .' She didn't finish the thought. 'This is as bad as it gets. It's *Leviathan*. I'm not sure why you're not taking this more seriously. *A demon made flesh*. The whole point of HMRC is to protect the country from demoniac threat. If I need to . . . well, there might be some difficult decisions ahead.'

Niamh frowned. The Helena Vance she'd grown up with would not be suggesting what she thought she was suggesting. 'What? You saying you'd kill that kid?'

Now Helena looked puzzled. 'To prevent *the Beast* from rising? Of course,' she said much too quickly. 'Wouldn't you?'

Chapter Seven

BIRDS AND BEES

Elle

Elle finished loading the dishwasher. She slammed it shut and waited for the whooshing noise to kick in. Her portion of lasagne was in the bin. Her throat was too tight to swallow, so she'd poked it around her plate before admitting defeat. They'd eaten early to allow Jez to take Milo to a five-a-side in Mytholmroyd at seven. Jez usually stayed to watch on the sidelines with a couple of other proud parents, although they'd all recently received a warning for their *overzealous* commentary.

It was now or never.

She washed her hands over the sink and then applied some Jo Malone hand cream. Expensive and needless, yes, but Elle liked to leave little treats to herself dotted around her home – rewards for maintaining it so well. When Jez did an equal share of the housework, she'd buy him nice smellies too.

Making sure the lounge and dining room were ship-shape, Elle followed the maudlin sound of Holly's music upstairs. Her kids shared the first floor and family bathroom now that she and Jez had *finally* moved into the attic conversion after much delay. They'd had to threaten to sue the cowboys who'd done the work in the end. Nightmare.

She'd finally begun to adjust to a life without that stress . . . and now this. It's always something isn't it?

'Holls?' she tapped on her bedroom door. There were no locks in Elle's home, because they trusted each other enough to knock. It was one of the House Rules framed above the downstairs toilet.

'Come in!'

Elle entered, bracing herself for her daughter's taste. It was an ugly mishmash of Pokémon, manga, German goth bands and modified baby dolls which look like zombies. Just . . . plastic *tat* everywhere. Still, Elle had read lots of books on stifling children, and thought it best to let Holly have her nest.

Before work started on the attic, they'd had a clear out, and Elle had come across her *Forever Friends* 1997 diary. The key long since lost, she'd clipped off the flimsy lock (how did she ever truly trust it to keep her secrets?) and reread her teenage thoughts. No, *thoughts* wasn't the right word: anxieties. She couldn't even pretend to remember the sheer intensity she'd felt in those pages: the very real dilemma of wanting to violently kill a lot of people while also desperately needing everyone to love her. Pages and pages of magenta biro, worrying she'd upset Helena for absolutely no reason.

And so she tried to go easier on Holly than she did Milo. If her own diaries were to be believed, being a teenage girl was a minefield of rules and traps. In 1997, apparently, an inch of fabric in the wrong direction was all that separated her from being a slag or a nun.

Her daughter was sat cross-legged on the floor, working in her sketchbook, right next to the expensive artists desk they'd got her for Christmas.

'Is there something wrong with the desk?' Elle asked. It did drive her mad when they didn't change out of their uniforms. Was it any wonder they always looked like rags?

'No. I just like the floor.' Holly held the sketchbook up. 'What do you think?'

Her angsty artwork depicted the body of a naked woman, covered in blood, with a bull's head. Elle raised an eyebrow. 'Oh, yes it's lovely. May I have it for the fridge?'

'No, it's for my coursework.'

'It bloody well isn't,' Elle said. 'Your art teacher will think we're abusing you.'

'Censorship,' Holly muttered, returning to her creation. Only then she stopped. 'What's up?'

That was what was up. 'What do you mean?' Elle prodded.

'You're being weird. You only come in here on laundry day, and that's not until Thursday.' Holly looked up at her and blinked. Her daughter was more like Jez than her. She *could* be pretty, but seemed to rebel against the notion, recently cutting her mousy hair into an unremarkable chin-length bob. Elle couldn't fathom it. Then again, even as a toddler, Elle had been lavished with praise for her looks. Her mother had entered her into the Bonniest Baby competition in the *Manchester Evening News* when she was two. She won as well. The big blue eyes, the white-blond hair and dimples. How could she lose? *Baby Spice.*

Later, she was the first girl in her class to get breasts, and boys started to offer her gifts and ask her out to the park. She didn't even notice the correlation at the time. Holly, perhaps thankfully, had never swerved that strange affirmation. It was all the sadder, Elle thought, when you lost it.

'I want to talk to you while your dad's out.' Elle perched on the edge of her unmade bed. How hard was it, honestly, to throw a duvet across a mattress?

'Mum, we already did the period chat and the sex chat, remember.' Holly carried on shading with a pencil crayon. 'Both really informative. Top Mumsnet marks.'

Elle felt sick. She remembered her grandmother taking her aside when she was six and telling her she was special. Why hadn't she done this years ago?

'What about Grandma?' Holly said suddenly, twisting round to face her.

'I didn't say anything,' Elle said quietly.

Holly pulled a face. 'Yes you did, something about Granny Device talking to you . . . ?'

'No, Holly, I didn't. And that's what I need to talk to you about. You . . . you, um, just read my mind.'

She frowned and then laughed. 'Yeah, good one! Are you drunk? You normally let Dad be the funny one.'

Elle felt it all build up inside her like a bottle of shaken pop. 'Holly, I'm a witch and so are you.' It all spurted out and trickled down the walls.

Holly sat very still. Her face said she was trying to process the joke, and she didn't get it.

The lid was off now, and all Elle could do was go on. 'Granny Device is a very powerful witch too, but your Nana – my mum – wasn't, you see. So I wasn't sure whether you would be or not.'

'Mum . . . ?'

Elle's eyes stung, but she wanted to get it all out without

74

crying. 'I should have told you when you were much younger, and I'm sorry for that. It doesn't make you bad or evil or wicked. It just *is*, but I wanted to shield you from it. When you were a toddler, I was involved in some troubles . . . and I wanted to keep you safe from all that.'

All the people she'd saved, all the people she hadn't. Who would wish that on their five-year-old? Holly still looked like she was waiting for a punchline, but she wasn't smiling any more.

'Mum . . . should I call Dad?'

'No!' Elle gasped. 'No, we can't tell your father. He doesn't know, and I don't think he'd understand.'

Holly now stood before sitting stiffly on her desk chair. 'Mum, you're freaking me out. You're not a witch. You shop at Next.'

Elle wondered, not for the first time, why HMRC didn't issue official guidance on this. A pamphlet or something. 'What am I thinking about?' she said wearily.

She pictured the lasagne she'd made earlier.

'I don't know. That's insane,' Holly said.

'Go on, guess.'

She vividly pictured sprinkling the cheese over the top before putting it in the oven.

'I don't know!'

'Just guess.'

'Mum, it could be anything. Um . . . lasagne?'

Elle wasn't sure if she was relieved or disappointed. This wasn't the life she wanted for her daughter. 'Got it in one.'

'What? As if. We literally just ate it so . . .'

'That's what I was thinking, Holls. You're what we call a sentient, which means . . .'

She sprung up to her feet. 'Mum, this is so cringe, can

we not? Like, I so wish I *was* a witch because that would be sick, but we are obviously the most boring people in the world, and this whole conversation is fu . . .'

'Um, don't you dare, missy . . .'

'Sorry, but come on!'

Elle sighed and scanned the room. The *Talk* was probably easier with younger kids: less cynicism, less backchat. *All* children quite organically believe in magic, until mundane life squashes it out of them. She swung her legs off the end of the bed and plucked a pair of scissors out of a stationary pot. 'OK, watch this.'

Elle held her left hand up and, clenching her jaw, sliced the scissors across her open palm. A red gash opened up.

'Mum!' Holly screamed, reaching to snatch the scissors off her.

'Wait!' Elle snapped. '*Watch.*'

Within seconds, her hand seemed to glow like there was a tealight under her skin. As soon as her body sensed trauma, it reconfigured the cells and proteins in her hand, sealing up the wound. At this stage, it was like driving the car. She could almost do it without really thinking. She took a tissue and wiped away what little blood had spilled.

'There. Good as new.'

Holly stared at her, slack-jawed.

'I am what we call a healer. I . . . heal things.'

Her daughter continued to stare.

'Well? Aren't you going to say anything?'

She finally snapped out of it. 'Mum. Do you have any idea how much cooler you just got?'

The hardest part had been getting her to shut up about it. She'd been expecting tears. Instead, Elle had to make

Holly swear on her life that she wouldn't tell her group chat. She'd slightly talked up the threat of witch hunters burning them at the stake, which, to be fair had been the case until relatively recently.

By ten, the house was finally settling, although she still felt nauseous. The genie was out of the bottle and wreaking havoc. She'd managed to keep her thoughts together long enough to make the packed lunches for school and rapid-wash Milo's kit so he'd have it for the match tomorrow.

There was comfort in routine.

Bone tired, and on an adrenaline comedown, Elle found herself staring at the walls, specifically the paint they'd chosen for the bedroom. She'd tried five different 'Duck Egg Blues' and this one, by lamplight, somehow reminded her of hospital scrubs. It might need repainting.

'What happened?' Jez asked, climbing into bed.

'What do you mean?' Elle avoided catching his eye in the reflection of her dressing table mirror, focusing on applying night cream to her face in small circular motions. She'd read somewhere that lymphatic drainage reduced puffiness and fine lines.

'What happened in the last episode?'

'Oh, um . . . they found the caretaker's body in the woods?'

Each night, they worked their way through a boxset, a TV fixed to the wall at the foot of the bed. Elle finished her nighttime skincare regime and tucked her pendant into her satin nightie. The small chunk of peridot attached to the chain contained the glamour enchantment. While she wore it, she'd appear as she wished for Jez to see her. Far less taxing than regenerating her actual body, although she had been known to do so for special occasions, like a wedding or a family portrait. To *constantly* hold back the ageing process would exhaust her to collapse within hours.

Niamh's judgement earlier still smarted. How was the charm any different from Botox or a facelift? At least this was *free*. She slipped under the duvet and snuggled up alongside her husband. These days, he kept his boxers on to sleep in. He wasn't quite as toned as he once was, and the hairline receded ever further, but she still definitely fancied Jeremy Pearson. Muscular, short for a man, strawberry blond hair. Great teeth.

He'd left school with two GCSEs, but buckets of charm – a definite twinkle in the eye – which had got him further than any exam would have. Back in the day, every straight teenage girl in Hebden Bridge had chased after Jez, but it was she who had won him, despite the scurrilous rumours about the Device family. And, seventeen years ago, she didn't even need an enchanted necklace to capture his heart. Not quite childhood sweethearts, but not far off.

Jez pressed play on the remote and the recap of the previous episode played. 'What was up with Holls?' he said, wrapping his arm around her so she could nestle in his nook.

'What do you mean?' she asked in a tone that bordered on am-dram.

'She was mad hyper when we got in. She been on the E-Numbers or summat?'

Deny everything. 'Not that I know of.'

'She was like Christmas Eve Holly. Manic.'

'Not a clue,' Elle lied. 'Oh, she is going to start going to Niamh for tuition though.'

'Oh?'

'Yeah. She's falling behind in maths and science. Niamh offered to help.'

'Ah, OK. Milo going too?'

'No,' she said, too quickly. 'I, um, just think it'd be too hard to plan around his football. And his grades are fine, I think.' She'd been lying to Jez for so long, she was fluent.

'Got it.' Jez settled down to watch the show.

Elle cuddled up closer and looked around their beautiful new bedroom, with its Velux windows, underfloor heating, en-suite bathroom and walk-in closet. No one, no one in this world, would risk losing everything she had with something as silly as the truth.

Chapter Eight

AND SO TO BED

Niamh

Night had long since fallen when they arrived back into Hebden Bridge. Ignoring the boy, Tiger darted through her legs, and into the garden as soon as Niamh opened the kitchen door. There were squirrels to be chased and fox shit to roll in.

She only really used the front door if the queen or pope were visiting, an odd habit she'd inherited along with the cottage.

'OK,' she told her silent companion. 'Here we are! This is it! Sorry it's not a mansion or nothing.'

He hovered tentatively on the threshold.

'Come in out the rain,' she said, guiding him in. 'Come sit by the fire and I'll fetch you a towel.'

If she was an elemental, she'd never have need of fire-lighters, but she quickly filled the woodburning stove in the cottage lounge and lit it. The boy – who social services referred to as John Smith – perched dripping wet on the sofa as she did so. She didn't want to call him by a name that had been forced upon him. A stubborn raincloud seemed to follow them all the way from Manchester and she couldn't help but wonder if it was *him* doing it.

Not wanting to upset the applecart, they'd taken the train. Teleportation was stressful enough for the most stable of witches. Helena – not quite trusting her decision perhaps – rode with them. He still hadn't uttered a single word, instead watching rivulets of rain on the train window, his forehead resting on the glass, while Niamh and Helena chatted books, films and coven gossip.

Now, she brought them both towels. He looked at the plush towel as if he'd never seen one in his life. He cautiously dabbed off his face and hair. 'Can I get you a tea or something? Chamomile tea is great before bedtime, or honey and lavender?'

She reached out once more with her mind, this time unfettered by countermeasures of Grierlings, but there was still only that onyx wall in his head. 'Well, I'll have one, so I might as well make you one too.'

As she made the tea, the reality of what she'd done sunk in. This boy, according to the oracles and the taxonomy of demons, was in league with one third of the unholy trinity. And she'd offered him a place to stay. She looked over her shoulder through the door and saw he'd moved from the settee to warm his hands by the fire. Gods, she'd left an elemental alone with an open flame. That might not have been her all-time smartest move.

She didn't dally with the tea.

As she carried it through, he was still warming his milky white hands. 'Can you control the flame?' she asked, trying to keep the nervous trill off her tone.

He squinted at the fire, like he was trying to make sense of it. Suddenly, the flames blossomed with a quiet *woof* and he leapt back. He's scared of his own power, Niamh thought, not the hallmark of a demonic mastermind.

Can you help me?

'That I can,' she replied aloud. She hoped if she spoke out, so might he. 'I'm so sorry about the way you've been treated. I can't imagine how scary it must have been.'

His pitiful bag of clothes was on the kitchen table. On the train, Helena had further briefed her on his recent past. Until the school burned down, he'd been at a care home in Edinburgh under the placeholder name. His most recent foster carers, after fostering him for a year or so, had found him 'concerning' and relinquished him from their home.

'We should have found you sooner,' Niamh admitted. 'There are people in HMRC whose job it is to locate junior witches and warlocks. You slipped through the net.'

He took a sip of the tea. He pulled a face.

'It's not the nicest, is it?' laughed Niamh. 'It'll help you sleep though.'

Were you always a witch?

'Yes. My mam was a witch, and my dad was a warlock. Mam told me and my sister we were witches, well . . . I was so young I don't really remember it to tell you the truth. I suppose I've always known.'

Where are your parents?

'They're both dead,' she said, nose wrinkling. 'Nothing witchy or magical. They died in a car crash when I was younger than you are. That's when we came to live here with our grandmother.' Time to take a shot. 'What about *your* parents?'

The walls in his mind came up so fast, Niamh almost fell off the sofa. That thread didn't want tugging on. 'Sorry,' she said. 'That's none of my business.'

What happens now?

An excellent question, and the poor kid deserved to know.

'Tomorrow, I'll get my colleague to cover me at the surgery and we'll go see a friend of mine, Annie. I trust her with my life, and she might be able to shine some light on the situation. She's the loveliest lady, and she'll almost surely feed us lemon drizzle cake. How does that sound?'

He nodded.

'Come on, I'll show you up to your room.'

She led him to the bedroom that she'd once shared with Ciara. It had twin beds pushed into either corner. Now it was a guest room, not that she'd had guests in years. The room smelled a little musty, unloved, although Tiger occasionally liked a nap on the bed. She found a spare toothbrush and showed him where the bathroom was.

'Do you have everything you need?'

He nodded again, but looked a little dwarfed, even by the poky room. She mostly used it as a dressing room these days, a place to keep excess clothing she couldn't fit in her wardrobe. It was a mess, really, summer dresses dumped on the armchair or slung over the mirror.

'It's gotta be better than Grierlings right?' She smiled and he perked up a little. 'I'm just next door if you need anything.'

She turned to leave, but then added, as an afterthought. 'Hey, you're not a flight risk are you? You're not gonna do a runner in the night?'

He shook his head.

'Good! Sleep tight. You're safe and sound here, I promise.'

Theo.

'Sorry?'

My name is Theo.

Well now that felt good. It was *something*. Vindication. Progress. It'd get Helena off her back. 'Nice to meet you, Theo. Rest up and I'll see you for breakfast.'

Conrad read to her in bed. *Dune.*

'What kind of name is Paul?' he said, putting the doorstop of a novel to one side.

Niamh was already dozing. He read to her to help her fall asleep. 'What do you mean? Paul's a fine name.'

'So the author went to the trouble of naming the planets Caladan and Arrakis and then gave the main character a crap name like *Paul*! Not very sci-fi is it? Like, I'd have called him Xylocarp or something.'

Niamh rolled over. 'That's a coconut.'

'What?'

'A xylocarp. It's a fruit with a hard shell.'

'Oh.'

Niamh realised she could hear water rushing, like she'd left a tap running. 'Con, did you leave the tap on?'

When he didn't reply, she opened her eyes and he was gone. The bedroom was dark, and her bed was cold. The water, however, continued.

Climbing out of bed, Niamh stumbled to the light switch. She flicked it up and down, but the lights wouldn't come on no matter how many times she tried it. The power was out. The thickness of the dark suggested they were hours from dawn. Niamh fumbled for the door handle.

She opened the door wide and, instead of the upstairs landing, the bedroom door now opened on to an unfamiliar room. Niamh held her breath. This wasn't right at all. Light was sparse, and she had to feel her way down a narrow hallway by touching the walls. The air smelled mildewed. The wallpaper was torn, peeling and sepia at the corners.

The rush of water continued.

She was in a dingy flat. Everything was right angles and low ceilings, soulless functionality. Only ashen light dribbled in through slit windows above the doors.

A baby was crying. It cut right through her.

A woman darted from a room on the left and Niamh pressed herself against the wall. She only saw her for a split second, but she was small, thin, with a mane of messy black hair.

Niamh at once sensed power, like money on her tongue.

With all that gruelling inevitability nightmares have, the scene chugged onwards like a rollercoaster heading toward the first summit. Niamh couldn't stop it if she wanted to. She followed the female shape into the room.

It was a nursery of sorts. A tatty bedsheet was stapled over the square windows and there was black mould creeping in from the corners of the ceiling. The crib, nonetheless, was new and filled with soft toys. A lullaby played from a moon and stars mobile dangling over the cot.

The woman hunched over the crib, her movements skittish, nervous. She reached inside and plucked out the infant. She seemed almost too frail to lift it, but she managed. The baby, Niamh thought, was between one and two years, not a newborn in any case. As soon as she picked it up, the baby stopped crying.

Hush now, she said. *There's a good boy. Mother's here.*

The woman cradled the child in her arms and swept past Niamh as if she weren't there. *I'm not here*, thought

Niamh, yet somehow she was. She'd never seen this flat or this woman before, but every detail of it felt solid. The woman's face was haggard. Her skin was sallow and pitted. There was a nasty red sore on her lip. Her long hair was greasy.

Niamh guessed she was younger than she looked. If she came to the surgery, Niamh would find her help. This was a woman who needed help.

Niamh, still a passive voyeur to this strange diorama, followed them across the dingy hallway. The water was coming from the bathroom. This room was in a similar sad state to the rest of the flat. The wall tiles were cracked and mouldy, and a split in the frosted window let in a biting draught. Only a feeble torrent of water trickled into the bathtub. Balancing the baby on her knee, the woman raked her pale fingers through the water, checking the temperature.

Satisfied, she pulled off the baby's romper suit and nappy and lowered him into the water. He fussed and cried anew. *Shhh, it's bath-time, baby.*

Only then, with her free hand, she took hold of the little boy's face and pushed him all the way under the water.

Niamh opened her mouth to scream, but no sound came out. She tried to reach out and pull the woman off the child but found she had no hands. She could only watch as the water danced over the baby's little face and . . .

She awoke hot, her nightie stuck to her back. Tears ran down her face.

And also, there was an earthquake going on.

A glass of water fell off her bedside table. The framed photograph of her and Conrad toppled. The whole cottage shook. Downstairs, Tiger started to bark. 'What the fuck?'

Niamh tumbled out of bed onto all fours trying to steady herself. She pulled herself up and clawed her way towards the spare room, somehow knowing this was something to do with *him*. 'Theo!' she cried. On the landing, a painting of the valley her nan had done fell to the floor, the glass smashing in the frame.

She almost fell into the guest room. She gasped. The boy hovered about a metre off the bed, twisting and kicking in his sleep. His face glistened with sweat. He made whimpering noises as he convulsed.

'Theo!' she cried again. 'Wake up!'

The window shattered inwards, soon followed by the free-standing mirror in the corner, showering them both with glass shards. Niamh screamed, covering her face. 'Theo!'

She grasped his arms and tried to pull him back down to earth, but he was stronger than he looked.

'*THEO!*'

She drilled the most powerful blast she could deep into his subconscious. It worked. His eyes opened and the cottage stopped rattling. He flopped back onto the mattress, limp. Tears ran down his cheeks too, and she understood her dream was also his dream. He'd transmitted it, unwittingly, she guessed, into her mind as she slept. To do that and not even *realise*? Just how fecking strong was he?

'You're OK,' she said unsteadily, getting her breath back. 'It was just a dream.' That was a whole lie and she knew it. It was a *memory*. Niamh knew the difference. 'You're OK now,' she repeated, trying to convince herself as much as Theo.

There was a cut on his cheek from the exploding mirror, and a smaller one on her forearm too. Just a nick. Even in the dark, she saw his skin glow and his cut sealed itself up. He gripped her hand and, a moment later, she felt a deliciously warm sensation flow from his skin to hers and then sink deep into her marrow.

The scratch on her arm faded to nothing, and the pain was gone. He was an elemental, a sentient *and* a healer. That was one more skill than she possessed. She fought to keep her face neutral. Niamh didn't often meet people more capable than she was, and she wasn't wholly sure she liked it.

Who are you?

His eyes glistened in the dark. *I don't know.*

Chapter Nine

VANCE HALL

Helena

As Niamh and Theo had arrived at the cottage, Helena too entered her childhood home. The grandfather clock in the hall chimed eleven as she gingerly closed the sturdy oak door behind her, even though there wasn't really a quiet way to do it. She assumed her parents would be in bed, although she had warned them she would be crashing. Not ideal for work in the morning, but there was no way she was leaving Niamh alone with such a rogue variable. She doubted she'd sleep well, worrying about Niamh, but Helena had trained herself to cope on an efficient five hours a night.

She tiptoed through the ground floor of the house, a gothic replica originally built for silk merchant Rudolph Garnett in 1864, which had been in the family since he'd married young Edith Vance shortly after. Witches do not, as a rule, take their husbands' names.

Helena now recognised her 'comfortable' upbringing, but hadn't then. What child didn't grow up in a seven-bedroom stately home? The rose garden, the duck pond, the treehouse and orchard were all she knew. One day, she assumed, she'd inherit this house, along with her sister. Sell it or gut it? Nostalgia and sentiment can be intoxicating, certainly, but the house was impractical, almost oppressive. The beams were too low, the leaded windows too fussy, the claret drapes too pompous. She much preferred the ease of her stylish townhouse in Chorlton.

She was greeted in the kitchen by a lingering fishy odour that reminded her it was Monday. Fish pie; meat-free Tuesday; lasagne (Week A) or shepherd's pie (Week B); pork chops; fish and chips; gammon and eggs (Week A) or pie and mash (Week B); Sunday roast. She flicked the kettle on before looking in the fridge for something, anything, homemade. The day had seen another trifecta of Pret meals: croissant, sandwich and the salad she'd just eaten on the train. On the top shelf of the fridge there was a clingfilm-wrapped plate of cold cuts she could fashion another sandwich out of. She sourced a bag of salad too and carried everything in her arms to the kitchen island.

Her mother levitated through the door and Helena dropped the lot all over the surface with a loud clatter. 'Mother! That's it, we're getting you a bell.'

'Sorry darling, didn't mean to give you a scare.' Lilian Vance floated into the kitchen silently, her slippered feet a couple of inches off the tiles. Helena often wondered if she *did* do it on purpose. Her stealthy party-piece. Her mother lowered herself into one of several wheelchairs she had dotted strategically around the house.

'I thought you'd be asleep,' Helena said. 'Would you like a drink? The kettle just boiled.'

'Chamomile, thank you. Will my granddaughter be gracing us with her presence?'

Helena smirked, smearing butter on to some freshly baked sourdough. 'Yes, the coven is going to teleport her in any minute now.' She carried two steaming mugs over to the breakfast table and then returned to finish her sandwich.

'Dare I ask what brings you here?' Lilian said, blowing on her tea.

'It's better you don't know. Where's Dad?'

'He's reading in bed.' Lilian was a beautiful woman, all poise and cheekbones, striking even in her silver years. If Helena aged half as well as her mother, she'd be quite satisfied. 'The whisper network is already chuntering away . . . some sort of unrest?'

'I'm sure it is,' Helena ignored her, taking a big bite of the sandwich. 'And no comment.'

'Don't talk with your mouth full. Is it the new Prime Minister?'

Helena fixed her mother with a defiant look as she sat down next to her at the table. 'Mother.'

'What?'

She sighed. 'The new Prime Minister is one more Etonian glory hound who thinks he's just won Head Prefect. As was ever the case, HMRC will continue to work with his advisers from a comfortable distance.'

Lilian smiled archly. 'No one ever said High Priestess was easy, Helena.'

What was it about this house? As soon as she crossed the threshold, she regressed to her seventeen-year-old self. She refrained from barking a surly I KNOW MOTHER in her face.

Helena sometimes wondered if it would ever be enough. Perhaps . . . perhaps if Lilian herself had served as High Priestess she'd have more empathy. As it was, she would forever be the daughter of one, and a mother to one, but never The One herself. A uniquely unfulfilling predicament. A lifelong backseat driver. Helena worked especially hard to keep such musings to herself. She said nothing. It was late, and she didn't want to say something she'd regret by the time morning rolled around.

'You look exhausted.'

'Thanks. I am. I've been up since four.' It was hard to believe the capture of Smythe had belonged to the same day. She wondered how his first night at Grierlings was going.

'Your grandmother always said the knack was in delegation, darling. You don't have to do everything yourself, Helena.'

Don't rise to it, don't give her what she wants. Some people enjoyed bickering the way others enjoy a brisk game of squash. Furthermore, Helena often found that if she wanted something doing right, she *did* have to do it herself. The youngest *ever* High Priestess of HMRC. She had so much to prove.

It was a chaotic time, but she remembered when people first started whispering her name in the midst of the war. The last High Priestess, Julia Collins, had been assassinated, and the feeling was that they needed someone in the thick of things. At first it had been wildly flattering but also lunacy. A star on the ascent, yes, and on the frontline in driving back Hale and his cronies, but a leader, no. The war took precedence over HMRC pomp and ceremony.

Only then Annie Device foresaw her coronation, then the oracles, and then Niamh and Leonie backed her, and her father, and some other well-heeled elders suggested her too. The idea gained traction. Helena Vance, granddaughter of one of the finest high priestesses the coven had ever seen. The fresh, young face of modern witchcraft. She tried it on and found it fit her well. In the end, even Lilian threw her tacit blessing into the ring, in her own way.

No one was immune to ego flattery, but it was the fight then, and the fight now. When she took that oath, she had meant every word. The coven was *everything*. Hale had threatened its very existence, and now so did that boy.

'You're doing a wonderful job, Helena,' Lilian finally said. 'Everyone says so.' Helena was all too aware of her mother's spies in HMRC. Many of them would never get their shot at High Priestess because of her, after all. 'But what is it young people call it? *Self-care?*'

Helena managed a smile. 'Thanks, Mum. I'll book myself in for a spa day when I avert the apocalypse.'

Lilian scrutinised her, trying to work out if she was kidding. Luckily, she was saved by an incoming teleport. The air crackled with static. Lilian seemed to sense it too.

The hairs on Helena's arm stood on end. A shimmering cyclone swarmed in the middle of the kitchen, until Snow stood, phone in hand. She didn't look impressed. 'Can you not do that please?'

'Kiss, please,' Lilian demanded, and Snow skulked over to oblige.

'I was in the middle of something, Mum, you can't just get the coven to kidnap me.'

'I can and I will.' Helena's patience was sorely tested. 'It's almost eleven, you should be in bed.'

'I was with my friends!'

Bother. 'Do we need to wipe them?'

Snow pouted. All mothers think their children are

beautiful, but Snow objectively was. Hair and skin were as white as her name suggested, with round doll-like eyes and full lips. Helena only wished she wouldn't spoil her face with trowel-loads of makeup. 'No. Witch friends.'

'Well then,' Lilian said. 'Where's the harm? Don't be petulant dear. It's unbecoming.'

On the contrary, Helena had raised Snow to speak her mind. In her eyes, *bossy*, *demanding* and *difficult* were misogynist lexicon for drive, ambition and initiative – traits she wanted to foster. Helena just wished her daughter would pick her battles outside of the home setting.

'I'm almost sixteen,' Snow went on. 'I can stay home by myself. If anyone tries to get in the house, I'll set fire to them.'

'There's the spirit,' Lilian chuckled as Snow helped herself to some Diet Coke from the fridge.

'Don't drink that before bed . . .' Helena lamented as her daughter defiantly took an enormous gulp. 'And also bear in mind our home isn't fireproof.' She didn't want to overinflate Snow's own ego, but Helena was quietly proud of how quickly Snow had taken to her craftwork. She was going to be a formidable elemental.

If she ever put her phone down.

'Why are we here anyway? Sorry, Gran. Obviously lovely to see you.'

'No offence taken, dear.'

Helena finished her sandwich and dabbed her mouth with a napkin. 'I can't say, but we need to be in Hebden Bridge tonight. Just in case.'

Snow and Lilian shared a glance. 'Just in case of what?' Snow asked. 'You can't say that and not tell us.'

'I can and I will.' Helena picked up her cup of tea and laptop case. She still had some paperwork to sign off before she could sleep. She pulled Snow into a hug and kissed her forehead. 'I worry about these things so you don't have to. Now, bed. Both of you.'

Helena took the weight of the world, and carried it upstairs to bed.

Chapter Ten

NIGHT TERRORS

Leonie

As children, they'd called it Bluebell Meadow. That was not its name, but it was a meadow and bluebells grew there. Leonie was there. White-pink blossom rained from the trees at the wrong speed. Everything was too slow – time in glue.

There was a bed in the clearing, and in the bed there was a woman. A woman who looked like Niamh but was not. Leonie had always been able to tell the difference. Her eyes were somehow more fox-like and Niamh had a faint scar in her lip.

The sleeping beauty had silver chains on both her wrists, tethering her to the bed.

As Leonie approached the bed, the meadow faded, replaced by sun-bleached floral wallpaper. The room smelled of lavender, of restorative *Virgo Vitalis*. The safe-house. Leonie hadn't visited in a long time. Too long. Once they had been allies. No, more than that. They had been best friends.

At the foot of the bed, Leonie felt a pit open up inside

her and all the hope drain out. Something awful was going to happen. Leonie felt the overwhelming urge to flee. The oldest part of her brain was on full alert: fight or flight. *Get out. Get far, far away.*

In bed, the woman looked restful. Leonie realised the face had changed. There was now a light scar on her lip.

'Where are you, Ciara?' Now there was a question.

Leonie *felt* her. She was close. This all felt a bit too real. Sentients had some very vivid dreams. Barely dreams at all.

Remembering the last time she'd seen Ciara Kelly conscious, and how *different* she'd been, she ought to be scared. Leonie held her breath and turned around, very slowly. She half expected to see Niamh's twin on the ceiling.

'Ciara?'

She felt a strong, icy hand seize her ankle from under the bed and—

Leonie woke up with a jolt. Startled, the cat darted off the foot of the bed and slipped out of the bedroom. Leonie's eyes tried to make sense of the gloom. She was in her bed, she was safe. She checked her phone and it was only just after one.

'What's up?' Chinara muttered, facing away from her. She was the lighter sleeper by far.

Her heart was beating too fast. Fuck, that had been a fucked up one.

'Lee?'

'Bad dream, babes.' No. More than that. That sickly dread lingered.

Leonie, still woozy, reached out across Camberwell, across Southwark, across South London. A dangerous thing to do in a city so populated. A lot of noisy minds make for a lot of noise. Truly London does not sleep and, as a sentient, she'd got used to a certain level of background chatter, in the same way she'd got used to the fact it never really got properly dark. The sky was always muddy with neon smog and the collective psyche of London was similarly murky. A lot of joy, yes, but the worst loneliness she'd ever felt too.

Leonie frowned. 'Something's wrong.'

Chinara rolled over and propped herself up on one elbow. 'What?'

Not wanting to sound like an antsy oracle, Leonie didn't tell her what she was actually feeling. What was the point in worrying her? Chinara had a big meeting in the morning. It wasn't fair. What Leonie felt was *doom*. That was it, the suffocating sense that something awful was going to happen. A catastrophe.

'I, um, just a dream,' she lied.

'Who was it about?'

'It doesn't matter.'

It was more like *what*. *Something* woke her up. Not Ciara, something else. Something bad.

Chapter Eleven

THE PROBLEM WITH PROPHECY

Niamh

One of the girls had laid, so Niamh made eggs for breakfast, all the while stepping on eggshells. So far, there had been no further incidents, but – for the second night in a row – Niamh had had precious little sleep. It's hard to sleep on high alert.

Already Theo looked better for being out of Grierlings. He'd showered and dressed in clean clothes and now looked like any run-of-the-mill teenager you'd see congregating around Hebden Bridge market. He remained timid as a dormouse, but accepted the breakfast of scrambled eggs on an English muffin, eating it hungrily.

'Do you want to talk about your dream?' she asked, regarding him over her largest mug of black coffee.

He shook his head and she didn't press him further.

'Tonight I've got some herbal remedies that'll help you sleep.' She added with a wink, 'and that'll keep the roof on if you have another nightmare.'

He appeared to blush and she assured him it was fine. Couldn't be helped. Accidents happen and all that. She'd already sorted a glazier to come and fix the window later that afternoon. He offered to wash the dishes, perhaps as penance.

'Come on then,' she said once he was done. 'Annie'll be expecting us.'

She was, after all, a very powerful oracle.

Niamh was in no mood for a ramble, so they drove the short distance to Midgehole. Annie's cottage – the old watermill – was far off the beaten track in the woods, nestled on the bank of Hebden Beck, the chatty river that wove all the way through Hardcastle Crags National Trust park, and down into the town. The whole mill seemed drunk, slumping into the forest it backed onto. Annie Device had been born in this cottage and it seemed to age with her. Both wore their years, yet the waterwheel continued to turn, although it no longer ground the wheat it once did.

Niamh and Elle often asked if she'd be happier living with one of them, and said they'd both be happy to have her, but she repeated her mantra: *I was born in this house, and they'll carry me out of it dead.*

No one, least of all Elle, knew how old she really was. Old. Definitely old.

The cottage was surrounded by *most* of the perimeter wall that had once surrounded the watermill courtyard. Nowadays, the crumbling wall, along with a soft enchantment, kept out nosy ramblers and tourists, walling off Annie's wild garden.

Theo hung back at the rusty gates as Niamh fought her way through the jungle of nettles to the front door. 'Come on,' Niamh said. 'There's really nothing to fret over, I promise.' Half consumed by reeds and vines, it did look every inch the Grimm witch's cottage, but Niamh suspected

Annie actively cultivated that appearance to keep folks away. She'd always taken one for the team. She was the 'witch of Hebden Bridge' so the rest of them could get on with it.

Every town has its witch, its gingerbread house.

Annie met them at the front door. 'Niamh, my girl, get your arse inside! Come on, don't let the warm out.' She had the most Yorkshire accent there had ever been, and ever will be.

Niamh was always surprised by how small Annie was now, quite sure the woman was shrinking. These days, she hunched over, and relied on a cane for support. She wore the wig Niamh had bought her two Christmases ago; a simple silver-white feathered bob.

'And who's this?' Annie said. Of course, she couldn't see Theo. She'd gone blind decades before Niamh had come to England, but she could certainly *see* him, and Niamh guessed she already knew the answer. There wasn't a lot that got past Annie Device. Her body was failing, make no doubt, but her mind was a steel bear trap.

'Annie, this is Theo.' She looked back down the higgledy-piggledy path as he hesitantly approached. 'I'm looking after him for a while. He doesn't say a lot . . . or anything in fact, but we need . . .'

The old woman chuckled. 'Oh I know what you need, Niamh Kelly, you need a great big fuckin' cup of tea. Now come on through.'

The cottage was filled with two things: diaries and cats. The cottage was Heptonstall's unofficial cat sanctuary and it smelled like it. Niamh saw Theo gag on entering the house, but gave him a quick look.

I know. We'll sit in the garden. Don't fear.

It was fair to say Annie's sense of foresight was rather keener than her sense of smell.

The diaries and almanacs, piles and piles of leather-bound volumes, were stacked on the stairs, against the walls and on the window ledges. Each contained intricate records of Annie's personal history and all the histories she'd been privy to; those of her ancestors and descendants. She was a custodian of both past and future.

Cats of all colours, shapes and sizes flocked to Niamh's ankles as they walked through the lounge. Familiars – those species with fleeting sentience: cats, toads, ravens, foxes – often sought Niamh out, knowing they could convene with her. She closed her mind off, unable to process so many overlapping consciousnesses. The meowing and mewling were loud enough.

Cats are *not* like dogs. They are fickle, easily bored. They love you intensely for a minute or two and the next you're dead to them. She stroked a couple of the friendlier ones and swerved the patchy ginger tom that hissed at her from the bannister. Niamh tried to neuter as many of Annie's cats as she could, but her feline army just kept expanding. 'We've just had kittens again!' Annie announced proudly, already feeling her way around the kitchen.

'Let me help,' Niamh said.

'Don't be daft. Sit yourself down. Are we in the lounge?'

She looked to Theo again. 'Let's go in the garden. I think it's nice enough.'

Stable doors in the kitchen opened onto a dandelion-strewn riverside patio where there was a rusty iron table and chairs. The garden was overgrown – not to mention covered in cat shit, but there was still the wishing well, and the swing hung, now forlorn and unloved, from the big sycamore tree. She, Ciara and Elle had spent many an aimless August day pushing each other back and forth on that swing, or – even better – leaning over the chair and twisting the ropes round and round before letting go, sending whoever was on the swing into a corkscrew spin.

Can I? Theo's shy voice popped into her head.

'I don't see why not. Careful though, that swing is older than I am.'

Theo carefully stepped through the undergrowth and tested his weight on it. It seemed to hold and he pushed himself off. He swung back and forth and he looked to her, a childlike surprise on his face. It was as if this was his first day on earth: eggs, swings, cats . . . everything seemed new to him.

Niamh thought back to his nightmare with a sourness in her stomach. If indeed he *was* that baby in the bathtub, he'd survived it – at least physically. That didn't tell her *how* he remembered the episode. Not even powerful oracles can remember their own infancy. For now, Niamh was operating on the assumption that the fraught woman with black hair was his birth mother, and she'd tried to drown him. That was surely the worst thing that could possibly befall a child. So it meant she'd take extra good care of him until it was time to give him back to HMRC.

A tiny furball kitten found him, and he stopped swinging to pick it up. Again, he looked to her for permission and she nodded. He carefully reached for the baby and picked it up, awe on his face.

Annie emerged from the kitchen with a tea tray and Niamh jumped up to help her. 'Here, let me get that.' She steered her to the table and rested the tray. 'How've you been, Annie? Sorry it's been a while.'

'You know me, love, can't complain. I'm falling to pieces, of course, but I shan't be complaining.'

Niamh smiled. 'The wig looks good. Suits you.'

'Oh aye? Shall I get myself down the Working Men's Club, see if I can ensnare a fancy man?'

Niamh laughed, but Annie *had* lived quite the colourful life. Niamh didn't doubt she'd fit in another husband, or indeed a wife, if she so chose. For one thing she was directly descended from the Pendle witches who'd been persecuted in 1612, which she wore as a badge of honour, regardless of the fact those witches had been sloppy enough to get caught. Pendle and Salem alike were a cautionary tale to all witches. *That* is what to expect when a coven descends into infighting and backstabbing.

In her youth, Annie flitted around the world, visiting as many overseas covens as she could, somehow finding the time to birth four children by four fathers. *I'm a 4x4 too*, she'd once said saucily, nodding at Niamh's Land Rover. Her youngest daughter was Elle's mother, Julie, born under the stars in a tent somewhere in the Nairobi Desert.

'Are we to walk while the tea brews?' Annie said. 'It'll do my hip some good.'

'Of course.' Niamh took her arm and they set off down the meandering garden path which looped around the entire mill. They spoke briefly of Holly Pearson. Annie had heard the news from Elle and, of course, was thrilled the Device line lived on in her. Niamh *strongly* suspected the information had not come as a surprise to the former Head Oracle.

Out here, it was a sensory feast; the colours, the scents. The garden may have looked like chaos – a wilderness of towering foxgloves and cow parsley, spiky teasel and columbine, bluebells and corncockles – but nature was never meant for symmetry. Annie's garden was messy equilibrium, a life-support system. Niamh sensed some very happy bees, worms and birds. Some of these flowers, Niamh understood, had no business flowering in late March, but a witch could convince anything to bloom if a witch knew the right words to say.

Niamh wondered sometimes if this was her future too. Fiercely single; just batty enough to deter nosy strangers; surrounded by animals and a handful of cherished friends. She could think of far worse fates.

'Shall we talk about the child?' Annie said, knowing all the while the purpose of her visit.

'Have you seen the prophecy?'

'Oh aye,' Annie said. 'And I had one of Helena's little minions on the blower too.'

Oh, is that right? Why had Helena denied that?

'Well?' Niamh lowered her voice. 'Is he this *Sullied Child*?'

Annie tilted her face skywards, basking in the meek sunshine. 'The child is a powerful symbol in divination,' she began. 'Life, unbridled potential, new beginnings. I've always felt, as oracles, we should be very careful about adding value – good or bad – to prophecies. Nothing's ever fully one or t'other. Sometimes change, although painful in the short term, is very much needed. The child was foreseen, that is all I'll say on that. Ooh, I wonder if I've got any biscuits in the tin. I bet they've gone soft if I have.'

'Annie!' Niamh's stomach was a tight knot. 'Helena seems to think there's a link between him and the . . . well did you see what they showed me?'

'Leviathan? Oh yes.'

She didn't seem nearly as anxious as she probably ought to be. 'And?'

'The unholy trinity made three weapons o' man: want, hatred and fear. The demons want us scared, Niamh, because fear makes us do some daft stuff. They enter into the reverie, make no mistake.'

It was true that demonkind speaks to humans on an individual basis, tailoring their appearance or promises to elicit the desired response from their victims. That's why they're so bloody effective. A personal demon, just for you, playing directly into your hopes and fears. 'But, all the oracles said—'

'If all the ruddy oracles said "jump off a cliff" would you do it to prove them right?'

'No. But I'd definitely get real cautious on clifftops.'

Now Annie laughed. The older she got, paradoxically, the more girlish her giggle got. She was like a naughty imp. 'If I had a shilling for every time I explained the nature of prophecy I'd be a very rich woman indeed. For us, even as witches, we read time in a straight line. Only Gaia sees it all upside-down and back-to-front. We tell stories and pass them down the line to the oracles before us and we receive the ones being passed down from tomorrow. But here's the thing: we tell 'em slant. None of us can resist adding a little relish, a little spice. And you've got to bear in mind two things: who's doing the telling, and who is the audience? They both matter very much. Both history and future are fictions. Only the present is real. Remember that.'

Niamh stewed on that while a wood pigeon cooed almost flirtatiously somewhere nearby. 'So you think the oracles in the future are . . . exaggerating? Or that it's what the oracles now want to hear? Why would they want to hear about Leviathan rising?' Her head was starting to strain. She might need a twenty-minute nap this afternoon.

'Who can say? I used to add a bit of spooky all the time. Much of life is tedious, Niamh, you've got to have a laugh haven't you? I do know that nothing's set in stone. Can you remember when they asked me to be High Priestess?'

Niamh laughed. 'No! Because it was about twenty years before I was born!'

'Well they did. HMRC did. It was seen that I'd be next.'

'And you didn't see it?'

'Oh no I did! Quite vividly saw myself getting up there in the fancy scarlet robe, and that ivy coronet on me bonce, but it weren't for me. I said "thanks, but no thanks", I did.'

Niamh had no idea. How, in all their years, had she never heard this story. 'I didn't realise you could turn it down.'

'Gaia likes surprises! She give us free will for a reason. I turned it down. They offered it to Clara Vance and, sure enough, the prophecies changed. Like a boulder falling in that stream, the water ran in a different direction. I were the boulder.'

'So the prophecy isn't certain?'

Annie stopped still now that they were back where they started, at the back of the cottage. She pointed at Theo, who now sat on the rim of the well, calmly playing with a pair of kittens, teasing them with a dandelion clock. 'All I know for certain is that that child heralds change. And not everyone is going to like that change.'

Niamh understood.

Annie now unhooked her arm from around Niamh's. 'Come on then. Let's not let them teabags stew.' She shuffled off down the path. 'Theo love, just be careful near that well.'

Niamh grinned. 'If you fall in there, you'll end up in Blacko.'

He rightly looked confused. Annie reached in her pocket for a two-pence coin and tossed it in the deep well. It gave a satisfying plop. 'Back in the fifties, I had a very close friendship with a married woman who lived in Blacko. We had the elementals make us a water conduit, so when her husband was back at parliament, I could sneak over in a jiffy.'

Blacko was a village in the Pendle Hills, about forty minutes by road, but mere seconds by water conduit. 'Does it still work?' Niamh asked incredulously. She'd been through it once when she was about twelve. Utterly terrifying. For a second, it had felt like drowning, pitch dark and airless, and then up she'd popped in the sister well, safe and sound. A rush, certainly, but not one she cared to repeat.

'Oh aye. While those old stones are enchanted, it'll do its job.'

Theo looked darkly fascinated. He searched the ground for a rock. He picked it up and let it drop into the black water below. There was another splash and then silence.

Niamh suddenly felt a chill. She looked to Theo. He caught her looking and, just for a split second, there was a certain flint in his eyes. And that was when *her* penny dropped. It wasn't a physical resemblance, but something in his mannerisms.

He reminded her of Ciara.

Chapter Twelve

WITCHCRAFT 101

Niamh

Niamh and Holly embraced for a long time.

'Every time I see you, you look more like a grown-up,' Niamh said.

The St Augustus school uniform, she noted, hadn't been updated a stitch since her time there, but Holly no longer looked like a little girl. 'Stop it, will you? You're a reminder of my own mortality! Do you want a drink or something?'

Holly entered the kitchen and dumped her school bag by the door. 'No thanks. Actually just some water? Mr Robson said in Biology that we're supposed to drink eight glasses a day, but I try not to use the toilets at school because the toilet attendant is definitely a nonce.'

Niamh laughed – because she hoped it was a joke – and fetched her a glass. Theo sat so quietly in the lounge, that Holly gasped when she realised there was someone else present.

'Oh, Holly, this is Theo. Theo, this is Holly. Her mam's my best friend. She's a witch too.' She handed Holly the water. 'Theo doesn't talk just yet, but he's telepathic like we are.'

Holly's eyes widened. 'I don't know how to do that yet . . .'

'That's what we're here for. Let's go in the garden and be nearer to Gaia.'

There'd been a little rain that afternoon, but Niamh told them that – in nature – there's no such thing as good or bad weather. Witches embrace everything Gaia makes. She shepherded them both out into the garden for her first lesson in years. She'd dug out a couple of copies of Patricia Kingsell's *An Introduction to Witchcraft*, although the textbook hadn't been revised since *she'd* been inducted and the most recent edition was from 1992.

'Who's Gaia?' Holly said. 'Is that like God?'

'Start with the biggies, why don't you? Hold your horses,' Niamh said as she settled herself cross-legged on the grass. 'Sit like me. Connect your butt to the earth.'

Theo smiled shyly.

Niamh tucked her hair behind her ears. 'I thought for lesson one we wouldn't actually practise any magic.' In truth, after his nightmare the other night, Niamh wasn't sure the cottage could take it. The last few days, thankfully, had been much calmer. Before bed, with Theo's permission, she made him a tea laced with a drop of *Sisters' Malady* to keep his power under control. A little chunk of amethyst under his pillow also aided restful sleep, not to mention safeguarding her new windows. 'Instead I want to teach you what it means to be a witch or a warlock. How does that sound?'

Holly grinned broadly. 'Sorry, but can I just say how mental this all is? I'm still getting my head around it. Like, I'm a fucking witch!'

'Don't swear, darl, or I'll have to tell your mam.'

Theo laughed quietly. That was a good sign.

'Witchcraft though? Amazing.'

'It *is* amazing, you have no idea. OK, close your eyes. I could *tell* you, but I thought it'd be more fun to *show* you.'

'You can do that?' Holly gawped at her.

'I can. And some day you might too. Just relax, feel the cool grass. Empty your head of anything you've got going on in there – homework or whatever. Just be as blank as you can be.'

'Shouldn't be too hard, Milo always says I'm vacant.'

'Holly . . .'

'Sorry.'

'Focus on your breathing. Just breathe in . . . and out.' She waited for total quiet. HMRC was conducting a lot of research on how distraction – social media and streaming services and the like – were impacting young witches. Certainly they weren't seeing as many Level 4s or 5s as they used to, and one theory was that novice witches lacked the meditative skills needed to hone their natural power. They simply couldn't sit still or empty their minds of anxieties.

When there was a calm synchrony to their breathing, Niamh reached out with the images that had been shown to her as a child. Her mother and father – both blessed – had told these tales to her and Ciara from the crib. They were the first stories she knew. It was like Annie said, all history is narrative. If you weren't there, it's a story.

Niamh began . . .

In the beginning, none of this was here. Nothing, total nothingness, is really hard to imagine, though. So let's skip to when everything changed. Before the

111

earth, moon and stars, there were powerful beings who lived in a realm we can't hope to understand. It was endless, eternal. If you want, you can call them gods or demons, although those are words we have given them. They didn't look like anything we know, and we don't have the words to describe them, so I won't even try. Simply put, they are beyond us. One day, one of these almighty beings – the most powerful of all – grew lonesome. She'd roamed eternity, and it was time to stop still a while. She made a home for herself out of herself; she became.

Everything there is was made from her: the atoms and molecules; the oceans and mountains; the trees and soil; the sun, the stars . . . everything. She forged herself into being. She started a glorious chain reaction. The life she created spawned new life, new species. It was unexpected, but she delighted in all the life she had made.

What she didn't know was that, as she fashioned the physical realm, other gods or monsters became trapped here too, and these great beings envied her creation and resented their earthly prison. If they couldn't have it, they'd destroy it in their bid to escape this reality. They weren't mighty enough to fight her, in fact they were weak in comparison, but they could sow seeds of malcontent in the most powerful of the creatures she made: us.

All of our worst traits: anger, hatred, jealousy and greed come from this poison in the well. We, as witches, call them demons. Oh, there are many of them – some powerful, some less so. They hide among us. Pouring words in our ears.

As the demons fanned the flames of war, and

murder, and famine, Gaia – the mother – fought back. She spoke first to her daughters, and later her sons. She taught us well, and showed us how to use her gifts. The tools were at our fingertips all along.

The demons spoke to us too, offering us earthly and sensual rewards for doing their bidding, to be their hands and voices. A selfish warlock or witch can live quite deliciously by using their powers for personal gain, but at what cost? If one takes out more water than one puts in, a pond soon runs dry. As Gaia grew ever older, she relied on her daughters to protect the colossal shell she'd made of herself.

The most powerful of her rivals was the demon king Satan. He tempted many a witch with delights of the flesh. A great divide erupted which engulfed early witch-kind. Covens united and, while they couldn't kill this overlord, they found a way to weaken him. Satan was split into an ungodly trinity of Master, Trickster and Beast. Three lesser demons: Belial, Lucifer and Leviathan. The first for hate, the next for want, and the last for fear. They were taken far away and contained – perpetually – in prisons of earth, fire, air and water.

Of course, that's not to say they don't look for ways out. The trinity still whispers to man and witch alike, but there's only witches who can guard the threshold between the world of demons and the world of mundanes. We're gatekeepers and protectors.

That's why, each year at solstice, new witches in this country make a promise to Gaia. We go to a sacred place in the Pendle Hill and swear our fealty to the mother. Without her, we are nothing, and have nothing. We sacrifice our lives to the cause: custodians of Gaia and her limitless creation.

It had started to rain more heavily at some point. Niamh opened her eyes to see Theo and Holly, both still entranced and soaking wet. Her hair was plastered to her face. Coming out of the reverie, she started to feel the cold on her skin.

Show over, her young pupils opened their eyes too. 'Wow,' Holly said.

Where are the demons? Theo asked.

Holly looked startled for a moment, hearing his question in her mind too. It was interesting that *he'd* ask *that* question. 'They are everywhere and anywhere,' Niamh said. 'They can live in the water, the air, the rocks. Demon is a very loaded word, they're just . . . otherly. It's certainly not like anything you've seen on TV. Mundanes hear them too, they just don't know what they're listening to.'

The pair looked at her, both processing the enormity of what she'd just imparted.

'Come on,' she said. 'Let's get out the rain. I'll make cocoa.'

She didn't even hear the van crunching down the track to the cottage, but she did see Luke's frame appear over the wall. She felt Theo bristle at once, surprised by the intrusion. Lightning snapped and crackled at his fingertips. Niamh grasped his shoulder. 'Theo, it's fine. He's a friend.'

Luke ran towards them. 'God, this weather!' he said, bursting through the gate. 'You all right?' He regarded Holly and Theo with some confusion.

'Yeah,' Niamh said, hustling them towards the door. Theo's mistrust seeped from him in stormy midnight-blue waves. She gave his shoulder what she hoped was a reassuring squeeze. 'Theo, this is Luke.'

Luke gave him a jovial wave. 'You good, mate?'

Theo, as ever, said nothing as she steered him inside.

'What you doing out in the rain?' Luke asked.

'We . . .' Niamh had never been great at lying on the spot. 'We just got back from a walk. Got caught out.'

'Ah, fair enough. I can't stop. I've got work to do but I were passing.'

Niamh quickly dried her face on a tea towel. 'What's up?'

Luke looked confused. 'Tonight?'

And now Niamh was. 'Tonight?'

'*The Exorcist*?'

How was it possible that six days had passed since she saw him last? 'Oh my . . . Luke, I totally forgot!' The look on his face really tore at her heart. 'I'm so sorry.'

'No worries. I should have texted really.'

'No, it's totally my fault. I've been busy.' Holly and Theo hung back like spare parts, watching this awkwardness unfold. 'I, um, Theo is my cousin.'

'Cousin?'

Cousin?

'Yeah, from Galway. He's come to stay for a while because his mam is real sick right now.'

Luke's expression changed at once. He turned to Theo. 'Oh, mate. Sorry to hear that.'

Theo nodded, playing along mercifully.

'He doesn't say much,' Niamh added for good measure. 'He arrived . . . unexpectedly . . . and the film slipped my mind.'

She read his disappointment loud and clear, but he also understood and believed her excuse. 'Honestly, it's fine. Totally understandable. It's on tomorrow night too if you can make it then instead?'

Niamh wasn't sure she could leave Theo alone. If Helena found out, she'd legitimately fire her into the sun. 'Of

course you can leave him alone,' Holly announced
suddenly.

Holly!

'What if I came over? Then he wouldn't be alone?'

I'll be fine, Theo added.

'We could watch a film,' Holly said. '*The Witcher*, or
Season of the Witch, or *The Craft* . . .'

Niamh gave them both a very serious look. The sheer
exhaustion of mentoring young witches came flooding
back. Sticking her arm up a cow's rectum was preferable.

Theo, I should stay with you.

Go with Luke.

Are you sure?

Yes.

'OK,' she said uncertainly, 'tomorrow night it is.'

Luke's demeanour brightened at once. 'Great! Shall I
pick you up at seven?'

'I'll meet you at the cinema,' she said quickly. Him
picking her up somehow made it feel more date-like,
reminiscent of fumbles she'd had in backseats during high
school.

'OK! Can't wait! *The power of Christ compels you!*'
He grinned.

'*Your mother sucks cocks in hell!*' Niamh immediately
wished she'd picked a different quote. Holly audibly
gasped.

He chortled. 'You leave my mother out of it! I better
go, I have a van full o' food.'

'I'll see you tomorrow.' Luke ducked out, and she turned
to her young charges as soon as he was out of earshot.
'OK then, let's talk about the *secret is ours to keep* part
of the oath, shall we?'

They both looked sheepish.

She did, however, like that they'd buddied up. Because she'd had Ciara, she'd never ever felt alone, and witchcraft always felt very ordinary. Now, Theo could see there were more like him. In fact, she could sense them figuring out the telepathy part, but chose not to listen in to whatever they were saying. That'd feel like reading his diary or something.

Although, this might be the opportunity she needed. While they were conversing, Niamh delicately skimmed his memories. If Holly was distracting him, she might be able to creep in unnoticed. She turned her back to them, filling the kettle to make the cocoa.

Concentrate.

There.

She saw only staccato flashes: his school ablaze, the grey-caped witches of HMRC arriving to take him away, being forced into that cage, and then . . . nothing.

Theo turned to her, fury briefly flashing in his eyes. The flame on the stove flared briefly and Niamh recoiled. She stared him out and he backed down at once.

Sorry, he said.

It's fine.

Niamh focused on the task at hand. She was going to need a bigger boat.

Leonie.

Chapter Thirteen

SATELLITES

Elle

Milo got home first. Like a tom cat, he only ever came through the flap when he wanted feeding these days.

'Mum, can I have twenty quid?'

She stopped stirring the risotto a moment. 'No. What? Why?'

He rolled his eyes. Her eldest was the spit of his father, but somehow less ruddy and more refined. Elle feared for the poor hearts of Year 11 girls.

'It's Cameron's birthday and we're going to Laser Quest and then Nando's in Manchester, but his mum needs to pay a deposit or something.'

'Milo, you already had your allowance.'

He pushed himself up onto the kitchen counter. 'Yeah, but I spent it on essentials.'

Elle added a good grind of pepper into the pan. 'Such as?'

'Drugs and hookers.'

'Don't even joke! Get down!' she slapped him off the worktop. 'You know where my purse is. If there's no cash, borrow some from the lottery syndicate pot and set a reminder for me on the Alexa.'

'Thanks, Mum.' And off he went.

Jez was next in.

'Shoes off!' Elle barked, able to tell without even looking from his heavy footfalls on the garden path that he hadn't removed them.

He kissed her neck. 'This smells good. Can you save me a plate?'

She stopped stirring, quite aggressively. 'What? Why? Where are you going?'

'I'm late with a car so I promised I'd drop it tonight. Sorry. I'll only be an hour tops.'

'Jez . . .'

'It's just an hour. I'll drop it off, get the bus to the garage, and drive back here.'

'Risotto goes funny in the microwave.' She resisted the nasal whine in her voice. *I wouldn't need to nag if you didn't give me reasons to nag.* She had made a personal vow to never be *that* old fishwife, but felt it setting in like rising damp. You wouldn't think he had a fully functioning mobile phone that could relay messages to her.

'It'll be lush. Back in a bit.' He kissed her fleetingly again and went back out the way he came.

Holly was last, and Elle could feel her vibrating with hot yellow energy from halfway down the street. She was quite literally buzzing following her lesson with Niamh, almost dancing into the kitchen. 'I'm home!'

'Well, I don't need to ask how that went,' Elle said, lifting the pan off the heat.

Mum, it was amazing.

'Stop that!' Elle snapped. One lesson in, and she could

already do that? It was hugely unnerving. She stuck her head into the lounge to make sure Milo wasn't eavesdropping. He was nowhere to be seen, off on his next adventure. 'I only want you to use telepathy in absolute emergencies. Understood?'

'Why?' Holly screwed her face up. 'It's faster than typing out a text.'

Elle remembered *Introduction to Breathing with Fearne* and took a deep breath in through the nostrils and let it out through her mouth. She was annoyed at Jez for spoiling dinner, not Holly. 'Holly, I'm not joking. It's part of the oath. What we are has to be a secret.'

She looked a little wounded. 'Even between us?'

'Yes. Well, no. I mean we have to be very careful.' Elle wasn't genuinely fearful of witch finders. They mostly existed online now. She was scared of the other mums finding out. She and Jez had *finally* been invited to one of Rose Hamilton's Nutri-Juice evenings and she wasn't going to blow it now.

One day, before too long, Milo and Holly would fly the nest, and Elle rather looked forward to a future of book clubs, flower arranging, wine tasting and spin classes. Elle had no intention of drinking (or selling) that Nutri-Juice tripe but Rose would be an influential friend to have. Worth subscribing for that alone. Elle had been a witch her whole life, and a mum for fifteen years. Now she just wanted to be a woman again.

'I'm sorry,' Holly said, picking a pea out of the risotto and burning her fingers. 'Ow! I'm just excited. This is the most exciting thing that's ever happened to me.' She now went to the fridge and picked out some pineapple juice.

'Get a glass,' Elle said, knowing what was about to happen. You didn't need to be a clairvoyant when you'd lived with someone for fourteen years.

Holly did as she was told without arguing, which must mean she was in a good mood. 'I mean, it's a freaking revelation. I always *knew* I was different. Like, girls at school are always like, *Holly Pearson, are you a goth? Are you a mosher? Are you gonna cast a spell on us?* Now I'm like, um, yes bitch, I will.'

No. Absolutely not. Elle felt sick. She wished, and it was a horrible wish, that she could wipe the last week from Holly's mind and have things go back to normal.

'Holly, no, that is enough!' she snapped. 'We do not use our powers that way . . . not ever.' A healer *could* inflict quite excruciating pain, but it stood against everything Elle believed she was.

'Mum! I'm kidding. God, you need to lighten up.'

She took her juice into the lounge and Elle was left alone in her magazine-worthy kitchen. This was her space, her personal HQ. It was the office, strategy room, canteen. She certainly spent more time in this room than any other, like a planetary body around which her satellites revolved. They drifted in and out of her orbit, and she remained fixed on her axis.

I wonder, she thought, if this is how Gaia feels.

Is this what it is to be Mother?

Chapter Fourteen

BLACK MASS

Leonie

There were better Chinese restaurants outside Chinatown, but The Jade Empress was convenient, and Chinara liked that they served dim sum all day. Leonie herself went for the tofu chow mein every time. Just the right level of greasy, but with no MSG high afterwards. It was a poky restaurant, almost claustrophobic, with red everything: walls, carpet, vinyl booths and paper lanterns. Plucked ducks hung in the window – a feature Leonie found gruesome.

'You want a bit of squid?' Leonie asked, holding it out on her chopsticks.

'Go on,' Chinara replied. Leonie was *mostly* vegetarian, but the odd bit of seafood didn't guilt her out too much. Probably because she'd never lived by the sea.

Leonie landed it in Chinara's mouth as her phone vibrated on the table. The notification told her it was Niamh. Well, damn. It had been a minute. She realised, however, that since her weird-panic-attack-thing the other night, she'd been expecting this. Well, she'd be expecting

Helena. Leonie wondered if Helena had asked Niamh to get in touch.

'Is it the coven?' Chinara asked as the waiter brought her a steaming basket of pork buns.

Leonie picked up her phone. 'No, it's Niamh.' She read the message. There it was. 'She wants me to go to Hebden Bridge.'

'To see the white people?'

Leonie laughed. 'No. Well yes. One white person in particular. The kid from the visions.' And all of a sudden, she was right off her chow mein. There was a nervy energy in her own coven about this random kid, and she didn't want to connect it to her sudden foreboding. It was pure coincidence. Because if it wasn't . . . well she didn't want to think about that.

Chinara dismissed it with a wave of her chopsticks. 'HMRC business.'

'Niamh isn't HMRC though, is she?'

'Babe, she might as well be.'

'She's never asked me for nothing before.' Niamh was Leonie's first girl crush. Chinara knew that because she'd told her when she was drunk one time. In hindsight, that was probably an error. And anyway, regardless of how many unrequited love songs Leonie had written about her in her *Powerpuff Girls* notebook way back when, Niamh was resolutely straight so that was that. What was even weirder was that she'd never fancied Ciara. Yes, they were physically identical, but Ciara was the only person who got sent to the Assistant Head's office more than she did. They were partners in crime, while Niamh was all daisy chains and lip gloss, and all the more alluring for it.

Now that she thought about it, that was some patriarchal bullshit.

Leonie poked at her food one last time before abandoning it.

'These visions,' Chinara said, her mouth full. 'They're nothing to do with us. Bri said she couldn't see our place in it all.'

Leonie shook her head. 'I know, I read her.' She paused. 'But I dunno if that means we *don't* have a place in it. Know what I mean? Everything's fucked up. The water's muddy, babe.' She'd never known anything like it. She was a big believer in gut feelings. The oracles told her what they saw, and their potential interpretations, but Leonie had always been able to rely on instincts and they always steered her right.

Usually, she dismissed them with a *it'll be fine*. Other times, you just knew to be worried. In 2019, oracles all over the world had seen the same portents of plague and unrest. Some governments heeded their witches. Others, notably, did not.

Now, though, this kid. A boy who would bring about death and destruction. An old-timey, textbook, doommonger prophecy. Her instincts were telling her . . . to feel weird. Just that, and nothing more. It wasn't good, like the planet was tilting and they were all about to slide. 'We need to wait,' she said. 'I'm all for doing, but sometimes the doing that needs to be done is just waiting.'

Chinara nodded slowly. 'You're right. But I maintain you're shit at picking your battles.'

Leonie grinned. 'You're not wrong.' She read the message again and put her phone away. 'I'll think about it and reply after mass.'

A little girl approached them. Leonie assumed she was the restaurant owner's daughter because she'd been doing some colouring in at the solo table near the door by herself.

'Hello,' Chinara said, smiling widely.

The girl held out a paper rose she'd coloured with a blue felt tip.

'Is this for me?'

She nodded and Chinara took the flower. 'Oh my days! Thank you so much. It's almost as lovely as you are for making it.'

The girl's head almost vanished inside her body and it was too cute to stand. She turned and scurried back to her table.

'Oh my goddess, how cute was that?' Leonie said.

'Yeah,' Chinara carefully folded the rose into her purse – a Louis Vuitton Leonie had got her for her last birthday. 'Is it time yet?'

'For mass?'

'No . . . for the talk. You said we could talk again in the summer.'

Leonie smiled, but simultaneously felt a different kind of dread kick in. 'Babe, if I'm wearing a coat, it's not summer.'

'I know, but we've got a lot to talk about. And if we're going to have two like we said, then . . .'

'Babe.'

'*Babies.*' Chinara's eyes twinkled.

Leonie laughed, but even she wasn't convinced. Of course she wanted kids . . . in like fifty years. Both Helena and Elle had babies in their twenties and they just *ruin* everything.

Last year, she and Chinara had fucked off to Jamaica and pissed about in bikinis for three weeks. They'd spent four days at Leeds Festival off their tits on pills. She'd flown to a yoga retreat in Bali on twenty-four hours' notice. A screaming baby in no way fit with their life. It was honestly a fucking riddle as to why Chinara was so keen to get started. 'How the fuck can we make children when we are children!'

'Speak for yourself! We are grown adults in our thirties. Spoiler: we're not kids any more.'

OK, Chinara was a legit grown-up, but Leonie wasn't so sure of herself. She finished her beer and wondered if she could conceivably get another in before mass and if that was a good idea. See? That wasn't the kind of thinking adults did. They would automatically know that running a huge event drunk was a dreadful idea. 'I just keep waiting for that day when I wake up and feel like a grown-up.'

'Lee, I'm a human rights lawyer, and I'm still waiting for that day. And, bitch, look at everything you've done. I see you.'

Founding a fifty-strong coven was far less intimidating than making a baby. It wasn't about her commitment to Chinara; they were in it to the death. It was just that, before her, Leonie hadn't thought one way or the other about children. It was like this prophecy: murky. She knew herself well enough to know what it was. It was fear, plain and simple. Her dad split when he found out what she was, and she was scared to hurt a child the way he'd hurt her. She had a therapist for a while, and you get a cookie for correctly identifying an emotion.

Speaking of cookies, they should probably get the bill. She flagged down the waiter.

'So?' Chinara asked. 'Should we start making plans?'

'Yes,' Leonie said, her heart leaping up into her mouth. 'We can definitely start *planning*.'

'I see what you're doing,' said Chinara. 'I don't mean plan to have a plan by next year, I mean let's start talking spunk, turkey basters, uteri.'

'Uteri? Or uteruses?'

Chinara threw a crumpled napkin at her head. 'Who gives a fuck? I mean it, Lee. Let's do this. There's never gonna be an ideal time, so the time might as well be now.'

The waiter brought the bill on a silver tray with the fortune cookies.

'Oh this should be interesting,' Chinara said, quicksilver in her eye, cracking her cookie open with her palm. She peeled out her fortune. '*Embrace change; don't fight it.* Well I think that's case closed. We're having a baby. Good times.'

Leonie scrunched her face. 'Yeah, sure, let's plan our lives based on cookie wisdom. Maybe mine will tell us who's oven we're using. You think?' She split her cookie open. '*A friend indeed helps a friend in need.* Oh, for crying out fucking loud.'

Chinara laughed even louder. 'Guess you're off to Hebden Bridge *and* having a kid. Big night for Leonie Jackman. Come on, let's roll or we'll be late.'

As they did every week, they slipped through the greasy, steam-filled kitchen and out of the fire escape. The Jade Empress was tasty *and* convenient. It was only a few steps across the alley to the stage door of the old Diablo Theatre. Chinara pounded on the door while she had a quick fag. *You'll have to kick the habit this time if we're going to have a child, Leonie.* After a moment or two, it opened up and Kane's face appeared through the crack. 'Oh my days! I thought you wasn't coming! You're late!'

'It's bang on eight!' Leonie said, pushing past them. By day, Kane Sanchez was a trainee mental health nurse, by night they were Kane *Dior* Sanchez, fierce fucking queen. Yes, the pronouns took some getting used to, but – like anything – the more Leonie practised, the less she fucked it up. 'Is it busy?'

'Yes, ma'am. Stalls are about full.'

'Oh wow.'

The three of them made their way through a labyrinth of backstage corridors, now a theatrical ghost town. The theatre, on Shaftesbury Avenue in Soho, had never reopened after the pandemic, but they couldn't tear it down because of its listed building status. It had been gathering dust and spiderwebs until Leonie had reached out to a bougie old witch who was on the board and asked if they could use it for Black Mass pro bono.

The theatre smelled musty, some of the seats had been torn out by squatters, and you could hear busy mice feet in the walls, but while she was tired, she was still a *grande dame*. The Victorian splendour was *faded*, but the Diablo had a certain end-of-the-pier dignity, and she had always been a fan of veteran drag queens, their wrinkles filled with warpaint. Leonie was usually immune to such sentimentality, but the theatre *was* somehow hallowed ground.

Some of the biggest names in vaudeville had played here – Rita Mae Brown, Josephine Baker – and now it was home, once a week, to Black Mass. Leonie was proud of her little play on words. Once used by the church to decry any sort of witchly activity as Satanic, Leonie now reclaimed it to describe her community gatherings. There had – as is the way with these things – been much, *much* discussion over whether the name was fully inclusive of *all* people of colour, but – in the end – it just stuck. People got that it was a pun more than a statement. It *worked*. Branding is everything.

She peeped out of the wings, stage left, and saw about eighty congregants tonight. It was never not mad. Five years ago, it had been her and about eight others . . . now look. She couldn't help but feel tipsy on pride, mixed with a chaser of panic. Sometimes the responsibility was a lot. They all looked to her for answers, answers she didn't always have. She was just a woman who'd stepped up in a moment of deluded bravado. Gods, this must be how men feel all the time.

Not everyone who came along to Black Mass formally joined her coven, but that was cool. Witches have lives too, and she felt no one should feel obligated to define themselves wholly by their heritage.

'You ready, babe?' Chinara asked.

'Yeah, go grab a seat.'

Chinara gave her a kiss for luck, and crept out of the wings, down the stairs at the side of the stage to the stalls. Kane tested the mic. One-two, one-two. 'OK, ready when you are.'

'Good to go.'

Kane held the mic to their lips. 'Ladies, gentlemen and those wise enough to transcend the binary, please welcome to the stage the queen of Diaspora and founder of Black Mass, Leonie Jackman!'

There was a whoosh of applause and Leonie rode it onto the stage. She always felt like fucking Oprah or Tyra or something. It was a bit cringe, but she heard – time and time again – how this community helped. She was *helping*, and each affirmation was another coin in the slot to keep her going. 'Thank you, thank you!' She waited for everyone to settle into their seats. 'Aw, thank you again! I cannot tell you . . . you give me so much life!'

More applause.

'OK, OK, OK! Boring shit first . . . fire exits . . .' She made like an air stewardess. 'And my colleagues Halima and Valentina are bringing around collection plates. Every penny goes back into Diaspora so we can keep the community going. Please give whatever you can afford, and if that's nothing, this one's on me.'

Chinara had had to, back in the day, force Leonie to do the collections. She hated being on the scrounge. Her mum had raised her to be against any sort of handout. *Leonie May Jackman, are you listening to me? If you haven't got it, don't spend it.* Esther Jackman had never even had a credit card. But, as Chinara was at pains to point out, Diaspora was *not* HMRC, reaping literally millions from the government through tax. If mundanes knew that their National Insurance was paying for Helena's minions to have Westwood capes, there'd be riots.

Running the coven was a full-time venture. Leonie previously had been a makeup artist, working on TV shoots or even the occasional wedding, but she simply couldn't do both. If she wanted to eat, she had to tax her congregation as much as she loathed it.

As the bowls went around, she read the community notices. Mrs Brown was running a tarot workshop every Wednesday morning. Mrs Mandela was now selling reptile familiars from her new flat in Peckham. Mrs Ramachandran was holding a feast this Sunday to celebrate her daughter Sunita's 'bloom' into witchcraft. All standard stuff.

'If you're new here tonight, and I see a few new faces, thank you so much for coming. You are so, so welcome.' New members had to be referred by an existing member, or screened by someone on the committee. No mundanes, no white people. Leonie felt those demographics had enough shit to entertain them on Shaftesbury Avenue.

'My name is Leonie. She/her pronouns. Little bit about me . . . I was only eight when I was taken from Leeds to

Pendle to train for HMRC. I know a lot of you were as well. I was taught by white witches about white witches, as we pretty much all are. I was told things were a certain way and I believed it, because I was, you know, eight!'

There was a sympathetic ripple of laughter through the theatre. Some of these witches and warlocks had gone to Pendle, or Manchester, or Boscastle for tuition, many of them hadn't. 'Because HMRC is very focused on tracing legacy bloodlines – finding witches they've already found – and because there's an undeniable racial bias concerning our "culture", a lot of witches of colour are never spotted in childhood.'

There was a soft boo.

'I know, it's horseshit. These white witches, these teachers at HMRC, see a little Chinese girl and just think *oh, that's what all Chinese girls can do.* Like bitch, she's fucking levitating! For whatever reason – OK, systemic racism – Black and Asian witches have always looked after our own. Even before Diaspora, only four per cent of witches in HMRC were from a minority background. That's why I broke away after the war. I knew there were girls and boys . . .' Kane coughed from the wings. '. . . and gender-fluid folks who need attention. It was a fucking emergency.'

This drew the loudest applause yet. Some witches rose to their feet and raised a fist in solidarity.

'Friends, we were lied to. And that's why we gather at Black Mass . . . to *share* and to *remember* and *celebrate* where we came from. The flowers and leaves are glorious: we are visible, and beautiful, but we mustn't ignore the roots. I want to go back to the beginning tonight if we can. Join me in contemplation. Let's share our stories.'

Telepathic connection with about a hundred people at once is about as difficult as it sounds, but Leonie had a system. She seated herself on the stage and started the ritual. With a piece of chalk, she first drew broad circles on the wooden slats to her north, south, east and west. She crossed each circle, a powerful symbol to enhance her natural strength.

She burned rosemary in a bronze dish with a chunk of rose quartz which soon blackened to produce a thick pungent fog. It billowed through the theatre, fast inducing a lucid dream state among the audience. She and Chinara, in the privacy of their own home, referred to the concoction as 'mind lube'. The congregation's minds opened to her like mussels on the boil and she could enter their psyche without resistance. The mist worked as a sort of conductor for her thoughts.

Leonie too let herself fall into the trance. It wasn't a one way street, and she did mean *share*. She conjured the stories she had been told and received those of her elders. Her head lolled back and her eyes first became cloudy, then as white as milk.

She was a conduit.

She saw nothing but their stories.

These are the stories of our people.

Once, long ago, there were three little girls. Not one among us remembers their names, and the place where they were born is no longer on any map. They walked, far, in search of what we now call the Nile.

One day, a sandstorm blew up out of nowhere and the girls became hopelessly lost. They feared they were for the desert's belly when, from out of the earth, a puddle seeped up through the arid sands. They drank deeply and, before their eyes, the water washed across the land, and trees, palms and vines unfurled. The oasis was ripe with life, with birds, dragons and insects.

A serpent, the sharpest green, slid down from the tallest gum tree and wove through the undergrowth to the water-hole to drink. To the girls' astonishment, the snake transformed into a magnificent woman. Rising naked out of the water, she was taller than any man, with the same vibrant scales as the snake, and with fierce black eyes and a forked tongue, yet the girls did not run or scream.

'Do not be scared,' the serpent woman said in a dialect the girls understood. 'Call me Mother, as I gave life to all.'

The girls knew this to be true and that they must serve and honour their Mother. She marked them as daughters by placing a drop of her own blood onto their tongues, and they saw the universal truths of the air, earth, water and fire – the ways of the beasts and spirits. The girls saw how everything stemmed from her, how she was the first and last. They saw where humanity fit in her intricate design. 'If you intend to fight nature,' Mother told them, 'first cleave off your right hand.'

The three girls were the first witches, and then the first elders, and the first ancestral spirits to tell their tale. Stories, like blood, ran through the centuries. Mother's name fell off many tongues in many lands: Abuk, Ningal, Pachamama, Asintmah, Isis, Lakshmi, Goanna and Gaia and thousands more for a thousand years. Warrior witches ruled the plains and mountains, the rivers and seas.

Only then, like a plague of locusts, came the colonisers. They devoured everything and laid waste to what they could not consume. The manifold ancestors of the three little girls and their clans were killed, enslaved, or driven into hiding. Our magic, our customs, our culture were deemed savagery. The fire of our glory was doused.

We call it the Motherland with good reason. Many of our brothers and sisters, to the tune of millions, were taken far over land and water, and the Mother wept for humanity's disgrace. But the colonisers, some of them witchkind themselves, with the demons of greed loud in their ears, craved our gifts, our power, our easy communion with the earth and sky. Some sought to learn, some sought to take.

We taught our white sisters the secrets because we understood our commonality. We understood that we were all of our Mother. The truth would reunite her long-estranged daughters with the sacred duty of the witch.

The word of Mother endured. The power endured. The power is ours.

Leonie's head snapped upright and her eyes returned to their everyday hazel. She saw the room once more, and not the tapestry of the past. 'So then, why the fuck is it,' she decreed aloud, 'the most influential witches in this motherfucking world are white women?'

Her words were a thunderclap, a clarion call. The audience were shaken from the dreamscape, soon on their feet applauding. Leonie pushed herself up to her feet and drew a deep cleansing breath in through her nostrils and almost – almost – burst into tears. But she didn't.

The applause went on and on. Chinara mouthed *nailed it* from the front row, and Leonie knew she ought to feel like a queen. So why, even knowing the stories of her ancestors, even knowing where she came from, did she not have a clue where she was going?

Chapter Fifteen

DATE NIGHT

Niamh

It wasn't a date, but Niamh made sure she left enough time to shower, change and put on some makeup after work. She told herself this wasn't for Luke's benefit as much as her own. She'd been in crisis mode: eating junk, sleeping fitfully, overly vigilant. Since Theo had arrived, she'd invested all her energy into looking after him, although – she was starting to think – she needn't have.

The boy was fine, and this task was beginning to feel like a fool's errand. For one thing, he was blissfully quiet, but he made for a great little housemate. He was keen to learn the contents of the herb garden and help with cooking, and quick to tidy up after himself and, most importantly, he made a cracking cup of tea.

Her poor partner at the practice, Mike, sorely needed a day off, and Niamh couldn't take any more leave to babysit. Not sure what else she could do, Theo went to work with her that day – *Take Your Sullied Child to Work Day* – and he was nothing but calm and helpful. She told clients that he was there on work experience and he was a perfect assistant: fetching things from the fridge and taking animals out to reception when humans came to collect their furry friends. It was hard to conceive of a time when he'd lead to the total destruction of the world. It was absurd, and she planned on telling Helena so.

A taxi waited, meter running, on the track outside. She cantered down the narrow cottage stairs and grabbed her dainty 'going-out' handbag – just enough room for a lipstick, a tampon and a bank card – from the bannister. She was, as ever, going to be late. 'Are you two going to be OK?' she asked Holly and Theo. The pair, thick as thieves, were in the lounge, devouring a pizza she'd had delivered from town.

'We'll be fine! Go! Have fun!' Holly said. Niamh noted she was wearing eyeliner and mascara, which wasn't like her. Are kids today as bad as TV shows made out? She wondered if she should leave some condoms out or something, but decided against it.

It was funny. In her day, all she ever wanted was to do spells with her friends and write fan mail to the Spice Girls, and yet here she was worrying for Holly's virtuosity. The patriarchy is so fucking contagious, even to women.

Behave, she instead told them both, and swept out the kitchen door.

As expected, Luke was already waiting on the steps of Hebden Bridge Picture House when the taxi pulled up. The imposing cinema, with its art deco stone columns on either side of the entrance, was probably her favourite building in Hebden Bridge. There was even a cute cocktail bar just next door – perfect for pre- and post-film analysis. She threw the driver a tenner and tumbled onto the kerb to greet him. 'Sorry!'

'No worries,' Luke said. 'We've got time.'

He gave her a chaste kiss on the cheek and led her into the lobby. On the way in, Niamh noticed a gorgeous young woman ogle Luke's physique. She couldn't be more conspicuous if she drooled. Niamh always felt a familiar sort of self-consciousness. She experienced the same thing with Conrad too, that *what's that Adonis doing with a weirdo like HER* judgement.

If she didn't know better, she'd think he was reading her mind when he said, 'You look very pretty tonight.'

Uncommonly tall, flat-chested ginger adolescents rarely grow into confident women, so compliments never really scratched the surface. She would always hear the girls at school first. 'Thank you. I put on mascara and everything.'

He grinned. 'I can see! I already got the tickets, by the way . . .' She went to argue, but he quickly interjected. 'But as this is not a date, you're in charge of exorbitantly priced drinks and snacks.'

'Deal! What are we having?'

He went for Diet Coke and salty popcorn, which Niamh felt was a personal attack, so she got her own sweet bucket. This meant there'd be no sharing, no danger of grazing fingers, which was fine because it wasn't a date.

She got her member's discount. She really did love the Picture House. It was a one-screen indie that made up for what it was lacking in mod cons with nerdy staff who knew their shit.

They'd been in their stiff auditorium seats for about ten minutes, waiting for the trailers to start, when they realised they were the only people in the screening. 'This is the dream,' Luke said. 'I always wanted my own cinema. I feel like a king.'

Niamh laughed, although half wished, just this once, the cinema was filled with screaming teenagers who played on their phones all the way through the movie. It would feel, yes, less like a date. That said, they were about to watch *The Exorcist*, so that ought to dampen the mood some. If it didn't, she'd have concerns.

Luke made small talk, ploughing into his popcorn reserves before the film even started. Niamh had been raised to wait – an exercise in self-control. 'How long will . . . um . . . what's his name?'

'Theo.'

'How long will he be staying?' Luke asked.

'I don't know,' she replied honestly.

'And he's your . . . ?'

What lie had she told? She lost track. 'Cousin. He's my mum's little brother's kid.' She did have an Uncle Damian back in Galway, her dad's brother as it happened, but she hadn't seen him in decades. She didn't even know if he had kids. If he did they weren't witches, or she'd have heard. That side of the family didn't vibe with the witch-craft stuff. Never had. Her father had been the Black Sheep.

'You never really talk about your family,' Luke said.

'You're one to talk!' Niamh deftly turned the tables on him. An image briefly entered Luke's mind: a miserable statue of a man and – in his heart – the doleful suspicion that he's a disappointment to his father. Like a lot of male mundanes, Luke deflected the thought like a shuttlecock. She wanted to reassure him – who wouldn't be proud of handsome, kind, entrepreneurial Luke Watts – but knew she must stay silent on it.

'There's not a lot to say.' Luke tossed a kernel of popcorn in his gob. 'Dad dead, Mum sunning herself on the Algarve.'

This time she vividly saw a leathery woman sipping an Aperol on a sun-drenched beach.

'You have a sister, right?' Luke said.

'Yes sir,' Niamh said, more sadly than she intended.

'And she's in hospital?'

'Yes.'

'Do you . . . want to talk about it?' Luke asked gently.

'Can we not? I don't want my personal tragedy to spoil the gentle family film we're about to enjoy.'

He laughed. 'That's fine. Families are such a headfuck. That saying is true: you can choose your friends but not your family, right?'

Once more the stern face of his father entered his head. The memories were gauzy, and Niamh wondered if these were old memories from many years previous. 'Daddy issues?' she asked, taking a punt.

'Something like that.' With a mechanical wheeze, the red curtains parted and the adverts started. He sank a little lower in his seat. 'You know, if it gets really scary, don't be leaning on me. I'm not your boyfriend.'

'Oh please! Don't *you* be hiding behind me. I can fend for myself.' She left out that she'd seen off demons far scarier than Linda Blair in her time.

She looked at his profile, his nose perfectly Roman. He caught her looking. 'What? You checking me out?'

'Don't you think, Mr Watts, that you should be here with a nice girl who doesn't come with a dead fiancé and comatose sister in tow?'

He guffawed – not like there was anyone to shush them. 'God, there's a question!'

'Luke, I mean it. Neither of us are getting any younger . . .'

He laughed again, so loudly it echoed off the walls. 'Is my biological clock ticking?'

She nudged him with her elbow. 'Well why not?'

'I'm not sure I've ever been asked that. Is this what it feels like to be a woman?'

Niamh laughed. 'You planning on having kids? If you are, you need to be courting!'

He shrugged his big shoulders. They were pressed side-to-side in the narrow aisle. 'You know what, I always assumed I'd have them at some point, but without meeting the right woman, it felt like it was jumping the gun to think about it too much. And anyway,' he added, 'I'm a bloke. I can fire out decrepit jizz until I'm what . . . ninety?'

He grinned and Niamh cracked up. 'You're a deviant!' She then added quietly. 'Half the girls in Hebden Bridge, and a fair few of the boys, would have you.'

'Nah,' he said. 'The rest of Hebden Bridge doesn't like horror films.'

The title screen – A WILLIAM FRIEDKIN FILM – faded in and Niamh settled as the overture of scratchy violin strings began.

She felt safe, and she admitted something to herself, secure in the knowledge there wasn't another sentient in miles.

I want him.

And even that felt like she'd committed a great and terrible sin.

Chapter Sixteen

WANING CRESCENT

Leonie

Leonie walked naked through the forest. No one would be around to see her at this hour. All she sensed from the neighbouring town were the soporific vibrations of sleeping mundanes. The nocturnal creatures though? They were vibing nicely.

Damp grasses poked between her toes as she picked through the undergrowth. She knew these forest trails like old friends, and they didn't shame her for being away so long. Gulping in swollen lungfuls of crisp night air, she rinsed her body of London's crud – some sort of rural dialysis.

Of course she'd agreed to come and help Niamh. Like Chinara had said, she could either mull it over and drive herself crazy for a week, or book the next train to Hebden Bridge. The Airbnb she stayed at, belonging to the guy Niamh ran her practice with, was cute, but she wasn't going to pass up all this open space.

Yorkshire had a lot more sky than London. Without the smog and light pollution, the sky was the purest black and the stars were truly diamonds.

An owl hooted and her heart sang along. Reaching the clearing they'd informally called Bluebell Meadow as kids, Leonie fell to her knees. She didn't know why, but she cried. Her whole body seemed to melt into the earth. It was quite out of her control and she could hardly breathe between sobs. This wasn't her home, but she missed it, craved it every day she was gone.

You often hunger for things that aren't especially good for you, and that's what she felt about this place. A place that hadn't really wanted her. Little Leonie Twist, the only Black girl in her class, dumped at Vance Hall, then briefly at Granny Device's cottage, then at the terrace house of their tutor, Edna Heseltine. Annie, goddess bless her, had tried but no one had made this feel like her home except Gaia.

Maybe that was why she cried. There's something singular about going home to visit your mum.

She sank her fingers into the wet peaty earth. Overhead, she had full view of the cosmos. She rolled onto her back and it felt like floating in a vast black ocean. Calmest waters. The crescent moon, almost too close for comfort, bore down on her. There was something knowingly sensual about its curves and Leonie touched herself with muddy fingers – both hands, one in, one on.

The earth responded to her sexual energy, one of the most powerful energies there was. Leonie felt worms writhe metres below. A beetle scuttled across her face. She closed her eyes and let roots and vines and creepers softly embrace her, pulling her down and down into the detritus. She wasn't scared as she went under. She felt wholly safe in her dark cocoon. Tonight she would sleep in Mother's lap.

Chapter Seventeen

FEATHER, SKULL AND STONE

Niamh

Niamh pulled up outside Mike and Grant's house in Heptonstall village and honked the horn. Whenever someone came to visit, she recommended her veterinary partner's Airbnb apartment, a self-contained studio flat underneath the main home. After a moment or two, the door to the annexe opened and Leonie emerged.

Niamh turned off the engine and jumped out of the Land Rover.

'Look at you!'

As ever, Leonie was stunning. How long had it been? Almost a year? More? Back then it had been silver braids, now she wore her hair natural and curly. How was it that Leonie got *more* beautiful with age, whereas she just looked more worn?

'How did you sleep?'

'Like a witch!' Leonie raced down the drive and threw her arms around Niamh. Niamh sucked in a lungful of her scent and already felt more centred from having another water witch close at hand. A witch can always tell her type. All witches jibe with some elements more than with others.

'I missed you,' Leonie whispered in her ear.

'Thank you for coming.'

'Of course.' With a true friend, it didn't matter how long they'd been away, you pick up where you left off. 'How are you?'

'I'm grand.'

'Irish grand or English grand?'

Niamh laughed. 'Split the difference! You ready to roll?'

Leonie said she was and they both got in the car. Theo waited in the backseat, nervously looking out of the window at petulant grey skies. 'Theo?' Niamh said. 'This is my friend Leonie, the one I told you about. She's a sentient too.'

Good to meet you, Theo. Leonie's voice cut through as clear as spring water.

Hello.

From him, Niamh sensed reticence, suspicion even. He was unsure around new people. Niamh gave Leonie a brief glance: *Go easy, we don't want to spook him.*

I'll get in.

If Leonie Jackman, a Level 6 sentient, couldn't get through to him, they were in trouble. There *were* only seven levels, and the last Level 7 witch died in 1982.

They drove north out of town, over the moors towards Pendle, catching up while Leonie incessantly hopped radio stations in search of the best music.

'I swear you have ADHD,' Niamh teased as she drove.

'Probably.'

'How's London? How's Diaspora? How's Chinara?' Niamh fired off questions like bullets.

Leonie wound down her window so she could smoke,

her hair billowing in the wind. 'London is expensive as fuck. Sorry Theo, language and adult content. Diaspora takes up literally all my time, but I love it, and Chinara is peachy . . .'

She wants a baby . . .

NO!

I know, right?

Are you going to?

One day, yes. Now, I'm not sure. Diaspora is my baby.

'I'm so happy for you guys,' she said aloud. 'Can we do a wedding please? You know I love a wedding!'

'Wedding? What? You Catholic now? We might have a *blessing* at some point. Wedding! Get that word off your tongue!'

'You know what I meant.'

The Spice Girls – 'Who Do You Think You Are' – came on the radio and Leonie jacked up the volume. 'Destiny . . .'

They sang along at the top of their lungs, with Theo looking increasingly disturbed, for the rest of the journey. As they arrived at Malham village, they saw Elle's Fiat 500 parked in the National Trust car park and pulled in alongside. Elle, Holly and Annie waited by the visitor centre in the meek sunshine. Niamh hoped the cove wouldn't be crawling with tourists, or she'd have to expend all her energies on cloaking them while Leonie read Theo.

Leonie climbed out of the Land Rover first and greeted Elle with a bear hug. If they'd been mundane, Elle and Leonie would have never been friends. They were chalk and cheese, well, earth and water in any case, but they were *more* than friends, they were sisters. As such, they tolerated a lot of each other's bullshit. It was important for peace, however, that they never talked politics.

'I've missed this face!' Leonie cupped Elle's face in her palms.

'I look like a hag.'

'Fuck off, you're still Baby Spice. Look at these cheeks!' She pinched Elle's cherub face.

'Get off!'

'And you can fuck right off if you think I'm gonna believe this fully-grown woman is Holly Molly Polly!' She grabbed Holly and pulled her into a hug too.

'Leonie the Pony!'

Elle sighed. 'Please don't use the f-word in front of my child . . .'

Finally she came to Annie, who stayed perched on a low wall, but took her hands. 'My sweet Leonie, how I've missed you.'

Leonie's demeanour cooled. Niamh could have sworn she saw a tearful shine in Leonie's eyes. 'I miss you too, Annie. All the time.'

Annie smiled. 'Our umbilical cord will always stretch as far as you need it, girl. Think on it.'

Interesting wording there. Niamh wondered if Annie saw that child in Leonie's future. She wouldn't ask. Another witch's future wasn't hers to know.

'Right then!' Annie announced. 'Grab the picnic and let's get moving. We're going at my pace, so we might get there by Christmas.'

They set off up the well-worn footpath towards the cove. Leonie led the way, Annie's arm looped through hers. Elle and Niamh closely followed, while Theo and Holly hung back, communicating wordlessly.

Niamh was glad they couldn't rush. It gave her a chance to *be* awhile. When there's always somewhere to get to, you can forget the journey, and Malham Cove was too beautiful to just *get to*. The many greens were lush, soothing, and the garlic-tinged mulchy air was a tonic, still dewy from the dawn. Of course, simply being in the company of other witches was restorative of itself. There was a reason they came together in covens.

Idling, they followed the path that ran alongside the meandering beck all the way to the huge stone bowl that loomed before them.

There was untold power here, locked inside the ancient limestone. Twelve thousand years ago, the ice age thawed and the melting icebergs formed the towering stone amphitheatre now called Malham Cove. Annie always said, *where there's years, there's magic*. All the power of Gaia herself was sealed in those rocks.

The perfect spot, in other words, to see what young Theo could do.

It was a weekday in March, and the patchy weather had kept most of the tourists away. Niamh spotted a couple of ramblers looking down from the top of the waterfall, but the odd mundane would be easy enough to shield.

They set up camp at the base of the rocks, near where the chatty beck vanished inside the cliffs. The water was crystal clear, pure enough to count the pebbles on the bottom. There was a grassy embankment, mostly shielded by hawthorn trees, where they laid out their picnic blankets.

Annie sat on a folding camp chair – *If I get down on that floor I'm never getting back up* – while the others sat cross-legged on the rugs, forming a circle around Theo and Holly. 'We are a sacred circle,' Niamh explained, pouring salt around the perimeter before taking her spot. 'We're a wall around you. So everything you do is kept within. Nothing can hurt you, and you can't hurt anyone either.'

'What she's saying is . . .' Leonie added with flare, 'do your worst!'

Holly laughed, but Theo looked troubled.

It's fine, Niamh told only him.

'This is a place of power,' Annie said. 'Can you feel it?'

'Yes,' Elle said. She combed her fingers through the grass. 'It's so alive.'

Niamh and Leonie placed their palms on the earth too. Elle was right. Gaia, always a lyrical whisper, roared here.

'Watch . . .' Elle said.

Niamh felt the energy pulse and channel through the soil, as Elle cast a summons down the root networks. Elle's skin glowed – a honey-gold light from within.

'Mum?' Holly asked nervously.

'Stay still child,' Annie warned her. 'Be still.'

Holly did as she was told.

Elle exhaled and the first daisies and buttercups erupted through the soil, blooming before the eye. Then came some larger wildflowers: pansies and milkwort and cranesbill. They emerged unfolding their dainty petals as if they were curtsying. Soon the whole circle was filled with colours and scents. Spring was in the air.

'That's so pretty,' Holly breathed, aghast. 'Did you do that?'

Elle opened her eyes to appreciate her handiwork. 'Easy really. It's all down there, waiting in the dark. I just encouraged them.'

'My turn,' Niamh said. She settled herself and let her mind wander into the cove. The witches were loud and present in her mind, but there was a cornucopia of life here. All sorts of voices. Some large, some minute. The smaller the creature, the easier to sway.

She steered a passing Cabbage White butterfly down

from the trees, and then another, and then a Red Admiral and a Common Blue and a Painted Lady. They fluttered down like autumn leaves and flew merrily about the sacred circle. Dozens of butterflies dipped and swooped, landing on their hair and clothes. She saw Theo smile as a bright yellow Brimstone settled on his hand. She smiled back.

'Look,' Leonie said. She focused and drew a timid doe out of the shadows. 'Come,' she said and it obeyed without question. The deer, with no sign of fear in her eyes, approached the circle and walked straight to Holly, letting her pet her.

'Auntie Leonie,' she said. 'It's so beautiful.'

'Bet you didn't know your Auntie was Snow White, right?'

'These are not tricks,' Annie said gravely. 'They demonstrate our oneness with Gaia. It is a privilege, not a game.'

'Granny, they know,' Elle said, gently defensive.

'We use our powers only when we need to. We're here to watch over the earth, not plunder it, or bend it to our will. Aye, it's tempting to lay in bed and open the curtains with your mind, but remember that's sucking the energy out of something else that sorely needs it. There's only so much power to go around, and the well must never run dry. But to defend the mother, or indeed the coven, yes, we must master – or mistress – our relationship with the earth.'

Niamh released the butterflies from her control and they fluttered away. Leonie, similarly, released the doe back into the trees. Holly waved her farewell.

'Now it's your turn,' Leonie said.

'Us?' Holly said. 'I can't do that.'

'Of course you can,' Niamh said. 'But we'll start small.' From her bag, she withdrew some tools of the trade: a feather, a bird's skull, a smooth grey pebble. She placed them between Theo and Holly. 'It's easy enough: a test of mindfulness.'

'Inanimate objects are easy,' Leonie added. 'Just as you would with your hand, reach out with your mind, and lift it.'

'First try the feather, then the skull, then the stone,' Niamh instructed. 'It's like a muscle. The more you use it, the better you get.'

She had seen already what Theo could levitate back at Grierlings, but what she wanted to learn today was whether he had any *control* of his power whatsoever.

'Holls, you go first.'

It took her some time, and she started to get frustrated. *It's not the same*, she said, going red in the face.

Don't listen for a reply, Niamh told her. *Just listen for its sound. Everything in nature has a sound. You know what a feather* feels *like, what does it* sound *like?*

'You can do it, Holly,' Elle said. 'Take your time.'

Holly seemed to appreciate this vote of confidence from her mother and tried again. After a moment or two, the feather twitched. 'Was that me?' Holly exclaimed.

'It sure was!' Leonie gave her a clap.

She tried again. This time, the feather levitated – or wobbled – a few centimetres off the blanket. Holly gained greater control, raising it level with her eyeline.

'Very good!' Niamh said. 'Now try the skull.'

Again, it took her a couple of minutes to find the skull, but she lifted it confidently off the ground. Niamh couldn't tell if Elle, who watched on with little expression, was impressed or not. She stumbled at the stone. She was able to find its core, but could only shift it an inch or so across the rug, not lift it.

When it became clear she was only going to exhaust herself, Niamh ended the test. 'It's fine. We'll practise in our sessions. Don't try that at home . . .'

'Yes,' Elle agreed, 'let's not.'

'Oh pipe down, Elle,' Annie laughed. 'You killed half the flowers in Hebden when you were training.'

'I'm sure I did, but I don't need rocks flying around my house!' Nevertheless, Elle gave Holly a warm hug, and assured her she'd aced her first test.

'OK, Theo, it's your turn,' Niamh said jovially as Holly returned to her position in the centre of the circle. 'Same rules. Feather, skull and stone.'

He nodded. He narrowed his eyes, focusing on the feather. Nothing for a second, and then it shot into the air like he'd launched it from a cannon. Leonie held out a hand to halt it. She brought it down, mentally handing it back. 'Control,' she said simply, kindly.

Niamh all too clearly remembered coming here with Mrs Heseltine twenty-five years ago. She recalled how their mentor had clipped Leonie around the ear. *Power is nothing without control, Leonie Jackman!* Horrid bitch. There had been a satisfying moment at her wake when everyone, at about the same moment, realised it was quite all right to talk about what a battle-axe she'd been.

'Control it,' Leonie said again.

Theo took charge of the feather. It jolted about in front of his face like a wasp.

'Don't fight it,' Niamh said gently. 'It's a *feather*, not a cobra. Hold it like one.'

He listened and the feather finally levitated, still.

'Very good,' Annie said. 'Now the skull.'

Theo focused on the skull. Nothing seemed to happen.

'Have you found it?' Holly asked.

They were so intently focused on the skull, no one thought to look up. A crow dove from the top of the waterfall. Its beak plucked at Theo's forehead. He yelped and rolled onto his back, covering his face.

Another raven swooped down on Niamh from behind. The first she knew about it was its talons in her hair. She jumped up and saw a swarm of jagged black shapes circling overhead. They cawed angrily. She realised what had happened.

Theo, stop. You summoned live birds. Let them go.

The flock blocked out the feeble sun and it was as if night fell over them. The birds descended. Holly screamed for Elle, but ravens tore at the girl, and she could only cower. 'Holly!' Elle shrieked.

'Fuck!' Leonie screamed, throwing her arms around Annie to protect her. They hunched together.

Niamh fell to her knees, trying to protect her eyes. She reached out for the birds, to stop them, but they were incensed, filled with rage. It was as if Theo had angered them, and they saw him as a threat to be destroyed. They continued to attack. Niamh's mind was hot red, panic on all sides, deafening.

Theo, she tried again. His mind was once more that black tar wall.

Leonie?

Yes.

I can't get in his head, can you?

No.

Can you shield me?

Yes.

The birds continued to bear down on them. Dozens of wings flapped, with feathers and clouds of dander raining down. Beaks and flint tongues and black eyes.

Carefully, Niamh regained her footing. The birds now flew around her. Leonie's shield was working. Niamh pushed forwards through the tornado, batting wings and claws away. She saw Theo and Holly cowering together, their hands and faces now covered in blood.

I'm coming.

She staggered to their position down by the beck, still fighting her way through. She fell to her knees and pulled Theo and Holly apart.

Theo, stop this.

I can't, I don't know how.

Then LET ME IN.

She took hold of his head in both hands and, with all the might she had, forced her way into his mind. And there was such a lot in there. So much noise. Care homes; the foster parent who watched him get changed; the teachers who laughed in his face; *that* bath; Helena's witches dragging him into a van and the cage and—

The birds.

GO.

And the birds went. As soon as they came, they left. They carried on about their business, circling back into the trees or over the waterfall. The last few black feathers drifted to the grass.

The stream continued to babble as they recovered their wits. Leonie checked on Annie. Theo looked shell-shocked.

'Is everyone OK?' Elle said, a cut on her forehead already healing. With nurse-mode kicking in, she efficiently strode to Holly. 'Let me see. Take my hand.' A moment later and Holly's cuts – little more than grazes really – were gone. Elle turned her attention to Theo, but his scratches were already sealing themselves up.

Elle's eyes widened once she saw what was happening,

and she looked to Niamh. 'He's an adept,' she explained, still out of breath.

Leonie's gaze was steely. 'The hell was that?'

Theo had already reverted to the cornered feral thing she'd encountered at prison, arms wrapped around his legs, eyes staring at nothing.

'I don't know!' Niamh snapped as Elle took her hand to work on her wounds. 'I don't know,' she said again, reining in her temper. She felt this was her fault. She was responsible for Theo, and he'd failed the most introductory trial of witchcraft. He wasn't the fool, she was, for thinking a week in her cottage had miraculously reformed him. Ciara always did say she was naïve – a hopeless Pollyanna.

Niamh looked haplessly to Annie as Leonie helped her to her feet. Although she rationally knew Annie couldn't see, her eyes seemed to be fixed on Theo. And she looked more shaken than Niamh had ever seen her. 'Now listen here,' she said matter-of-factly. 'I don't know what you are, child, but you are something new.'

If Theo heard her, he didn't respond.

'Get up,' Annie commanded, but he continued to clutch his legs. 'I said GET UP.'

Snapping out of it, and embarrassed, he stood up. Annie approached him, Leonie guiding her over to his position. She took hold of his chin with one hand and wiped away his tears with the other. 'What are we gonna do with you, eh?' she paused, and Niamh wondered if she was seeing the future unfurl in her third eye. 'You're a rare bird you, aren't you? Pun intended.'

I don't want to hurt anyone.

'Good. That's a start. Potential is cheap. A stone can be a spade or a spear, you get me?' He said nothing. 'Are you prepared to work? *Really* work? Let Niamh shape you?'

Yes.

'Right we are, then.' Annie let go of this face, seemingly satisfied with his answers.

Niamh felt the scarlets ebb out of Theo, replaced by soothing blues. A chill wind blew across the dell and she held herself tight.

Annie took her cane from Leonie and poked Theo in the chest with it. 'A beginning,' she said, 'often signals an end. That's the thing with dawn . . . you must first get through the night.'

Annie hobbled towards the path out of the cove. Niamh looked despairingly at Elle, then Leonie, who could only shrug. It looked like the field trip was over.

Chapter Eighteen

SCARS

Helena

In days gone by, a witch could communicate with her coven by enchanting a crystal. Aquamarine or turquoise were the most effective. The stone acted as a conduit for their sentience, hence the archetypal 'crystal ball'. Nowadays, Helena preferred the ease of video conferencing from the comfort of her home study.

It was one of those unicorn days when she'd made it home before sunset, and had a homecooked dinner with Snow, but there was still plenty of work to do before she could watch *Real Housewives* in bed. Niamh's wi-fi really was terrible. The image kept freezing on her friend. 'How's it going over there?' Helena asked.

'Everything's fine,' Niamh said spryly, apparently using her laptop in the cottage kitchen.

'Is it?' Helena took a sip of hot water and lemon. It was a detox week, which probably wasn't helping her mood.

'Yeah.' Niamh was positively straining to appear casual. 'I'm running basic trials to establish his power level.'

'And what's your analysis?'

Niamh shrugged. 'Too early to say. I think the trick is in controlling his power. I can say for definite that he's an adept. I've seen sentience, healing and elementalism in him.'

Helena felt her jaw tighten. 'Anything else?'

'Like what?' She laughed a little. 'That not impressive enough?'

'Do we know anything more about him? Can you read him?'

'I've seen bits and pieces.' She lowered her voice. 'He's had a really difficult life, Helena. Really tough. More than enough to explain what happened at his school.'

Was Niamh insinuating that she couldn't empathise? 'That's all very well,' she said tersely. 'But a boy shouldn't be able to master more than one discipline. He should barely be able to master one.'

'I'm not sure he's mastering anything at the moment. He's all over the shop, and that's partly on us. He should have been in training since he was in nappies.'

'Niamh, I'm serious.'

She smiled. 'Oh you're always serious! Helena, it's fine, we're fine. It's all under control. Relax!'

They finished up and bid each other a good evening. Helena waited for the screen to go black before looking to Robyn Jones, who sat silently at the far end of her office. She'd remained silent for the duration of the call, on the reading seat underneath the window – not that anyone ever read on it. The shelves and rows of bound leather esoteric volumes in the home office were mostly for display, truth be told.

'Well?' Helena said.

'She's lying,' Robyn said, abrupt as ever. She was a tall,

sturdy broad-shouldered Welsh woman. Helena believed she used to compete nationally in shotput, or hammer, or javelin – one of the throwing ones – before she'd come to HMRC full-time.

Helena reclined in her fancy new chair. It was supposed to stop her becoming a keyboard Quasimodo, but it was an ugly thing. Why could no one perfect the equilibrium between style and function? She took another sip of water and mused, tapping her nails on the side of the mug. 'Perhaps I should have just asked her outright why Leonie was there.'

'Something went badly wrong at Malham Cove. They were well shielded but I saw them all panic. I don't know what they were trying to do, but a flock of birds attacked them. And I forwarded you the reports of seismic activity the night he arrived in Hebden Bridge.'

'It's *him*!' Helena snapped, slamming the mug down. Shit. She wiped away the spilled water with her palm before it could stain the wood. 'Why the hell is she defending him? Does someone have to die before she wakes up?'

Robyn was still as a statue.

'Continue the surveillance and tell me *everything*.' Helena speed-dialled the overnight staff at the offices. 'Teleport Robyn back to the safehouse in Hebden Bridge please.'

Robyn stoically waited for the coven to send her back. A moment passed and she was gone. At least she could rely on *some* of them to do as they were told.

Helena was too furious to even check her inbox. She wanted to smash something. Instead, she went to the globe in which she kept the emergency booze and broke out a twenty-year-old bourbon. She poured herself a good glug into a tumbler and frosted the glass with the tip of her finger.

It didn't work.

She still *really* wanted to smash something.

On an empty bookshelf she scanned the photographs she cherished enough to frame. They were dusty. She'd be sure to bring that up with the cleaner. The first was on her wedding day to Stef. Although she knew this was problematic, she had never looked better nor thinner than she had done in the run-up to that day. Strange that now all she saw when she looked at this picture was her protruding collarbone. The wedding day itself was a dizzying blur; she scarcely remembered it.

Her mother, of course, had questioned *why* she wanted to get married at twenty-three when she was such a promising young witch. No one knew Stefan Morrill like she did though. For one thing, he'd been ten years older than she was, but moreover, he was a force of nature. That was a blessing and a curse. To be loved by Stef was to feel like you had your own personal sun shining on you. When they got together, she felt almost *bombarded* with love. She'd never felt anything like it. So when he proposed one night in Manchester – flash mob and all – how could she say no?

Next to that picture was Snow as a baby, soundly sleeping on Stef's broad chest. That one really got her. It hurt, but she never wanted it not to. The next picture was one she treasured: one of the only photos in existence of Betty Kettlewell, the very first High Priestess of HMRC when it was founded in 1869. She was a stern woman, her billowing black dress buttoned all the way to her throat. She looked like a leader.

The final picture was another from her wedding day.

Her bridesmaids. It was chilling how fast the matching 'bandage' dresses had dated. At the time, Helena had thought making them wear the tight knee-length gowns was progressively sexy, but now they looked so cheap.

It did hurt though, seeing them now. Niamh, Leonie, Elle.

Niamh was supposed to be her *friend*. So why was she taking his side?

A fire in her blood. It felt like her bones were swelling, desperate to erupt from under her skin. Outside, she heard a distant grumble of thunder. She closed her eyes. She was better than this. She had everything in hand. Another growl from the skies.

Niamh and Leonie and Elle and Granny Device out for a picnic. How merry.

It was Tammy Girl all over again.

Lightning flashed and the lamps in the office dimmed as the power faltered. This time, the thunder sounded like the sky was snapping in two.

Get it together, you stupid bitch.

It was ridiculous, and shameful, that she still felt so sore about that day. It was . . . what? Twenty-one, twenty-two years ago? Elle's mum had taken Elle, the twins and Leonie to the Trafford Centre not long after it first opened for a day of shopping, burgers and milk-shakes. Helena, quite pointedly, wasn't invited because Julie Device *didn't like how Helena bosses our Elle around all the time.* Helena only knew about the trip at all because Ciara had blabbed about where she'd got her new embel-lished flare jeans.

It had hurt. It had hurt more than when Mark Braithwaite had commented on her 'wrestler thighs' on sports day. The night Ciara told her, she'd cried and cried and her mother couldn't understand what the big deal was. They could go to the Trafford Centre any time.

In the end, Lilian called Julie and that only seemed to make things worse, although Julie backpedalled and said there was simply no room in the car. From that point, Helena always felt she had to play the cupcake angel every time she went over to the Device house for tea or birthday parties. Grovelling and snivelling, pleases and thank yous. It was humiliating.

Even now, in her beautiful office in her beautiful townhouse, she physically squirmed, mortified about the whole thing. Why did it still smart? Why would she – after having a baby, winning a war, losing a husband – even still *remember* a fucking trip to Tammy Girl?

You know what? It didn't matter.

Let them have their secret day trips. She had her *work*. It was her work she'd be remembered for. The youngest ever High Priestess was about to save the earth from the most powerful demon threat in centuries. A demon in human form, but a demon nonetheless. The work was what mattered.

'Snow!' she shouted.

'What?' her daughter hollered from the living room.

'Come here please.'

'Why?'

Helena gritted her teeth. Best not to scream when she was about to ask a favour. 'Because I said so.'

Snow slumped across the hall wearing some flannel pyjamas and with her hair neatly plaited into braids so it'd be beachy in the morning. 'What? I'm watching *Botched*.'

She seated herself back at her desk. 'I need to ask you a favour.' The bourbon was spot-on – oaky, mature.

Snow didn't look impressed. 'What favour?'

'It's a big one, and you might not enjoy it, but you'd be doing your mother *and* your coven a huge service.'

That was enough to intrigue Snow. She set herself down on the foot rest. 'OK . . .'

'I need you to spend some time at your grandparents' 'house . . .'

'How long?' she asked, very cautiously.

'Not long, until solstice perhaps.'

'Ew! No way! That's weeks, and Grandma only buys, like, one type of cereal.'

Helena sighed. This was exactly what she'd known was going to happen. 'What if I tell her to buy the cereal you like?'

'Mum, no! That's bullshit! What about my friends? I don't get it! Why do you want me to go there anyway?'

'If you calm down, I'll explain.' She waited for Snow to de-escalate. 'I'm going to ask Auntie Niamh if she'll train you in preparation for your oathtaking, but actually, what I need you to do is keep an eye on that boy I told you about. You'll go to the lessons she's running with him and Holly Pearson, and report everything back to me.'

Snow pouted. 'Why?'

'Because I think he's the human embodiment of Leviathan.'

Her daughter laughed. 'What? No way! Mum, that's a reach.'

'I hope you're right, but I fear he's bewitched your Auntie Niamh, and Auntie Elle, and maybe even your Auntie Leonie. Snow, I'm relying on you to tell me the truth. Because my friends, it seems, are lying to me. Now, will you do it for me?'

Chapter Nineteen

SORORIA

Niamh

Through the kitchen window and over the sink, Niamh watched Holly float three pencils over the garden table, keeping them spinning in a circular merry-go-round. Theo watched on. His eyes were so hooded with heavy black lashes, it was hard to read him even the mundane way. The two were intensely quiet, no doubt talking telepathically. What is it teenagers talk about nowadays? She dreaded to think. Every day, Niamh thanked the universe she'd come of age mere moments ahead of social media and camera phones.

She read the email one more time, and put her phone on charge on the counter before going outside to join her mentees.

'I can only do three,' Holly said sadly, not taking her eyes off her pencils. 'I'm shit at this.'

'You're not at all,' Niamh said. The fact she had any telekinetic ability whatsoever said she was on her way to being a Level 3 sentient. At some point, she'd have to put them through the Eriksdotter Test: the standardised measure of supernormal ability. It was a tedious affair, a series of controlled challenges to establish their precise level. Niamh had never understood why HMRC felt the need to rank something so mercurial.

'I'm doomed to float stationery. Great. Wicked Witch of WHSmith.'

Now. How to break it to them? She took a seat at the garden table. 'Next session we have a new pupil,' Niamh announced, aiming to keep her tone jovial. Helena must think of her as a simpleton. Snow was being sent to spy on her, plain and simple. 'Snow Vance-Morrill wants some help to get ready for her oathtaking in June.'

'Snow?' Holly said, grimacing.

'Not a fan?'

Holly transmitted something to Theo, who, in turn, smirked. 'No,' Holly said curtly.

Niamh pursed her lips. 'Please don't gossip behind my back. Gossip to my face. I like gossip.'

'I didn't realise *she* was a witch,' Holly said, with a disappointment that suggested being a witch felt less special now.

'She's going to be a powerful elemental. I said I'd help out. Looks like I'm mentoring baby witches again.' She wondered if she should speak to Mike about going down to two days a week at the clinic. Working during the day, being on call, and training the students was a lot of plates to spin. The only upside was that she was too busy to see Luke. He'd asked if she fancied seeing another film – *The Eyes with No Face* – but she'd declined. She was truly overwhelmed, but it certainly provided a convenient excuse.

Because she did *want* to see him. Last thing at night, when the cottage was quiet and Theo was asleep, thoughts of Luke slid under the duvet with her. From nowhere it seemed, she wanted to have him in a very physical way. Perhaps it was the seasons changing. As spring blossoms, so does the libido. She wanted to feel his heft on top of her. She wanted to kiss his rough jaw. She wanted his big hands pawing her body.

Is this how I get over Conrad, she thought. With sex? She likened it to being ill. For a long time afterwards, you have no appetite. So much so, that when hunger returns, you're almost taken by surprise. Suddenly she was famished, and it was probably safer if Luke wasn't around to . . . eat. She wouldn't sleep with Luke for the same reason she didn't get shitfaced on sambuca shots every Saturday any more. It wasn't worth the hangover the next day.

'Does she *have* to come?' Holly continued to whine. 'I like things the way they are.'

Niamh wondered if what she was really scared of was competition – for both witching accolades and Theo's attention. Without question, Holly doted on Theo. Niamh didn't even need to read her to know that. Niamh supposed he had a certain brooding teen Heathcliff quality and could see why a goth-adjacent teenage girl might be into that.

Regardless, she had tried to talk Helena out of it. Snow had been honing her skills from the crib, so there was no real need for her to have tuition. It seemed Helena's mind, however, was made up.

Still, there were certain duties a witch must perform, even if she wasn't formally on Helena's staff. 'A coven is a sister-hood, Holly. In any coven there might be women you wouldn't pick as friends, but our ties go deeper than that. In the oath, we swear that our bond is everlasting and exceeds our humanly relationships. The coven is sovereign.'

Holly considered this. 'So you don't have to actually *like* every witch?'

Niamh shook her head. 'No! Gods no! Even when you don't like a sister, you still love them as one. We call it *Sororia*, the most special type of love. There are witches I dislike, witches I fundamentally disagree with on all manner of things, but I would fight for them, protect them, champion them . . . because the goals of the coven – to protect Gaia, her daughters and her creations – are more important than our petty personal bullshit.'

What about me? Theo said suddenly and Holly's pencils crashed to the table.

'What about you?' Niamh asked.

Am I in the coven?

Just this week, since the day trip, the question of Theo's future had started to trouble her. Although he was still sedated at night, during the day – if he refrained from using his gifts – there weren't major issues. He didn't *need* to be here. Not really. The warlocks could just as easily place him with a mentor.

'Well, next lesson, we can go into the history of it all, but warlocks have their own coven. They call it a cabal. Someday, when you're ready, you'll join the cabal, but there's no rush. I'm very happy working with you on getting your power under control.'

He looked so disappointed. She didn't even need to read him. Another foster parent who'd shunted him along like a human pass-the-parcel when the music stopped. She took his hand. 'It's gonna be fine. We'll figure it out.'

That evening, for the first time that spring, it was warm enough for them to have dinner outside. Niamh watched over Theo as he prepared fusilli pasta in a sauce, picking fresh tomatoes from the greenhouse and basil from the garden. Like most sentients, Niamh was mostly vegan aside from the eggs her chickens laid. As a vet, she'd spent time on farms and, suffice to say, those creatures know what the abattoir is, and are greatly afeared of it.

Eating animals just wasn't fun after that. And dairy cows spend their days frantically wondering where their calves have gone. So milk wasn't so much fun either.

The pasta was lovely, and she mopped up every last drop of sauce with some crusty bread. It was a school night, but she allowed herself a small glug of red wine. She imagined what the summer would be like, and wondered if Theo would still be staying. She was getting quite fond of his company. For one thing, it meant the evenings where she had a bag of Kettle Chips dipped in ketchup for dinner were a thing of the past.

'You full?' she asked Theo. 'We save ice cream for later?'

He nodded, lost in thought.

'What's up?'

Do you have a real sister?

I do.

You think about her a lot. She looks like you . . .

'Identical twins,' she said and nodded at the chicken coop. 'We used to be one egg. It blows my mind on the regular.'

Where is she now?

Uncomfortable, Niamh gathered up their dirty plates.

Sorry. That was rude.

'No,' she said, and sat back down. 'It's fine. She's . . . she's in a sort of private hospital . . . slash prison.'

You miss her.

She could chastise him for poking around in her head, but she'd been poking about in his enough, and she

167

doubted her feelings regarding Ciara were particularly well buried. 'I do. But it's a very complicated story.'

Sororia.

'That's the one.'

You should go see her. You think about it all the time.

Niamh huffed through her nostrils – a wry laugh. 'The longer I leave it, the worse it gets, but I also know that going will be . . . fucked.'

Now Theo laughed. *You should still go. I could go with you?*

It was a sweet offer, until a dark thought entered her mind. Fucking Helena was making her paranoid. But it would be quite the ploy though, wouldn't it? To get to Ciara through her. Her sister had consorted with all kinds of demons in her heyday.

'I think it's one of those heroic things I have to do alone,' she said, keeping the suspicions under wraps. This time, she did collect up the crockery and started towards the back door.

She wants to see you too.

Niamh dropped the bowls. They shattered on the patio into smithereens. She turned to look at him. *What did you say?*

His eyes were dark, expressionless. *I hear a voice like yours, but different somehow. I couldn't understand it at first. It's very weak and distant, almost like an echo. She's calling your name.*

Niamh fought the urge to stride over and slap his face because there was no way he could be telling the truth.

She's calling out to you. I hear her.

Chapter Twenty

THE HOTEL CARNOUSTIE

Niamh

Eight Years Earlier

One by one, they materialised on the overgrown lawns, once a golf course, at the front of the hotel. High winds rippled through dunes of grass and the sky was as grey as the HMRC capes they each wore.

'Are you sure you want to do this?' Helena asked.

'Yes,' Niamh said, although she very much did not.

'Here, have a sip of this.' Leonie handed her a tiny glass bottle with a cork stopper in the top. '*Excelsior.*'

She wouldn't normally – it was made from coca leaf and ginseng, and highly addictive – but on this occasion she tipped a drop or two on her tongue. The bitter, almost earthy, tincture would make her alert, sharpen her senses and elevate her gifts. She'd take all the help she could get.

'Helena?'

'Certainly not!' Helena shook her head dismissively and strode towards the derelict hotel.

'What? You think *they're* going to play by the book?'

169

Leonie followed, stowing the bottle back inside her cape. Niamh thought of Elle, presently in Dorset, healing the witches Hale had mangled during his capture.

'I don't want to cloud my mind,' Helena retorted. Since Stef had drowned, there was a definite sense that Helena was powering through, saving her tears until the end of the war. Niamh felt the same way. She would power through today as she had done yesterday and the day before, because they were *that* close now.

Niamh felt a sharp pain in her stomach as she tried to match their pace. She didn't want to be here, although she'd always known, in her heart, that sooner or later this day was inevitable. Later, she'd hoped.

It was one of the last things she remembered about her mother before she died. Niamh had perched on her knee while her mum brushed her hair. 'How does Ciara use her powers?'

'What do you mean?'

'Does she ever use them to . . . hurt people?'

All those years ago, Niamh hadn't really understood the question, or why her mother would ask it. She understood now. Ciara hurt people.

Helena stopped and waited for her to catch up. 'Seriously, Niamh. No one would blame you for not wanting to go in there. We can wait for backup to arrive.'

'No,' Niamh said firmly. 'Once they hear Hale's been caught, they'll run. It has to be now. This is our shot.'

Helena nodded, choppy winds whipping hair across her face. She couldn't fault Niamh's logic. Instead, she offered an alternative. 'I could just blast it? I could level the whole building.'

'Helena, you can't,' Leonie said.

Niamh didn't doubt she *could*, but that wasn't right. 'I

know it sounds like pure melodrama, but this is something I think I have to do. I need to see her with my own eyes. I need to hear her say it.'

The others said nothing for a moment. 'You're amazing,' Helena told her.

'So are you.'

Here they were. The end of the war. A day Niamh had longed for, but had never quite been able to picture. Or maybe she was just scared to hope. Two widows. They were ragged, exhausted and weak, but they'd made it. Hale was on his way to Grierlings. One last mission to make sure his acolytes couldn't continue his work. Then, then she could start to sift through the pain of losing Conrad. She'd put it all into storage, ready to unpack when they'd caught Ciara.

'Let's finish this,' Helena said in earnest, and led the way.

The hotel was a ruin. The external walls were covered in a colourful spaghetti of graffiti tags, the windows boarded over to keep out trespassers. That had failed, evidently. It was hard to believe this dump was the stronghold of criminal masterminds. Once, it must have been majestic, overlooking the raw wilderness of the North Sea, but the sun had set on the golf resort a decade ago.

It was a ghost town, filled with ghosts. Every cell in Niamh's body recoiled from it, urging her to retreat. Unnatural acts were being performed. She could feel it. Her natural powers were responding to the abuses within the hotel.

The trio reached what was once the main reception. A huge 'CONDEMNED – KEEP OUT' notice was plastered across the double doors. 'If you can, take them alive,' Helena said. 'We can use them to find out where any stragglers are hiding. Use *Sandman, Medusa* or just take them out telepathically. If you *have* to, sever them.'

Niamh and Leonie nodded. Once, to sever a witch or warlock – to slice them from consciousness – would have seen any sentient in the Pipes, but they had both resorted to it more than once since the troubles broke out. Unthinkable then, but funny how even the most dreadful things can become thinkable. And in such a short amount of time. It was shameful, Niamh thought, and there would be a time – soon – for fallout.

War was no excuse. Ever.

'Leonie,' Helena said. 'I need a field all around the hotel. No one teleports in or out.'

'Got it.'

'Stay here. If anyone tries to run . . .'

'Got that too,' she said gravely.

Helena motioned for them to take a step back and summoned a blinding bolt of lightning from the clouds. She lifted her hands to receive it and then directed it at the doors. They blew inwards, splintering into kindling. 'OK, if they didn't know we're here, they do now. Let's go. Be. On. Guard.'

Niamh and Helena ascended a flight of grimy marble stairs.

'Wait!' Leonie said. They stopped. 'Remember . . . it's *Ciara.*'

Niamh sighed. That could mean so many things: *she's our friend, our sister* or *she'd kill you in a heartbeat.* All were true.

'Come on,' Helena took Niamh's hand.

The art deco interior of the hotel was somewhat better preserved than the outside, but only just. A once ornate skylight over the main reception desk was broken and the lobby had been flooded many times over. Vines snaked through the missing panes, feeling their way down the walls like tentacles. It smelled stagnant, pond-like. It was dark, lit only by reedy light peeping through the spaces between the boards over the windows.

'It's huge,' Niamh said. 'They could be anywhere.'

'Can't you sense her?'

Niamh closed her eyes and let her mind wander down the corridors, up the stairwells and lift shafts. 'There are three of them,' Niamh said. 'All powerful . . . and *she's* here.'

She'd know her sister's chaotic energy anywhere: garnet red, swirling with blacks and midnight golds.

'Can you find her?'

'Upstairs.'

Helena nodded and Niamh led the way. If she could feel Ciara, Ciara could feel her. The first sweeping staircase led to a mezzanine of sorts where, once, you'd have helped yourself at the breakfast buffet, taken afternoon tea, or a whisky after a quick round of golf.

The bar was permanently shuttered and the tables and chairs were coated in thick black mould. In a building this big, they could be hiding, like rats, in any dark crevice. Niamh felt her heart sag. Perhaps this wasn't the end after all.

'Do you hear that?' Helena whispered.

'What?'

'I heard something.'

Niamh closed her eyes again. Before she could even start, she sensed – a sixth sense everyone can tap into – something overhead. She opened her eyes and looked up to see a blond female form scuttering across the ceiling like a spider.

'Helena!'

Realising she'd been rumbled, the witch leapt directly towards her. The *Excelsior* perhaps kicking in, Niamh raised her hand and – using telekinesis – swatted her to one side the way you might a mosquito. The blond crashed into a velvet booth with a nasty crash and howled in pain. Even so, with catlike agility, the witch was on her feet in a second, limping for the stairs.

'Stop!' Niamh said, sinking her claws into her mind. The witch froze but screamed in frustration.

'Cassidy Kane,' Helena said, glancing at Niamh. 'Well that's interesting.'

There had been rumours the American elemental was associating with Hale, but nothing had ever been proven. Until now. Niamh took some satisfaction in how bedraggled she looked. She'd always been known as the perky, pretty face of the far-right, a subscriber to Hale's credo of witch dominance over mundanes.

'Let me go you dumb fuck,' she snarled, resisting Niamh's control.

'Yeah, good one,' said Helena. She made a beeline for her and, without ceremony, blew a handful of *Sandman* into her face. Cassidy's eyes rolled back into her head and Niamh released her. She folded to the floor.

Helena spat on her. A special torment awaits witches who betray a coven. Maybe not in this world, but the next. A witch's body returns to the earth, to Gaia, but her soul . . . well, who knows? Cassidy Kane's was going nowhere good.

Leonie, sleeping witch on the mezzanine.

I'll keep her there.

'Leonie has her,' Niamh told Helena.

'One down,' Helena said.

There were two storeys of bedrooms and conference

174

rooms, all connected by metres and metres of endless tartan carpet. It made Niamh's eyes go funny. Each corridor turned into a new one identical to the last. It was darker up there, too.

'Can you make the lights work?' Niamh asked.

Helena directed some electricity back into the husk of the hotel, but the light fixtures stuttered and buzzed with only the most feeble light.

On and on the maze of hallways went. Niamh lost track of which rooms they'd already been past. She couldn't feel life in any of them. It was like that old game show where you had to pick a door and hope for a prize.

'Maybe we should split up,' Helena suggested.

'No. Helena, you'd be blind . . .'

Suddenly, someone shoved them both over. They clashed with each other painfully, went down in a knot of legs, fists and feet.

Ciara hovered over them. 'Tag. You're it.'

With a dismissive flick of the wrist, she sent them careening down the floor to the end of the hall. The friction on her back was agony until Niamh's head rammed into the fire-escape door. She felt her brain rattle in her skull. Seeing glitter, she sat up and held out her hand. 'Stop!'

'No,' Ciara said casually, blocking Niamh out of her mind. Her twin continued to glide down the long corridor, her bare toenails scraping along the carpet. The lights strobed and it was like seeing her move inside a zoetrope.

Niamh recoiled, pushing herself up. They were hardly twins now. Her sister was thinner than she'd ever seen her, gaunt and hollow-cheeked, her jet black eyes sunken in her skull. There was a slackness to her, her head lolling side to side on her toothpick neck. Her nails were long and yellowed with nicotine.

'Ciara, stop,' Niamh tried again, climbing to her feet.

'Stay down,' Ciara said, knocking her back down with a finger. Her voice was unnaturally deep, channelling whatever demonic entity she'd invoked. Niamh sensed an inky presence squatting behind her sister's, her power was greater than she'd ever known it.

Ciara was gaining on them. Helena released a lightning bolt directly at her and, with a cry, Ciara was repelled the way she'd come. The jolt was enough to release them from her control and Niamh helped Helena up. 'Quickly!'

'Did I kill her?' Helena gasped.

By way of an answer, Ciara's cruel laughter echoed down the hall. 'Well that was rude.' She now stomped down the corridor towards them.

Helena gritted her teeth and summoned the strongest gust of wind she could, holding Ciara back. Ciara stood her ground, looking thoroughly bored. 'Can you get in her head?' Helena yelled over the squall.

Niamh reached out, trying to force her way in to her sister's mind.

'Can you not, please?' Ciara said. 'Oh, Helena, you have a little something on your face . . .'

Niamh turned and saw a honeybee crawl across Helena's cheek.

Helena batted it away. 'What is it?' She saw the bee and her eyes widened. She was deathly allergic to them. From a crack in the wall, a swarm oozed, buzzing angrily around Helena. She swatted them away, panicking. As they beat her back, the winds died down and Ciara was free.

'Helena!' Niamh screamed, trying to grab for her cloak. 'It's just a glamour! It's not real!'

Too late. Ciara was free. She giggled and tore apart the

floor beneath Helena's feet. Too concerned with the bees to use her powers, Helena plummeted. Niamh looked through the jagged chasm her sister had made and saw Helena lying far below in an empty swimming pool.

Her body was motionless.

Without flinching, Niamh jumped through the gap, levitating all the way down to Helena's side. There was blood on the tiles. 'Helena?'

Her essence was still there. She was alive, but hurt, badly. Niamh placed her hands on Helena's forehead and tried to heal her.

Leonie, I need help.

'You couldn't just feckin' let me be, could you?' Ciara asked, sitting on the tip of the diving board, swinging her legs gaily. 'Had to find me and do the whole sisterly talk thing. Let me guess: *it's not too late, Ciara, we all still love you. You can make good choices.*'

From the bottom of the pool, Niamh looked up at her sister . . . and also just *past* her sister. An idea was formulating, and she hoped Ciara wouldn't hear it over the crimson rage in her head. 'This isn't a fucking intervention, Ciara.'

'Am I not even worth that?'

Niamh's jaw felt hardwired. 'You're so far past salvation . . .' Poolside, behind Ciara, a red firehose slowly and steadily uncoiled.

Ciara laughed harshly. 'Well that's not very sisterly! What would Julia Collins say about that? Oh wait . . . she's de—'

Niamh's mind seized the hose and, viper-like, it struck out. She wrapped it around Ciara's neck and, at the same instant, dragged her off the end of the diving board. Down she fell.

It would have snapped her scrawny neck, but as soon as she knew what was happening, Ciara tried to float to the side of the pool. Gravity was on Niamh's side, however, and she tugged Ciara down by her feet until the rubber noose was tight around her neck. A horrid noise gargled on her sister's tongue. She dangled a metre off the bottom of the deep end, legs thrashing. Her hands fumbled at her neck, desperately trying to loosen the hose. 'Niamh . . .' she rasped. She wasn't so jovial now.

Niamh now took her time. She walked slowly across the crackled tiles of the swimming pool. With every step she took, Ciara's power diminished. This was the first time they'd been face-to-face in two years and now they were mere inches apart. There was only one question: 'Why did you do it, Ciara?' Her voice trembled.

She struggled less, giving in. *Why did I do what?* Her face was turning scarlet.

A sob broke free from Niamh's lips. 'Why did you kill Conrad?'

Ciara's black eyes were full, for a second, of the purest hate Niamh had ever witnessed. And then a choked sound that could have been laughter, and spittle spraying in her sister's face. 'I did it . . . for the craic.'

Cunt. Niamh levitated off the floor and grasped both sides of Ciara's head and squeezed with all her might. She broke through her barricades and started obliterating everything she saw or felt. Ciara's mouth hung open in a silent scream.

Their tenth birthday helium balloons. Gone.

Spice Girls live at Sheffield Don Valley Stadium. Gone.

Trying on their oathtaking capes for the first time. Gone.

Her first kiss on the swings in the park with Joe Gulliver. Gone.

Their parents. Gone.

Niamh tore through her sister's mind, plundering every single memory. They all went black.

A witch is made of her stories, and the stories of those who went before her. This is what it was to sever someone.

Suddenly, Niamh's arms clamped at her hips. A force greater than her dragged her down to the earth with a thump. Ciara slumped down also, the hose slack.

Niamh tried to scream, but she couldn't move her mouth. Instead her feet stepped back, one stride, then another. She didn't have control of her body – a hex.

'Stop!' Leonie cried, sprinting down the edge of the pool, both hands outstretched. Call it mind control, brain-washing, imperium, puppeteering – all different words for the same thing: a hex. Leonie had a hold on Niamh's body and, as the more powerful sentient, wasn't letting go. Niamh felt tears stream down her face, salty on her lips.

Ciara was now in a heap on the floor. A foul-smelling black cloud seeped out of her mouth, eyes and nostrils; the demonic entities she'd invoked fleeing before they could be exorcised. They dribbled into the cracks in the tiles, seeking some rock or root to take sanctuary in.

Leonie loomed over them poolside. 'For fuck's sake, Niamh. You don't want to hurt your sister,' she said gently.

Oh, but she did. And how she had.

Chapter Twenty-One

BLOOD

Leonie

Desperate times call for desperate measures. At least, that was the mantra Leonie recited as she made her way down the third floor walkway of St Leonard House towards the flat of Madame Celestine. This was a 'bad part of town' but Leonie actually quite liked the brutal pebbledash high-rise council blocks that dominate much of South London. They were certainly preferable to the curvy glass monstrosities that councils were replacing them with.

She passed dozens of identikit flats, like popcorn chicken of London life – kids screaming in the rec area below, barking dogs, blaring TVs – until she came to one that was especially pungent. There was a wreath of dried palm leaves on the door and a basket for offerings. It was presently about half full with fresh cut flowers, some peppers, coconuts and a mango. Leonie took a deep breath and knocked three times.

She wouldn't be here if it wasn't *absolutely* necessary. She hadn't even told Chinara she was coming because, as openminded as she was, she wasn't down to fuck with

this. The notion of triggering has become much maligned
... *blah blah blah, woke snowflakes* and all that, but
Chinara – as a kid – had seen shit. It was kinder to leave
her out.

There was a peephole in the centre of the wreath. 'Who
wakes the spirits?' A muffled voice spoke through the
door.

'Leonie Jackman from Diaspora. I'm here to see Madame
Celestine.'

There was a pause and the door opened. The smell of
sage and eucalyptus was overwhelming. Leonie entered
the living room-cum-waiting room, where Celestine's clien-
tele waited for their readings. A slight teenage girl, no
older than thirteen or fourteen, beckoned her inside. 'Wait
here,' she said. 'I will see if Mistress takes callers.'

Leonie didn't sit because she was uncomfortable and
wanted to pace. Dozens of tealights flickered in red jars,
filling the room with crimson light. Red for danger.
Between the candles, rows of empty eye sockets stared
her down from a shrine made of human skulls. The walls
were lined with masks representing various gods and
goddesses.

She wasn't one to judge. Make no mistake, this wasn't
her approach to witchcraft, but that was the whole point
of Diaspora – to expand and include. There were as many
ways to be a witch as there were witches. Madame
Celestine – government name Dolores Umba – had been
quite literally blacklisted from HMRC thirty years ago
because she wouldn't practise the *polite* sort of witchcraft.

'Why does the *queen* of Diaspora darken my doorstep?'
Her booming voice announced her arrival as she swept
into the room past a bead curtain. She was a formidable
woman, her waist cinched by a boned corset to accentuate

her buxom figure. She was tall already but her headwrap made her look Amazonian.

The word *queen* was sour on her tongue. The advent of Diaspora had, for want of a better phrase, pissed on Celestine's candle by offering a more mainstream alternative to Celestine's methods. She was not Leonie's biggest fan, needless to say. 'I'm not here to talk about Diaspora . . .'

'Good. Cos I got nothing to say on that. I seem to remember someone arriving in London and saying she didn't need any help from Madame Celestine . . .'

Leonie shrugged. 'I'm just here as a customer. I want a reading.'

Celestine threw her head back and laughed throatily. 'You think I'll be doing you favours, child? After the disrespect you showed me?'

'My money spends as well as anyone else's . . .'

That was the language Celestine spoke. A witch for hire. Again, Leonie wasn't there to judge. Before there were doctors there were witch doctors and before that there were just witches. A girl's gotta eat. 'For you, child, I charge double-time. Call it reparations.'

'Deal.' At least she knew she was being scammed, unlike a lot of her other clients. Dolores – as far as Leonie had concluded from doing a bit of digging – had come to London as a refugee, fleeing war in the Congo in the nineties. HMRC put her on a watchlist after she advertised her skills as an exorcist. In truth, Leonie knew that what HMRC didn't understand, it feared. HMRC was nice scones-and-jam *English* witchcraft. No menstrual blood. No sacrifices. No sex, please. We're British.

'I'm gonna enjoy this,' Celestine smiled. 'Come on through.'

She held aside the curtain, and Leonie followed her into

what was, by rights, a dining room. The walls were smeared in greasy black paint with symbols painted in vivid red. The windows were crudely boarded over with haphazard planks of wood and there were yet more skulls, canopic jars and petrified animal parts on bookshelves.

This was all designed to scare mundanes – a fairground ghost train.

The reason Leonie *did* take issue with Celestine's business model was that it involved telling mundanes they were cursed or possessed and then charging them to remove or exorcise it. That said, her customers came to Celestine in distress and left . . . less distressed, regardless of all the theatrics. This was, Leonie supposed, a sort of alternative therapy, and every other therapist in London charged a lot more than Celestine did.

Moreover, Celestine was also a bloody good medium. She hit the spots oracles couldn't. Leonie had had enough of waiting to find out what was on the horizon, and of feeling under the thumb of some nameless doom. She wanted spoilers.

Leonie took her seat at the small round table at the centre of the candlelit room. Celestine sat opposite on a throne entwined with roses and lilies and took up a fat cigar. 'What has brought you to Madame Celestine? What troubles your pretty head?' She puffed on the cigar and exhaled a plume of smoke in Leonie's direction.

Reluctantly, Leonie reached into her tote bag and extracted her offering. Celestine unwrapped the package.

'And what do you call this?'

Leonie blinked. 'It's a dove.'

'It is dead.'

'I know. I'm a sentient. I'm not going to sit here while you slaughter live animals.'

Celestine smiled. 'Stupid local girl. Without a blood offering, how do you hope to appease the spirits?'

Besides sentients, elementals, healers, and oracles, there is a type of witch HMRC would *never* teach children about, wouldn't even admit to. Necromancers. Witches of death. 'There's plenty of blood in that bird,' Leonie said.

When the daughters of Gaia left the motherland they travelled far, absorbing and assimilating a myriad of cultures and customs. Leonie, once, had sworn an oath to *a* coven, but Diaspora recognised – in theory – that there are a thousand covens worldwide, and countless more witches. And it wasn't her place, or Helena's, or anyone's, to define the right or wrong way to be a witch.

Yet she did. She was a liar and a hypocrite. You know what? She *did* judge. There was ugly shrapnel in Leonie's gut and it was called *shame*. When people saw her, a brown-skinned witch, this is what they thought she was about: blood rituals, and spirits, and demons. *You gonna voodoo me, Leonie?* Stereotypes she'd fought against her whole life. But here she was judging Celestine for living her life. She judged herself for judging Celestine.

'Severine!' Celestine barked and the girl, her assistant, hurried in. '*Va m'en chercher un vivant, et mets cette merde morte à la poubelle.*'

The girl took the dove and Leonie realised that Celestine really was going to make her pay. A moment later the assistant returned with a guinea fowl struggling in her hands. She gave it to Celestine who held it firm.

The witch tossed back her head and laughed a husky, deep-throated laugh. 'The girl disapproves of Madame Celestine.'

'I do not,' Leonie said.

'Keep your deceitful tongue outside my house.'

Leonie was shamed. 'I'm sorry. You're right, I do disapprove. But I also respect your talent and I need you. That is the truth. I swear on the goddess.'

Celestine chuckled. 'Very well. What is it you wish to know, *bébé reine?*'

'You've heard the Sullied Child prophecy?' Celestine nodded. 'I met him last week. He's powerful. Far too powerful. I admit I was scared.'

'Even you, *queen?*'

'Yes, even me. HMRC believes he is in league with Leviathan. I want to know what the spirit world sees.'

The death witch laughed again. 'Oh I see! The girl doesn't like it when she's not the top of the totem!'

Leonie shook her head. 'That's not it. I need to know . . . if this threat is real and if I need to protect my coven. If it was up to me, I'd have nothing to do with their white-witch drama.'

The loudest laugh yet. 'Child, I hear that! As you wish. But be ready to hear things you might not like.'

'I'm ready.'

She lay the fowl on the table and casually picked up a cleaver. Leonie focused on anything other than the rising panic in the little bird. It knew.

But it was over fast. With one blow, its head was off, blood spurting from the hole in its neck. Celestine got to work, etching symbols on the table in the blood, before then wiping her red thumbs over her eyes.

Leonie had *heard* what invocation looked like, sounded like, but hadn't seen it for herself. Invocation was the ghost story witches told at sleepovers. Letting something slither inside your body, you could see why teenage girls in particular found it so scarily compelling. She was determined to look without flinching. She was the head of a coven, for crying out loud, not a teenage girl watching her first 18-certificate movie. She would *not* look green in front of Celestine.

As an oracle, Celestine was at best a Level 2, but her death rituals took her power to a whole new and uncharted realm – souls. When a person dies, their body is recycled but even a witch doesn't quite know what awaits the spirit. Well, not *most* witches. Because HMRC in the UK, and Coven Intelligence America across the pond didn't formally acknowledge the existence of necromancers, it was impossible to know how many operated in the world. Witch academics spoke of necromancy as if it were something savages practised in the past, in mud huts, in some monolithic Africa.

Celestine started to circle in her seat, muttering in French under her breath, no doubt summoning the spirits. Leonie was ready. Once you open a door, anything can step through. She remembered that fucking day at the Hotel Carnoustie – that black shit dribbling out of Ciara's face. If you let a demon into your body, it doesn't always want to leave.

Leonie clasped her hands together on her lap. Celestine's chanting grew louder and her rocking more aggressive. Her neck and shoulders spasmed and Leonie wondered if she was getting the full tourist experience until something moved in the corner of her eye.

A breeze stirring the candlelight? No. A tall shadow swung around the wall and a gentle wind ruffled Leonie's hair. She looked behind her, but there was no one else in the room.

'*Je convoque les esprits! Je convoque les esprits! Entendez moi! Entrez moi!*'

Disembodied shadows now encircled the table, some

impossibly tall, others the size of children. They seemed to congregate around Celestine.

Suddenly, the medium sat stiff and still. Her eyes turned white and her mouth sagged open, her tongue protruding and limp. A throaty groan rumbled up from her chest, deep at first and then high and strangled. Leonie forced herself to watch as saliva dribbled down her chin and dripped onto her cleavage.

Celestine's neck snapped to one side. A voice emerged from her mouth, but it was not her own and her lips didn't move. '*Leonie? Leonie? Can brown people get sunburned?*' It was the voice of a little girl. A little girl had once asked her that question at a caravan park in Skegness.

Leonie was speechless.

The voice changed. Now an old, a very old woman seemed to speak through Celestine in clipped RP tones. '*You're asking all the wrong questions. That's the problem with you lot.*'

The voice changed again, huskier, gravelly. '*Mira con más cuidado.*'

The old posh woman returned. 'In my day we didn't have a word for it, of course.'

The little girl came back. 'Why don't you have a dad?'

'My sweet Leonie,' said a voice that sounded a lot like her grandmother. 'A child will change everything. It will change you.'

'*Mira de nuevo.*'

'Just listen to her,' said the old lady.

A man's voice cut through with a strong Creole accent. 'You'd think you of all people would have worked it out by now.'

'Deaf!' screamed the old woman. 'Deaf and blind!'

Celestine groaned, her eyes bulging. She slumped on her throne, and a new voice emerged. One she recognised. *'Leonie? Can you hear me?'*

So familiar, but so far away. So distant. It took her a moment to place it. 'Stef?' she whispered. Stefan, Helena's husband. It couldn't be. She remembered his corpse floating, pale and bloated, caught in a hedgerow during the floods. She felt dizzy, like all the blood was leaving her head.

His voice now came, almost backwards-sounding, through Celestine's mouth. *'Leonie. You need to stop her. You need to stop Helena before . . .'*

Then Celestine shot out of her chair, banging her fists against the table. Her eyes were now jet black. 'YOU CANNOT STOP HIM.'

A warm, stinking belch of sulphuric wind whipped around the dingy room, blowing the candles out. Leonie pushed herself back, sliding off her seat to the floor. 'Celestine!'

'HE WILL RISE AND EVERY LAST MUD CUNT WITCH WILL BURN.'

'Celestine! Stop!' Leonie screamed.

The medium's eyes bled, blood rolling down her cheeks. 'LEVIATHAN WILL RISE. *SATANÁS PARA SIEMPRE!*'

Leonie raised a hand against the hurricane and focused everything she had on throwing Celestine back. Whatever was inside her was powerful, but she managed. The woman flew backwards, crashing into the boards over the window. She cried out and slumped to the floor in a heap.

The winds and the stench dissipated and Leonie scrambled to her side. 'Celestine? Are you OK?'

Celestine sat up and straightened her headwrap. She looked blankly at Leonie for a moment, as if trying to remember where she was. 'I am fine,' she said, although she seemed far from it. Leonie helped her to her feet and she smoothed down her dress. 'You can leave now.'

'But . . . I haven't paid you yet . . .'

Celestine seemed numb, her face ashen. 'I don't want your money, and I don't want your problems, local girl. You have no business bringing your shit to my door. If you got any common sense in that head of yours, you'll leave this matter well alone. That ungodly *thing* I just felt inside my bones, it is not here to play. It's old, and it's hungry, and it has got a mouth full of teeth. You hear me, *bébé*?'

Leonie nodded. 'Loud and clear.'

Chapter Twenty-Two

THE WAR

Niamh

Her already cluttered kitchen was starting to resemble a school room. Snow sat incongruously between Holly and Theo, poised and ready to go with a gleaming new notebook and pens.

'I have a question,' Holly asked.

'Go on,' Niamh said, carrying a mug of lemon and ginger tea to the table.

'You know how my mum's a healer? How come Snow's grandma needs a wheelchair?'

Snow screwed her face up like she'd swallowed something bitter. 'Are you an idiot?'

'Snow, enough.' Niamh shut her down, already lamenting the loss of the cosy threesome she, Holly and Theo had so quickly established. 'Holly and Theo haven't had the training you've had. We have to go at their pace, OK?'

'Sorry,' said Snow. 'To be fair, I asked the same thing when I was like eight. She had something called a herniated disc when she was having my mum. Brutal, right?

Healers helped her for years, but without their magic, it just gets worse right away.'

Niamh nodded sagely. It was a valid teaching point. 'Understand this: witches work *with* nature, not against it. I'm sure a powerful witch could keep herself – or himself – young and fit forever, but what a shocking misuse of Gaia's power. It's in our nature to age and die, like all things must. We're not gods.'

'Well that's my next question,' Holly said. 'You know how you're dead powerful and stuff?'

'I do.'

'Why don't you, like, get some jumpsuits and do the whole Marvel thing?'

Snow tutted again, but Niamh thought that was a perfectly valid question too. 'For one thing, mundanes don't relish the idea that there's people – especially women – stronger than them, so for a long time they rounded us up and well . . . it was safer to keep to ourselves, look at it that way. Only a very few people in government are aware of us, and they've signed the Occult Secrets Act. Our truce with mundanes now dates back to the start of HMRC . . .'

Theo looked pensive. Niamh gently probed Theo and there was a saltiness, a leaden feeling of . . . disappointment. Deflation. She didn't push further. 'You good, Theo?' she instead asked. He nodded.

'Very well, then,' Niamh went on. 'Today I want to go into the history of HMRC because it does make a difference to how we function. I think it's important you know who we – *they* – are.' She forgot, for a moment, that she wasn't from HMRC any more. It was happening a lot just lately.

She placed her palms on the table, a chunk of fool's

gold between them all. 'Join hands,' she told her students. 'Focus on the rock. I'll share the past as I understand it. You ready?'

Her young acolytes nodded. Even Snow was rapt now. They took five minutes to synchronise their breathing and Niamh spoke in her most soothing tone. 'Open your minds. See as I see . . .'

We'll never know exactly when the first witches migrated to these shores. There's evidence as early as the Stone Age that there were witches and warlocks here who harnessed Gaia's energy. Certainly as long as history has been recorded there have been witches. Healers, medicine women, shamans, seers. We've had many names, and we were revered, exalted even, in ancient times.

You can chart the decline of witches against the rise of monotheistic religions. One by one they appropriated magic into spirituality. 'Spells' became 'miracles'. Only certain brands of miracles became acceptable. Although, you will note, many Judaeo-Christian beliefs overlap with ours.

Was Jesus a warlock? No one knows, but it's thought he communed with nature, healed the sick and came back from the dead so . . .

Where was I? As religions all around the world began to persecute witches, we were driven into hiding. We developed secret languages and symbols, formed covens and cabals and operated in the shadows.

Now. Cast your minds back to 1522. A year which, in hindsight, changed the path of British witches forever. A powerful young witch called Anne Boleyn discovered her considerable sentience, and trained with a coven in France. Anne was different from other witches because she was born of nobility. She was a powerful girl when girls weren't meant to have power, and she wouldn't settle for marrying her cousin. Instead, she set her sights on the throne.

Who can say if she enchanted Henry or if she was just a firecracker in the sack – by far the easiest way to bewitch a man, if I'm honest – however, when Anne failed to provide a male heir, the king moved on to the next. Some people accused Anne of witchcraft, others of adultery and incest. Either way, by the time she was beheaded, Anne had firmly established a secret coven within the court of Henry VIII.

She also had a daughter, Elizabeth, who eventually became Queen of England in 1558. By all accounts she was not as powerful as her mother, but she understood the value of the coven, even if she publicly distanced herself from poor headless Anne. You'll not find it in any history books, but it was Elizabeth who founded the first official Royal Coven in 1560. She was wary of witches, it's said, but knew there was no one better to protect her when she was surrounded on all sides by vipers at court.

Everything was going swimmingly until Elizabeth chose – and I respect her choice, obviously – to not have children. If she had, however, I think we'd be having this lesson in a school rather than in my kitchen. As it was, James, the son of her distant cousin, ascended to the throne. He was no warlock, and was terrified of the coven. He feared they'd kill him and place a witch on the throne. In 1604 he passed the Witchcraft Act.

Knowing they'd be executed, the witches of Elizabeth's court fled, forced back into hiding while King James oversaw witch trials up and down the country. It was the worst time. Over five hundred witches were hung, burned or drowned between then and 1717, when the act was finally scrapped.

Of course, during these years, both throne and parliament knew of witches and what we were capable of. Some witches were offered plea deals if you like – their lives for their service. We were enslaved, forced to assist or we'd be burned at the stake. That went on for a hundred years until Victoria's long reign.

Around that time, spiritualism became very fashionable among the middle classes. As you know, once rich white people start doing something, they very quickly make it legal. Victoria was no different and, when her beloved Albert died, she called on a coven to help her commune with his spirit. Her 'personal coven' also foresaw the final four assassination attempts against the queen, saving her skin, and – increasingly – she relied on oracles to guide her.

Obviously witches and the church make for uneasy bedfellows. Victoria decreed that the crown must be protected by witches, but covertly. The church and the coven would exist separately from state, but work alongside one another. In 1869 – officially – Her Majesty's Royal Coven was formed. Since that year, there has always been a verified coven working with the government. That's not to say there aren't others – look at Diaspora – but HMRC is the strongest and largest. When we take the oath, it's HMRC we pledge our service to.

If you look hard enough at old photographs, we're

there in the background – healers in the trenches, suffragettes, Bletchley Park oracles, land girls and resistance fighters. Why is it we help in times of crisis? We have a gift. We are stronger than mundanes, plain and simple.

We could – and some witches think we should – enslave or dominate our ungifted siblings. But at HMRC we decided, long ago, that we help and protect mundanes. Regardless of how we've been treated in the past, they are equal in Gaia's eyes. She doesn't favour a witch over a flea. We don't think our powers make us superior. They make us responsible. We are guardians, custodians, not weapons. That's why we fiercely maintain our independence from politicians. They'd have us blowing up countries left, right and centre. They'd have us hexing world leaders, the way Russia did with—

'But what about the war Mum talked about?' Holly asked.

Niamh blinked and joined the room. Theo and Snow too left the trance state. 'I was getting to that part,' Niamh said. 'It's important you know, because it shows how close we were to the coven imploding for good.'

'What happened?' Snow asked. 'Mum doesn't like to talk about it.'

Niamh hesitated. Helena might not thank her for this. 'Are you sure you want to hear about this, Snow?'

'Yes.' Snow nodded, determined. 'I want to know how my dad died. I don't even remember him. He's just memories the oracles have shown me, but they're not mine.'

'You deserve that much,' said Niamh. 'Ten years ago now, we were at the big party after the oathtaking. After the new witches were sworn in, they lit the bonfire as usual. We took off our capes and danced. That's the tradition; we celebrate our freeness in fire and air.

'At the time, we had a High Priestess called Julia Collins. She was a good, and fair, woman. She oversaw my own oath way back when, and your mother's. I was dancing around the fire, and I sensed it, you know. I knew something was wrong, and I said so. I stopped dancing and turned to see Julia. She was stood on the sidelines, watching the fire, clapping and singing along. All of a sudden her smile fell, she took the silver blade from the altar, and slit her own throat.'

Holly and Snow reacted with shock. Theo listened, waiting for her to go on.

'I saw the way her face changed. She'd been hexed. That's when a sentient takes control of another person's body. To this day, we don't know exactly who hexed her, but for a witch to assassinate another witch is highest treason. You do not betray the coven. That's the greatest sin there is.

'For some time before that there'd been tension. Dabney Hale, a well-bred warlock from a good family was garnering a lot of support from both warlocks and witches. He felt HMRC had run its course. It was old; it was stuffy; it was at the beck and call of idiot mundane politicians. He formed his own coven based on a philosophy of witch supremacy. Hale believed, like I said, that witches and warlocks are stronger than mundanes. We shouldn't be lurking in the shadows, we should be the ones ruling the world.

'And he wasn't the only one. Turns out that once someone like Hale, someone handsome and refined and wealthy, is bold enough to step up and say it aloud, there were plenty of others who'd been sitting on that opinion too. Including my sister, Ciara.'

'That blows,' Snow said.

'Yes, Snow, it really did. With Collins gone, HMRC fell into chaos and Hale and his cabal took advantage. They launched attacks on mundanes – floods and fires, they summoned demons to provoke violence and murder; outbreaks of infection, stirring discontent and paranoia and fear of the unknown. They used sentients to turn people against vaccines and then conjured old diseases like measles and syphilis. They stoked ideological divisions, ripping families apart. They'd been plotting it for *years*. Hale's ultimate goal was to get himself into power. He'd create a myriad of "natural" disasters and then present himself as the saviour. Humanity would bow down before us.

'Those of us who were left at HMRC had no choice. We had to go to war against witches. A civil war. None of us *wanted* to kill witches – we're already so few – but what choice did we have? To subjugate mundanes – despite everything they've done to us – was, is, wrong. We have to know, I think, the difference between right and wrong.

'So we did what we had to do, your mums, Leonie and I. We fought for what we thought to be right. Wherever possible we detained the terrorists – most of them are at Grierlings – but we, I, had to kill some too. As the younger witches in the coven, it was up to us to lead the charge. I think I was only twenty-four when Collins died. Too young.'

'And my dad?'

'He died in the Somerset Floods,' Niamh admitted. 'Trying to save mundanes and stop rebel witches. My fiancé, Conrad, was killed by . . . a sentient. Some of them came after us, of course, once they knew what we were doing. Conrad wasn't even a warlock. He was just there. And that's war for you,' she said sadly.

'Hang on a second,' Holly said. 'If there was like a huge war, wouldn't people know about it?'

Niamh shook her head. 'Oh Holly, you have no idea. Even during the war, some mundanes started fussing about witchcraft. It was even in the tabloids. And you know what happens when people get wind of witchcraft . . .'

'Witch hunts,' Snow said.

'Precisely. We, at the coven, took the difficult decision to erase the memories of the general population. The Prime Minister gave a national TV and radio broadcast that allowed every sentient we had to—'

She'd have gone on, but, behind her back, there was a thud at the back door. She turned just in time to see Luke's face through the window, but missed Theo recoil in surprise.

All she saw was a flash of lightning in her periphery. 'Theo! No!'

Too late. A bolt shot from Theo's hands, obliterating the back door and blasting Luke across the back garden. The crate of veg he was carrying spun into the air, oranges and onions raining down. Niamh sprung up, her chair clattering over the tiles. She ran to the garden to where Luke lay, motionless, on the lawn.

He was utterly still, eyes closed. Fresh blood covered his face, she guessed from the shattered glass in the door. Niamh placed a hand on his chest, trying to find a heartbeat. 'Holly,' she said gravely. 'Call your mother *now*.'

Chapter Twenty-Three

THE SECRET

Elle

Even a mundane mother knows when her children aren't kidding. So when Holly rang, she heard *it*, that siren, in her daughter's voice at once. Something was badly wrong. Elle abandoned her trolley in the middle of the Sainsbury's aisle and raced back to her car.

She'd finished her rounds for the afternoon, but hadn't as yet got home to change out of her drab community nurse uniform. She stalled the car to a halt next to Luke's van in the lane outside Niamh's cottage, and grabbed her first-aid kit out of the boot. It was a long time since she'd done trauma nursing – not really since the war – and the sheer dread came soaring back like she was stretching old muscles, that horrible sensation of not knowing quite what horrors awaited, but that horrors awaited.

She saw Luke's body on the lawn; Theo crying on the back step; Holly comforting him, an arm around his shoulder; Niamh leaning over Luke, doing what she could to heal him. There was a reason she'd given all this up for a life of changing dressings or removing stitches in the comfort of people's homes.

Elle stepped over spilled fruit and veg and hurried to their position on the lawn. 'What happened?' she said shortly, time of the essence.

Snow Vance-Morrill hovered at her side. 'Theo has, like, magical Tourette's or something.'

'Welcome back, Snow.' Elle politely ignored that.

Niamh pulled a stray hair out of her mouth. 'Lightning bolt. But I think the door took most of the blast. I've done what I can but . . .'

Elle surveyed Luke. There was a nasty shard of wood sticking out of his groin and gashes on his face. 'Step back.' She knelt beside him and held her hands over his chest. 'He has a heartbeat and he's breathing. He'll be fine.' Life emanates from all living things. The more vibrant, the more alive. Luke was skirting closer than she'd like to the fine line where she wouldn't be able to get him back.

She heard Niamh exhale deeply. 'Can you heal him?'

'Yes.' It wouldn't be pleasant for her; she'd have to transfer a lot of radiance from herself into him, but his vital organs were all intact from what she could sense. She cupped his cheek in her left hand and touched her right fingers to the earth. She could borrow energy from the soil too. Elle closed her eyes and let her mind trace where he was most hurt.

It's nature's nature to heal. All Elle did was hurry the process along. She often thought of her powers as a biological fast-forward button. She directed white blood cells and plasma to where they needed to be. She imbued cellular matter with energy to regenerate faster than they ever could by themselves.

That splinter in his groin, however, was in the way. She

went into her kit and found some latex-free gloves. She snapped them on efficiently. 'This isn't going to be very pleasant,' she warned them before swiftly extracting the stake with a moist squelch. Luke moaned and stirred. She moved her left hand to his forehead and sent him back to sleep, sending a surge of melatonin through his system.

There were still tiny wooden splinters in his leg, but the healing process would expel them. Bracing herself, she offered Luke as much of her own healing energy as she could. The wounds on his face sealed up first, followed by the nastier incision over his hip crease.

Elle slumped over, spent. The floor felt like it was tilting, spongy like a bad mattress. She was out of practice. She'd need a minute. She admired those witches who secreted themselves away on A&E wards. They were brave and selfless, but she – for she had tried it for a month or two after she first qualified – found it simply too sad. Too many patients arriving on that ward were beyond her capabilities.

'Mum? Are you OK?' She felt footsteps cantering towards her.

Elle rolled onto her back and absorbed as much energy out of the grass and soil as she could. She felt the cool air on her face. She stared up at the clouds – white galleons on a deep blue sea – and felt her heart rate return to normal. 'I'll be fine. Just give me a second.'

'You're amazing,' Niamh said softly, kissing her forehead, and transferring some of her own radiance to Elle at the same time. 'Thank you.'

'All in a day's work.'

'You gonna wipe him now?' Snow said, apparently underwhelmed with her exertions.

Holly helped Elle to sit up, and she looked to Niamh. 'Do you think he'll remember?'

Niamh looked torn. 'What am I supposed to tell him? A bomb went off in my kitchen?'

Elle glanced back at the cottage. Theo was still perched on the back step, surrounded by the carnage he'd created. He was watching intently, eyes red and puffy. The poor kid was a walking disaster. It was like when her mother adopted a stray mongrel in Cyprus and it destroyed her home out there too. 'Well you can hardly tell him you're a witch.'

'I know.' Niamh focused and touched a finger to his temple to speed the process along. A second later and it was done. He wouldn't remember anything.

Elle took an anti-bac wipe from her kit and started to clean up any tell-tale blood. 'How will you explain the hole in his crotch? You could say you tried to tear his pants off.'

'Don't start,' Niamh warned her.

'What?' Elle said, batting her eyes.

'Come on you lot,' Niamh said, trying to jolly up the troops. 'Let's *carefully* move him into the lane. We'll say he fainted.' It was a feeble cover story, but Elle couldn't think of anything better off the top of her head.

Luke's body levitated off the ground and obediently followed Niamh. She looked tired, Elle thought. This daycare stuff was taking it out of her.

Niamh held out a hand to Theo. 'C'mon. It was an accident. But that's my window *and* door now. I'm going to start charging if you're not careful.' She gave him a wink as she pulled him up. 'You lot gather up the food. We need to make it look like he dropped it in the lane.'

Snow collected the crate, but Elle saw Theo and Holly deep in psychic conversation. Theo took her hand. Holly, not quite subtly enough, shook her head. What she'd give

202

to be a fly on that wall. The boy was a liability. Luke would be fine – this time – but she didn't fancy Holly getting in the way of a lightning bolt, even if it was an accidental one.

Elle wondered if she'd let this flirtation go on long enough.

She waited until Jez took Milo to training to pounce. Some nights, Elle insisted they ate at the family table, reminding them that she wasn't operating a takeaway restaurant. It caused nothing but arguments – because she enforced a strict no-phones policy on such evenings – but she stuck to it regardless.

Holly poked at her portion of blackberry and apple crumble long after her father and brother had left. 'What's the matter?' Elle asked. 'It's your favourite.' She'd made it, essentially, as a bribe.

'I'm not hungry,' Holly said.

There was a time when Elle had been fearful of Holly and anorexia. Like a lot of teenage girls, she'd been through a phase of thigh-gap measuring and flesh pinching. Worse, Elle knew it was behaviour Holly had learned from her in a roundabout way. She wished she could go back and stop herself from whining about size twelve, 'bikini diets' or calorie-counting in front of her daughter when she was little. Luckily, each Instagram diet obsession lasted only a few days before her daughter hungrily accepted whatever food Elle prepared. Anyway, she had the metabolism of a whippet.

She wasn't entirely sure how worried she should be about self-harm – at least one of her gothy friends was a cutter – and she had been on the fence about potential lesbian tendencies until Theo turned up. Of course Elle had noticed the eyeliner and mascara emerging, and the requests to borrow her hair straighteners. What else could it mean? She *assumed* Theo had knocked Holly back and that was responsible for her surliness, at least this week.

'Holls?'

'What?'

'Is there something you want to tell me?' She tried to keep her tone light, difficult after the intense afternoon they'd had. She had wakened Luke on the lane next to his van, befuddled after being wiped, but otherwise fine. He was embarrassed they'd called a nurse more than anything. They'd left him in the cottage kitchen, with Niamh attempting to explain how *firemen* had hacked apart her back door due to a suspected gas leak.

'No,' Holly said. She couldn't look more suspicious if she tried.

'Holly. I like to think you could come to me with anything. I'm not a scary mum am I?'

Holly laughed. 'No! You are definitely not Scary Mum.'

Elle wondered if they were both thinking of Lilian Vance. 'Then what is it? Since Theo came along, you two have been thick as thieves, spending all your time sending little psychic messages – yes I noticed. Something's going on. Mums know these things. Even non-witch ones.'

Holly looked weighed down by whatever it was she was carrying. If this Theo kid was Leviathan incarnate, there was no way he was dragging her daughter down. 'Holly . . . ?'

'Mum, I can't say. I promised Theo.'

'Promised him what?'

There was a big pause. 'Well that's the thing . . . no I can't, Mum. A promise is a promise.'

She rose to leave the table, but Elle stopped her. 'Holly, sit down. I know a promise is a promise, but this is serious.

Theo isn't a houseguest, he's here because HMRC think he's dangerous. If you know something that could bring harm to the coven then . . .'

Holly looked like she might cry. Elle knew this was turning into an interrogation, but she was too close now to stop. 'God, Mum! You've got it all wrong!'

'Then what is it?' And then she played her trump card. 'Look. Niamh can't read Theo for whatever reason, but I'm willing to bet she can read you. So either you tell me now or I get her to do it.'

Holly was beaten and she knew it. A tear rolled down her face. Elle remembered how monumental friendships are when you're fourteen. The approval of a girlfriend was more important than anything else. It's a misconception that teenage girls are boy crazy. On the contrary, she remembered how they'd always run boys past each other, vetting them, before agreeing to go with them.

She stood and fetched a kitchen towel for Holly to dry her face. 'Now,' Elle said gently. 'What the hell is going on with that boy?'

Holly sort of sob-laughed. 'Well that's the thing!'

'For Gaia's sake, Holly, what?' Not even meaning to, she clutched Holly's hand and her anguish flowed into her. She fought the urge to cry too.

'Mum, I really liked Theo but . . . but he . . . *she's* not a boy. Theo thinks she's trans.'

'Oh.' The noise popped out of Elle's mouth involuntarily and she dropped Holly's hands.

'I can't believe I told you. I *swore* to Gaia I wouldn't say anything. She hasn't told anyone else *ever*. Mum, you have to *promise* you won't say anything to anyone.'

Elle handed her another sheet of kitchen towel. 'Honey, I promise.'

Chapter Twenty-Four

DAUGHTERS OF GAIA

Niamh

'Holly made me *promise* I wouldn't tell you this,' Elle said the second the waitress walked away with their order at the Tea Cosy.

Niamh blinked. 'Is *this* the emergency? You have *gossip?*' Niamh was still in her vet scrubs, having dashed out of the clinic to respond to Elle's urgency. 'Elle! I have appointments!'

Elle gave her a stern glare. 'This is not gossip. It's important.'

'Go on then . . . you have five minutes.' Niamh guessed it was something to do with what had happened yesterday afternoon. Theo was at home right now waiting for the joiner to fix the door. She hoped he wouldn't electrocute her too. That was one of many nice things about Hebden Bridge – a selection of super reliable lesbian craftswomen. The pleasingly analogue noticeboard outside the indie bookshop was a true community hub. The business cards and fliers gave away something of their secret: women's yoga, herbalists, gardeners and choirs. The witching clues were there if you knew where to look. Niamh had never lived anywhere else where so many mundanes, at the very

206

least, *suspected* they were in the presence of real witches, and didn't seem to mind.

The waitress brought their lattes over, and Elle waited for her to leave. 'OK, this is big . . .'

'Elle . . . I have horny cats to spay.'

'Theo is transgender.' It blurted out of her mouth.

Niamh waited for follow-up. 'I beg your pardon?'

'It's true. He . . . or, as it transpires, she . . . told Holly so.'

She ran some maths in her head. Had he . . . she . . . said anything? Even hinted? 'OK . . .' she mused, swilling it around her head like she was at a wine tasting.

'Explains a lot doesn't it?'

'Does it?' Niamh said. The tearoom seemed to carousel around. She felt tipsy.

'Well it explains his . . . her . . . power for one thing.' Elle lowered her voice and scanned the tearoom. There were only a couple of others in the café at present: a man with a very cute French bulldog and a teenage girl tapping away on her phone in the corner.

Niamh massaged her temples. Would a trans witch be on a par with a cisgender witch? If she googled it would that help? Unlikely. 'You're right. It makes some sense. God, I didn't think anything of it.'

'What?'

'He . . . *she* . . . a while back, she asked about whether she'd be allowed in HMRC, and I said she'd have to go to the cabal and she seemed properly gutted.'

'There you go.' Elle sipped her coffee triumphantly. 'I was shocked for a while last night, but it's not a big thing these days is it? There's a trans boy in Holly's class at school. They seem to take it in their stride.'

Niamh waited for the room to stop spinning. Of all the

fucking foreboding apocalyptic portents about that kid, being *transgender* was minor-league stuff. She actually breathed a sigh of relief. Her shoulders inched down for the first time in weeks. 'She's trans. OK. That's almost mundane shit. Can you remember that lady at school? The one who worked in the bursar's office?'

Elle was confused for a second and then recognition flashed in her eyes. 'Oh yes! What was her name? Daphne!'

'That was it.'

'Bless her heart. I haven't thought about her in years. I wonder what happened to her? The boys were so horrible about her, can you remember?'

Niamh paused. 'We all were. We were right little shits. We used to make fun of her too, Elle. You know we did.'

Elle scrunched her face, but didn't deny it. 'Things are different now.'

'Are they? I hope for Theo's sake you're right. Kids can still be vile though. I hear the way they talk sometimes.'

'I sometimes eavesdrop on Milo and his friends. I think they try to outdo each other.'

Niamh felt her schema shifting to accommodate this new truth. It was clicking into place. Everything about Theo was unstable, turbulent. Niamh had assumed the chaos was in his – *her* – home life (she had to get on top of that) but it seemed there was a storm *inside* of her too. What's more fundamental than your gender? The way people describe you, treat you, greet you, on a daily basis. It was no fucking wonder she couldn't control her powers. Imagine discovering that not only are you a girl, but you're also a witch.

And, on top of everything, her mum had tried to drown her and Helena had her kidnapped. Niamh felt a sudden rush of anger. Her chest felt hot and prickly. Theo needed protection, not persecution. This changed everything.

'Are you OK?' Elle asked.

'Sorry, yes. Just thinking to myself. This is big, Elle.'

'I told you it was an emergency!'

Niamh smiled, but now faced the unenviable job of finishing the rest of the working day with this news on her mind. 'Thank you for telling me.'

'Don't tell Theo Holly blabbed though. I think she idolises hi . . . her.'

'I won't. Fuck. What do I do with this? Do I ask Theo outright?'

Elle shrugged. 'Tell Helena I guess?'

For whatever reason, that solution didn't fit. Surely better that Theo's a girl than in league with Leviathan? Still, it seemed too easy somehow. Solving this case couldn't be so straightforward . . . could it? 'Can we wait a while?'

'Why?'

It was a reflex, a hunch, more than anything. 'I think . . . I can get through to her, get her to open up. If she's a girl, she could make a phenomenal witch. I don't want to tell Helena and have her swoop in and ruin the work we're doing.'

Elle nodded. 'Sure. You're the boss.'

'Elle, I am categorically not the boss.'

Elle giggled and Niamh downed the rest of her coffee. It was bitter, too much foam. Her head was messy. If *she* was confused, how must poor Theo feel? She didn't know what would happen next. She didn't know if she could do anything to help, but Niamh decided, right there that morning in the Tea Cosy, that she would be *there* for Theo. Whatever that looked like.

She was a sister, after all.

As she left the Tea Cosy, Niamh saw a Green & Good
van parked on the other side of Market Street outside the
Turkish restaurant. It could be any of his drivers, but
Murphy's Law dictates . . . sure enough, Luke emerged
from the front entrance, swinging an empty crate.

He clocked her and raised an arm in greeting.

'Good luck with that,' Elle said and kissed her goodbye.

Niamh thanked her for her sentiments and crossed over
to face him. Summer must be on the horizon because she
clocked the influx of tourists, the North Face and Berghaus
cagoules and suspiciously new hiking boots. It was lovely
for the village traders, the cafés and gift shops, but Niamh
always felt slightly aggrieved at sharing their hidden pearl
with outsiders.

'Morning!' she said brightly. 'How's it going?'

Luke stowed the crate in the back of the van and turned
to her. It was sufficiently spring-like for him to have dug
out his cargo shorts for the first time this year, revealing
muscular calves. 'Yeah, I'm good. Still a bit weirded out
about yesterday though.'

'How are you feeling?' Niamh asked. She shoved her
hands in the pockets of her scrubs, trying to hide her
guilt.

'I feel fine!' he said. 'It's so mad. Never in my life have
I fainted.'

'You know what I bet it is? 5G.'

He bellowed. 'You're not serious?'

'No! I dunno, low blood sugar?'

'I'd just eaten.'

'High blood sugar?'

His brow furrowed. 'Are you OK? You seem wired.'

She pointed back at the café. 'Ah, my poison is caffeine,
not sugar.'

'Look. I'm sorry for collapsing on you.'

'Any time,' Niamh said without really thinking it through. 'I mean . . .'

Luke smiled broadly. 'I got it. You know what, Niamh? One of these days, I'm gonna figure out what's going on in that head of yours.'

Niamh smiled. 'You think you're ready for the big secrets?' She knew, in her waters, that he wasn't. It was different with Conrad, back in Dublin. That had felt like a perfectly natural stage of her petals unfurling at the start of their relationship. They'd mutually revealed their secrets, while exploring each other's bodies and lives. This was different.

'I can handle whatever you got,' Luke smiled, and she felt it between her legs.

'Really? OK, come here . . .' He leaned closer. 'I'm Spider-Man . . .'

He laughed louder. 'I see! Not Spider-Woman?'

'There's a Spider-Woman?'

'Oh aye. She's a looker too.'

This was getting hard. Her hands wanted to loop around his neck and pull him in for a kiss. 'I need to get back to the clinic . . .'

'Aye. Good to catch you.'

'Don't you be telling anyone about my secret identity, will you?'

'Cross my heart.'

She backed away down the high street, feeling the way you feel in the prelude to sex, the anticipation, like pink lemonade all over. *Hope to die.*

Chapter Twenty-Five

EAVESDROPPINGS

Helena

It was only correct that Helena should have the best corner office in HMRC. Double aspect with windows on two sides overlooking the redbrick and steel sprawl of Manchester. The Beetham Tower – still the tallest building for miles – gleamed in a hazy, tangerine late-afternoon sun.

There was still plenty to clear from her desk before she could leave for the day: sign-off on repairs for the damage caused in the Smythe sting operation; check-in with Sandhya about prep for solstice; a quick Zoom meeting with Sanne Visser, the notoriously – and perhaps ironically – frosty head of the International Global Warming Action Coven.

But first, and most importantly, the Sullied Child.

Her intercom buzzed. 'Yes?'

'Incoming teleport,' her secretary said.

'Thanks, Karen.'

The hairs on her arm stood on end and there was a familiar bonfire-night odour as her daughter's particles started to swirl around the centre of the office. Her expression was sour. 'I hate teleporting,' she whined before she'd even fully formed. 'I swear it triggers my IBS. Can't I just FaceTime you like everyone else?'

Helena stood to give her a cuddle. 'Can't I see my daughter?'

Snow rested her head on her chest. 'You're the one who exiled me.'

Helena smiled and returned to her seat. 'How's your grandmother?'

Snow helped herself to a lemon sherbet from the bowl on Helena's desk before slumping into the visitor chair. 'I'm not allowed to talk when the weather forecast's on. I'm like *hello, we can literally control the weather*, but whatever, Gran, go off.'

Helena couldn't help but laugh. It was comforting to know her mother was unchanging, a standing stone. 'You said you had news?'

'Yes!' Snow said excitedly. 'I think you'll be very proud! I did spying!'

Helena grinned. 'Spying? Like James Bond?'

'Only way cuter. Look!' Snow concentrated and gradually her skin and hair darkened. Her eyes went from blue to brown and her delicate nose widened. Her daughter now looked Mediterranean, Spanish or Italian perhaps.

Helena *was* impressed, but a little shaken. 'Where did you learn to do that?'

'It's just a glamour.' Snow's voice remained the same as ever. 'Jess's big sister taught us.'

Jess *and* her sister, both daughters of an old Manchester witch family, were bother with a capital B. 'Please don't use glamours, Snow. Mundanes can see through them occasionally, they're not always convincing and . . . and

213

well, they're common.' She didn't want to use the phrase *peasant magic* but that went without saying.

The girl who didn't look like her daughter rolled her eyes – a very Snow gesture. 'I had to get close to them though.'

'Who?'

'Auntie Niamh and Auntie Elle.'

'You wore a glamour to spy on *Niamh*?' Snow nodded. 'Then you're very, very lucky she didn't realise it was you. That was thoughtless, Snow . . . and you shouldn't really be spying on your aunts.'

The strange face smiled. 'Don't you wanna know what I heard?'

Helena sighed. 'Can you drop the spell now please?'

Snow shook her head and the illusion faded until she looked herself once more.

'Go on. If anyone asks, we never had this conversation.'

Snow smirked slightly. 'So, I went to the cottage this morning. Theo was there while Niamh was at the vet's . . .'

'She left him *alone*?' Helena clenched her teeth.

'Some woman was there fixing the door where he blew it up.'

Helena's eyes felt like they were going to fall out of her skull. The twists just kept coming. 'I beg your pardon? He blew up the door?'

'Mum!' Snow threw her hands up. 'Will you let me finish?' She gestured for her to go on. 'Anyway, I went to the vet's and Niamh was heading for this café in town. I followed her and bought a coffee and a cinnamon swirl. I was sat close enough to hear what they were saying and . . . guess what?'

Was she really going to make her guess? 'Just tell me please, Snow.'

'So, you are going to die . . . Theo is *transgender*!' She was pleased as punch with this mighty slice of information.

'I'm sorry? What?' Helena said. The first whisper of a migraine lingered at the front of her skull.

'You know . . . like trans. He wants to be a girl. Well, he is a girl inside, he just needs the outsides to match or whatever. Can you remember that girl Laurel at school? She was trans and . . .'

'Thanks, Snow. I'm not totally clueless. I do know what transgender means.' She stood and crossed to the window. She felt her blood bubble and, right on cue, ugly black clouds started to form over the Manchester skyline. They spread like a bruise. The jigsaw pieces started to form a picture, and she didn't like it. Quickly she saw how deep the roots of the weed went . . . the implications of a transgender witch. Well, it could be huge. It would change *everything*.

Or would it?

She turned back to Snow. 'Has he actually started his transition?'

'Maybe we should use she/her pronouns . . . ?' Snow suggested. Helena glared. 'How should I know? Probably not if she hasn't even told people. Niamh only knows because Holly blabbed to Elle. Shady bitch.'

Helena mused on this information for about five seconds and made a decision. Sometimes good leadership is taking counsel, listening to those around you, and on other occasions it calls for someone to step up and act decisively. Balancing the two had always served her well. Her instincts hadn't failed her yet.

'You know what, Snow?'

'What?'

'It occurs to me I've been spending an awful lot of time

215

on this, and I really needn't have bothered. I'm going to wash my hands of him.'

'*Her.*'

She stared her daughter down. 'We'll see.'

Helena pressed the intercom button. 'Hi, Karen? Can you set up an urgent meeting with Radley Jackman, please?'

Chapter Twenty-Six

VALENTINA

Leonie

Leonie met Niamh at Euston Station because although her friend was one of the most powerful witches of her generation, Niamh was anxious about coming into London and getting lost. They hugged on the concourse and Leonie wondered if people thought they were a couple.

Niamh assured her the journey down had been a blissful three hours of catching up on some reading – the latest Atwood – and piss-poor train coffee with a side of Haribo Tangfastics.

'Is Chinara working?' Niamh asked.

'Yeah, she's in court today, but they sometimes finish up early so she might meet us for a drink before you head back.'

'Good! I really want to see her!'

A human tidal wave surged towards the 11.36 to Birmingham New Street so Leonie took her hand and guided Niamh out of the throng. Euston was, without question, the *worst*. They took the Northern Line to Leicester Square – field-mouse Niamh all the while dazed and confused by her surroundings.

London is a mood. A bad mood. Her trip to Hebden Bridge a couple of weeks back had reminded Leonie how much she missed the amiable frame of mind outside the capital. Here, if someone stood on the wrong side of the escalator she snarled at them and telepathically urged them to get it together or leave the city forever. And the pace, gods, why was everyone walking so fucking fast all the time? Niamh had to canter to keep up with her Underground pace.

Emerging into what passed for fresh air and daylight, they strolled through Soho, early for their lunch with Valentina. 'So this is the gay village?' Niamh asked.

'Once upon a time,' Leonie said sadly, gesturing at multiple Prets. 'And not so much for lesbians. Although if you want, like, a rubber catsuit for Luke, Clone Zone is still just over there . . .'

Niamh laughed. 'I'm not sure that's Luke's kink.'

'Do you know what is?'

'No!' Niamh said with finality.

The news about Theo had gone some way to calm her down after the traumatic evening at Madame Celestine. She still hadn't even dared tell Chinara she'd been. *Some* of the messages that had channelled through Celestine now made a fragment of sense: *we didn't have a word for it in my day* or *you'd think you of all people would know*. Some of the messages – the one from Stef and . . . the other one – still very much haunted her. *That* voice was the last thing she heard before she went to sleep at night.

Theo was trans. And the spirit messengers were right; it should have been the first question she'd asked Niamh when they saw how much power was in Theo. *Are you sure he's a he?* Leonie should have known better than to assume anything about someone's identity. Every time a hotel receptionist or waiter referred to Chinara as 'her friend' she wanted to punch them.

'Have you said anything to Theo yet?' she asked, small talk done.

'No.' Niamh chewed her lip. 'Do you think I should rip the plaster off? I don't want to land wee Holly in the shit, but I could just say I'd read it in him . . . her. Fuck me, I need to get better with that.'

'You really do. We have a sentient in Diaspora that uses they/them pronouns. That was a trip at first, it just takes practice. Chinara and I have a swear jar at home for every time we get their pronouns wrong.' Leonie steered Niamh towards Mildred's – some of the nicest veggie food in London.

'Thanks so much for this by the way, Leonie, I owe you one. Did you tell her why we're coming?'

'I did,' Leonie said. 'I've prepped her.'

'Thanks. It's pure embarrassing that I've never really thought about trans witches.'

It was, Leonie thought, although she kept the thought to herself – nothing more than a reflection of her privilege. She wondered if Niamh had spent much more time thinking about the role of Black witches. She *was* Irish, she mused. They had shit to contend with for years – although Celtic witches had always been somewhat revered at HMRC so it was a tough one to call.

'It's just over there,' Leonie pointed to the other side of Lexington Street and waited for a black cab to go by. 'Don't feel too bad about it; you're out the loop. But if HMRC aren't having conversations about intersectionality yet, they fucking should be.'

They entered the narrow restaurant, greeted by the smell of the sweet potato curry that Leonie was craving hard.

They were shown to a table at the back of the restaurant, only waiting a couple of minutes before Valentina appeared to join them.

Thing was, Leonie thought, when a trans woman looks like Val – who resembled a frigging glamour model – it's no effort to understand them as a woman. That being said, she felt there shouldn't be a pressure on *any* woman to conform to 'rules' of gender. Too many Black women down the years had been mocked for appearing 'mannish' for her to value any nominal notion of 'femininity'.

Valentina strutted past diners – turning heads – in a pleather pencil skirt and pussy-bow blouse. Her mane of hair was relaxed and dyed a rich caramel blond. In short, Leonie absolutely would under different circumstances. Who wouldn't?

'Hey guys! Sorry I'm late.' Her day job was around the corner at the sexual health clinic, something to do with HIV prevention.

'No worries,' Leonie said, leaning over the table to kiss her. 'Valentina, this is my best friend Niamh from school.'

Val gasped and stroked a lock of Niamh's hair. 'Oh my gosh. Is that your real hair colour?'

Niamh laughed and said it was. They air-kissed and settled to eat. Valentina's voice *travelled* so Leonie subtly established a shield around the table so they could speak freely.

'This is so nosy,' Niamh explained, blushing. 'Thank you so much for this.'

'Darling, it's fine. I don't mind at *all.*'

'I don't know if Leonie told you, but I'm living with a young person who thinks they might be transgender . . . and, well, I just don't know where to begin.'

Leonie felt a turgid moss-green frustration pouring off

Niamh in waves. She kept forgetting that Niamh wasn't HMRC any more. She had volunteered to shoulder this . . . *burden* wasn't the right word, because no human life is a burden, but it was certainly a *responsibility*. If she could help Niamh out on this, she would. Setting up a lunch was the least she could do.

'It's fine, darling, I'm happy to help. I'm an open book! What is it you want to know?'

'I guess,' Niamh said thoughtfully, 'did you know you were a witch or a girl first?'

Valentina shared her childhood in Manaus. 'Darling, I knew I was a girl as soon as I knew there was a difference between boys and girls. I look at boys and I am like, *uh . . . nah-nah*. My mama was like, *honey you're a boy* and I was like, *oh no bitch! I beg to differ!* My avó, my grandmother – she was a witch, a sentient, and she could read it in me when I am four or five years. She said it shine off me like the sun. It was only later, when I am ten or eleven, I started to realise I could do things as well.'

'Read her,' Leonie told Niamh.

'If you don't mind?'

'Open book!'

Leonie watched Niamh focus. 'Gosh.'

Everyone has a unique energy in the way they have a unique fingerprint, but there were undeniable masculine and feminine energies. That didn't automatically mean that all men and all women have the same aura – some cis women had distinctly masculine energy and vice versa. Valentina's aura, however, was as present as her perfume. Leonie was frankly surprised the *mundanes* in the restaurant couldn't feel it too.

'I know, right?' Val laughed. 'Can you imagine anyone trying to make me a boy? Good luck with that, honey,

221

you can't hold back the tides! Hold that thought while I go pee.'

Valentina excused herself and Niamh turned to Leonie. 'So does she . . . um . . . ?'

'Have a vagina?' Leonie exploded. 'Niamh! Does it matter? Is it our business?'

Niamh blinked her green eyes, incredulous. 'Thank you, Miss Jackman. I was *going* to say, how does her *power* compare to a cisgender witch?'

'Oh, OK.' Leonie flagged the waiter down so they could order when Val returned. She only had forty-five minutes. 'Well it's interesting. She's an E4.'

'Level 4, really?'

'Uh-huh.' Warlocks very, very rarely attain above a Level 3, so Val's level was more in line with a cis woman than a cis man for sure. 'She's a force of nature. Told you.'

Her heels clopped back toward the table. Niamh said, 'Well then maybe that explains why Theo is so powerful? It all makes sense.'

'I hear you,' Leonie said as Val slid back into the banquette seat. 'But it doesn't explain *everything*. We don't know where she came from, why she's so powerful without training . . .' Leonie left out the stuff she'd learned about Leviathan at Celestine's. Theo being trans didn't even start to explain what the oracles were seeing.

'No,' Niamh reasoned, 'but it means I can send Helena your way if she tries to argue . . .'

Leonie cackled. 'You bitch! Don't you dare!'

The waiter came to take their order. The lunch was a lovely diversion, but it was just that. Intuition was a motherfucker, and Leonie couldn't relax. Even now her fingers drummed at her knee nervously. Something bad was coming their way. Something involving Theo, Helena and the king of the demons. Maybe she should just tell Niamh what she'd heard in Peckham.

Niamh and Valentina continued to chatter as the waiter took their menus. Niamh asked if Valentina knew of other trans witches, and she replied that she definitely knew of some in the CIA – America had more readily embraced trans witches. Leonie had only one question, which had lingered since the night at Celestine's: do we need to get the fuck away from all this right now? Seriously, Chinara hadn't taken holiday in months. Was it time to book two plane tickets, pack some rucksacks and get a cat-sitter in? Something – some piece of the puzzle – was still missing and nothing made sense.

As if she'd accidentally performed some sort of summoning, first her phone and then Niamh's vibrated on the table. The group chat. It was Helena. 'What does she want?' Leonie asked, putting her phone away out of politeness.

Niamh checked the message. 'She . . . is coming to stay at her mum's next week and wants to arrange a girls' night at the Lamb and Lion. Wait . . . she's typing. Oh, she says she'll get HMRC to teleport you.'

Fuck. Well that was her best excuse shot to shit. 'I . . . dunno.'

Niamh looked wounded. 'Oh, go on. Why not? I think she feels left out that we went to Malham without her. The four of us haven't been together in . . . well I can't even remember the last time. Last Samhain?'

'Maybe. I'll check with Chinara.' Pin it on her. It was awkward. Niamh, Elle and Helena rose-tinted their childhood, and regarded their unit as some aspirational Taylor Swift girl squad, *Sex and the City*, Instagram clique, but Leonie saw their past differently. She had grown up with those girls by chance, not birth, and she had been forced to assimilate. Her adolescent growing pains were borne of bending backwards to whiteness, to middle classness. They had welcomed her, but kept her in her box. Did any of them once ask which fucking Spice Girl she *wanted* to be? Just once, she'd have liked to have been Baby. What had bonded them then no longer existed and like the continents, she'd drifted. Other than coven shit what would they even talk about?

We'll reminisce about the good old days, Niamh's voice filled her head, her friend able to sense her reticence.

Leonie smiled but said nothing because the old days weren't that fuckin' good. Her most primitive urges, far below logic or friendship, were telling her to grab Chinara, and run. Fight or flight, and this wasn't her fight.

Chapter Twenty-Seven

GIRLS' NIGHT OUT

Niamh

It was funny, thought Niamh, how she always made much more of an effort when she was going out with her girl-friends. A compliment from a woman means twice as much as one from a man. She wore makeup less and less over time, but she still enjoyed the language of it. Like witchcraft, it was a tongue spoken predominantly by women – a secret Esperanto most men couldn't follow.

She licked lipstick off her teeth and rummaged through her dresser drawer for the partner to her silver hoop earring, wondering if she could pull off mismatched ones. She gave up and settled for some gold creoles instead.

She looked herself over in the mirror: tea dress, velvet blazer and old cowboy boots. Stevie Nicks would be proud. A spritz of perfume – basil and bergamot – and she was done. She was surprised at how excited she was. It was the faint flavour of her life before the war; date nights with Con, nights out with the girls. Before the babies had come along, she used to see Elle or Hels all the time, she'd go over on *weeknights* just to chill and watch *The Apprentice* or old episodes of *Charmed*. It's funny how much life had slowed down, how she'd adjusted to her own company. Now, if she left the house two nights in a row . . . gods, busy old week.

Downstairs, she heard Holly make her entrance, talking aloud to Theo. That must mean Jez was outside in the car with Elle. She hurried down to the lounge. 'Hi Auntie Niamh!'

'Hi, darl. Theo, you got everything you need?'

She nodded. Niamh had been practising, but still wouldn't be saying anything until Theo – or whatever her name was – was ready. She didn't want to hijack her. Like, they'd *figured* Leonie was gay years before she told them, but you can't chase a flower out the ground, you have to let it bloom on its own clock. Well, unless you're a witch, but that was a whole other thing.

'OK, there's money for pizza on the counter. Don't drink, don't smoke, although if you have to smoke, make sure it's something green, yeah?' They both laughed. She brushed a stray hair off Holly's face. *Thanks for being such a good friend to Theo*, she told her.

Holly blushed, batting off the compliment. *It's OK.*

Niamh said no more and hurried out to meet the car waiting in the lane. Elle, from the passenger side, reached over her husband and honked the horn. 'Get your skinny bum in the car!' she yelled. 'The girlies are waiting!'

Oh gods. *Girlies.* Oh, Elle. Niamh jumped in the back-seat. 'Hi Jez!' she forced a cheery greeting for Elle's sake.

'You all right, love?' His car smelled of engine oil, not unpleasantly.

'I'm good! You?' They only ever had small talk. And that's what you get, Elle, when you only share half of yourself with your husband.

It was hard to like Elle's husband, not only because he was dull and never did his share of childcare or housework, but also because Niamh could see inside his head as if it were a greenhouse, visible on all sides. Once or twice a week, Jez went to the Harmsworth House Hotel and had anal sex with Jessica Summers, one of the receptionists.

She and Leonie had argued – at length – about whether or not to tell Elle. It's the ultimate friendship conundrum: *if you knew your friend's partner was cheating, would you tell them?* To Niamh it felt too much like kicking over a sandcastle. She could also read Elle, and Elle was, for the most part, happy and content. Niamh feared knowing the truth would only cause her misery. Leonie favoured scaring the absolute shit out of Jez so that he never strayed again. Niamh could, if she so chose, give him some very unsettling nightmares.

She observed them. Jez doted on Elle. That was a thing, she'd once read. Cheating creates a feedback loop of guilt, each indiscretion prompting the cheater to try harder at home. Niamh shook it off. Sometimes she *loathed* being psychic. She'd give anything to not know. It was none of her business.

Niamh knew she was lying to herself. Elle was her sister. Of course it was her business.

Jez drove them into town, to the Lamb and Lion. It was a bit old-mannish, but it was the only pub in Hebden Bridge that was run by a witch. Pamela Briggs had served under Julia Collins at HMRC until she retired. With Jez sent packing for a night in charge of the remote control, Niamh and Elle entered the Tudor tavern, Niamh ducking under the heavy black beams. Pamela greeted them from behind the bar, all blue mascara and cherry mahogany hair dye, and signalled them towards 'The Snug', a private room with its own fireplace out back. Helena must have booked ahead of time.

It was a Friday night, still the fallow period between the quick-one-after-work shift and the on-a-bender crowd. Later, it would be heaving, so Niamh was pleased they had their own space. Helena and Leonie were already here, a couple of sips into their first glass of wine. In the end, Leonie hadn't taken *that* much badgering.

'Hello girlies!' Elle rushed in for hugs and kisses. They'd apparently all got the memo about their Sunday best. Elle looked like a fifties bombshell, Helena was *very* Posh in her jumpsuit and fuck-me heels, and Leonie wore a fur coat that looked like she'd skinned the Cookie Monster.

The pang of friendly nostalgia hit her like Christmas morning. She ached from wishing Ciara were here too, that history hadn't happened the way it happened.

'I wish she was here too,' Leonie said and Niamh realised she was thinking too loudly again.

Niamh shook her head as she sat down at the big round table. It was as old as the tavern, carved from Pendle oak.

'Let's drink to absent friends,' Helena said, pouring wine for her and Elle.

'I think it'd be a little hypocritical to toast to my sister's health,' Niamh said, holding up her glass. 'But I'll drink to peace.'

Helena dipped her head. 'To lasting peace.'

Niamh took a big glug of red wine.

Soon, their lips and teeth were bluish. They ate tapas, and Elle came running in with shots of tequila, salt and lemon for afters. 'Shots!' she cried and everyone protested. 'No! No arguments! I get one night off every *decade*, or at least that's what it feels like, so tonight, girls, we are getting DRUNK. Got that?'

Leonie gamely knocked back her shot and grimaced. Niamh followed suit.

'Is Holly with Theo?' Leonie asked.

'They're babysitting each other,' Elle said.

'Theo's fine,' Niamh said defensively. 'Nothing's gone wrong since the Luke incident.'

Everyone looked to Helena. 'No coven chat tonight, I beg you. Gods, I think I've earned a weekend off. Although – while I remember – I brought this for you, Elle.' She reached into her handbag and withdrew a glossy white HMRC pamphlet: *Explaining Witch Life to Your Child or Children.*

Elle fanned herself with it. 'Little late, babes, but thanks anyway . . .'

The pair laughed, flicking through the leaflet and mocking the staged pictures.

Can you read Helena? Leonie popped into her head.

What? No. Why? Niamh hadn't even tried.

Her head is weird.

Maybe because she knows you're trying to read her mind?

Leonie rolled her eyes and poured herself another glass of wine.

Niamh was already tipsy and it was a gazillion times harder to use her powers when she was drunk, even more so if the person you were trying to read was half-cut too. It was foreign cinema without subtitles. Nevertheless, she read Helena. Her mind was tranquil, a coolly metallic lilac shade. Guarded, yes, but relaxed. Quite standard for Ms Vance.

'Can you remember how we used to dress to try to get served in here?' Elle peered over the top of her glass. 'Jailbait or what? If Holls went out like that, I'd have a seizure.'

'What were we thinking?' Niamh said. 'Pamela fully knew we were underage. Like, who were we trying to fool?'

'And standing outside Spar trying to lure men into buying us fags like sirens. It's honestly a wonder we weren't murdered,' Helena added.

Leonie laughed. 'We were five *witches*! Goddess help any man who fucked with us.'

'Oh, we were so well behaved though!' Niamh popped the last green olive in her mouth. 'Wee angels we were.'

'Hardly!' Helena laughed. To be fair, Ciara was a handful *long* before she got into the demonic shit.

'I always think that! We proper wasted our youth!' Leonie exploded. 'If I had my time over, I'd fucking hex all the teachers at school. Bunch of cunts.'

'Imagine Edna Heseltine's verdict on that . . .' Helena said.

'*No spells outside of the coven . . .*' Elle's impression was uncanny, including index finger waggling in Niamh's face.

'*A sinful witch is Satan's bitch . . .*' Leonie laughed.

Elle held her hand up to take a turn. 'Can you remember when you got stung in the woods, Hels, and I used my powers on you and she *told me off*? Like, hello!'

'Fucking hell, she was a piece of work!' Helena shook her head.

'The only funeral I've ever been to where I could actively *feel* the joy,' Niamh said.

Three bottles of merlot became four, then five. Their here-and-nows were different these days, so the past was fertile ground to camp out on. First boyfriends (or girlfriends); school friends; teachers who shagged sixth-form students; who was gay now, and a gay guy who ended up marrying a woman. Twist.

230

It all clicked back into place. Niamh briefly skimmed Leonie and she was having a blast, any reservations erased, and her volume creeping up with every unit of alcohol. Pamela came in and brought them desserts on the house: sticky toffee pudding and ice cream. She was in love with these women. *Sororia.*

'I'm so glad we did this,' Helena said. 'Thanks for coming up, Lee.'

'I'm glad I did. I'll try come back up for solstice too.'

'Holly wants to take the oath this June,' Elle admitted. Helena said she was pleased. 'She's taken to it all so quickly. My head is spinning.'

'I was shitting myself,' Leonie said.

'I remember that night so clearly. Up in the treehouse,' Niamh added.

'Look!' Helena reached into her handbag – Chanel, no less – and pulled out an equally lovely wallet. She leafed through some credit cards and pulled out three photos: one of her wedding day, one of Snow's early school pictures and a faded dog-eared image of them.

It was from that night. In Vance Hall, on the back patio. They'd been allowed to try on their robes ahead of the big night. Seeing Ciara's gappy grin felt like a great fucking cleaver between Niamh's ribs.

'That is some cute shit right there.' Leonie took the photo off Helena and passed it to Elle.

Elle gasped. 'Oh Lee, you were adorable!'

'Right?'

Niamh took it from Elle. '*We could have been anything that we wanted to be.* What's that from? That musical.'

'Bugsy,' Helena told her.

'We had no fecking clue, did we?' Niamh soaked it in. 'Everything that was coming up at us at a hundred miles an hour? Adulthood is a fecking steam train and we had no idea we were in its way.'

'Thomas the Wank Engine?' Leonie offered.

'Would you have wanted to know in advance?' Helena said. 'Or just enjoy it the way we did?'

'Ignorance was bliss,' Elle said. 'And today kids have the internet to ruin their lives when they're little anyway, so we don't have to.'

Helena pushed the bottles and glasses into the centre of the table.

'What are you doing?' Niamh asked.

Helena pushed her bottom onto the table and swung her legs into a folded position like a Buddha. 'Let's form a circle. Like we did back then.'

'I'm so too drunk!' Leonie said.

'How am I gonna get up there in this skirt?' Elle pointed out.

'Oh come on! We haven't done this in years!'

Bones creaking after weeks of neglecting yoga, Niamh hoisted herself onto the big old table and crossed her legs. 'What if someone comes in?'

'They won't!'

Leonie helped Elle up onto the table, her pencil skirt allowing her to kneel. 'I hope you know I'm going to pass my hangover into you,' Elle smiled.

'OK.' Unspoken, Helena took the lead, the way she always had. 'Join hands.'

Niamh held her hands out; right palm up, left palm down. On one side Elle touched her fingers and Helena was to her other, Leonie opposite. She closed her eyes and focused on her breath. Her mind engaged her lungs, taking longer, deeper breaths.

She – they – all started with the first element: air. She

pictured herself as a bird flying high overhead, weaving, soaring through the cloudscape. More than picturing it, she felt it. Air is *freedom*.

Air begets water.

Air freezes and melts, releasing water. Gooseflesh crept across Niamh's arms despite the fire in the Snug. She saw water fall to the hills, trickle over rocks and travel down the mountain before meeting rivers and then the sea. Water is *serenity*.

Water feeds the earth.

Roots drink it in – live, vividly green and opulent. Earth is *life*, but plants, as all things must, wither and die, enriching the soil, transferring their lifeforce into other plants, trees, grasses which in turn feed us.

Earth becomes fuel.

A spark and earth becomes fire. Niamh felt the hunger and dominance of fire. Fire is *strength*, destructive and brilliant at the same time.

Unified, the witches formed a single current. From her right, Niamh sensed pure Helena. A fire witch; bold scarlets, confident, independent but, yes, arrogant, egotistical, terrified to fail.

Like a carousel, Leonie's energy came next. A water witch like her, but also entirely unlike her, Leonie was chaotic as a waterfall, overflowing and ebullient. Even Leonie was scared of her own undertow.

And dear Elle. An earth witch: all the greens, all the time. Calm and solid, reliable, certainly, but unyielding, stubborn. Everything buried as deep as she could manage it. With Elle, Niamh had only ever seen the topsoil.

Finally, her own flow came back around to her. It felt like nudity, being so exposed to yourself, but the good kind of nudity: no judgement, and free from the yearning of desire. Not exposed, but *open*. Niamh was black-blue. A lake, a reservoir, vast and still. Untold depths, intimidating to the others. None could see the bottom.

Niamh realised the hard table was no longer beneath her rear. The kinetic energy running through them had lifted them about a metre off the wood. It held them steady though, a reflection of their expert balance and control. She felt safe. They'd been creating a cell since they were nine or ten years old. They knew each other like a pair of favourite jeans. It fit just right.

I'M GIVING YOU EVERYTHING! They sang at the top of their lungs as they staggered down the high street, jelly-legged. ALL THAT JOY CAN BRING!

'Shut the fuck up! It's after midnight!' someone yelled from one of the flats above the shops.

They fell apart laughing. Niamh had to hold Elle up with one hand, and carry her heels in the other.

'You shut the fuck up!' Leonie screamed back. 'Shall I hex him?'

'NO!' the others clapped back in an instant.

Helena checked her phone. 'OK, Lee, your magic Uber's here.'

Leonie stood in the centre of Market Square by the hideous metal sculpture. 'I fucking *love* you girls, yeah? See you soon . . .' Before there was even time to say their farewells, Leonie was teleported back to London by the night shift at HMRC.

'Sure you don't want to come with us?' Elle slurred at Helena. 'There's room . . . ?'

'I'm in the opposite direction,' Helena said. She didn't seem quite as messy as the rest of them. 'It's fine. There's a cab waiting.'

Niamh and Elle made sure Helena was safely despatched in the direction of Vance Hall. The pair then zigzagged to the spot Jez had promised to wait. 'Oh Jesus,' Jez said, getting out of the car to greet them. 'Good night then?'

'Best!' Elle said. 'I love you. Did you miss me?'

'Oh aye, don't know how we managed, love.' He gave Niamh a wink and plonked his wife into the passenger side. Niamh had hardly clipped her seatbelt on when Elle's head rolled to one side, soundly asleep. 'She's such a lightweight,' Jez said.

'She'll feel this one in the morning,' Niamh said with confidence as the car wove uphill towards the cottage.

Jez engaged her in more small talk, but Niamh was busy admitting to herself that she wasn't going to take off her makeup before bed. She was allowed to do that, under her own rules, twice a year. Tea, toast, pint of saviour water to fend off her own hangover, and then straight into her bed. Excellent.

That was until she saw Holly running down the lane towards the car. 'Is that our Holls?' Jez said, applying the brakes.

Elle stirred. 'What's wrong?'

The girl was clearly distraught. The headlights picked out the tears staining her cheeks. She stepped out in front of the vehicle, waving it down.

All of a sudden, Niamh was stone-cold sober. She scanned the cottage for Theo.

Nothing. She was gone.

'Jez, stop!' she cried, though he was already pulling over. 'And *sleep.*'

Jez went out like a light and the car stalled. 'Niamh?' Elle muttered, but Niamh was already on the road, racing towards Holly.

'Holly? What on earth is . . . ?'

'They took Theo!' she wailed.

Her stomach lurched and she took hold of Holly's arms. 'What? Who did?'

'The warlocks! Uncle Radley and the warlocks! They came and they blew something in my face and I couldn't move! I'm so sorry, Niamh, I'm so sorry! I couldn't do anything!'

Niamh pulled Holly into an embrace as Elle joined them still barefooted, and also suddenly sobered. 'What the hell is going on? Come here, baby.'

Niamh passed the sobbing girl to her mother. 'They took her away,' she said, the words like broken glass in her throat. 'They *stole* her.'

And then, although fire blazed in her veins, a rare clarity. *Fucking Helena.*

Chapter Twenty-Eight

RESCUE

Niamh

'Niamh! What are you doing?'

She ignored Elle's cries, instead falling to her knees on the kitchen tiles. She flung open the cabinet under the sink and rifled through a clutter of bottles and boxes and cartons.

'Niamh . . .'

'Just take Holly home,' Niamh snarled. 'Jez will be waking up.'

Losing her patience, she swept everything aside, bottles of disinfectant and cleaner rolling across the floor. There. At the very back of the cupboard was an inconspicuous Scottish shortbread tin. She leaned into the cabinet to retrieve it and then emptied out the contents into a heap. This was where she secreted her more contraband potions: pure *Digitalis*, *Poppy Tears* and the like.

'What are you looking for?' Elle and Holly lingered on the threshold to the kitchen.

'This.' Niamh held up a small brown glass bottle of *Excelsior* that hadn't been touched in years. She forgot, did it get more or less potent past its use-by date?

Elle's mascara was smudged. She looked weary. 'Niamh, you can't be serious.'

'Take them home,' she repeated.

She unscrewed the stopper, the seal a tad crusty. She dropped five pipettes' worth onto her tongue. 'How many warlocks were there, Holly?'

Holly shook her head. 'I think I saw four . . . maybe five?'

'Niamh . . .' Elle warned again.

'Five. Fine. How long ago did they leave?'

'Maybe ten minutes . . . more perhaps.'

Quite a head start. No time to spare, she made for the door, but Elle blocked her path. 'Niamh! You can't take on five warlocks by yourself.'

Niamh stared the shorter woman down, pushing past her to the garden. 'I won't let her get away with this. Seriously, Elle, take Holly home. She's been through enough tonight.'

'But what about you?'

'If I need you, I know where to find you.'

Elle was pale. 'I'll wait up.' Reluctantly, she steered Holly towards Jez's car. 'And what about Helena?' she asked nervously.

Niamh glowered at Elle, biting her tongue so as not to take out her fury on her. She wasn't sure what she'd do to Helena, truth be told. This whole night had been a scam to get them out of the house and isolate Theo. She was sure of it.

In the car, Jez stirred. Niamh was too preoccupied to care how Elle explained that one. Instead, Niamh shielded herself from him and levitated onto the cottage roof, landing unsteadily against the chimney for support. The brickwork was damp to the touch, rough with lichen.

She found her footing on a ridge and surveyed the dark valley. A sliver of orange streetlight snaked into a vast midnight-blue night. They could be halfway to Manchester by now. Niamh tried to empty her mind of anger, the noisiest of emotions at the best of times, and listened.

Hebden Bridge was nesting, bedding down. Much of the town was already asleep.

Theo!

She blasted it from her mind as powerfully as she could. Any sentient for miles would hear her.

It would have been so perfect if she'd replied, but that was wishful thinking. Theo was chaotic and – if she knew Radley Jackman – he wouldn't want any uncontrolled variables. Theo would have been drugged, probably with *Sandman*. The anger threatened to bubble up again, and she pushed it down to her guts.

Instead, she closed her eyes and cast her mind as far as it would go. It was like looking for a specific pebble in a sizable pond. The stone she sought, of course, was a rare gem, and that would aid her. Mundanes murmured, but she knew from having Theo in her house for the last few weeks that, even when sleeping, Theo's resonance thrummed.

Where are you?

The cool night air was laced with a promise of lily and wisteria. It blew through Niamh's hair and she allowed herself to be still. She was silent.

There.

It was distant, and she could be mistaken – it could easily be a different witch – but she sensed *something*. Yes, yes, it was her. It was like the pieces of Conrad's clothing she'd kept in the closet. They'd long since lost his scent, yet they somehow carried him.

Niamh took flight.

She was not *flying* in the birdlike sense of the word, rather she used her telekinesis to propel her body through the air. The air pummelled her face, revitalising her. She was awake now, ready, the drunken fuzz under her skin gone. All she could do now was sniff her out, let Theo's signature guide her like a bloodhound.

As she careered over the rooftops and spires of Hebden Bridge, the trace grew stronger. As predicted, they were most likely heading in the direction of Manchester – back to the cabal headquarters.

Keeping herself aloft was hard, punishing, but she keenly felt the *Excelsior* kicking in. Her heartbeat was faster, her mouth dry. However tiring the flight was, she was bolstered by the tincture. It was exhilarating, not exhausting.

She left town behind, heading south through Eastwood. The silver road was half-obscured by dense tree canopies, only intermittent streetlights peeping through. The traffic was sparse, only the occasional taxi ferrying people back towards Todmorden after a night out in Hebden Bridge.

What Niamh was looking for was a maroon van. She'd seen it in Holly's mind. Theo's troubled mind grew louder and louder. She was fighting, struggling against whatever potion she'd been given.

Keep fighting, Theo. I can hear you.

The van. She saw it. It was pelting much too fast through the country lanes, lights on high beam.

Got you.

Halting herself, Niamh suspended herself over the highway. She'd feel bad about it later she was certain, but she psychically took hold of a rotten elm on the roadside and tore it out by the roots before letting it crash into the path of any oncoming traffic. She needed the road to herself and didn't want them retreating the way they had come.

Obstacle in place, she cannoned on, struggling to keep up with the speeding van. They were getting away and she was starting to tire. She needed to make contact with earth, and fast. One last push and she hurled herself forward. It was not graceful, but who cares? There was no one around to see her.

Niamh sailed over the top of the van, travelling slightly faster. She surpassed the vehicle, flying further down the tarmac. When she was a few hundred metres ahead of them, she let herself down, staggering down the street in a clumsy landing. Still, she remained upright, and came to a standing stop. She turned to face the van, planting her feet wide and bracing herself.

This was going to hurt.

They sped towards her and she was blinded by the headlights.

She reached out with both hands and readied herself.

She caught hold of the van, its forward motion almost knocking her off her feet. She grit her teeth and pushed back.

If she couldn't do this, it was going to mow her down.

She heard herself scream. She felt it burn in her shoulders and back. She was slowing it down, but it was still coming at her.

Her thighs and calves blazed in pain.

Only one thing for it: she lifted the wheels off the tarmac. She held the van aloft, heard its wheels spin against the air, the engine rev uselessly. Opening her eyes, she saw a warlock driving and a shocked Radley in the passenger seat. Niamh lifted it higher, and the passengers lurched forwards, pinned by their seatbelts.

At least one of them was a sentient – the driver. *What the fuck are you doing?*

Niamh! Radley. *What the hell?*

Turn off the engine! Now!

Radley again. *Niamh, put us down!*

Turn off the engine or I will crush the van like a can of Coke with you all inside it, I swear to Gaia. She could, but she wouldn't – not with Theo inside.

Radley's eyes widened and he barked an order at the driver. The engine went dead, which was fortunate because Niamh estimated she could have held it up for another ten seconds at most. She let it down with a thud, the tyres bouncing.

Behind her, down the lane, she snapped off a couple of sturdy overhead branches to block traffic coming from the other direction.

'Get out!' she cried aloud. Fuck, she badly needed to recharge, her heart beating way too fast and hard. The body can only take so much. She could feel some residual energy seeping up through the asphalt, but she'd get more from soil or grass. If the warlocks tried to fight her, she honestly wasn't sure she could take them.

'I said get out!'

Radley fought his seatbelt and fumbled with the door handle. 'Niamh, how dare you!' he shouted, furious. 'This is official cabal business.'

'Give Theo to me now,' Niamh growled.

He marched to her position, the officious twat. 'Absolutely not! This is an outrage and I shall be reporting this to Helena V—'

Niamh found enough power to push him up against the bonnet. He gasped. 'Did she tell you where he was?'

'I'm not at liberty to—'

'*Speak.*' She grasped hold of his mind. It had been a *long* time since she'd flexed her muscles like this. A part of her – although this could be the *Excelsior* talking – was enjoying this. She was *strong*. She'd forgotten just how strong.

'Yes, Helena arranged the collection.'

'Thought so. Does she know Theo wants to transition?'

'To what?'

'To a girl, you idiot.'

Radley looked genuinely bewildered. 'I don't know what you're talking about. She just said there was a powerful young warlock who belonged with us at the cabal. She said he was dangerous, and that he'd resist, which he did.'

Niamh forced him back against the car. 'Can you blame hi . . . *her*? You kidnapped her!'

There was a cry from inside the van. There was a mighty thud as someone was apparently hurled against the wall.

'I guess she's awake.' Niamh released Radley. 'You might want to let her out before she kills your men, Rad.'

Niamh had known Radley Jackman since he was eight years old. He'd always been a whiny pain in the ass. Then again, they'd never let him play with them, so she could understand some of the simmering resentment.

'I can't do that Niamh . . .'

There was an ear-splitting squeal from within the van. Theo – but not from her throat, from her mind. The same hideous scream she'd first heard in that cage at Grierlings. It cut through Niamh's mind like exploding glass. She clamped her hands over her ears as she fell to her knees. Radley too curled up into a foetal ball on the road. It was as if the banshee cry was coming from inside her skull.

It hurt, it hurt, it hurt.

Theo! She winced, trying to get through. *It's me . . . please.*

243

It went on. She felt hot blood gush down her nostrils. *Theo! I'm here! You're killing me! THEO!*

The horrific howling stopped. Niamh unfurled herself and saw Radley cowering near the van.

'She's a powerful adept,' Niamh said, wiping the blood off her nose with her sleeve, 'and she's a girl. This is not your fight. Let her out *now*.'

Radley told the driver to open up. Niamh poised herself, ready to fight. There were, what, three warlocks in the back with Theo? Five in total. Honestly, she wasn't sure she could take them all on.

The driver slid open the side-loading door and Niamh realised she had nothing to worry about. Theo was hand-cuffed to a mighty lead weight by a silver chain, but there were three unconscious warlocks at her feet. Niamh was oddly proud for a moment, but then her teacher-student mindset kicked in.

'He killed them!' Radley rounded on her.

Niamh skimmed them. 'They'll be fine. They're alive. Heal your men, Rad.' Radley moved to do so. 'Wait. First get those cuffs off Theo.'

'I can't do that, Niamh.'

'Are you mad? You just saw what Theo can do . . .'

'It's not up to me!'

'I wasn't aware you followed HMRC orders now.'

That pushed the right buttons. 'I don't! But this is a warlock matter.'

'Theo isn't a warlock!' Niamh muttered, glancing up at Theo in the dingy van. She was very aware she was essentially 'outing' Theo before she or they had plucked up the courage to talk to her about it. Theo looked more scared than anything right now, still woozy, no doubt from the *Sandman*.

'That's not up to you.'

'It's not up to fucking Helena either. Theo?' Niamh said. 'Where do you want to be? With me or at the Warlocks' Cabal?'

With you!

The voice boomed so loudly, indiscriminately, that the driver and Radley heard it too. Birds were shaken out of the trees.

'Well there we go then. I'd say that was fairly definitive, wouldn't you?'

'Niamh . . .'

'What the fuck, Rad?' She lowered her tone, trying to appeal to the human hidden away inside him. 'You're talking about taking a minor into custody against their will. I have accepted full responsibility for Theo, OK? Now, get those cuffs off. Please?'

Shame Elle wasn't here. He'd always liked her the best, he'd comply a fuck of a lot faster with a bat of her lash extensions. With a great sigh, Radley relented. 'Do it.' The driver boosted himself into the back of the van to free Theo. One of the unconscious warlocks was starting to come around too.

Theo emerged like some befuddled creature woozy from anaesthetic, eyes squinty, puffy. Unsteady on her feet, she almost plummeted off the van and into Niamh's arms. 'For the love of . . . are you OK?'

What's . . . ? She couldn't even form a whole thought. *You're gonna be fine. I got you.*

Radley paced, hands on hips. 'Helena isn't going to be happy about this . . .'

Niamh glowered at him. 'Don't you worry about Helena Vance. I'll deal with her . . .'

Chapter Twenty-Nine

BOTH SIDES

Helena

So this was how it was going to be. She had hoped, although she knew it to be false hope, that Niamh would *tolerate* her chosen direction. It seemed, according to Radley's text message, that it wasn't to be on this occasion.

With only the cabinet lights illuminating the kitchen, Helena poured herself a bourbon on the rocks and awaited Niamh's inevitable arrival. She hoped it wasn't going to be too histrionic. It was late and everyone else was soundly asleep. She'd changed into a silk gown and pyjamas as soon as she got home.

It was good bourbon. It took some skill, Helena thought, to drink as little as she had all night, dutifully playing mother by keeping everyone else's wine glass topped up while nursing her own solitary drink. She'd wanted to keep a clear head, knowing this eventuality might well come to pass.

On cue, the back door smashed open, the lock shattering, splintering the frame. Helena winced and closed her eyes. She'd bill her for that.

Niamh levitated across the threshold, her pupils black and unnaturally dilated. Helena sighed deeply. So it *was* going to be histrionic. 'Really, Niamh? Can we not?'

'Did you know?' she demanded.

'Did I know what?' Helena took another sip of bourbon until, with a swipe of her hand, Niamh snatched the tumbler out of her grasp, propelling it against the wall above the Aga. It shattered, the bronze liquid trickling down the back of the range. 'Oh, for crying out loud!'

'Did you know she was trans?'

Helena held up a hand. 'I'm not talking to you when you're like this. Look at you, are you high?'

'You knew. Snow told you.' Niamh read her, and Helena doubled her efforts to occlude her thoughts. *Pick a salient memory: Stefan. The war. Ciara even. Conrad.*

'Can we please discuss this in the morning when we've both—'

'We'll discuss it now.'

They were doing it now then. 'Very well. Am I safe to get another drink or shall I put this one in a plastic beaker?'

Niamh lowered herself so her feet touched the floor. Progress. Helena took two tumblers from the cupboard and hoped a stiff drink would calm her friend down. Niamh stood on the opposite side of the kitchen island, and Helena imagined herself as a barkeep in a western movie. She refrained from sliding the bourbon over the wooden top.

'Why, Helena?' Niamh said, her tone softening. 'Don't you think that poor kid has been through enough?'

She took a large slug. 'I wanted to get shot of him.'

'*Her.*'

'Oh come on, Niamh . . .' she said wearily.

Niamh stared her down. 'No. You go on. What do you mean?'

'Theo, whether he likes it or not, is a boy. He will grow up and become a warlock.'

Niamh downed the bourbon in one greedy glug. That was expensive stuff to drink so fast. 'I think that's for Theo to decide don't you?'

Helena rolled her yes. 'Niamh, it's after midnight. Can we not discuss identity politics now?'

'No, I think we should. It's important. I've been to London and met with another transgender witch in Leonie's coven and—'

Helena laughed bitterly. 'Oh I should have guessed!' Some elastic band holding Helena's patience together snapped. That happened sooner than she was expecting, she was almost surprised. 'Of *course* Leonie has trans-gender witches in her *woke* coven!'

'But don't you see? That means Theo isn't the first . . .'

'Theo is *male*,' Helena hissed, cutting her off. 'It's really very simple. Witches are *female*.'

'Oh, for sobbing out fuckin' loud, have you heard your-self?'

She knew Niamh was getting riled up because she was suddenly ten times more Irish than normal. Her face screwed up with anger. It wasn't fetching. 'Who the fuck are you to tell people their fuckin' gender? You're not even fuckin' psychic, hun, I am.'

Helena threw her hands up into a stop sign. This was such a waste of air. Had everyone gone blind and stupid? 'So if Theo randomly says he's a girl, we're all meant to simply accept it?'

'Well why not? You said you were High Priestess and we all fuckin' accepted it.'

'Well that's charming.' She wasn't going to be goaded and nor would she unravel semantics. 'Be real, Niamh. You can't be seriously telling me I'm supposed to let a boy take the oath? Let a boy into my coven?'

'No,' she said with infuriating calm. 'Because Theo is a *girl* if she says she is.'

'In that case I'll be Beyoncé.'

'Really?' Niamh sighed loftily.

'Maybe we can bob into town and ask Dave the butcher if he fancies becoming a witch? Or what about your lovely Luke? I'm sure we can all look past the beard and pretend he's a woman.'

Niamh said nothing.

Helena recharged her glass. Perhaps that was a little childish of her. 'How can he possibly be a witch? He'll never bleed.'

Niamh threw her head back, exasperated. 'That's such an old witch's tale! I was reading minds *years* before my first period, as you are fully aware.'

Helena threw her hands up. 'I don't care! I don't! If he wants to call himself Sheila and wear a dress, I'm fine with it, I am. What I will not do is let him or any male into my coven. End of.'

Niamh took a deep breath and unclenched her jaw, apparently choosing her words carefully. 'Helena, we are *witches*. We're meant to be better than mundanes. We know, intimately, the infinity of nature, its bottomless variation and wonder, and you can't fucking conceive of Theo as a girl? You can turn *fire into ice*, but you can't believe a boy could become a girl? We are not of our bodies, Helena; they change, die and rot. Our magic, the thing that defines us has no sex, and I think you know it.'

Helena looked into Niamh's eyes and saw that she had

truly drunk the Kool-Aid. 'Well that's a lovely sentiment, Niamh, but what happens when we're at solstice or Beltane and we're dancing naked around the bonfires and there's a penis jiggling about? Did you think of that?'

'Oh, for fuck's sake!' Niamh exploded. 'This is bullshit.'

'It is not! This is real life, Niamh!'

'One – when was the last fuckin' time you danced naked around a fire, and two, what exactly about Theo's crippling shyness suggests she has any inclination whatsoever to strip off in public?'

'Or what about . . .'

'Stick your *What Abouts* up your arse, Helena. I'm not having some fucking philosophical debate. I'm talking about *Theo*. A young witch who needs our help.'

Outside lightning forked across the sky. It started to rain, tap-tapping on the window pane. Helena glared at Niamh. 'A *powerful* witch that might kill us all. Did you forget that part? I want that child – whatever it is – far, far away.' She had hoped the cabal, and spending some time with young warlocks, might straighten Theo out. She hadn't thought much beyond what would be necessary if the charade went on and his powers continued to grow. Radley was supposed to buy her some time. They'd spoken about a special centre in Arizona for unruly warlocks which sounded ideal. With any luck, the centre would have crushed it out of him.

Niamh's expression was grave. 'Have you actually spoken with her? Spent any time with her? I've been around some fuckin' *dark* witches. My twin sister is one after all, and I'm telling you Theo poses no risk to the coven. She just fucking wants *in* on the coven.'

'And that *is* the risk to the coven!' Helena now shouted before remembering her family upstairs.

Thunder growled. Helena wondered how easy it would

be to take Niamh down. They are both Level 5s. It posed an interesting thought experiment, one she hadn't really considered since she was about thirteen: *who'd beat who in a fight?* Superman or Batman? Pink Ranger or Yellow Ranger? Niamh or Helena? 'Listen. Humour the kid all you want, but I'm never going to induct a penis into HMRC, regardless of who it's attached to.'

Niamh's brow creased. 'What if Holly Pearson, what if Snow, came out as a trans boy? Would you still induct them?'

'Yes . . . no . . . I don't know!' Helena was flustered. Perhaps the second bourbon was a mistake.

Niamh seemed to supress a bitter laugh. 'You are so critical of Leonie, but did you stop to think *why* she had to set up Diaspora? Or why people were so quick to leave HMRC? We have to evolve, Helena.'

Just fuck her. Fuck this. The more she thought about that skinny flat-chested thing dragging up and playing at witchcraft, the sicker she felt. It did. It *repulsed* her, made her flesh crawl like there were lice burrowing inside it. She couldn't shake the vision of him squishing his penis into girl's knickers. As a mother . . .

'You know I can read your fuckin' mind, and that's disgraceful,' Niamh spat.

The coven, any coven, by its definition is of female unity. To let a male in was *repugnant*. A fox in the henhouse. 'Have you forgotten,' Helena said, 'what men have done to witches? Witch finders, nearly all men, drowned us, lynched us, raped us, burned us alive. Warlocks are constantly grasping for our power in the one space in this entire fucking world where women, against the odds, actually dominate. And if you say *not all men*, so help me, Gaia, I'll scream.'

Niamh pushed herself off the counter. 'I hear you loud and clear, but Theo isn't a man! You know what? I'm wasting my breath. We could stand here all night but what it boils down to is: do I believe her? I read a trans witch in London, and saw very clearly who she is, and what she can do, but that's not important. It's like this: if someone tried to tell me that something about myself wasn't true, I'd tell them get to fuck, and so would you. If Theo says she's a girl, I believe her.'

Helena laughed. 'It's that easy is it?'

She shrugged as if it were the most obvious thing in the world. 'It could be if you let it.' Niamh turned towards the door.

She wasn't going to let her just walk away with this matter unresolved. 'This isn't over, Niamh.'

'I'm not playing intellectual ping pong over your kitchen island. It's boring, and it's late.'

Helena slammed her palm onto the worktop. It hurt. 'That child is dangerous.'

Niamh looked back. 'Theo does not belong to you or HMRC, and neither do I. Leave us alone. I mean it.' On that note, Niamh slipped out into the night.

You think I don't? Helena made sure she heard her final thought.

The sky over Vance Hall was split by lightning.

Chapter Thirty
BURN IT OFF

Niamh

Luke's text message came at the exact best/worst time. *How was the big girls' night out?*

Niamh walked in the rain. The water cooled her down for one thing, but she was too drained to contemplate using her powers to get herself home. Her blood was lava. The *Excelsior* wouldn't wear off until dawn.

She checked the time. A little after one. Why was he awake so late? She supposed it was a Friday night. Ah yes, *Late Night Horror Film Fridays*. His wee ritual.

She tapped out a reply: *You still up?*

After a moment or two he responded: *Yep. Why?*

Niamh paused, standing stock still in the leafy lane that led to Vance Hall. Great thick splats of rain ran off the leaves onto her head. There were no streetlights this far out of town and her phone was a beacon in the dark.

She needed to think this through.

Actually, she didn't.

She first dialled Elle.

She answered halfway through the first ring. 'Where are you?' she whispered.

'Just left Helena's.'

'Did you kill her?'

'Did I fuck— Are you mad?'

There was a notable pause. 'I haven't seen you like that in years.'

Niamh kept walking down the lane and ignored that statement. 'Why are you whispering?'

'Everyone's in bed.'

'Theo too?' Niamh wanted to spare Theo that clusterfuck at Helena's, and couldn't risk leaving her home alone, so had asked Elle to host an emergency sleepover.

'Asleep. I think he . . . she . . . was still pretty out of it on whatever the cabal gave her. I gave her a cup of sweet milky tea and a chocolate digestive, but she passed out on the settee before she'd drunk half of it.'

Every stray thought in her head enhanced by the serum she'd taken, Niamh really *felt* how much she loved Elle in that moment. If she was with her, she'd have kissed her hard for ages. 'Am I to leave her there?'

'Yeah, there's no sense in waking her, is there? Collect her in the morning?'

'Good shout.'

'What about you? Are you OK? Do you want to stay here too?'

Niamh *loved* Elle. 'I'll be grand. Don't worry about me.' She wished her a goodnight before hanging up and dialling Luke.

Luke lived in a converted mill in Pecket Well, the tiny village that nestles on the hills above Hebden Bridge. Niamh felt her bones respond to – hum with – the oldness of the brickwork as she took the stairs to the third floor. She'd never been to his flat before, but she often admired the building and its chimney from afar, and wondered who lived here. Luke, it transpired.

He'd buzzed her into the building, but she found the door to his flat shut. She gave it a discreet, one-in-the-morning tap with her turquoise ring. Luke answered, wearing marl sweat-shorts and a plain black tee.

Something inside her twisted, not unpleasantly.

'I had no idea you were such a night owl,' he said with a broad grin. 'Come on in.'

He moved aside to welcome her. She entered, feeling prom-night nervous now that she was actually here. In her head, it was going to be one of those cinematic *say nothing* moments, and she'd be naked under a trench coat and cast it aside brazenly. Now, in the real of it all, she'd forgotten the lines.

'You're soaked. Let me grab you a towel . . .'

He darted off and she continued into the open-plan loft. It was cute. The whole top floor of the mill was divided into an airy living room and kitchen, with a bedroom and bathroom walled off at the side. A pair of archway windows were eyes over the slumbering valley.

'This is cool,' she called as he appeared at her side with an unnecessarily enormous towel. It was *such* a bachelor flat; scented with gruff leather furniture, gym shoes and a hint of whatever deodorant was on offer that week. She did a quick scan. She had a theory that if left to his own devices, every straight single man will have . . . yes, as suspected, the ubiquitous Stormtrooper helmet was proudly displayed in an alcove on the bookcase.

'Are you OK?' Luke said, wrapping the towel around her shoulders. 'You sounded kinda weird on the phone.'

Even with a terrycloth barrier between them, his touch sent ripples across her inner pond. 'I'm fine,' she said.

'You wanna talk about it?'

She thought she did, but now found herself tongue-tied. 'What are we watching?' Niamh nodded at the equally huge flatscreen TV. It was paused on some black and white film.

'*Witchfinder General.* 1968. Seen it? It's on BBC Two pretty much every Friday night.'

'No,' she said. 'Triggering,' she added more quietly as he padded, barefoot, to the sofa area.

'It's a stone-cold classic. Want me to start it again?' He hovered at the kitchen counter. 'Or can I get you something to drink?'

No. The other kind of thirsty. Perhaps she was capable of the movie kiss after all. She cast off the towel and walked directly into his personal space. She was tall, but he was taller. She nudged his chin with her nose, the way a cat nuzzles for attention.

If he was surprised, he recovered quickly. He cupped her jaw with a broad hand and their lips met.

Oh, it was good.

We are not of our bodies, she'd told Helena, but sometimes you absolutely could be. In fact, right now, she rode on the sensuality of it all because she didn't want her thoughts, her head, her history, to burst in like a disapproving nanny and tell her this was a dreadful idea.

The kiss was good. His rough stubble on her face, his hot lips on hers, the promise of a tongue. He was something real.

He lifted her onto the kitchen counter, and she was deaf to whatever it was she knocked to the floor. She spread her legs wide to allow him the closest closeness. The grey shorts didn't leave a lot to the imagination and she felt his stiff cock press against her.

Her dress was wet, and cold, and she wanted it off. She started at the top with the buttons, until she was naked aside from her knickers and cowboy boots. A look.

He took her breasts in hand and kissed her nipples. He tested the waters, biting them, feeling out how hard she wanted it. She wanted it pretty hard. She steered him southerly, although he didn't especially need the encouragement. He pulled her pants to one side to get at the good stuff.

Fuck. Yes.

Clitorises are good, but have you tried having someone lick one while you're high on magic potions? Niamh closed her eyes, tipped back her head, and sailed on it. There was, she felt it, a vibrant purple-pink electric pulsing through her. Could he see it too? It emanated from her.

Pleasure, my old friend, I have missed you.

She felt like a bubble bath. She seeped over the work surface and into the brickwork, back into Gaia.

That baffling craving kicked in; she wanted him inside her. She pulled him into a kiss, tasting herself on his lips. He unhooked her pants and she wriggled free of them. She stopped to pull his shirt over his head, and the shorts down over his bum – a lovely bum it must be said – and guided him in. Gaia doesn't make mistakes and they clicked together, accompanied with that singular sensation: sort of pain, but not pain at all.

They kissed and he began, groaning, whispering the right words in her ear. She said nothing, no need for human words at that moment. Instead she leaned back, opening like the lotus. She strummed herself while he gained momentum. He pounded her, fast but not frantic.

She watched the way his chest and torso moved, animal somehow. His arms were strong and muscular. She was white hot all over, close to boiling point – her orgasm's little way of letting her know it was close. Pressing herself close to him, she wrapped her arms around his neck, her back arched.

It doesn't happen very often, but their bodies came at the same time without advance notice. He shuddered and she shattered, exploding, before imploding back into one whole. Spent, she flopped her head onto his shoulder, getting her breath back. He tasted salty, of fresh sweat. She kissed his neck.

He said something, but she didn't hear it.

For now she would sleep.

That was exactly what she needed. Fleetingly, she was complete.

Chapter Thirty-One

THE MORNING AFTER I

Niamh

She was being punished, make no qualms about that. With the *Excelsior* comedown ramping up, and retrograde Saturn in Aries, Niamh skulked past Luke's neighbour, who also happened to be one of her clients.

'Morning, Mrs Marshall . . .' Niamh said. Ginger, the smushed Pekinese at her side, also judged her.

'Well, good morning, Dr Kelly.' Prim bitch.

She held the doors open for Niamh and she fled the mill shamefaced. Last night's dress was dry but creased and, with no makeup remover at Luke's, she sported a pair of kohly panda eyes.

It was early, but she'd had no inclination to stick around for eggs or pillow talk. She wanted to be there when Theo woke up. That was her excuse and she was sticking to it. She'd left Luke half-asleep in bed with a gentle farewell.

This was all very retro. *Walk of Shame* or *Stride of Pride* after sex with someone new. Very freshers' week. She didn't feel as guilty as she thought she would, although she'd woken up with Conrad very much on her mind, wistfully so. It wasn't inherently good or bad, but it was sure different. The hangover was all Luke.

What to do with him now?

Was that a huge mistake?

What did it all mean?

The thought of it meaning anything was intimidating, dizzying, more than she could process now.

She stopped halfway down the lane and vomited over the dry-stone wall into the pond – the Pecket Well itself. Her puke formed scum on the surface. She looked over her shoulder and saw Mrs Marshall was still watching her through the glass on the mill door.

Let *that* witch hunt begin. In a town as close-knit as Hebden Bridge, she might as well have taken out a billboard on the way into town: THE VET FUCKED THE VEG GUY!

And what did it mean for her and Luke? Once you open a dam, you can't put the water back. There was no undoing what they'd done.

She went home first, quickly changed and washed her face. She then took the Land Rover over to Elle's, where the house was moving at a leisurely Saturday morning pace. Once inside, she found Theo, Holly and Milo amiably watching *Steven Universe* in the lounge while Elle made bacon sandwiches in the kitchen. Jez had gone for a run.

'Are you OK?' Elle said, pouring her a coffee and trying to force-feed her a croissant. 'You look like you didn't sleep a wink.'

'I basically didn't. It took a while for the *Excelsior* to wear off. I laid in bed twitching most of the night. Elle, will you do something for me?'

'Of course, anything.'

Niamh lowered her voice. This was pure mortifying. 'Am I pregnant?'

Elle lifted the bacon off the stove at once and glared. 'Whose bed were you twitching in?'

'Who do you think?'

'Luke?'

Niamh just nodded. Checking no one was watching, Elle held her hands over Niamh's abdomen. It took her only a second. 'No. Not yet, anyway.'

'Can you make sure it doesn't?'

Over in the blink of an eye. 'Done.' Elle pursed her lips. 'Less invasive than the morning-after pill, wasn't it? Shall I call the kids through and I could do my safe-sex talk again?'

Niamh laughed ruefully, although her head was starting to feel like it was full of Polyfilla. 'I know. It was stupid. I blame the potion.'

'Cop out. Are you OK?' That was the thing with Elle, she didn't do judgemental. Nurses see all four corners of life, day in, day out. Nothing much shocks them.

Niamh nodded. 'How's Theo?'

'Seems fine. A little shaken maybe.'

Niamh breathed a sigh of relief. She'd been pregnant once before, during college. She'd felt it – 'sensed' wasn't the right word – it had no sentience of its own at that point. Only twenty, and in the third year of vet school, there was no way she was becoming a mother back then. Using her latent healing powers, she'd simply reabsorbed the cells back into her body. She still thought about it though. She could have had a child the same age as Holly by now.

In a way, she supposed she did. 'Theo?' she called. 'You ready to head out?'

Theo nodded and gathered her things. That was the other hangover kicking in: Helena, HMRC and Theo. Some days are born to be a struggle. Niamh sensed she had to do it today. She would need to have The Talk.

Chapter Thirty-Two

THE MORNING AFTER II

Helena

'Don't you think she's being unreasonable though?' Helena asked, her phone – on speaker – perched next to her bowl of granola and blueberries on the patio table.

'No,' Elle replied. 'I think you went too far, Helena.'

'I knew you'd take her side.'

She tutted. 'It's not about sides. You went over her head *and* used *Medusa* on my daughter. What do you want me to say?'

Helena winced. 'I never told the cabal to drug Holly. That's on them.' On the other end of the line, Elle was silent. 'You don't seriously think this Theo kid is a girl do you? Please tell me *some* of us still possess common sense.'

She heard an audible sigh. 'I don't see what harm it's doing. I'm seeing my granny later. I'll ask her what she sees.'

Was there a sex change in the kid's future? It made little difference as far as she was concerned. Moreover, Helena still hadn't forgiven Annie Device for not agreeing to help with this shit in the first place. 'So you're sitting on the fence? That's great, Elle, thanks.' Helena had assumed that, out of all of them, Elle would understand. Salt-of-the-earth Elle, who didn't even like admitting she was a witch, was sure to call a male spade a male, right? Evidently not.

'Hels, I don't think this is about Theo. It's about you.'

Helena took a sip of black coffee. 'What's that supposed to mean?'

'I don't know . . .'

'No, go on. Spit it out.'

'It's just . . . well, Helena, you . . . um . . . you don't need me to tell you that you like to be in control . . . and not everyone wants to be controlled. You're the High Priestess, but you can't control Niamh, or Lee or Theo's bloody gender. You just can't. I'm not saying that to be mean, I'm really not. I think . . . if you keep pushing at people, sooner or later, they push back.'

Helena squinted at her phone, glad she wasn't on video. What the fuck was that supposed to mean? 'Is that a threat?'

'What? No!' Elle practically shrieked. 'Helena Vance! Learn to take criticism! I'm saying what you did last night was a bit OTT! That's all!'

She was about to argue, but her father pushed her mother out of the patio doors to join her. 'Elle, I need to go.'

'OK. You should apologise to Niamh.'

'I am sorry that Holly got caught in the middle of things last night.' She truly meant that. They swapped farewells and Helena hung up.

Lilian settled herself at the table and reached for the coffee although her father seemed to be on the move. Geoff Carney, now retired from the cabal, was fairly powerful for a warlock, but patience was by far his greatest gift. He'd have to be, surrounded by Vance witches. 'I'm just going to bob down for the papers,' he said. 'Do we need anything from the shops?'

They didn't, and he took off, keys to the Jag swinging as he went.

'That sounded fraught,' Lilian said archly.

'It's fine.'

'Still bossing your little friends around, I see.'

'Mother, can we not?' Helena looked up at the old treehouse, still clinging on to the branches. It had weathered well, all things considered. She wondered if her parents would take it down now that Snow was older. It had been up there so long, she didn't really see it any more. It was part of the tree.

'Elle's right. You *do* need to learn to receive feedback without getting defensive. Gosh, I remember your poor ballet teacher.'

Helena felt her shoulders creeping up. She so badly wanted to tell her that she'd been in a relationship with criticism since she was born. Did her mother *know* she was like this?

'I know what you're thinking.' Lilian smiled, pinching the curl off a croissant.

'I didn't realise you were a sentient now.'

'Sarcasm isn't at all becoming, Helena. You think I'm too hard on you. I probably was, but look at you now.'

Helena simply looked at her, truthfully too worn to argue. Last night with Niamh had drained her.

'A coven is a sisterhood, certainly,' Lilian went on. 'But it takes something more than popularity to lead, Helena, dear. I saw it in you, you know, long before the oracles did. You were going to *be* someone.'

Helena gulped painfully, her throat like a cactus. Praise from her mother was so alien to her, she might prefer the endless nit-picking.

'Your friends are darling. I love them all dearly, but the High Priestess can't let friendship cloud her judgement. She's a fortress. Sometimes she has to make difficult choices that people won't like. She must even prepare to be hated, if it's for the greater good.'

Helena would *not* cry in front of her mother.

'*That's* what I saw in you all those years ago, Helena. Oh we all swear our oath to the coven, but when push comes to shove, how many of us are truly willing to be inconvenienced? You've always been willing to pay the price, to make the necessary sacrifices. Not everyone is willing to do what must be done. I'm not. I hate it so, but I obsess over what people think of me. I envy you. It's a gift.'

Helena was scared to reply in case her voice broke. 'It's my job.'

Lilian shook her head. 'It's so much more than that for you, Helena. It's a *cause*, a vocation. Mark my words, your name will be up there with the very greatest of witches.'

'Thank you, Mother.' Helena felt very young.

'I'm not so bad, am I?' Lilian gave her a wink. 'Now. Do what must be done.'

The Greater Good. Elle was right. She couldn't control Niamh, or Theo, but she could control the coven. She was the most influential witch in the United Kingdom, and here she was sore over name-calling. Almost embarrassing. She had all of HMRC. She had *power*.

What did they have? They had *nothing*.

Chapter Thirty-Three

THE MORNING AFTER III

Leonie

Leonie fell down flat on the dewy grass and looked up at the sky. It was wishy-washy blue, still spring. Leonie was ready for summer, when the tarmac went spongy and London stank of burps. She wanted to drink cool beers under the shade of a tree and get high. She wanted tan lines.

This, however, was bullshit.

'Get up you pussy!' Chinara prodded her with the toe of her Nikes.

'Fuck off. This was a terrible idea.'

'It'll cure you.'

'It won't. I'm gonna be sick.'

'OK,' Chinara glared down at her. 'Either you finish this run, or we go home and start looking for a sperm donor.'

Leonie sat up. Some people are quite jolly on a hangover. Leonie was not. 'That is some coercive fuckery, Chinara Okafor.'

She grinned. 'Yeah, but you're up so . . .'

'Can we just go get some pancakes instead? Or waffles?'

Chinara held out a hand for her. 'Up you get . . .' Leonie allowed herself to be hoisted up. 'Let's get brunch. I did think this would help though.'

Leonie kissed her. 'I know, and you're a hero, you are. But, babe, I may legitimately still be drunk.'

At this time on a Saturday morning, Burgess Park was fairly empty aside from joggers, dogwalkers and one of those 'boot camp' training sessions where a terrifying personal trainer barked orders at a group of minted-looking young professional types. The trainer was quite hot actually – the bitch clearly did her squats.

'The trainer?' Chinara asked. 'Yeah I clocked her too.'

'Behave. Fuck, I'm too hungover to contemplate a three-some. Wow. Heavy night.'

Hand-in-hand they ambled past the class. 'Good night though?'

'Yeah, do you know what? It was. I had way more fun than I thought.' Leonie took a deep breath in through her nostrils and hoped it'd rinse off her liver. 'There's something about being with your childhood girl gang, you know? I am someone new now, and I don't think I'd ever go back, but when I'm with those girls . . . they're all fucking mad . . . but it's magic.'

Chinara looked a little disheartened.

'Oh, fuck, sorry babe. I didn't mean . . .'

Chinara gave her hand a squeeze. 'Hey, it's fine. I made friends here too. I know what you mean.'

Chinara was only eleven when a fire had raged through her township in Unwana. The way she told it, she'd been terrified and scared, racing through the narrow alley-ways looking for her mother and sister who were at her auntie's. The apartments were tightly packed and the fire gobbled the place up like it was kindling.

Leonie had seen all this play out like a movie in Chinara's mind: the skinny little girl in her pink *Power Ranger* t-shirt looking up at the sky and commanding it to rain.

And man did it rain.

It's the first lesson of magic: *you can't make something out of nothing.* Leonie could so vividly hear that in Annie's Yorkshire drawl. On that day, Chinara *did.* In an empty turquoise sky, clouds appeared from nowhere. The heavens turned black and torrential rain fell on the township, dousing the flames.

Lives and homes were lost that day, but Chinara saved many more. It would have been perfect if only she hadn't been witnessed screaming at the sky. Igbo women love a gossip and soon word spread . . . 'Chinara Okafor is a *witch.*'

Even her own mother was terrified of her and, positively brimming with Christ's love, exiled her to live at her auntie and uncle's house in Onueke. There, she was treated like shit, not much better than a fucking servant, until her father – himself a low-level warlock on the DL – brought her to England as a refugee. HMRC isn't *all* bad, and they have an immigration policy for witches or warlocks being persecuted in other territories.

'There's something about your past, man. It's like crack. I keep going back for more.'

Chinara laughed. 'We're all in recovery from our childhood. Amen to that.'

'Where are we going by the way?' They were now adjacent to the pond towards the north exit of the park.

'That diner place if you want waffles?'

'Oh yeah, good shout.' Leonie's phone vibrated where is was tethered to her bicep in a jogging cuff thing. She freed it and saw she had a message from Elle.

Morning! How's the head? 1. Niamh got some with Luke last night! Finally!

She finished it off with several aubergine emojis. 'Oh my days!' Leonie laughed.

'What?'

'Niamh got laid! At last!'

'Oh thank fuck for that. Good for her.'

'I'll call her later, make sure she's not self-flagellating.' Leonie was about to reply but then saw Elle was typing and waited.

And 2. Helena got your brother to kidnap Theo from Niamh's!!! WTF?

The second message stopped her dead in her tracks. WTF indeed. 'The fuck?' she said aloud.

Chinara stopped too. 'OK, that's less good. Did she fuck the wrong person?'

'No. No, it's not that.' Leonie fired a quick reply to Elle: *I beg your fuck???*

Elle was excellent at replying. In fact, if you wanted Niamh, it was sometimes quicker to text Elle. *Helena doesn't want trans girls in coven?*

Leonie tossed her head back. Honestly, that bitch was fucking exhausting. 'Fuck my life.'

'OK, please explain,' Chinara said, getting irritated.

'Well it seems that Helena Vance is a TERF. Why are people so fucking disappointing?'

Chinara understood. They continued their stroll. 'Theo?'

'Yeah. She tried to dump him – fuck, *her* – on the cabal. On my brother, specifically.'

'That's shitty.'

'You think?'

Chinara looked a little smug. 'You know, Lee, I am

constantly surprised at *your* surprise in the ongoing oppression conducted by cis white women.'

Leonie bristled. 'What? You having a laugh, I literally set up my own coven.'

'You have a blind spot with your friends. Of course fucking Helena Vance is a white supremacist.'

'I don't know if she's that bad . . .'

'Why would the people who benefit most from white supremacy be hustling to get rid of it? People like Helena are pretty cosy with the system exactly as it is. She's a gatekeeper, deciding who gets in or out. I present Theo as evidence.' Always the barrister.

Leonie sighed. She was right. There'd been some – although only a few – dissenters over her decision to let trans witches (well, Val and Dior) into the inner sanctum at Diaspora, but she just didn't get it. Like, Leonie under-stood that women were forced to compete for a measly smattering of professional positions, but failed to see how there was a cap on the number of women who could be women. 'I think that as white witches . . . as white women, full stop . . . they're so used to men treating us *all* like shit that they can't acknowledge their privilege.'

Chinara barked a harsh laugh. 'Fuck that noise! Right – if Helena was given a choice, would she choose to be Black?'

'No!'

'Would she choose to be gay?'

'I doubt it.'

'Would she choose to be trans?'

Now Leonie laughed. 'Clearly fucking not.'

'There you go then. She is *very* fucking aware of how the system is stacked.' Chinara rested her case. Leonie found Helena guilty of all charges.

Chapter Thirty-Four

THE MORNING AFTER IV

Elle

Elle was in her bedroom, sniffing laundry. She loved it when it had dried on the line and not in the tumble dryer. Jez clomped up the stairs, back from his run. 'How was that?'

Jez peeled off a sweat-soaked vest and tossed it at the wash basket. 'Not bad. About 6k today. Got a stitch.'

He wrapped his arms around her waist and kissed her neck. Short and muscular, Jez wasn't all that much taller than Elle. 'Jez! You're minging!' It was a reflex, really. She actually didn't mind the smell of fresh sweat, and she was still dressed in trackpants herself.

'Think we've got time for a quickie?' he said, sliding a hand under her waistband and into her pants.

'No!' She promptly withdrew the hand.

Sex increasingly felt like a weird quirk of her twenties: a striptease to lure in a man and convince him to stick around. Clearly, the strategy had worked, although passing two children through her vagina meant it was very hard to regard the area as anything other than a crash site. Elle had acted as a midwife many times and, while birth is undeniably miraculous, it's also acutely traumatic. A part of her body that had once brought her great pleasure became associated, overnight, with the worst agony of her life. In the beginning of her own labour, she'd been able to deploy her powers to take the edge off, but by definition, birth is expelling something that's become a part of you, and to heal would be to keep it inside. To allow the birth to progress, she'd had to give in to the pain.

Elle understood that one of her wifely duties was to keep Jez satisfied. He wanted more sex than she did, so she'd have to meet him in the middle. When they did have sex, it was very nice, and Jez always ensured she came, but these days it just felt like there were a million other things she could be doing with the time. She certainly wasn't going to sacrifice a chunk of her Saturday morning to it. She'd been having sex routinely since she was sixteen and doubted it had any surprises left in store. Sometimes, she tried to remember if she'd ever really *enjoyed* sex, or whether she'd preferred the attention that sex could fetch her.

'Maybe tonight?'

Jez slapped her bum. 'Fine. Schedule me in.' He made a move toward the shower room, only to linger in the bathroom door. 'Elle?'

She looked his way. 'What?'

'How did we get home last night?'

Panic fizzed in her stomach and she fought to keep her face breezy. 'What do you mean?'

'I dunno . . . I just feel weird. I remember picking you up in town . . . and you staggering around like a proper lush.'

'Thanks for that.'

His eyes darted absently, the cogs in his head whirring. 'But then I don't really remember what happened next . . .'

She feigned a laugh. 'Christ. A bit young for dementia, Jez.'

'I'm not kidding, Elle,' he said tetchily. 'Did we go to Niamh's?'

'Of course we did! We dropped Niamh and picked up Holls and Theo and came straight home.' This was what Holly called *gaslighting* and Elle knew it was awful, but didn't see what other choice she had. 'You hadn't been drinking had you?'

'No I bloody hadn't! Well I had one sad Corona while I watched a film with Milo.'

Elle planted her hands on her hips, wary she looked a bit panto. 'I don't know what to tell you, babe.'

He looked troubled. She'd have to get Niamh to wipe him. In time, she thought, Holly might be able to do it too. 'There's not something going on is there? With Niamh?'

Elle frowned. Why wasn't he letting it go? 'Are you asking if we're lezzing off?'

'No! Just . . . sometimes, I see you two . . . and Helena and Leonie too. The way you look at each other as if you're psychic or something. It's like you're this little gang, speaking a made-up language that I can't understand.'

Elle smiled and walked over to him. She kissed him on the lips. 'Babe, we do. We're *women.*'

Below the belt – literally – she slipped her own hand into his sweaty briefs. His cock was shrivelled and damp from his run. 'What you doing?'

'Come on then . . .'

'Serious?'

'Yeah!'

'Let me grab a quick shower, I'm gross.' Not needing to be asked twice, Jez practically smashed through the shower glass in urgency.

Elle closed the bedroom door and climbed onto the bed to wait. OK, she'd lied, but Jez was going to get a shag out of it. She figured they were even.

The pharmacy shut at twelve on a Saturday, so Elle didn't even shower before whizzing over to her grandmother's cottage to drop off her prescription. She parked haphazardly on the country lane and trotted down the steep zigzagging stone stairs that led to the old water mill. She had such mixed feelings about this house. As a child, when she and her big brother had been left here during the holibobs, other kids had loitered around the crumbling garden walls.

Is your nanna a witch?

Are you a witch too?

Can you cast a spell on us, Elle?

She remembered how they used to find sticks and spear chunks of dog or cat poo before tossing them over the wall at her. They called it 'shitsticks'. It'd be funny if it hadn't ruined her childhood. She wasn't sure if Annie really understood why she never wanted to play in the gardens. The only girl in school who wished the holidays away.

She's pretty for a witch.

Have you got warts?

They ran away from her in case she gave them warts. All except Jez, anyway.

She knocked on the door out of politeness before heading in. 'Granny! It's only me!'

'Oh hello love!' Annie called from upstairs. 'I'll be down in a jiffy.'

Her grandmother's house was rank. She'd once arranged for a cleaner to come once a week, but the poor woman quit after a single visit. Elle didn't blame her to be honest. Everything wore a wheezy blanket of cat fur.

On a fold-out table in the living room, a fountain pen rested in the trough of one of Annie's open diaries. Elle idled over, wondering if she dared sneak a peek. Of all the witches, Elle felt most sorry for oracles. The blindness and hair loss was bad enough, but to be able to see the future – what a total nightmare.

She stopped herself. *If you dwell too long on the future,* Annie always said, *you'll never get there.* The mantra had served her well. Of course she was desperate to know how Milo and Holly were going to turn out, but she wanted them to make their own way there. It went deeper than that, if she was honest. Sometimes Elle couldn't quite believe her luck: loving husband, gorgeous kids, nice house, good job. Sooner or later, something was going to go wrong. She was a community nurse, all she ever saw were things going wrong.

Now reliant on the bannister, Annie hobbled downstairs. 'Are you all right?' Elle said, going to assist her.

'Gerroff! I'm fine!'

'I wish you'd come look at one of those residential flats in town. They're ever so nice you know.'

Annie scowled. 'Raisin ranch.'

'They're not! You have your own flat all by yourself.'

'And what about the cats, eh? No. I'm stopping here.'

Elle shook her head. 'Oh, I know. But I'll keep on pestering.'

'Aye you will. You want a tea, pet?'

'I better not. I've said I'll run Milo into Halifax this afternoon.' She reached into her handbag for Annie's medication. 'Here you go, I've put your meds on the table. Do you need anything else fetching?'

'Oh, next time you do a big shop, I'll have some of those . . . actually, never you mind.'

'What?'

Annie lowered herself into her favourite armchair, her knees creaking. 'No, you're OK.'

Elle hoisted her bag back onto her shoulder. 'Okey dokey, then. I'll be off . . .'

'Elle, love, wait.'

She turned back. 'What's up?'

'Have a seat a minute.'

Elle perched on the sofa, the enormous Maine Coon certainly wasn't shifting up to make space for her. The thing was like a frigging lion. 'Are you OK?'

'Nothin's up,' Annie said. 'You just sounded like you needed a sit-down.'

Elle laughed ruefully. 'Gran, I could *always* use a sit-down. It's non-stop.'

'You work very hard, my love. Unpaid labour, too, most of it.'

Elle looked at her hands, at her rings. She knew that Annie was bewildered by her choices. Not openly disappointed, but they were always joined in conversation by the version of herself she *could* have been. Of Annie's four children and five grandchildren, somehow she was the only magical descendant. The last of the Device witches until Holly. 'I like looking after everyone,' she replied, honestly.

'I know, and you're only just getting started. You're still a young 'un.'

Now Elle really laughed. 'I'm staring down the barrel of forty, Gran!'

'Not even halfway!'

Elle glared at her grandmother. 'Is that an official vision? Because I don't wanna know!'

Annie leaned forward. 'Oi! You listen here. When everyone around you was telling you what to do, who to be, you made your own mind up. Elle, love, I've always, *always* respected that. You went your own way. And I've no doubts you'll carry on sailing up your own little river. I believe that without needing to see the future.'

Elle was taken aback. 'Well, thank you, Gran.'

'You are so much stronger than you think you are.' Annie sighed. 'And that'll come in handy.'

That was never good. Elle felt a familiar turn in her tummy. 'Have you seen something?'

Annie nodded, her face stern. 'Oh aye. The cards are turning faster now.'

'What does that mean?'

She nodded at the chess board set up on the coffee table. Elle knew that she sometimes played with Niamh, she wouldn't know where to begin. 'Pieces are moving into position; decisions making ripples in the pond.'

'Gran, you're scaring me. Is this about Theo?'

'In part.'

She lowered her voice. 'Is she a girl?'

Annie tutted. 'Well I saw that the second she stepped in my cottage, but she's a pawn in a much bigger game that's been going on a lot longer than she's been alive.'

'Gran, should I get Niamh over? This sounds important . . .' She fumbled for her phone. This wasn't Elle's business, or at least she hoped it wasn't.

'I will see Niamh, but I want you to hear it too, Elle. You're on that chessboard too.'

Fuck that, thought Elle. Like Annie said, she'd made

her choice almost twenty years ago. She was a witch in name only. 'Gran, can we not with the enigmatic oracle stuff? You know it does my nut. Can you just tell me straight? Should I be worried?'

Annie's brow furrowed. 'Oh, yes, my love. We all should be. Every last one of us.' Her eyes widened. 'We saw a storm front coming and I thought, I must admit, that it might not make landfall but . . .'

Elle felt nauseous. '. . . it will?'

Annie nodded. 'Leviathan *will* rise.'

Chapter Thirty-Five

DIFFICULT CONVERSATIONS

Niamh

The only thing for it was to sleep it off. Niamh took a nap on the sofa in the lounge, dreaming fraught hungover dreams. She tore through Hebden Bridge at night, drained of any magic, breathless, desperately asking a cast of faceless villagers if they'd seen Theo. All the while, an unnaturally elongated Helena stalked the foggy streets, also hunting Theo. And then Helena became Ciara, and then Conrad, and things got even more confusing.

It took her a minute to realise the knocking sound was in real life and not in the nightmare. Tiger jumped off her lap and started to bark. There was someone at the door. Groggy, Niamh pulled off her blanket and shuffled to the kitchen. Her tongue felt furry, her breath inexplicably meaty.

Fuck. It was Luke. She recognised him through the glass panel in her new back door. She wondered briefly where Theo was. Possibly having a kip upstairs? The exertions of last night had wrung it out of them both.

Niamh cleared her throat and opened the door to come

face-to-face with a bouquet of buttery yellow roses. 'Oh god, Luke, I look like total shite.'

He smiled and made a fuss of the dog. 'You don't at all. Can I come in?'

'Of course.' She stood aside to let him in. 'Tea?'

'Please. These are for you.' He handed her the roses. 'Where's Theo?'

'Upstairs I think.' She ought to go check no one had kidnapped her again really.

She rested the flowers in the sink and looked for a vase. She found a scuffed tin jug that'd do, and filled it with water.

'Google reliably tells me yellow roses are for friendship.'

She winced and looked at him. 'We don't have to do a post-mortem do we?'

'No. Well yes. Look . . .' he lowered his voice. 'Last night were boss, but if I thought it was going to fuck up our friendship, I'd take it all back. That's what the flowers are for.'

Niamh bowed her head slightly. 'Consider the air cleared.' It wasn't of course. She still had no idea what came next. It was the terrifying empty Word document when you have an assignment due.

'Are we good?' he asked hopefully.

She admired the roses in their new vessel. 'We are. And the flowers are gorgeous.' There was an expectant silence. The room held its breath for a kiss. 'Luke, I wish I could tell you our future, but I can't. I want you to know how much I love having you in my life, because I do, but I'm not sure if it's fair.'

He frowned. 'What do you mean?'

'You're waiting for me. And I know that sounds arrogant, but that's what it looks like from where I'm standing, and it's a lot of pressure.'

Luke leaned back against the worktop, trying to keep it casual as she filled the kettle. 'OK, let's run with that. What if I am? It's not like there's anyone else on the scene.'

'That's because you're not looking . . .'

'Niamh Kelly, I'm a catch! I deliver veg to a lot of single ladies!'

Niamh laughed. 'But what if it never happens?'

'What if what never happens?'

'I don't know . . . the *vision*: you and me, Mr and Mrs, happy families.' All the things she'd already had with Conrad.

'Who says I want those things?'

She fixed him in a sceptical stare. 'You watch a lot of movies. Of course you do.' Movie love rarely deviates from the template: two people (either sex to be honest) meet, overcome an obstacle and, as the credits roll, we assume a lifetime of contented monogamy lies ahead. That's how you *win*. Friends, career and family can rot once you land in a marriage.

'OK, I do, but I'm only thirty-two, Niamh. I've got all the time in the world.'

She and Conrad on their final holiday in Santorini, cocktails in hand. As the sun set over the caldera, talk turned to their engagement. *There's no rush to plan the wedding is there? We've got all the time in the world.* The sadness was always inky in her heart, just waiting for something to swill it around. If only there were some valve to expel it.

In her fragile state, she briefly imagined herself wiping Luke for good. She could do it, too. Remove herself entirely from his memory. She'd get her food delivered by someone else and he'd move on to some other woman, left only with a strange tip-of-the-tongue sensation of the desire he'd once had. Erasing her own lingering feelings, of course, was that much harder.

'What?' he said when she said nothing.

'I'm honestly not sure why you bother.'

He reached out to touch her but she flinched. 'I think you're the best one I've met. Sorry it's not more poetic.'

She gave a half-arsed smile. 'I quite like that as it goes.'

Maybe she should kiss him again. Last night it had been something. But if she kissed him now, she couldn't blame the *Excelsior* which was such a perfect alibi. With expert timing, she heard footsteps on the stairs and Theo trotted down into the lounge.

'You're awake,' Niamh stated.

'Hey, mate,' Luke said.

It was probably her imagination, but there was an increasingly feminine chord to her aura, or maybe it had been there all along, and Niamh simply hadn't been looking in the right places. 'Thanks for the flowers, Luke. I actually have plans with Theo right now . . .'

We do?

'No worries, I'm meeting some mates down the pub for the rugby anyways. But . . . don't you worry about me. I'm happy.'

Niamh wasn't sure she'd stretch to happy personally, so she instead said she was glad. It seemed to be enough for him and he ducked out of the back door.

Is this a relationship? Neither was seeing anyone else and she thought about him first thing in the morning and last thing at night. Perhaps that was her problem – the *vision* was the only relationship on the movie menu. What if there was some breed of relationship where she didn't have to be Luke's Mrs? Something built on their own definition of a couple. What if this *was* that relationship?

It was confusing, so she did what she always did: focused on needy strays. She turned to Theo. 'Yes, we do have plans. We need to talk about what happened last night.'

Theo nodded and sat down on the floor by the wood burner. Niamh finished off making the teas she was going to make for herself and Luke and took it to her. She mirrored Theo's pose, sitting cross-legged on the rug. 'Light a fire,' she said.

Theo put some logs in the burner and lit them with an easy wave of her hand.

'You're getting so good at that,' Niamh said. She took a sip of much-too-hot ginger and lemon tea before beginning. 'You have every right to know what that was all about.'

Helena wants me to go to the cabal.

Yes, she does. Do you know why?

Because I'm a boy.

'Well that's the thing isn't it?' Niamh was determined to keep Holly's name out of it. 'Are you?'

Theo's eyes dipped at once, her cheeks flushing.

'Don't get upset,' Niamh said, fearing for her windows. 'You know I can hear your thoughts . . . and you've been working really hard at keeping me out, but I get the feeling that you've been thinking about your gender for a long old time now.'

Theo looked to the ceiling, trying to keep the tears from spilling.

'Can we talk about it?' Niamh said. 'I want to help you however I can. I want to use the right name or pronouns or whatever. Basically I don't wanna fuck it up. I probably will, but I don't want to.'

I . . .

Go on . . .

Instead, Theo closed her eyes and took Niamh's fingers in her own. Understanding, Niamh closed her eyes too and emptied her mind. At first, hazy half-formed images came to her – nothing she could make sense of, but they started to make sense.

A classroom filled with infants. Noisy, chaotic. A small child playing in the sand tray with some other little girls. She has long black hair, a fringe covering much of her round face. In her hand is a plastic doll of a girl dinosaur. Rather, a T-Rex with a pink bow. 'You can't be that one!' a loudmouthed brat tugged the dinosaur out of her hand. 'It's for girls!' The first little girl grabbed it back, trying to regain it.

Only then a teacher, a plump woman in retro hipster glasses, intervened. 'Theo! Stop that! Why don't you come play with the other boys?' Theo – the first girl, it transpired – was led away, not gently, by the hand.

A sweaty, boiled gammon face. A middle-aged man, Scottish, bearing down on her. ACT LIKE A LADDIE, YOU FUCKIN' FAIRY.

Next she saw a slightly older child on the fringes of a football field. A match was going on around her. She instead looked to the adjacent field where a group of girls played hockey. She was so transfixed, that she missed the football rolling her way. PASS IT YOU FAGGOT.

And then all the girls, the obsessions: Miley, Ariana, Beyoncé and so many more who Niamh didn't know – just snippets of their faces and the rush of joy they'd brought her. Then the faces of girls at school who'd look upon Theo with utter disdain, the girls who'd feared her difference.

Niamh opened her eyes at the same time as Theo. She offered a sympathetic smile. 'Well that was shite,' she said kindly and Theo smiled back. 'I cannot pretend to imagine what it's like to be you. I've always quite liked being a girl if I'm honest. I wouldn't want it any other way.'

Theo looked so tired, like someone who'd had a tooth-ache her whole life.

'What do you want to happen next?' Niamh asked.

I don't know.

'OK, let's try a different question: who do you wanna be in like . . . five years?'

She dwelled on this a moment and then took Niamh's hand again. Niamh closed her eyes and, after a moment, when nothing entered her head, she opened them again. She gasped. In front of her sat an entirely different person. She was reminiscent of Theo, but now outwardly looked like the girl she was on the inside. The ebony hair was longer, almost to her waist, falling in thick waves. Her face was beautiful, not down to bone structure or features – although those were beautiful – but because she seemed so entirely at ease. Open, effortless as a summer daisy.

This is who I am in my head.

The glamour faded and the grungy teenager re-emerged.

'What's the fun of living in your head?' Niamh said, fighting back tears. That was a deeply personal thing she'd shared and she felt honoured. 'You can be her in real life too, you know?'

Can I?

Niamh took her hands and spoke very seriously. 'You are a *witch*, Theo. You can be whoever you want to be.'

Chapter Thirty-Six

CHAIRWOMAN

Helena

Sandhya came to her office as if she were delivering the last rites. 'They're here, ma'am.'

Helena inhaled slowly, centring herself. She'd kept them waiting a while quite deliberately. It reinforced her busyness, her importance, that her time was more valuable than theirs. 'Is there coffee in the boardroom?'

'Yes, ma'am.'

She'd just got off a sobering Zoom call to a breakaway coven in Sydney. It transpired – pun intended – that there was a widening rift in the Australian Coven Association since they passed a motion last year to allow trans witches to swear the oath following pressure from the Indigenous Witches Collective. Some tedious fuss about how the Aboriginal equivalent of Gaia has no gender so nor should a witch. For fuck's sake.

'We just didn't feel safe any more,' a witch called Heather had told her. 'Like how do you know they're telling the truth? They were basically saying any bloody man could sign up, whether he'd had any surgery or not.'

'It is the erasure of women as a category,' another said. 'If anyone can be a woman, women don't exist.'

Helena could only agree and sympathise. As the call went on she found herself squirming in her seat. They sent her pictures of some of the beefy 'ladies' who'd joined ACA's ranks. It looked like a bad drag show; balding gorillas in floral dresses. But whereas Heather had formed a new coven, hideously titled *Coven XX*, Helena would *not* see HMRC splinter *again*. Diaspora was bad enough.

Still stewing, Helena swept down the corridor with Sandhya at her heel to Boardroom 1. Power dressing served a double purpose: it made Helena feel more intimidating and, one hoped, intimidated others. She wore a 2017 jade Celine trouser suit with zebra Jimmy Choo pumps. Her hair was pulled back into a severe knot and her lips were fire-engine red. She meant business.

They were already gathered around the conference table. The fucking board, every last one of them like gravel in her shoe. In smaller covens, a High Priestess is answerable to her sisters directly, but in something as sprawling as HMRC, there was a requirement to have a board of directors to keep the running of the coven in check. Mostly, it was financials, but today Moira Roberts had instigated an emergency meeting.

Well of course she had, the vinegar-faced shrew.

'Good morning everyone,' Helena said, launching into the room *Devil-Wears-Prada* style. 'Sorry, I'm late, I was on a call.' She made sure to obfuscate the truth from Moira, the sentient in the room.

They were a sorry lot to be so influential. Radley Jackman, as Head Warlock, was obligated to be there. Moira, the Chief Cailleach of Scotland, took the other head of the table – on purpose, no doubt. Next to her was Seren Williams, the Headmistress of the Bethesda School of Dance, the closest thing there was to a school for young witches. There was Priyanka Gopal of Psyence UK, and Baroness Wright, and finally the only one Helena actually tolerated, Sheila Henry, the stout lesbian from Hebden who founded Witch Pride.

Helena took her seat and Sandhya brought her a coffee before sitting to her right with her laptop, poised to take notes.

As the chairwoman of the board, Baroness Wright called the meeting to order. Her recent facelift hadn't gone entirely to plan, Helena felt. She looked somewhat mummified by her own skin. 'Thank you all for teleporting in at such short notice . . .' Wright was so plummy that the first time Helena had met her, she assumed the woman had a speech impediment. 'I know we're all awfully busy . . . this is an emergency meeting, as such there is no formal agenda, although there will be time for any other business at the end . . .'

'Oh, let's cut the crap shall we?' Moira piped up. That didn't take long, thought Helena. 'I've got covens calling from New Zealand asking if the apocalypse is coming, and here we've got Helena trying to kidnap children. Forgive me if I'm a wee bit confused . . .'

Helena had no choice but to remain calm. Realistically, these were the only people who could chair a no-confidence vote in a High Priestess. 'Very well, you deserve an explanation.'

'We're all ears,' Moira sneered.

'As you're well aware, the oracles have foreseen a critical occurrence. The probability of demonic interference is high. As oracles outside of the UK are *not* receiving such compelling visions, there's a likelihood the uprising will happen on our turf and will fall under HMRC remit.'

'And what of this child?' Sheila said, red-faced and out of puff. 'The coven in Hebden Bridge is saying Niamh Kelly caused a motorway pile-up?'

'That categorically did not happen,' Radley interjected.

Helena raised a finger. 'Radley, I've got this, thanks. I have reason to believe the child who destroyed the school near Edinburgh is the fabled Sullied Child; a male child who will find a way to free Leviathan from his earthly prison.'

Baroness Wright spoke. 'What evidence do you have of this?'

'He is powerful beyond any male witch I've ever seen, including Dabney Hale.'

'Niamh told me she's transgender,' Radley said and Helena shot him an acidic glare. After the other night, she'd downgraded him from a nuisance to literally good for nothing.

'She's a she? She intends to transition?' Moira sat up straighter. 'Then why would you palm her off onto the cabal?'

'This does change things, Helena,' Sheila added. Helena was surprised. She didn't think a fifty-odd-year-old lesbian would be keen to defend a transgender.

Helena held her tongue. 'Regardless of the child's identity, they were *born* male so they fulfil the prophecy. All Niamh has been able to ascertain is that the child is a powerful menace.'

'How powerful?' Priyanka asked.

'She very nearly took out all of us, including Niamh,' said Radley.

'Niamh is a Level 5 adept!' Seren, a touch hysterical at the best of times, looked like she might faint.

'Precisely.' Now Helena turned to Radley. This was news to her. 'You believe Theo could defeat Niamh?'

'It's all in my report, Helena, but yes. She emitted some sort of psychic alarm that disabled even Niamh.'

Helena sat back, exonerated. 'Well there we are then. There aren't many witches in the UK more powerful than Niamh Kelly and a *male* child has somehow risen above her. I'm sure, then, you can understood why I took the action I did.'

'Without consulting the board . . .' Moira put in archly.

'Covens are getting panicky,' Sheila said plainly. 'We lost many lives in the war and none of us are getting any younger, Helena. I'm not sure we've got another fight in us. You've got gossip about Leviathan rising and, pardon my French, people are shittin' themselves.'

'They have no need to. Everything is in hand.'

Moira laughed callously. 'Oh aye? So where's the kid now?'

'He's with Niamh.'

'Because your midnight flit ended with Niamh taking out half the cabal. Is that right, Radley?'

'Not in the slightest, Moira.'

'But your plan failed? Helena, why are you incapable of accepting fault?'

Helena could feel her skin crawling, crackling with static. She wanted to fire a million volts at the smug bitch and melt the fucking smirk off her face. 'Theo is contained in Hebden Bridge.'

Sandhya stopped typing and looked at her, no doubt sensing her lie, which meant Moira did too.

'I have a team of four headed up by Robyn Jones at the safehouse there. I can remain at Vance Hall and send more witches if necessary. It's all under control.'

Moira's green eyes sparkled at the far end of the table.

She was really, really enjoying this. Why wasn't a mystery. A lot of people had felt after Collins was assassinated that Moira Roberts was the most obvious candidate for the role of High Priestess, and that her appointment would resolve any notion of a divide between English and Scottish witches.

Well, it sucks to be her. And, as she was nearing sixty, Helena doubted Moira was going to get her turn.

'I don't envy you this,' the Scot said. 'But you have more oracles in here than anywhere else in the world. Figure out what the risk is and stop it before it starts.'

'Oh, I think it's already started,' Radley said quietly.

Helena marched down the hall towards the oratorium in a rage. Sandhya had to trot to keep up with her stride. 'Are they in trance?' she snapped.

'I'm not sure,' Sandhya said.

'They fucking should be if they're not.' Helena stopped at the big double doors and banged hard with her fist. She was about a second from ripping the doors off their hinges when a meek oracle opened up. Helena didn't ask to enter.

The oracles cooed like pigeons, unsettled by her sudden entrance. 'Enough is enough,' she barked, taking the stairs two at a time to where Irina Konvalinka was seated in the lotus position, half hidden, as ever, by the strange twilight of the room.

She rose to her feet. 'Greetings.'

'No!' Helena held out a hand. 'Enough cryptic crossword clues. Tell me what is going to happen and tell me now.'

Irina considered her with an infuriatingly calm Mona Lisa smile. 'We have shared our consolidated wisdom.'

'You've shared shit!' There was an audible gasp. 'Tell me what is going to happen precisely and when.'

'You know that's beyond our reach.'

'Then what fucking good are you? There's, what, thirty of you, and I'm totally by myself in this. What am I supposed to do? Tell me!' There was a horrible silence and Helena held back tears of frustration. She really wanted to cry. But she would not.

Irina was no doubt about to impart some more tedious poetry when a very young, waiflike oracle stepped out of the shadows in the back rows. Helena had inducted her at solstice either last year or the year before, she couldn't remember which. She couldn't remember her name either. Her eyes were haunting, reminiscent of some nocturnal marsupial. She still had some wispy blond hair, combed over her scalp like Trump.

'What is it, child?' Irina asked.

'I have seen,' the girl said earnestly, clearly scared to speak up.

'Remind me of your name,' Helena said.

'I'm Amy Sugden.' Ah yes, that was it. A sad girl from a family near Bradford who are petrified of her.

'What have you seen?' Helena asked.

'I've been having the same dream every night, Ms Vance. I didn't know if I should say anything or not.'

Helena looked briefly to Irina. 'How powerful are you?' she asked Amy directly.

'She is a Level 3,' Irina answered for her.

Middling. 'Show me.'

Konvalinka seemed displeased that Amy had kept these dreams from her. Some oracles worked best while unconscious. Straining for visions can be like willing an orgasm, Helena had been told – far better to let it happen. 'Show us all,' the chief oracle said.

Amy's eyes widened further. 'Please, miss, I don't know if I should. The dreams . . . they're horrible.'

Irina snatched her hand. 'Very well, then just show us. We do not dream in secret, child. You know this.'

Amy offered Helena her other hand. She closed her eyes.

The visions crashed into her mind without grace or finesse. It was like the floor was tipping ninety degrees under Helena's feet. She almost toppled into Amy's dream.

She was standing on a grassy slope. The skies were as grey as lead. The fields were much of a muchness, but after a second, Helena recognised the familiar incline of Pendle Hill, and the exposed side with the copse above her.

Dotted along the landscape were bonfires, ready to be lit. Only as the milkiness of the vision came into clarity, Helena saw there were not bonfires. They were pyres. She remembered the local farmers burning their cows during the foot-and-mouth outbreak in 2000 – great big mounds of blackened, burning flesh.

Only this time, it wasn't livestock. It was women.

Helena tried to scream but found she had no volume. She tried to run, but instead swooped towards the nearest pyre. Women – witches – piled on top of each other, dead. Bent over backwards and upside-down was an unmistakable shock of white-blond hair. It was her daughter, mouth hanging open like a dead fish. At the bottom of the pile was Niamh's red hair, half trodden into the mud. Leonie's grey face and expressionless eyes were splayed on the top of the heap.

The macabre sculpture burst into flame and Helena recoiled. One by one the pyres caught fire, illuminating the hillside.

There was nothing she could do except watch as Snow's skin blistered and peeled back from her skull. The smell was horrific, more real than any dream could be. Helena was powerless.

How many witches were there? It could well be all of them. Was she on one of these pyres?

On the top of the hill, through the smoke, a figure emerged. Helena had never really thought how Leviathan would appear to her – demons were something you *felt* not saw – and yet she knew it was him. He was vaguely humanoid in shape, but his limbs and torso were unnaturally elongated. His arms reached the ground so that he prowled out of the woods upright but also on all fours. Almost as tall as the trees, he wore a veil over his face, but Helena could see an inhuman skull against the sheer silk. From his head grew two mighty horns, like those of a stag.

Helena felt a sharp stab of terror in her side. She almost doubled up from pain. This was the source of all the fear in the world, standing right before her. She looked again and now the beast became the child, Theo. He was naked and pale, with the same horns on his head. He overlooked the valley with a satisfied smile on his lips.

He would end them. He would end them all.

In the oratorium, Helena pulled back from Amy's vision at the same instant Irina did. Helena was too stunned to speak. Amy looked almost embarrassed at revealing her vision.

'Who else has seen this?' Irina hollered, her voice echoing around the chamber. No other oracle spoke. 'Anyone?'

'It was so real,' Helena said, mostly to herself. 'Snow . . .'

'Helena, stop.' Irina's expression rested somewhere between shock and caution. 'Heed my words, Amy is a young oracle. These visions are disturbing, yes, but those events are unverified, unsubstantiated in the almanacs.'

Helena would not be patronised. She saw what she saw. Her mouth was dry, her eyes sore. 'The Sullied Child was foreseen a hundred times over. You yourself warned me. How much more evidence do you need?'

There was nothing Konvalinka could say to that. They had seen the school burning, they had seen where this would lead. What sort of a leader would she be if she laid back and let this tsunami wash over her. She was elected High Priestess because she was the strongest willed, the most unyielding witch in England.

She would not yield now.

It was time to act. She would rather be known as a hard-faced bitch than the witch who did nothing while demons eviscerated an entire coven. A new course of action had been brewing in her mind for a few days now. It wasn't going to be . . . pleasant, but it would get the job done, once and for all.

'No more delays,' she told the women in the oratorium. 'This stops *now*.'

Helena turned on her heel, only to feel Irina's needly fingers clutch her wrist. She spoke just loudly enough for Helena to hear. 'When they learn of your plans, the girls from the treehouse will stop you.'

That stung. Helena almost swung for the oracle. She cooled herself. 'And just who do you think is going to tell them my plans?' Irina said nothing, because Helena already knew the answer. Annie Device would tell them.

Helena looked from Irina to Amy Sugden, to Sandhya. Her friends no longer mattered. They weren't little girls any more and nostalgia, ultimately, is flavourless gum. 'Let them try to stop me,' she said and she stalked out of the dome.

Chapter Thirty-Seven

HALE

Helena

She felt mildly ridiculous, waiting until nightfall and driving herself to Grierlings, but she didn't want the coven to know of her visit. She told only Sue Porter, and asked her to ready the prison doctor. Driving her own car felt slightly alien. She drove so rarely these days.

Along with a butch, bulldog-faced guard, they made their way to the East Wing of the men's block. It was after lights out. Only a sickly, greenish emergency light illuminated the long corridors. Heavily diluted *Sandman* was pumped through the AC to subdue the prisoners, so Helena, Sue and Dr Kiriazis each wore a face mask to prevent them nodding off.

Dabney Hale was located at the furthest reach of the prison where he couldn't get inside the heads of any other inmates. No one was taking any chances. There were nights, many nights, where Helena questioned why they'd let him live. Quite vividly she imagined locking him into the Pipes and throwing the lever.

Everything happens for a reason sounded like the sort of Christmas cracker wisdom a particularly poor oracle would spout, but perhaps *this* was why she'd spared him the death sentence. Perhaps on some level she'd known he'd come in handy one day. This was, just maybe, Hale's place in things.

Sue Porter unlocked and unbolted the door to Hale's quarters. The door and locks, like most in Grierlings, were made from fibreglass, a material that didn't respond to any form of magic. The guard went in first with a mundane pistol in hand. Magic was all well and good, but guns got the job done too. Kiriazis went next and Helena followed, removing her mask.

If the coven at large knew just how luxuriant Hale's 'cell' was, there'd be riots. There was no way to justify it except that Lord and Lady Hale pumped hundreds of thousands of pounds in donations into HMRC. His parents fled the UK in shame – not that that was the official version of events, of course – for Grand Cayman years ago, but Helena maintained civil terms with them. Lady Hale, ever penitent, was on a number of charity boards with her. After all, they couldn't be held responsible for what their son became.

Helena knew that was a lie too, but sometimes you have to sell yourself these little balms to soothe the guilt of inequality. This room had once been the prison library. He'd kept it as such mostly. The shelves on the lower level were still filled with thousands of volumes, but the iron spiral staircase now led to his sleeping area.

Thick church candles flickered. It was quite the cosy nook. A pair of matching armchairs and a coffee table were positioned before a lethargic fire crackling in the hearth. He was going to be here forever, with no chance of parole. She supposed him having a few creature comforts wasn't going to change that. He suffered. Good. Perhaps death was letting him off the hook.

With heavy metallic footfalls, he descended from the mezzanine. 'Goodness me. It's been a long time since Helena Vance came by of an evening. What a treat.' His voice was smeared in sarcasm, but he also wasn't lying.

Every woman can be forgiven her ill-advised teenage dalliances. At eighteen, one thinks a twenty-four-year-old boyfriend is a status symbol, not a creep who dates girls because they're more malleable than their contemporaries.

He was no less handsome in his forties than he had been in his twenties. If anything, the lines around his eyes and few extra pounds suited him. He had a neat beard now but the blue eyes still fizzed the exact same way they had done when Helena was a girl. Those eyes had convinced a great many people of a great many things.

Charisma is a kind of magic, a very dangerous and unquantifiable weapon.

Kiriazis had her instructions. The guard met him at the staircase and thrust him forward. He wore the same grey jumpsuit as the rest of the prison population. Kiriazis rolled up his sleeve and injected him with *Merry Dance*, a heady cocktail of ethanol and guanine that would make Hale susceptible to her will. There's no such thing as a truth serum, even for a witch. Helena wondered if she should have brought Sandhya with her to read his mind, but she'd decided against it, feeling that the fewer people who knew of this visit the better.

'Was that really necessary?' Hale didn't resist, but moaned, rubbing his arm.

'Thank you,' Helena said to the others. 'You can leave us now.'

'Are you sure that's wise, Ms Vance?' Sue fretted.

Helena assured her it was and ushered her out. She was left alone with the man who killed her husband, albeit indirectly. Instinctively, she flexed her fingers to summon lightning, only to feel the singular impotence that came with Sister's *Malady* in the air.

Hale flopped onto one of the armchairs. 'Helena, you are looking sensational. CrossFit?'

Helena took the other chair. 'Peloton,' she admitted.

'You've never looked better.' Being able to flatter with such sincere abandon is quite a skill, but she was gratefully immune now. Perhaps it was a good thing she'd rinsed Hale from her system while she was still at school. 'Is there a reason the High Priestess has dropped by this late in the evening? Don't get me wrong, I'm not complaining. The company isn't great around here.'

'It's not a social, Dabney. You killed my husband.'

He looked genuinely hurt. 'I did no such thing. I've never killed in my life.'

The worst thing was she couldn't argue with that. He was clever enough to make sure he got others – Travis Smythe, Ciara and many more – to do his dirty work for him. The warlock Charles Manson.

'I greatly admired Stefan Morrill,' he went on. 'And I never set out to hurt you, or any witch. I like to think you know that.'

Helena laughed. She could see *why* people fell for his shit. 'God, you really can't admit fault can you? You should have been a politician. I always said so.'

'No more so than yourself, Helena.'

She also wouldn't rise to his bait. She wasn't here for intellectual banter, either. 'When we spared you the Pipes, it was part of a plea deal. Life imprisonment in return

for the whereabouts of your conspirators *and* your exper-
tise in future coven matters.'

Hale made a steeple of his fingers. 'Yes, I remember that
part quite well, thank you. I assumed now that you've
rounded up Smythe, we'd be done.'

'This isn't about the war.'

He perked up. 'Oh?'

'I'm assuming someone as learned as yourself is familiar
with the prophecy of the Sullied Child?'

'Of course. One of my faves. High doom content.'

Helena aimed to be as casual as she could. She *needed*
him, but certainly didn't want him to know that. 'We
think the time is upon us.'

'Gosh!' He engaged, apparently glad of the drama. 'The
boy child to end all witches.'

He didn't need all the plot points. 'Something like that.
I'm going to kill him.'

Hale rocked in his armchair, laughing like they were
old soldiers down the pub. 'Gods, I've missed you lot,
stuck in this naughty boys' home! Witches! Brilliant! You
glorious Valkyries, all hair and lightning. I pity mundanes,
I do.'

Helena fixed him in a sceptical glare. 'You pity them
so much you wanted to rule over them like a fucking
fascist despot.'

'We're better than them, Helena. You know that as well
as I do. Why are we cleaning up after them? It's beneath
us. We should make the rules, not follow them.' He
reclined, balancing one leg on the other. 'But then you do
that anyway, you always did.'

'HMRC . . .'

He grinned wolfishly. 'Oh come on! You ignore government! You treat mundane politicians like simpletons.

Rightly so, too. They are terrified of us. They ought to be.'

He was right. Her job, really, was to make sure witches and warlocks *behaved*. It was the eternal conundrum: witches were far more powerful than mundanes, but there were vastly *more* of them. Who'd win in a fight? No one, except Hale and his cronies, ever wanted to find out.

'So what is it you need me for?' he asked. 'Who is this little Damian, anyway?'

Helena certainly wasn't going to risk putting Theo and Hale together. That was what he did: turned people into weapons of mass destruction. 'I need to know how you did it.'

'How I did what?'

'Don't be coy, Dab. When we dated you were a fairly strong sentient. Level 3, perhaps. Then you take your gap year or whatever and return a Level 6 adept.'

His eyes flashed. 'I met some hugely inspirational people in Bali.'

'Oh, who didn't? Come off it. This child is powerful. Perhaps even more powerful than you were.'

There. He flinched. His ego wouldn't enjoy that. 'Is that so?'

'Frankly, he makes you look like an amateur.'

'Helena, let's save some time. How do you *think* I did it?'

She shrugged. 'You invoked demons.'

'Obviously. Which one?'

There were countless demons sponging off Gaia, trapped in her infinite nooks and crannies. 'You want me to guess?'

'You *know* me, Helena, intimately. Do you think I'd let just any foul, rancid entity occupy my body?'

He had a point. She remembered his disgust, many

moons ago, as she'd tucked into Chicken McNuggets while high on weed. The HMRC presently held the fourth edition of *The Modern Grimoire*, by far the most rigorous and accurate hierarchy of demons in the western world. Helena shrugged, running a list of the more potent demonic entities rumoured to run close to the surface of this reality. 'I don't know, Moloch? Mammon?' Mammon, a demon that fosters an obsession with money and material greed sounded about right for Hale.

Hale grinned again. 'Think bigger.'

No, Hale didn't want money. His family had more of that than he could spend in three lifetimes. He wanted *power*. The word came to Helena's lips almost of its own accord. 'Belial.' It was a statement, not a question. She felt a hollow open up inside.

'Bingo.'

Helena wasn't sure if he was kidding. Such a thing was . . . preposterous. 'You invoked the Master?'

Hale didn't flinch. 'Oh yes. You just thought it yourself. He turns men into weapons. *All the spirits of his lot are angels of destruction. They walk in the laws of darkness; towards it goes their only desire.* It's in the Dead Sea Scrolls. I became his sword.'

Helena stifled a gasp of horror. How could he possibly be inside her head? With all the protections Grierlings had to offer?

'How?' She could only muster a whisper.

'What's that? Prudish, prim Helena Vance, everything over the underwear, wants to know how I got royally fucked by one third of Satan?'

She said nothing in case she gave herself away.

'Well, my dear, you'll need an industrial vat of lubricant . . .'

'I'm serious, Hale.'

He leaned forward, very serious. 'You in the market for a demon guard dog, Helena? That's not how it works. Belial doesn't serve the witch, the witch serves the master. And how I served him. I miss it, having him fill me.' He sat back, the cat with the cream.

This was dirty work, make no doubt, but no one plays fair. No one. Every athlete dopes, every shortcut gets you there quicker. What kind of fool would she be if she was the only sucker playing by the rules? Rules she never wrote in the first place. 'This is pure business.'

'That's your problem, Helena. All work, no play.'

'I need a weapon to destroy this child. It's for . . .'

'The greater good?'

'The greater good,' she repeated. 'Now either you can tell me, or I can have sentients get it out of you the hard way.'

'Tease. You're going to have this conversation wiped from my head aren't you?'

'Of course.'

He raised a finger and summoned a leather-bound volume from the top shelf. It floated to Helena's outstretched hands. 'They let you keep books of demonic invocation?' she asked, her voice shrill.

'I wish. Look in the back.'

It was a fairly standard book of forest wildlife, in Latin, but tucked in the spine was a business card being used as a bookmark. Helena pulled it free. 'What is it?'

'An address for a rare book dealer in Rye. Archibald Frampton. He has a highly contraband collection of illicit texts. Real top-shelf stuff. You'll be appalled. Can I watch your face while you read them?'

'Absolutely not, but thank you for your invaluable

service to HMRC,' she said sarcastically. She slipped Frampton's address into her pocket and went to exit.

'Helena, wait,' Hale said, suddenly serious, no bolshy veneer. 'You don't want to invoke Belial.'

'Don't I?'

Hale stood between her and the door. She shouldn't have let that happen. She was trapped. 'You're a good woman. If things were different . . .'

She laughed harshly. 'I'd be Mrs Helena Hale?'

He shook his head and came closer. She felt his breath on her ear. 'If I had my time over, I might do things differently. He is absolute power. There's nothing of me left, Helena, I lost myself entirely to Him. You see here a shell. A woman like you is too good to lose by far.'

She was so tired. She could feel those tears behind her nose again. Not tonight, though. *Good. Goodness. Moral purity.* Such admirable traits, but traits that would see her daughter, her coven, burn in a field. Goodness is both abstract and subjective. 'I have to do this,' Helena said quietly. 'I've got to stop the prophecy from coming true.'

'Whatever the cost?'

'I think so.'

Hale looked almost disappointed, his smirk gone. 'That's what I thought. Good luck with it.' His mouth curved once more. 'Now! Before you go, do you fancy a quick fuck? It's been an age, and I always felt you and I had unfinished business.'

With her limited capabilities, she slammed him into the bookcase with a sharp, stiff gust of wind. 'In your dreams.' She banged on the cell door to be let out.

'I know you want to,' Hale said, picking himself up. And, of course, she did.

Chapter Thirty-Eight

THE PROBLEM WITH PSYCHICS

Niamh

There was a newfound light-footedness to Theo that was lovely to behold. Any sentient can tell you that secrets weigh more than your routine thoughts, and Theo had been carting a whopper around. Now she moved brightly around the cottage, galloping up and down the stairs, chasing the dog in the fields, feeding carrots to the ponies that stuck their heads over the back wall. Her head, once such a quagmire, was now occupied – mostly – by whatever song had been on the radio in the car.

Presently, Holly and Snow were in the back seat of the Land Rover while Theo was up front with Niamh. Halifax was about a half hour's drive from home through Sowerby Bridge and had malls with all the high-street stores that Hebden Bridge didn't. Niamh actually loved that Hebden Bridge was all quirky independent shops, but could see why Holly, Snow and Theo wanted a day of grubby capitalism. There had been days, when she was a teenager, that Niamh had wished she could sit outside a McDonalds with a McFlurry and flirt with boys instead of preparing for life in HMRC too.

As for Snow, it didn't seem fair to punish her for her mother's opinions, although Niamh was hyper aware she could well still be relaying messages back to Helena. Well, good. Let her tell her that Theo is a regular teenager who likes shopping and burgers and gossip and laughter. Maybe that's what Helena needed to hear.

For now, Theo was sticking with Theo, but was keen to try she and her pronouns, albeit uncertainly. Niamh had assured her that there was no need to be certain of anything. Most of the *adults* in her life were still clumsily figuring out their personal riddles. She felt it a tad steep that Theo was expected to have her ducks in a row at fifteen simply because she was trans. The way Niamh saw it, using different pronouns made fuck all difference to a single soul in this world aside from Theo. And for her, it seemed to mean a whole lot.

Niamh parked up in one of the shopping-centre car parks and they first went for veggie burgers before hitting the shops. Niamh, Snow and Holly acted as a human shield to allow Theo – androgynous anyway with her long hair and kohl eyes – to peruse the 'girls' clothes' shops.

What the feck were 'girls' clothes' anyway, thought Niamh. There she was in skinny jeans and a stripy t-shirt. She looked like a ginger *Where's Wally*. Now that Theo identified as a girl, was she meant to don a pink tutu or something? Still, Theo seemed utterly transfixed. Waves of sugary glee washed off her, it was quite potent and Niamh took a step back. They'd agreed a budget back at the cottage and Theo's head had spun with gratitude.

Kid in a candy shop. Niamh was delighted to be Willy Wonka, albeit less creepy, she hoped.

Theo seemed especially keen on accessories and jewellery. She asked if she could get her ears pierced and Niamh saw no reason why not and gave the consent the girl in the piercing parlour required. Theo only winced slightly as the girl punctured her earlobes and Niamh mused about how far they'd come in just a couple of months.

While the kids picked out juices at the insanely overpriced juice bar, Niamh gave Annie a quick call. 'Hello! I'm just in Halifax with the kids. Is there anything you need?'

'Oh hello love, glad you called actually.'

'Yeah? What can I get you?'

'Oh, nothing like that, but I have a message for you. You were in my dreams last night.'

Niamh groaned. 'Oh, go on then, what now?'

'I dreamed about fire and water. You were trying to push at fire with your hands. Just remember that's not how to douse a flame.'

Niamh adjusted the knot of hair on her head. 'OK?'

'Aye, that was it. I don't know when you'll need to know that but know you can't fight fire. Water extinguishes fire just by merit of being water.'

That was no more or less enigmatic than any of her visions. Niamh filed it away for later. 'Got it. But do you need anything in town? I can drop by later.'

'No, I'm all right, thanks pet. I've everything I need.'

Niamh saw the kids trip through the faux marble mall, noisily taking up their space, giant smoothies in hand. 'Well, how about I cook something delicious tonight? OK, how about I cook *something*? I can pick you up on our way home.'

'That's very kind, love, but I've already got a visitor tonight.'

'No worries, soon though.'

'Aye.'

'OK, the kids are back and we have about ten more identical high-street stores to plunder. I'll come by for tea tomorrow, OK?'

'You will. I love the bones of you, Niamh Kelly.'

Niamh smiled, feeling a warmth inside. 'I love you too, Annie. Speak soon.' She hung up and addressed her gaggle of girls. 'OK, which polyester hellhole is next?'

The next store was, for want of a better word, *witchy*. Its signature style was grungy smocks in monochromatic hues. Snow said this was her favourite and it seemed to be up Theo's street too. Theo picked out her first dress – a modest, billowy affair with spaghetti straps.

Can I try it on?

Of course.

The changing rooms were tucked away in the corner, so she and Snow both took items in the two spare cubicles. Niamh and Holly got comfy on the distressed leather sofa, no doubt set aside for husbands and boyfriends to evaluate their partners' fashion choices.

As the girls changed, the third booth opened up and a familiar woman stepped out. It took Niamh a minute to remember who she was. It was only when she saw Holly stare after her that the penny dropped.

It was Jessica Summers, the receptionist from Harmsworth House and the woman Jez Pearson regularly fucked in the arse.

Holly's face was a picture of confusion. 'Niamh? Who was that?'

At once, Niamh put up a vast white wall around her thoughts. 'Who?'

'That woman with the long hair. I've seen her before.'

Niamh was torn between lying to the girl and protecting her. The knowledge about Jez's affair had only brought her turmoil. 'I . . . she, um, lives in Hebden Bridge. I've seen her around too.'

'No,' Holly said wistfully, the tiles sliding into place. 'She's in my dad's head. I've seen her. And then abject horror spread across Holly's face as she read Jessica's mind.

'Holly, don't do that!'

But it was too late. If she'd seen what Niamh had seen in Jez's mind it was all over. 'Is my dad . . . ?'

'Holly . . .'

'Is he having an *affair*?' An *affair*: the word only someone who'd seen them in soaps, but had never had one, would use to describe one.

Niamh took both her hands in hers. Panic was gurgling up inside her head, a nasty orangey-brown hue. 'Oh Holly, my sweet girl. This is why your mother worries. Being one of us isn't always fun. Sometimes you see the real person behind the mask, and it's not always pretty. In fact, it usually isn't. We're all a little bit monster, you know?'

A tear rolled down Holly's face, her mouth an almost perfect upside-down U. 'Does my mum know?'

'No.'

'Did you know?'

'Yes,' Niamh said simply.

'We have to tell her!' Holly said, tears now falling freely.

'Holly wait. Listen to me. Can you read your mother?'

'A little bit. She tries to hide her thoughts from me.'

'Me too, but does she seem happy to you?'

Niamh gave her a sad, crumpled tissue from the bed of her handbag and Holly wiped her face. 'Yes, but . . .'

'But nothing. Do you think telling your mother would make her more or less happy?'

Holly's mouth gaped like a fish.

'Exactly,' Niamh finished for her. 'Your mum loves her life. She's got you and Milo and your dad and Annie. I decided a long time ago to use my gift to make people more happy, not less. It's hard sometimes, we put such a high premium on the truth when we're kids. But as you get older you realise you don't wanna hear the truth. The truth, more often than not, is feckin' awful.'

'But . . .' Holly was flailing, both inside and out. 'How am I supposed to talk to my dad now? I *hate* him.'

She didn't, though, and being a witch wasn't all herb gardens and crystals. All witches must learn the hard way that their powers come with a huge catch. Oracles living out of time; elementals finding every sad day is met with rain; healers navigating the inevitability of sickness and death; and sentients hearing things they'd rather not hear. It's not a tap you can turn on and off.

Instead, Niamh did what she always did. She used her gift to make someone more happy, not less. She cupped Holly's cheek in her palm and delicately placed a fingertip to her temple.

It took only a moment and the memory of Jessica Summers was wiped from Holly's mind. For how long depended very much on Jez's dirty mind. As Holly got older she'd learn not to peek in people's heads uninvited. No one, as a rule, is thinking anything nice.

Niamh wiped away her tears. The curtain to Theo's cubicle slid open and she shyly emerged in the black dress.

Holly's head snapped up. 'Oh wow!' she said enthusiastically. 'That looks so cute!'

Niamh remained on the sofa in the man crèche. She'd just done a terrible thing. She inhaled through her nostrils and reassured herself that it was for a greater good.

Chapter Thirty-Nine

QUEEN HEREAFTER

Helena

It was dusk as Helena reached the periphery of Hardcastle Crags. She saw her phone buzzing on the top of her handbag and willed Sandhya not to hang up. 'Wait, wait, wait . . .'

She parked up and grabbed her handset. 'Hello.'

'It's done,' Sandhya said simply.

'Can you show me?'

It would *probably* have been easier to FaceTime, but on this occasion, Helena wanted to see it for herself. She closed her eyes and waited a moment, turning off the engine of her father's Jaguar. Her own idle thoughts clouded over and took shape, receiving Sandhya's sight in her mind's eye.

The Mermaid Inn in Rye was a toffee-tin medieval tavern dotted with history. The ghosts of smugglers who ran rum, whisky, tea and coffee all over the south of England were still said to haunt the bedchambers. Helena wasn't sure she believed in ghosts, but the beams and bricks dated back to 1420, plenty old enough to channel terrific energy, so it remained popular with witches and warlocks.

Sandhya descended into the cellar from the timber-framed dining room, now filled with confused tourist diners who would each require wiping. She passed several HMRC witches in their official capes, the women trying to keep everyone calm following the raid.

Jen Yamato guarded a white-bearded man, hands now in silver cuffs. 'You can't fuckin' come in here and take my stuff, that's my fuckin' stuff!' he spat through nicotine-yellow teeth. Archibald Frampton, Helena presumed. The smugglers had never left.

Yamato read him his rights. 'Mr Frampton, you are under arrest on suspicion of being in possession of controlled demoniac items. You do not have to say anything, but it may harm your defence . . .'

Sandhya left Yamato to it and looked down through an open trapdoor in the beer cellar. As she carefully climbed down the ladder, Helena saw what she saw: a concealed cubbyhole stocked with a myriad of leather-bound volumes, shrunken skulls, human and animal embryos in canopic jars, brown bottles filled with what looked like controlled potions. It was an entire black market for the discerning witch.

Show me the books.

Sandhya turned her attention to the bookshelf. *A Treatise on Demons, Daemon Wiccecræft, The Satanic Lexicon, Crowley's Book of Shadows, The Sumatran Grimoire, Invocation of the Spirit, The Gospel of Lilith.*

There. *The Gospel of Lilith* was said to contain the most detailed recount of how Satanic Trinity had been captured, divided and contained. Helena said nothing as Sandhya continued to scan the shelves.

Seize and impound them all. Deliver everything to the HMRC vault.

They had enough evidence to put Frampton in Grierlings for a decade at least.

Good work, Sandhya.

Helena dragged her mind back into the vehicle. It was like waking yourself from an especially vivid dream and it took her a minute to sober up. Spots of rain started to tap on the windscreen. Helena took a deep breath. Some parts of her job were awful. She'd never really understood the phrase: was it the book or the buck that stopped with her?

But that's why she was High Priestess. She remembered what her mother had said: she was willing to do the things that others were too weak to contemplate. She looked inside herself, finding that steel. Helena Vance was *strong*. Helena Vance was *brave*.

She could do this. She had to.

What job doesn't come with bad days?

She locked the car and took the treacherous forest stairs down to the watermill. It had been a long time since she'd been here. A palpable nostalgia started to mist up in her and she pushed it back. She remembered the swing, and the wishing well and the cats, and the sleepy rush of Hebden Beck in the background.

No. It was only a house.

Find the steel.

She knocked on Annie's door. 'It's open, love,' the old woman called from inside.

As ever, she was greeted by the odour of cat piss seconds before the first cat came to see her. 'It's just me,' Helena said, finding Annie sat in front of a roaring fire, a pot of tea already brewing next to the chess board between two mismatched cups.

'Oh aye, I knew you'd be paying a visit.' And that was *why* she was paying her one. Annie wore a candy-pink wig and a lemon mohair cardigan. Her pale grey eyes stared into the hearth, the flames dancing across her gaze. Kindling snapped and cracked. 'It's Earl Grey with lemon isn't it? Have I got that right?'

Helena couldn't drink the woman's tea. 'Do you know why I'm here, Annie?'

'I do.' She didn't look away from the fire.

'Did you tell anyone I was coming?'

'No,' Annie said with a sigh. 'You'd have killed them too.'

'Then you should also know how sorry I am.' Helena was surprised at the calm in her voice, and in Annie herself. The whole cottage had the expectant hush of Christmas Eve.

'Is that right?'

'Yes. You have to believe that.' Her insides felt heavy, waterlogged. She so dearly wished there was another way. The next few days were critical and – fact was – Niamh, or Leonie, or Chinara could stop her from completing her mission. And that wouldn't do when the stakes were so high. A couple of regrettable tasks, and then things could go back to normal. But if Irina could see the things she was contemplating, then so did Annie. The difference was that Irina wouldn't alert them.

This was not what she wanted. No one would want this.

Helena prided herself on having an analytical, problem-solving brain, but even she couldn't see a way around this . . . hurdle. A sentient can't wipe memories that haven't happened yet, or she'd simply get Robyn to erase the future from Annie's head. If only it were that simple.

Now Annie turned to face her. 'Helena, my love, I know what you *think* you have to do, I've seen the path ahead of your feet, but I do hope you might change your mind.'

The sadness in Helena was a tumour, growing and swelling in her chest the longer this went on. But it was the least she could do, to hear her out. 'What do you see?'

Annie huffed down her nostrils. 'The problem with your lot is no one will ever admit they're wrong. If you're out for a walk on the moors and it starts to rain, you turn back, you don't keep on flipping going until you sink in the mud, do you? Helena, pet, it's not too late to turn back.'

She repeated herself. 'Please. Tell me what you see, Annie. Do I stop Leviathan?' If she succeeded in this, not a witch on earth would blame her for what she was about to do.

But she stubbornly shook her head. 'There is nothing in this world that doesn't change with time. I remember when you became High Priestess, we all saw fifty glorious years. A golden age for witches.' Helena remembered it well. It had been Annie who championed her appointment. 'But then – as you know – a few years back, things changed because all things are destined to do so. To prominence came a *Sullied Child*, the catalyst who would change everything.'

'For the worse!'

'Life is impermanent!' Annie hissed, spittle flying from her lips. 'Everything changes, and nothing stays the same. The more we fight change, the more it fights us.'

Helena felt like there was cement in her veins. 'I can't let what it is to be a witch die.'

The old woman ignored her. 'And those are our spider-webs on the breeze. One where Theo becomes a powerful witch, possibly the most powerful witch in a generation, and one where Helena Vance ends a child's life, and we revert back to that glorious dynasty we all foresaw. But here's the thing with threads: they all get tangled up in the storm. Who knows where one ends and another begins? What if they're a knot, one that can't be undone, whatever action Helena Vance takes.'

'What does that mean?'

'I already said, love . . . the arrival of Theo changed your fate, and removing her might not change it back. You create a new thread, a strange new yarn. You have no way of knowing.'

Helena was too hot. It almost felt like the fire was in her chest. She reached out a hand and extinguished the flames in the hearth. 'I have to take a stand.'

'Why, love?' she asked, very sincerely.

'Because it's what I believe is right.'

She gave a distasteful tut. 'All these abstract things people fight about: *borders, beliefs*. Ephemera. You're kicking over sandcastles, dear. Just know they will fight you back,' Annie said, her mouth a grim line.

Helena knew just who she meant. 'How will they know? Niamh, Leonie and Elle don't work for HMRC. They don't have access to my oracles. You were the only one who could warn them, and you chose not to.'

Annie nodded and finished her tea. 'Aye, I know that too.'

Helena noticed the first cloud of Annie's breath in the air. 'You never did like me, did you?'

Annie said nothing, which said a lot.

Helena went on. 'I used to think it was because you didn't like my mother or because we came from money, but now I wonder if you always knew this day would come.'

The old woman pulled her cardigan closer around herself, shivering so hard she convulsed. Helena, of course, did not feel the chill. 'This bleak thread was always there for Gaia to see, yes, but make no mistake, Helena, this is a choice you're making.'

The cats, one by one, retreated for the stairs or catflap, the cottage becoming much too cold for comfort. The windows frosted over.

'I don't see any other way.' Helena felt her voice wobble. 'I so wish this were avoidable.'

Annie's lips turned blue, delicate ice crystals forming on her eyelashes and brows. 'Please . . . it doesn't have to be this way . . . I'm not ready to go, Helena.'

The woman had had her years in abundance. Helena had to think of the future, not the past. Annie, as an oracle, should know that better than anyone. Progress is painful, there was always going to be collateral damage. Helena closed her eyes and plunged the temperature below minus thirty. 'It's for the coven. I'm so sorry.'

Outside the ramshackle cottage, the waterwheel froze to a halt, thick with ice.

Chapter Forty

ANNIE

Niamh

Last night, Luke had come over and they had watched some made-for-Netflix trash about a possessed rocking horse while the kids all had a sleepover at Elle's. More importantly, they'd had red wine and a Chinese takeaway *without* having sex. She had wanted to, and it would have been an easy transition from seated on the sofa to horizontal on the sofa, but she wanted to prove a point – to herself, not to him.

Things were changing. She had not foreseen Theo's arrival – who could have? – but perhaps she was the catalyst she'd needed: something huge to snap her out of the routine she'd clung to since Conrad died. Make no mistake, she'd very much needed that routine. Some days it had only been that rigid track that stopped her from derailing entirely. Safe, certainly, but stagnant.

Now that Theo had taken a sledgehammer to her carefully curated snowglobe existence, perhaps she could rebuild and factor in Luke too. What an odd little family they would be: the Irish witch, the Yorkshireman and the transgender teen prodigy. She'd watch *that* direct-to-Net-flix film.

As Heptonstall village stirred, Niamh stopped by the new trendy bakery and picked up a couple of loaves for Annie as well as some coffees and cinnamon buns for breakfast. Theo was still at Elle's – apparently they'd stayed up much too late dicking around with Snow's Ouija board – so she'd pick her up after she'd seen Annie.

She drove to Midgehole, parked up and navigated the stone stairs. The May sky was almost summer blue, but the steps were wet. It must have drizzled in the night and Niamh took care not to slip. When she reached the water-mill, it took her a moment to realise the wheel wasn't turning. That wheel, as Annie was keen to tell anyone who would listen, had only stopped twice in over sixty years.

Niamh frowned. Why there were *icicles* rapidly melting on the mossy green planks was anyone's guess. 'Annie?' Niamh called, knocking. 'Did you know the wheel's stuck?'

There was no answer, so she let herself in. She recoiled at once. It wasn't the smell this time, it was the temper-ature. The cottage was bitterly cold. 'Annie?'

Annie, despite their protestations, had never had central heating installed, but there was a fireplace in every room. That said, last night had been warm enough to sleep with the window open an inch, so Niamh was at a loss.

Her body was so small, Niamh almost overlooked her. She was folded over in her armchair next to the coffee table. 'Oh gods . . .'

Niamh dropped the brown paper bag from the bakery and went to her side. She was stiff, and cold, her wig in her lap. Not flinching, Niamh put the wig on her scalp, because Annie would *never* be seen without it. Not ever, and certainly not now. Niamh rearranged it on her head, smoothing it around her face. One slipper was on, one was off. A cup of tea was capsized on the stone floor.

The cats nervously approached, mewling, almost asking Niamh why their mother was motionless. Their little minds were curious, confused.

The initial numbness wore off. How could this be? Niamh felt everything, everything hopeful and joyous, drain out like there was a puncture in her. 'Oh Annie, no,' Niamh said. 'Not you.'

Her skin was deathly pale. Niamh summoned as much healing energy as she could to her hands, but it seemed to flow around Annie, as if she were a pebble in the beck. There was no life in her to redirect.

Instead, Niamh awkwardly embraced her, resting her head on Annie's itchy cardigan. 'Fuck. Annie, I'm so sorry. You shouldn't have been alone. I'm so so sorry, Annie.' As tears clouded her vision, she tried to access what was left of Annie's mind, desperate to know if she was scared, or sad, or even aware of what was happening. There was nothing, the fat nothing of death. 'Annie, please come back. We love you so much.'

Niamh's mind wandered to *that* place, urgent and outraged. She could. She could if she wanted to, she didn't for a second doubt she could. But she would not. She *should* not. A witch must not peek behind the curtain.

'Did you know?' she breathed in Annie's ear. 'Did you know how much we love you? I hope you knew.' Tears ran off her cheeks and splattered noisily onto the book on her lap, one of her many diaries. She had died writing her final visions. That was Annie.

Niamh took the book from her knee. There was only one word scrawled – a childlike scrawl at that – on the otherwise blank page.

The word was *Ciara*.

Chapter Forty-One

THE WITCH'S GRAVEYARD

Elle

For centuries, a witch could not be buried on consecrated ground. This was for no other reason than superstition and prejudice. Many women, some of them witches, some of them not, and a great many illegitimate babies were instead buried on the fringes of church graveyards, just beyond the perimeter wall.

Elle knew her grandmother wouldn't have wanted a church burial even though those laws had long since gone. Instead, they gathered at Annie's ancestral home – the Demdike Cottage on the estate of Malkin Tower Farm in Blacko, some thirty minutes outside Hebden Bridge. It had been many years since Annie – or any witch – lived where the original Malkin Tower had been, but the present owners knew her grandmother well and had agreed without hesitation to allow the burial to take place in the garden.

Niamh, sitting to her left, clutched her hand. They were seated in a broad horseshoe shape around the grave. The hole in the ground was tucked away in a quiet corner on the hillside. In time, sheep would graze over her, as she looked out over the Lancashire hills. 'She'd love this,' Niamh whispered. 'Everything is perfect.'

Elle nodded, because if she tried to speak, she'd cry. Niamh was right, something told her Granny would approve. *Malkin Tower*, she had once told Elle, *was called that after 'mawkin'. Do you know what a mawkin is? It's a nasty old word for a slovenly woman, a classless woman or a whore. That's what they called us.*

The whore's tower where the Pendle witches had held their masses was long gone – although the remnants remained on the farm – but it felt right that Annie was back with her ancestors. The mawkins. Annie was a proud mawkin.

Elle took a deep breath. She had to get through this day. Just six more hours and she could break, hide under the duvet for a week.

Her mother, Julie, had flown back from Cyprus, and was presently seated next to Milo on the far side of Jez to her right. Although her brother only lived the other side of Bradford, Elle had arranged the whole funeral alone, with Julie on hand to tell her how wrong she was getting it. *A field!* She'd wept. *We can't bury my mother in a field!* She'd relented only hours before Niamh was going to convince her in a slightly more underhand fashion.

Julie wept noisily, sobbing into a handkerchief. It was all very reality TV. Julie had been mortally embarrassed of Annie, ashamed of the family name, taking three different husbands' surnames and eloping to Cyprus with a waiter some fifteen years ago, not long after Elle had married Jez. She hardly knew Milo and Holly and didn't like them making a mess of her house in Limassol. In Julie Loukanis's world, things had to LOOK GOOD and it wouldn't LOOK GOOD if she wasn't the saddest person at her mother's funeral.

The service would be carried out by Tom Redferne, another descendent of Pendle. He was a gentle, middle-aged warlock. A primary school headteacher by day and shamanic leader by night. He and his husband very much spurned both coven and cabal, something Annie had always respected. He'd reached out to Elle the day after Niamh found her, ten days prior.

'And now we pop our beloved Annie back into the earth,' he said in a chirpy Scottish accent. 'She will once more be at one with Gaia. Annie will live on in the worms and birds, in the air we breathe and the water we drink. We don't know where her quintessential Annieness is now, but we will each of us remember how she enriched our lives, how she steered us right. Through our own kindness, humour and wisdom, we will share Annie with those dear to us too, and then our children will teach their children. In us, Annie Device lives on and on. Let's face it, there's no getting rid of that old witch, is there?'

There was a polite chuckle. Elle did not chuckle. She was stony. Everything was unacceptable. She wouldn't let her mother see this. She let go of Niamh and Jez's hands. Without saying a word, she stood and briskly walked to the cottage. She let herself in through the back door and went directly to the bathroom. She folded down the toilet seat and sat on it.

She cried. She tried very hard to make no sound, and it came out in strange raspy stabs. She hadn't even had time for a cup of tea with her that last time she'd seen her; when she dropped off her medicine. Too busy with some trivial shit that she couldn't even remember now. She was a goldfish.

In her haste, she'd forgotten to lock the door. She didn't even know Niamh was there until she felt warm hands rubbing her shoulders. 'Let it out,' Niamh said. 'You're emotionally constipated. It can't be good, doll.'

Elle clung to her friend, finding a nook in her armpit and burying herself there. 'How?' she gasped. 'She was all alone, Niamh. None of us were there. She was all alone. They're saying she died of hypothermia! Hypothermia! How? I let it happen.'

She cried and cried, shaking with anger. How could this have happened? Never had she failed so badly. So blind. So ignorant. So stupid.

'It's not your fault,' Niamh said, rubbing her back. 'It's not your fault.'

Elle couldn't see who else's fault it was. And everyone knew. All those people sat outside knew. Everyone could see her for what she really was. A bimbo. A scrap of cheap tinsel. A fucking selfish bitch. A rotten, shallow imbecile. A callous, self-involved princess. The one thing she was meant to do well in this world was care for people. And she'd failed. She bottled the scream. Elle felt her insides squirm like eels, her innards repulsed at their host.

She had let Annie die in the cold.

All those spiteful children back in the day were right. Elle Device *was* a witch.

They took some time in the cottage bedroom. Working diligently in silence, Niamh reapplied the makeup Elle had cried off. 'Will people be able to tell?'

'It's a funeral,' Niamh said. 'They'd judge you more if you didn't cry.'

Elle smoothed down her black dress, the best of the twelve black dresses ASOS had delivered, and checked herself over in the mirror. If she was a pariah, she'd at least look nice. She'd aimed for Ginger Spice from the UN Ambassador years.

Why did it even matter?

This whole day felt like a circus somehow. A gory carnival for everyone to do and say the right things. To LOOK GOOD.

'Are you ready?' Niamh asked.

'Let's get this over with.'

The pair trudged downstairs, stopped every few paces by well-wishers. Annie was so well loved, dozens of witches and warlocks – and mundanes for that matter – had come to pay their respects from all over the world. Padma Baruwal, the High Priestess of India, was here. Helena hadn't left her side all day, which was about the only thing keeping Niamh from making a scene. About a hundred mourners milled around, diluting their chit-chat in sombre, library tones. Julie was with her half-brother and half-sister. Elle's eldest uncle – Annie's first son – had died in the Korean War which gave some indication of just how old Annie *really* was.

Elle had never quite understood the notion of the wake. Like, *you're dead, here's a mushroom vol-au-vent.* Weird. They fought their way through the kitchen, now a forest of finger foods, and into the yard that backed onto the field. Elle was surprised to see Luke stood with Jez, both gripping bottled beers self-consciously. Jez was dressed head-to-toe in black: black suit, black shirt, black tie. He looked like a bouncer.

'Luke!' Niamh exclaimed, apparently surprised to see him.

She kissed him chastely on the cheek. 'I didn't want to crowd you,' Luke said, his deep voice almost rattling through Elle's bones. 'But I wanted to be here. Elle, I'm so sorry about your grandma.'

Elle remembered herself. 'Thank you, Luke. Thank you for coming.'

'Lotta ladies here,' Jez said, trying to inject some levity. 'I was feeling outnumbered until Luke pitched up.'

Elle mustered a smile and gave Jez's hand a squeeze. He was trying so hard. Since Annie died, he'd gone into overdrive to try to cheer her up. Somehow it made her feel worse. She wasn't a car he could jump-start with cups of tea.

Up on the hill, she located Holly with Theo, Leonie and a few others up at the grave site. They'd formed a circle which meant they were trying something.

'What's Hol up to?' Jez said, a frown crinkling his brow – a reminder it was almost time for their biannual Botox appointment.

Luke too looked baffled. Niamh looked like she was about to say something, but Elle hopped in just in case. 'You know Leonie. It'll be some hippie nonsense. Let's go see.'

They left the boys to their beers and headed up the gentle slope of the farmer's field. 'You might need to wipe them,' Elle said. 'Again.'

Niamh shook her head. 'Not unless I absolutely have to. Elle, their heads will be Swiss cheese at this rate.'

'Can you wipe me, then? Just get rid of this whole year, please.'

Leonie, Chinara, Holly, Theo, Snow and Tom Redferne were crouched around the grave in a rough circle, hand in hand. 'What's the craic?' Niamh asked.

'We're folding her back into nature,' Chinara said softly, not looking away from the fresh mound of dirt. After a moment or so, shoots of grass sprouted up into daylight, blades unfurling for the gauzy sunshine. The muddy brown rectangle was soon a vibrant green. A few buttercups fought their way to the surface too. No one would ever know she was here, aside from the smooth, oval pebble with a subtle 'AD' engraved on it.

'I think something beautiful will grow here in time,' Tom said as they let go of each other. The Regeneration Ceremony was complete.

Leonie stood and pulled Elle into a tight embrace. 'No blame, no guilt,' Leonie said, reading her.

Elle said nothing because she'd only just redone her makeup.

'I mean it,' she went on. 'She fucking adored you. And I adored her.'

'She loved you too,' Elle said.

Chinara took her turn to hug Elle. 'Did Lee ever tell you about her pre-thirtieth breakdown?'

Elle smiled. That sounded so unlike Leonie. 'No!'

'I was proper shitting myself about getting old. And then I remembered Annie,' Leonie said. 'I thought about her life . . . everywhere she'd been, and everything she'd done. If that's what being "a crone" is all about, bring it.'

'I wish I'd known her better,' Chinara said, always so poised. Quite the opposite of her girlfriend. 'It sounds like she lived a lot of adventures.'

Elle nodded. Part of the reason she was such a personal disappointment. She looked back at her mother in the garden below, forcing guests to eat shitty prawn tempura and it was painfully clear which genes she'd inherited. Closer, she saw Helena making her way uphill to join them.

Leonie tensed first, putting herself between Niamh and Helena.

'Oh, hi,' Niamh said bitterly once she was in earshot. 'Did you come to kidnap my foster child again?'

Leonie, of all people, issued a quiet warning. 'Not now, babe.'

'I come in peace,' Helena said diplomatically. 'Elle, the ceremony was beautiful. Annie through-and-through.'

'Thank you, Helena.'

'It's so sad,' she went on. 'And Niamh, at times like this, we're reminded of what's really important in life: family and friendship. I do hope there's no hard feelings over . . .'

Niamh clung protectively to Theo's hand. 'If Annie was here, she'd tell you to go fuck yourself.'

'Niamh!' Leonie snapped. 'Bish, chill. Fuck's sake.'

'What's the deal, Helena? You don't expect us to believe you're not going to try something? We've known you forever and you don't like to lose.'

Elle stood alongside Leonie and Niamh, and thought about how that must look: like taking sides. As such, she repositioned herself between the two factions, not committing to any one stance. It didn't help, however, that Helena had really perfected that brand of smug, infuriating calm politicians used on BBC Breakfast. 'We can talk more, further down the line, but now is a time for mourning.'

'Let's talk now,' Niamh said. 'I'll start. Don't you think it's weird how our mostly healthy friend died of hypothermia in *May* with a basket full of firewood next to her hearth?'

'Niamh . . .' Now Chinara moved in to put some distance between them.

'What on earth are you suggesting?' Helena's eyes blazed and Elle felt the hairs on her arms stand up as the ions around them charged.

331

'Leonie, can you read her?' Niamh demanded.

'Niamh, you need to calm the fuck down. This is mad inappropriate, and if *I'm* saying that, you're in trouble.'

'But can you?' Leonie looked torn. 'Because I can't see anything. Helena, you've got so many walls up in your head, it's Fort Knox. Why? Why are you so keen to keep us out?'

'Are you seriously standing on Annie's grave and asking if I . . .'

Elle snapped. 'Will you just fucking stop? The pair of you!'

'Wow, my mum said fuck,' Holly muttered.

This was perfect, thought Elle. The last fortnight had been horrific, why not throw in a casual murder accusation? A cherry on the shit cake. It felt very soap opera. She was determined to keep it together. 'You know what, some of you were probably closer to my granny than I was, I'll admit that, but she would *not* want us fighting.'

Both Niamh and Helena paused, sheepish.

'She used to say *the patriarchy loves the sound of women bickering among themselves.* Isn't this *sad*? We used to be such good friends! Now, we can't even get together for an afternoon without World War III breaking out!' Leonie tried to take her hand, but she snatched it back. 'No! I know you all think I'm an idiot or whatever, but I really don't see why we can't just get along.'

She stood between Helena and Niamh. How could either of them possibly counter that? Instead, they stared each other down a moment longer, before breaking the staring contest. 'I'm sorry,' Niamh said, begrudgingly, the exact same way she had after she'd given Helena's Barbie doll some Sharpie lipstick.

Helena conceded. 'We're all hurting, Niamh. I am too.'

Niamh gave a curt nod. And that was that then. She'd averted the storm.

But Elle wasn't an idiot, not a jot, and she knew full well what was still brewing. She'd averted the storm *for now*. Like any mum she knew there were only so many times you can glue, stitch and patch things which are broken. Sooner or later, they go beyond repair.

Chapter Forty-Two

MATTERS OF OPPRESSION

Leonie

The third bottle of pinot noir may have been an error. Niamh was *drunk*, and on the threshold of Bad Drunk. Her teeth were blue and lips purple. Witches drink. Not *all* of them of course. To Leonie, it was very natural – grape and grain, fermentation. Witches had imbibed at rituals for as long as anyone thought to write anything down. The three of them – her, Chinara and Niamh – lounged around Niamh's dinky cottage snug, the crusts of a takeaway pizza idle in greasy boxes.

Niamh, down on the rug, was slurring. 'I mean, you sorta start thinking about why you're friends with someone you know? Like why *am* I friends with Helena? She's pushy, she's posh . . . I bet she's Tory too.'

That, thought Leonie, had never been in question. Small 't' if not capital 'T'.

'She does like her money . . .' Chinara added, her eyes peering over her wine glass from the sofa.

Niamh went on. 'All we have is years, you know? We've invested more years than we can walk away from. Does that make sense?'

It made perfect sense, and Leonie had asked the same thing of all of them many times. If they hadn't been bound by the oath they'd taken all those years ago, Leonie assumed she'd have remained friends with Niamh and Ciara – but very much doubted she'd have anything to say to Helena or Elle. 'It makes sense,' she said, tucked up under a blanket with Tiger at the other end of the settee. 'She's harmless though, right?'

'No one with that much power is harmless,' Chinara replied sombrely.

Her girlfriend, as ever, was right. She did have a blind spot regarding Helena. For whatever reason, the wine wasn't even touching the sides tonight. Leonie had felt nun sober since she'd got the news about Annie. Everything was sober, nothing was funny, nothing was fun. Someone had let all the air out of her tyres and now all she could do was grind herself along the asphalt.

Theo was upstairs reading an impressive pile of theoretical textbooks on the Craft, as well as some notable *Book of Shadows*, including Valentina's personal one. Leonie had brought it for her as a gift with her permission. The change in the girl had been evident as soon as Leonie had clapped eyes on her. Those tumultuous inky clouds in her head were now a melba sunset shade. A sense of resolution. The end of a marathon.

'OK,' Leonie went on. There was a hole in one of her socks and her big toe was poking through. 'I know you were hella mad earlier, but you don't *really* think that Helena is capable of causing harm? She wouldn't want to fuck her manicure!'

Niamh considered this. 'Gaia knows. God I'm too drunk for this. But . . . it's Helena! She's . . . ambitious.'

'Oh, fuck yes.'

Niamh went on. 'She's . . . determined. She's confident. Those are the good parts. But she's also dogmatic. And self-righteous. And inflexible. All-in-all, a bit of a cunt, to tell you the truth, Miss Jackman. She won't let this Sullied Child thing lie. No way.'

'You don't seriously think she hurt Annie though?' Leonie said, surprised at how immature her voice came out. She didn't want to believe that *anyone* could bring harm to that woman.

They looked at each other for a long time. Niamh said nothing, but Leonie saw a deep, almost acidic, uncertainty in her. Fuck, Niamh really thought she had it in her. 'She wouldn't,' Leonie said quietly.

'Fucking white women,' Chinara said abruptly, sloshing wine onto her crotch. 'No offence.'

'None taken,' Niamh said, toasting her.

'I have looked deep in myself to try to understand this fucking TERF shitshow, and I must say I am at a loss.' Chinara topped up her glass.

'I'm not,' Leonie said, holding out her glass for a refill. Perhaps this would be the one that sanded off the edges. 'This is said with no offence, Niamh—'

'None shall be taken . . .'

'Some white women struggle to see past their own oppression,' Leonie said. 'Look at the fucking suffragettes. Did they campaign for the rights of Black women? Or poor women? Did they fuck. Like, I get it, to be a woman in the patriarchy is inherently traumatic.'

Niamh folded her legs and shoved a cushion under her rear. 'You got that right.'

Leonie was on a roll now. 'From the second we're born we're made to feel insecure about our bodies, our choices, our lives. Then we hit puberty and all of a sudden we have to be both sexual and chaste at the same time, while our bodies are going fucking mental. We start leaking, for fuck's sake. Then, after we're covertly trained to conceal our excellence at school, we get to go work for men who don't understand literally any of those dilemmas, and think they're innately more skilled than us. They want you to be like men, but also not like men. It's a fucking trap. We're fucked as soon as the doctor says *hun, it's a girl.*'

'True, but I wouldn't choose to be a boy,' Chinara said. 'Would you?'

'Fuck no! I can love being a woman while also recognising it's traumatic. I fully think men are traumatised by masculinity too, but I don't know a woman who hasn't suffered because the system is fucking rigged.'

'I don't think women are defined by shared trauma,' Chinara said thoughtfully. 'We're *marred* by it, but I knew what it was to be a girl long before I experienced trauma. Like when did you know you were a girl?'

Leonie shrugged. 'I just knew.'

She turned to Niamh. 'Me too.'

Leonie took a sip of wine. 'And I'm betting Theo *just knew* too.'

'Yep, I saw her childhood. She knew.' Niamh nodded. 'You'd think, as witches, we'd fare better in the world, but I remember as soon as I got to college, one of the first year lecturers would talk to us as if we were simple. Like I remember him saying, *oh it's not all puppies and kittens, girls.* I was like *well fuck you mister*, and shoved my hand right in that cow's ass. All the way to the shoulder, just to prove a point.'

'Thanks, Niamh. Thanks for the visual.'

Chinara grabbed a handful of leftover M&S crisps Elle had forced them to take home from the wake. 'Maybe that's why Helena wants to police the coven. It's the last matriarchy.'

Leonie grimaced. 'Oh, fuck that. Who asked her to be the fucking ticket inspector? I do not doubt that Helena Vance has been through misogynist shit – even in her position – but she won't look past that. I have never *once* heard Helena acknowledge that life is *more* fucked for me,' she looked to her girlfriend, 'or you, because of our race, or because we're lesbians . . .'

She was getting angry. She stopped and took a breath, although she was comfortable in knowing Niamh was not the sort of white woman to tell her to *calm down* or *don't get angry*. She was reminded – as she often was when she least expected it – why she'd founded Diaspora. She turned to Niamh with a sly grin, 'Or you, because you're ginger as fuck.'

Niamh laughed ruefully. 'Truly, my bondage is great.'

'I want you to know . . .' Leonie reached for her hand, 'I am a ginger ally,'

'That means so much, thank you. We are *witches*,' Niamh said with more than a hint of pissed exasperation, 'and I know a fecking witch hunt when I see one. Scapegoating trans women, of all people, is the latest in a long line all the way back to Pendle. Poor women, old women, sex workers, Black women, lesbians, Muslims, travellers . . . and now trans women. Trans women! It's so baffling! I can honestly say the existence of trans people has never impacted on my entire life. As far as I know, I've encountered *three* of them, each a delight.'

'Amen to that. Have you *seen* the new Prime Minister?

Trans women are the least of our worries,' Chinara said. 'I've represented trans asylum seekers at work. No one would choose that path unless it was life or death.'

'And that's what it boils down to,' Leonie said. 'Helena's life is so fucking cushy that she has all the time in the world to muse on the potential theoretical, philosophical, academical ramifications of trans lives. Theo just wants to fuckin' *be*. Don't quite seem fair, does it?'

Maybe she was a *little* drunk. The cobbles outside Niamh's cottage were suddenly a lot harder to navigate. Her legs felt elastic.

'You OK there, Wobbly?' Chinara said.

'Fine, thank you!' She looped her arm through Chinara's. Just in case.

'You think she'll be OK?'

Leonie sucked in a big dollop of Yorkshire air. 'Oh, she'll be all right. She'll sleep it off.'

'I meant about Annie . . .'

'None of us will ever be OK about that, babe. I feel scared.' There was a long silence, Chinara giving her the time to do her thinking. 'Annie always knew what to do. Not just the future, but what we should do with it. It's like when you can't get signal for Google Maps. I don't know where to go. I don't know where I am.'

Chinara clutched her hand tight. They were safe to do so here. In Hebden Bridge, there was little (there's never *no*) danger of homophobia. It was the lesbian capital of the country. 'You can guide each other. You've got a lot of sisters.'

Leonie shook her head. The sky was obscenely starry again. 'I wanna go home.'

Chinara scrutinised her. 'You sure? I think Elle and Niamh could use the support.'

She did not doubt that, but there was some massive shit coming. The sort of massive shit that would block the U-bend and require a plumber.

'What?'

'Something's not right,' Leonie said, stopping in the silent square at the top of Heptonstall village. She thought back to that nightmare, all those weeks ago. That sense of total dread. And Ciara's presence troubled her too. What did that mean? She knew it wasn't possible, but what if – what if Ciara was somewhere else right now, someplace where time wasn't linear? Perhaps it wasn't just Gaia who could see what had been and what would be.

'I know that sounds like woolly oracle talk, but I'm telling you, my Spidey sense is fucking tweaked. Something is off here, and I wanna get out.'

'Leonie, listen to me,' Chinara said, very seriously. 'The war is over now. Life is good and we can put down roots. Nothing is going to happen to us. I sometimes think you do this—'

'Do what?'

Chinara folded her arms defensively. 'You create these coven dramas to avoid us making plans for the future.'

'No, I fucking don't!'

'Please don't raise your voice,' she replied. 'But I think it's true. It's always something, Lee. I understand. Adult life is perhaps even more terrifying than demons. *Those* you can fight. You can't fight growing up.'

'No . . .' Leonie could weep. She felt so misheard. OK, maybe that was a little true, but not this time, not now. This time it was real, she wasn't crying wolf. It was like smelling smoke, just a whiff on the wind. She hadn't been able to stop since Niamh had commanded her to read Helena at the funeral. 'It's Helena,' she confessed.

'It's always one of them.'

'Chinara, I mean it this time.' She took hold of Chinara's arms and looked her dead in the eye. 'Look at me. I'm serious.'

Chinara relented. 'Very well. What about her?'

'I . . . I didn't want to say this to Niamh, but there *is* something weird going on in her head. It's so quiet, so empty, like it's been sterilised with bleach. She's keeping her mind blank, working insanely hard to appear relaxed. Why?'

Chinara sighed deeply. 'I think you know her a lot better than I do. But I'd guess she's very used to being around sentients all day.' She smiled slyly. 'You think I don't put up obstacles for you?'

'Yeah, and don't you think I know it?'

'Leonie, I love you and I trust you. Where you go, I go. It's your call.'

They were only around the corner from the B&B. Leonie pulled Chinara towards home. Her head swam. OK, that last glass of wine *had* done the trick. 'Tomorrow, we're out of here. I don't know what she's up to, and I don't care.'

'Lee . . .'

'I don't. Let fucking HMRC eat itself. It's nothing to do with us. It never was.'

Perhaps some things were scarier than adulting after all.

Chapter Forty-Three

WOMEN

Niamh

Niamh dreamt stressful dreams of missing flights, losing Theo, offending Leonie and telling Elle about Jez's side piece. It was probably the wine, but also guilt. Many times, she dreamt of visiting Helena. In these vignettes, sometimes Helena apologised to her, and sometimes Niamh offered an olive branch.

She woke up more exhausted than when she'd gone to bed, with a dry mouth and bad breath. She hit the snooze button twice and decided her hair could get by on dry shampoo for one more day. It was a surgery day, but things were not right between her and Helena. Witches are, by definition, more intuitive, and Niamh woke up to the new day with a new mindset.

She couldn't leave things the way they were, and the longer she left it, the worse it would get.

That lunchtime, still in her scrubs, she left the clinic and drove into Hebden Bridge. She parked at the back of the Mill Croft building and cut across the main street to Venus Nails where Helena had told her she would be. A bell tinkled as she entered the beauty salon and she saw Helena was already receiving a manicure from a petite Thai woman in a facemask. There was only one other customer, getting her brows threaded.

Another nail technician greeted Niamh in a crisp white uniform. 'Hello, Miss, do you have a booking?'

'No . . .' The manicurist said she could fit her in, and Niamh took the station next to Helena. Niamh had to wear her nails short, a professional hazard of putting your fingers inside animals all day long, but they could still be a nice colour. 'Thanks for meeting me,' she told Helena.

The High Priestess seemed wary, even colder than usual. 'You're so dramatic lately, I didn't want to miss the third act.'

Niamh guessed she deserved that. She had now literally flown into her mother's kitchen and screamed at her at a funeral. 'I was surprised you're still here.'

'Getting a few things ready for solstice while I'm in town,' Helena said curtly.

The girl got to work on Niamh's nails, filing off the wonky edges. 'I wanted to apologise,' Niamh began. She infiltrated the minds of the manicurists, gently diverting their attention away from their conversation.

'I should think so. It was really fun explaining your outburst to my Indian counterpart. She saw everything, you know.'

'I'm sorry. Again.' Niamh had tried to prepare a script in her head all morning only now she was tongue-tied. Stage fright. 'You know, we've been friends a really long time.'

'We have.'

'This stuff with Theo seems like a real stupid reason to fall out, don't you think?'

Helena looked over. 'Well, I'd say that very much depends.'

Niamh had vowed to herself that there would be no more raised voices on this. 'OK, let's try a different approach. I think Theo's inclusion in the coven could be a positive thing.' Helena went to interrupt, but Niamh ploughed on. 'No, bear with me on this. I know you were hurt when Leonie established Diaspora, so why don't we take this opportunity to signal that HMRC is a modern institution that welcomes LGBTQ witches? Get ahead of the curve, like.'

Helena winced. 'We're going around in circles, Niamh. You're asking me to induct a transgender into a coven of women.'

At the word *transgender*, something flickered in the mind of the woman doing Helena's nails and Niamh realised she too was trans. On hearing the word, she became alert, like a deer sniffing the air for danger. Well that said it all, didn't it? A migrant trans woman from Thailand who had to serve the all-powerful Helena. Niamh, oh-so carefully, drew the woman's – Pranpriya was her name – attention away from their conversation, instead focusing her on the task, literally, at hand.

'Yeah, I think you should. HMRC has a reputation for being old and fussy. Let's modernise.'

Helena at least went to the effort to feign thinking, briefly casting her gaze to the ceiling. 'No. I don't think so.'

'What colour would you like, Miss?' Pranpriya asked Helena.

Helena scanned the acrylic nails glued to the colour board. 'Red please. Number twenty-three.'

There was a trace of sentience in Pranpriya. She was

– probably unconsciously – resisting her attempt to shield their conversation. Niamh wondered if she was aware of her ability. 'Oh, come on, Helena. Theo can be a test case.'

'I said no.' Helena *did* raise her voice, just a shade. 'It's very simple. Covens are for witches, cabals are for warlocks.'

'Theo is a witch. She says she is a girl and I believe her.'

'And I do not. I'm sorry, Niamh. Call me old-fashioned, call me names. I don't care. You can stick a pointy hat on his head and give him a broom if you want, but that child will never be a witch.'

'Can we not insult trans people please? Can we at least keep this civil?'

'I am being civil!' Helena said, admiring her new scarlet nails. 'But you want me to sacrifice my beliefs to be politically correct, and I'm just not prepared to do that. That *thing* will grow into a man, with all the correlating male appendages and I won't allow that in my coven.'

Niamh read Helena. Her head was a swirling grey mass. An oil slick on water, and just as dirty. This was hatred. Out here in Hebden, Niamh didn't see it very often and when she did, she was startled at how ugly some heads were. It was cancerous too, hate, how it infected reason and kindness. Sometimes it stemmed from a misguided sense of breathless panic; the notion of cuckoos coming to take *what's ours*. Sometimes it was fear of difference, plain and simple, and all witches knew what that was like. So why didn't Helena?

But Niamh, employing the rational part of her brain, knew hate was learned. The seeds had to be sown somewhere. 'Helena, what happened to you?'

Helena looked away from her nails and glared at her. 'What is that supposed to mean?'

'Who hurt you?'

There. A split second. The most fleeting glimpse inside Helena's head. A blink. Stefan, and the unmistakable green-brown sludge of *fear*. Stef hurt her. She was scared of him.

'Helena? Did Stef . . .'

'What? No! That's ridiculous.'

Stef had been ten years older than Helena, and very much an alpha at the cabal. Niamh had always assumed they were well-matched in that regard. It seemed unthinkable to Niamh that someone like Helena Vance could . . . but that's the thing with assuming, isn't it? 'Helena, you know you can tell me anything, right?'

'This is outrageous,' Helena said, but she was more flustered than Niamh had ever seen her. 'I can't believe you're dragging Stef into this absurd conversation. He's been dead for almost a decade.'

Helena's mind was now panicked, shards of memories flashing in a rapid slideshow. Some were the Stef Niamh knew: the bombastic, gregarious showman, always ready with a filthy anecdote. She saw a glimpse of the lavish surprise party at the Lowry he threw for Helena on her twenty-third, and his very public proposal, flash mob and all. But she also witnessed a Stef she had not seen before. A secret Stef.

The more she tried to keep Stef out of her head, the more he surfaced.

She felt Helena's anguish; the tears; the wrought knots in her stomach; the dread that he would arrive home in a bad mood. He was not a shouter, but a *sulker*; the excruciating torment of the Silent Treatment; a man who threatened to hurt *himself*.

To see such turbulence in Helena of all people was

terrifying. How hard must she work to keep this hidden? Niamh felt a tear pool in her eye. All those walls in Helena's mind suddenly made a lot more sense. 'Helena . . .'

'Enough!' she pounded her fist atop the workbench, and both manicurists recoiled. The skies outside grew black as night. Helena spoke through gritted teeth. 'I will not have you drag my dead fucking husband through the dirt to serve your sick little agenda.'

Niamh shook her head. Helena should not be forced to speak on this. 'I . . . OK. But I need you to see that Theo is not what you're scared of. That's just not fair, Helena. She is not that *thing*, that thing we all fear. She's a confused teenage girl who needs all the help she can get.'

Helena's rage faded, although her head ran scarlet. 'We'll have to agree to disagree. Like when you preferred NSYNC to Backstreet Boys.'

Niamh was momentarily speechless. 'I don't think that's quite the same, and you know it. This is a fundamental thing. It's about a person's right to live as themselves.'

'You're not going to change my mind, Niamh.'

'Very well,' Niamh said sadly, 'then I think we're done.'

'What does that mean?'

'I . . . I respect the work you do at HMRC,' Niamh would not mention Stefan again, 'and I am truly, truly sorry if I ever failed when it came to being there for you, but I'm not sure I can be friends with you, Helena.'

'I beg your pardon? You're breaking up with me?'

'Not what I said. My door is always open to you, always, but only if you can extend kindness to Theo.'

Helena's flint eyes were impassable. Niamh peeked inside once more and there was only ironclad certainty. She was right and Niamh was wrong. That's all there was. She'd turned to stone.

Pranpriya flinched, getting gel nail polish on Helena's thumb. Helena tutted. 'Sorry, Miss,' she said, and efficiently wiped it clean.

The other girl hadn't actually started on Niamh's gel nails yet. 'You know what, I'm OK,' she told her. 'I'll pay in full anyway, but they'll just get ruined at work. Thank you.' She took her hands back.

'If that's how you want to leave things,' Helena sighed, 'I suppose you've made your choice.'

'No. Theo had no choice in who she is. *You* made the choice to exclude her.'

Helena's polite demeanour slipped for a split second and her mouth curled into an ugly shape. She said nothing.

'If you won't help us, just stay away from us. You have no business in Hebden Bridge any more.'

'You are not his legal guardian, Niamh,' she said smugly.

'Is that a threat?'

'Just stating facts.'

'So am I. Theo can stay with me for as long as *she* likes. I'll apply for guardianship if need be. If HMRC comes anywhere near us . . .'

Now Helena smiled. 'Is *that* a threat?'

Niamh collected her handbag, phone and car keys from the little salon table. 'Yes, it is.'

Chapter Forty-Four

INVOCATION

Helena

Night is thickest between two and three in the morning. Dawn is hours away and no one has any honest business being awake.

Helena banked on it.

Naked and barefoot, she strode into the pasture. The sky was overcast with thin cloud and the waxing moon was oddly lilac. Despite her preparedness, she was nervous, her stomach a tight knot.

There had been many, many instances over the last couple of weeks where she'd questioned this course of action, swinging back and forth like a pendulum, but she always came back to the oracle's visions. She'd been back to Amy, the young oracle, numerous times and the portent remained the same: the total annihilation of all witches.

She had no other choice.

People. People *let you down*. It's a nice surprise when they don't, and Helena knew she had HMRC at her disposal but – as evidenced by the betrayal of her friends – you can only ever truly rely on yourself. Even Annie had once told her we enter this world as we leave it: screaming and alone.

Annie.

No. Focus.

If Helena was going to do this, she would need rare firepower. You fight fire with fire, any elemental can tell you that. She needed a weapon. She needed to become a weapon. A weapon that, if needed, could better Leviathan himself.

And, as far as any witch knew, there were only two demons in the world who could match him.

As per the rules, she carried everything before her in a wooden chest wrapped in black silk. Everything had to be handled meticulously, treated like the Christmas china. The chest and its contents had lain under her bed for seven nights, familiarising itself with her essence as she slept.

She was too anxious to notice the cold. Even in late May, the core of the night was cold and pearls of dew formed on the grass. Helena knelt and placed the chest before her. She unwrapped the silk and opened the lid. A muscular oud scent greeted her, hitting the back of her throat.

If she stopped, even for a second, to dwell on things now, she'd lose her nerve. She did what she'd always done: she *got on with it*.

First things first. She took out a paper bag filled with salt and poured it all around her in a circle, about two metres in diameter. A *Zisurrû* was especially useful when summoning; when one put out a call to the spirit realm, anything could – and would – respond. Tonight, Helena sought only one, highly specific, conversation. The circle ensured she'd be safe from any curious gatecrashers during the conjuring.

She unfurled a second silk, and took out the bones. They belonged, once, to her grandmother. The texts had been vague in the ingredients: the 'bones of the ancestors' could well mean anything, but Helena thought it best to take it literally. Exhuming her grave had been easy enough. She'd simply manipulated the earth to bring them to the surface. As instructed – and she'd learned the method word for word – she scattered the bones randomly onto the ground in front of her.

This was all part of the test. Was she worthy of Belial? A tinge of arrogance cut into the doubt – if *Dabney Hale* was deemed acceptable, she definitely was.

She was dreading the next part. From the chest she selected the small, blue glass vial containing the exact measurement of *Jugo de Bruja* she would require to enter the trance state. This meant losing control, something Helena wasn't a fan of. From this point forward, it was all out of her hands. All she could do was pray her sober foreplanning would compensate for however she reacted to the hallucinogen.

It tasted rancid, like drinking a muddy puddle, with the consistency of cold espresso. She winced and swallowed it back hard. She paused in case she vomited it straight back up, but after a second, she shuddered and it stayed in her stomach. Already, she felt a spicy warmth radiating from her gut.

She moved fast. She wanted to complete the ritual before the drug kicked in.

The dagger was at the bottom of the chest. She'd been expecting something more bling, more ceremonial, but it was old, sharp and efficient, the blade no more than an inch thick. This next part wasn't going to be especially nice, she understood that, but already her heart seemed to be pumping hotter blood to her head. Was that the point? The *Jugo de Bruja* was a distraction from what was to come?

Don't dwell on it.

She jabbed her left index finger with the dagger's tip. Despite the drug, it hurt. Like it was lipstick, she smeared her blood carefully around her mouth and then on her tongue, ensuring both were well covered.

This brief unpleasantness would all be worth it. It had to be.

Her head, or the field, or both, started to carousel around her. One last step. She took a small tinder box from the chest. No going back once this tin was opened. She pressed it between her palms and set her intention.

Hear me now, oh Master. Send forth your emissary. Grant me an audience.

Oh-so-gingerly, Helena worked the lid off. Satisfied the yellow-tailed scorpion wasn't going to leap out at her, or try to flee, she set aside the lid.

It was a tiny thing really, why was she so scared of it?

She took it by the tail, which wasn't yellow aside from the vicious-looking stinger, and held it aloft. If she was worthy, she would not be harmed, and Helena knew she was worthy. Closing her eyes, she lowered it to her lips, feeling its legs kicking, tickling her skin.

She opened her mouth and the scorpion crawled onto her tongue where it seemed to hesitate. Helena dared not breathe. Of course, she'd made doubly sure that scorpion venom was different to bee venom, and yellow-tail stings aren't *usually* fatal, but she didn't want to find out . . .

After what felt like hours, the scorpion moved. It continued down her tongue. Instinctively, she fought the urge to spit it out, her gag reflex kicking in. She pressed her hand to her mouth, feeling its spidery legs tickle her throat all the way down to her stomach.

And now she waited. There was a moment of stillness. Somewhere in Pendle Hill, an owl hooted. There. That wasn't so—

It felt like she was being stabbed. Helena screamed, she couldn't keep it in. Her whole body spasmed violently. She flipped over onto her back, her spine arching in agony. Oh god, she couldn't bear it, it was worse than childbirth, like every last bone had grown barbs and was trying to slice itself out of her flesh. Her limbs jerked up and down, minds of their own. She felt her legs, her bottom, her shoulders slam into the ground as she flailed like a fish out of water. She twisted over, her face now smashing into the damp grass.

Quivering all over, she felt herself leave the ground. Her head whipped back and forth, quite out of her control, and her neck cracked painfully. She panted, her lungs felt too small.

And then she bellyflopped back to the earth. She lay a moment on her back, shivering all over, her skin soaked with cold sweat and mud. She checked to see if she could breathe. She could. For a second, it had felt like drowning. She blinked her eyes open. They were now black as ebony, but her sight was clearer than ever, as though she had night vision.

And she knew exactly what she had to do. She twisted herself over and onto all fours. Helena let her hands go where they wanted to go. With inhuman speed, they darted from one bone fragment to the next. Soon, they began to take shape, forming a series of runes written in no book, not even *The Gospel of Lilith*. Like some secret password, they could only be told. Helena didn't know what she was doing, but her hands seemed to.

Before she knew it, it was done. She didn't even know what the shapes meant – they were in some ancient script of the demons, not meant for man. She sat back and admired her craft. Her body was sore, but she also felt *alive*, the way she did after an especially punishing spin class. She wiped slick hair off her face.

Squinting at the horizon, she saw a shape emerge from the trees. She allowed a brief, relieved, laugh. She'd done it. It had worked.

Taking its sweet time, the bull majestically paraded down the meadow towards her. She'd been expecting a white bull, and it *was*. Its hide was pearly, gleaming under the moon. He was quite beautiful. She hadn't expected that.

As he approached, she took the final item from the chest. The sacrifice. A serious ask calls for serious payment. *You can't make something from nothing.* Magic *has* to be balanced. She was asking for great strength, so that power had to be returned.

The haul from Rye had solved the problem for her. The human foetus was wrapped in a separate silk. Helena set it down, unfurling it and presenting it to the bull. This was the last place where it could all go terribly wrong. The emissary might not accept her offering – it was not a live sacrifice – but Helena could not bring herself to slay a live infant.

Of course it's blood. It's always blood. What has more life than blood, and what is purer than the blood of youth? That is why it's *always* blood.

The bull slowed as he came close to the circle. Helena sat back on her heels, before bowing to the beast, palms facing up, her forehead pressed to the earth. Total submission. She dare not look, but she felt hot breath spray from the creature's nostrils as he stooped to pick the embryo up with its teeth. She heard it chew and, when she sat up, his white mouth was red.

He'd taken it.

She was worthy.

With an odd clucking noise that took her by surprise, Helena started to cry. She had always known. *I am worthy.*

In her right hand, she gripped the dagger, and drove it hard into the bull's neck.

The head had not come off as easily as she'd hoped, and you aren't allowed to – she assumed – use a chainsaw. She had to hack away at steely sinew and bone for over an hour. And it had been so full of blood; it spurted from the veins long after the heart stopped beating. Head to toe, Helena's skin was rust red, sticky and wet. Her hair swung about her face in matted ropes as she entered the woods.

She held the bull's head aloft by the horns, letting his dead eyes lead the way.

Around her, the forest teemed with life. She felt them all: the beetles, the worms, the aphids, the adders. She understood how they were linked in a vast web of life. She was supreme. Nothing here could better her. She was primed. A perfect killer. A predator. A *witch*. Mice and spiders fled out of her path as she prowled through the undergrowth. Underneath it all, we are animal.

The bull head led her to a very average oak surrounded by many other average oak trees. Only this one *was* different. It began to glow from within, a phosphorous green emanating though its gnarls. The long limbs creaked, and the branches moved. Helena watched as the bark and roots slithered like tentacles, parting to create a hole at the heart of the trunk. A foul, sulphurous stench hit Helena and she staggered back. A vile belch from the earth's bowel.

Trying to breathe through her mouth, she followed the instructions from *The Gospel of Lilith* and placed the severed head inside the oak cavity. Vines and creepers squirmed over the dead flesh, binding it to the tree.

Helena took a step back. This *had* to work. She'd done everything right. She would not fail now. Only success would make this worthwhile. 'Master Belial,' she said aloud. 'I submit to your will as a worthy vessel for your power. Now hear me.'

The bull's dead eyes stared into nothingness.

'Hear me!' she cried at the top of her voice.

There was a green spark in his eyes and the bull's head came to life, the thick neck flexing and the lips peeling back over yellow teeth. The beast gave a mighty roar.

'Who dares demand an audience with Belial?' The voice rumbled through the entire forest.

'You know me, Lord. I summoned you here to this place, imbued you with the strength to manifest. I am your servant Helena Vance, High Priestess of the United Kingdom.'

The bull eyes considered her. 'You are insignificant.'

Helena hadn't expected it to be easy. The bull glowered at her, now so much more than a severed head. She'd seen Ciara, and others, invoke demons, but she'd never *seen* a demon face to face, even if that face was borrowed, as Belial's was in this realm. She had to prove herself. He could still say no. 'I am worthy. I completed your tests.'

'You are a grain of sand in all this.'

'Then make me strong,' Helena said. 'Fill me with your infinite power.'

'It seeks power.'

'Yes.'

'It has war in its heart. It sings the song of Belial.'

What had she expected? Belial was why men went to war. As long as men had roamed this earth, this demon had sown seeds of division, of vengeance, of malcontent, of tribalism. He'd put weapons in so many hands.

'I want to win a war,' she said.

'The sword of witches.'

'Yes. I will finish it.'

'You will start it,' the bull retorted.

'I will save witchkind.'

'It is witches that imprisoned Belial in this carnal prison.'

'Through me you will be free. I will serve you well.' She would become a weapon, stop Leviathan, and no one would ever know.

'A witch would trick Belial.'

'I would serve Belial.' It was a lie. She served no man, no demon, but man's greatest weakness was his arrogance. There isn't a woman in history who considered herself less than a man, but there's a trick to allowing men to *think* they're in control. A coward's strength, but strength.

'It would be the vessel.'

'Yes.'

'It would know untold strength, but it would belong to the Master in perpetuity.'

She had seen Hale and she did not believe the demon. Demons were terrifying, but they were weak in this reality, wholly reliant on their subjects. He would accelerate *her* power, not the other way around. Nonetheless, if she wanted to defeat the Sullied Child, she needed an upgrade. 'I accept your terms.'

'Does it?'

'Yes.'

'Come closer.'

Helena took a step towards the oak, the pungent cloud of gas still billowing from the wound in the tree.

'It is weak,' Belial said, dismissively.

'She is not,' Helena snarled, suddenly furious. 'She is sacrificing *everything* for her coven. I have lowered myself to consorting with demons for the cause.'

The bull chuckled. '*There* she is. Pompous, arrogant, entitled. But willing, certainly, willing.'

'Make me into a sword.'

The bull seemed to smile. An unnerving and uncanny thing to witness. 'The vessel is virgin.'

'Yes.'

A low gravelly laugh shook the forest. 'Witch, your first time is a *big* one.'

Helena saw a spark of green jade in the bull's eyes before she felt an ice cold, viscous, gel-like substance hit her mouth, her nostrils, her eyes and ears. Sap. It was sap, gushing from the tree. She choked and choked as it gushed down her throat. The force of it lifted her clean off the ground and held her there. It surged around her body, squeezing into every orifice. She gagged, gasping for air. She couldn't move. It filled her stomach, her guts, her skull.

It touched every inch of her, inside and out.

She couldn't breathe, she couldn't—

Helena woke up with a start.

She was naked still, but in her room at Vance Hall. The

curtains were open and dawn had broken, which suggested some hours had passed. She scanned herself over: she was clean, her hair still damp. She had no memory whatsoever of getting home. The last thing she could recall was choking on the thick suffocating goo, her feet kicking at thin air.

She heard footfalls on the stairs and looked to the open bedroom door. She wanted it closed.

The door slammed shut.

Helena gasped. She saw her water bottle on the window sill. She merely lifted her hand and it shot into her palm with a satisfying slap. She looked at it with awe. 'I'm an adept,' she said, barely audible.

It had worked.

Like a cat, she stretched out diagonally across the bed, arching her back. Every cell in her body felt charged, electric. Oh, she liked this.

And yes, Belial liked his new vessel too. He liked it greatly.

Chapter Forty-Five

SUMMER PROMISE

Niamh

How can you not know how to make risotto? Luke had said. Because it's a frigging faff, Niamh had told him. Nurturing rice like it was a baby, gently massaging it with a wooden spoon. Who on this earth has the time?

It was mightily disconcerting though, seeing Luke take command of the kitchen the way Conrad once had. She'd always loved that dance: a pinch of sea salt, a grind of pepper, the way he instinctively knew which herbs to fetch from the garden. Perhaps that was her type, she mused, men who cook well. It certainly fulfilled a need.

It was plenty warm enough to have dinner outside on the patio overlooking the hills. This year, the seasons were progressing nicely from spring to summer, incrementally, the way it used to when she was little, without the freakish abnormalities they'd come to associate with global warming. Hebden Bridge, down in the valley, had flooded no less than three times in three years, but this year – thus far – seemed more forgiving.

Theo sat, quiet as ever, at the outside table, still reading the grimoires Leonie had brought up from London. She was as committed a student as Niamh had ever taught. Finally, the control was starting to emerge. It all figured: a messy mind makes for messy magic. How could a person who'd been through what Theo was going through possibly keep their shit together? Chaotic energy makes for chaos.

Luke, perfecting that waiter thing of carrying three pasta dishes at once, brought the risotto to the table. 'I could get used to this,' Niamh said, and then wished she hadn't because it sounded like a line from a romcom.

Luke swerved that, instead teasing her. 'I can't believe you can't make risotto. I present asparagus and pea risotto.' He handed a dish to Theo. 'There you go mate.'

Niamh spoke only to Theo. *Can I say something to Luke? I don't want him to misgender you and 'mate' feels quite laddish, don't you think?*

Sure. I don't mind.

'Luke, I've been meaning to talk to you about Theo, actually.'

He took his seat and grabbed a piece of garlic ciabatta. 'Oh, aye?'

'So. Theo is going through some changes and, from now on, would like us to refer to her as a girl.'

Luke, an open book, registered surprise only for a moment before sucking it all back in. 'All right, then. Ah, is that why you've come up here?'

That was plausible. Theo nodded. 'That's right,' Niamh added.

'Cool, cool,' Luke said. 'You changing your name, or stopping with Theo? You could do Thea, I suppose?'

Theo blushed. *Tell him I'm sticking with Theo.*

'She's Theo. For now anyway. I like it. The artist in *The Haunting of Hill House* was called Theodora.'

361

'I like that,' Luke said cheerfully.

So do I.

'She likes Theodora too.'

Theo smiled shyly and picked at the risotto, almost one grain at a time. She ate like a nervy sparrow, like she was pinching scraps from the table.

If some sort of picture was to develop with Luke, he had a right to know – partially – what was going on. Maybe even, if things went much further, it'd be time to ease him into the witchy malarky. 'So Theo's going to be staying a while longer.'

'How much longer?' It wasn't suspicious as much as curious. Gods, Niamh already came with so much baggage, what was one more satchel?

Niamh sensed Theo waiting on her response even more keenly. 'As long as she wants.'

Theo didn't need words to thank her because she almost tasted the sugar rush of gratitude, so strong it was.

They finished dinner (accompanied by the first rosé of the season) and played a card game called Skulls. It was easy enough for Theo to play without words, and they made a private vow not to read Luke's mind, however much of an advantage that would give them.

The sun set and they moved inside to watch TV. The first rosé and now their first boxset. The dog nestled between Niamh and Luke on the sofa while Theo read, making notes in the margins. Niamh felt more content than she had done in a long time. What if this was life now? *There are far worse lives to have.* That's what true love is all about: it's not about drama and tears, it's about risotto and boxsets. She'd felt lucky to have that sort of intimacy once, twice felt almost greedy.

She took the chance to speak to Theo while Luke used

the bathroom upstairs. *Theo, how would you feel about Luke staying over sometime? Not tonight, but sometime.*

She seemed distracted, her thoughts staccato, jittery. *Can you hear that?*

What?

Theo's forehead wrinkled, smelling the air, wolf-like. *There's a new voice.*

Niamh listened, really strained. There was nothing at first, and she almost told her so, until she did hear something. Hear wasn't quite the right phrase, more *felt* it. Something cold, something old, like the black air and musk inside a deep cave. *I see what you mean.*

What is it?

It was odd is what it was. *I don't know.*

Theo's eyes widened. *I'm scared.*

Now Niamh grew concerned. *Of what?*

Something isn't right. I think she will come for me.

'Helena?'

Theo nodded.

'She won't. And if she does I'll stop her. I'm more powerful than she is. Always was.'

She wished she could say that satisfied Theo, but she still looked fraught.

Theo, it'll be fine. I promise.

I've never lived anywhere nice before. I don't want it to end.

Niamh scooted over onto the arm of the easy chair and wrapped her arms around Theo. She was still brittle, but no longer flinched from her touch. *No one is taking you anywhere.*

Chapter Forty-Six

CALL TO ARMS

Helena

'Don't argue, please,' Helena said, folding a swimsuit into a case on Snow's bed.

Snow made a strange noise – a mix of whiny swear words and exasperation. 'I don't want to go to Boscastle! It's even worse than Hebden Bridge.'

'It's very scenic,' argued Helena. Poor Snow had only been back in Manchester a few weeks and now she was being shipped off again. It was for her safety though.

Snow looked at her as if she were simple. 'Man, do you know what I look for in a holiday? This sucks, why can't I just stay with you?'

Helena ceased packing and glared at her daughter. She harboured a powerful desire to punch the whinging bitch so hard she broke her jaw. And she didn't doubt she could. She tempered the urge. *It's Snow.* 'I have a lot of work to do. It's the half-term holiday, it'll be lovely and your grandparents are delighted to be able to take you away. You used to love the holiday home.'

'I used to love One Direction. Things change, Mum.'

I could snap your neck, you wretched—

'Please, Snow, do it for me. Please.'

Snow paused and reconsidered her approach. 'Something's going on, isn't it?'

'No. Is it that strange that your grandma and granddad want to take you away for a break?'

'It is a bit, yeah. It came out of nowhere, and Grandma's supposed to be judging the flower show in Todmorden, so it doesn't really make sense to be honest.'

Snow was cleverer than she looked. 'Her plans changed.'

'You want us out of the way, don't you? Why?'

'That's not even vaguely true,' she lied.

'Is it something to do with Theo?'

'What makes you think that?' She slathered syrup on her voice.

Snow shrugged. 'I dunno. Like when Auntie Niamh went schizo at the funeral and stuff.'

Helena stroked Snow's lovely hair off her lovely face. She loved this girl who had expanded her heart. She felt it very strongly. She felt everything strongly at the moment; hungry all the time, ravenous. She would kill for Snow, the way she should have killed those who harmed her husband. She would have shown no mercy now.

She was the most powerful creature on this sorry planet. It was delicious.

'You have nothing to worry about, sweet Snow.'

The girl grimaced. 'Mum, you're being extra.'

Helena raised a brow. 'You have no idea. Now, finish packing and await the teleport to Cornwall. I need to get to the office. Have a lovely time. I'll join you if I can the day after tomorrow.' Helena kissed her on the forehead and then slapped her bum. 'Get cracking. Love you.'

'I love you too,' Snow said.

The girl is suspicious.

As Helena left her bedroom, she subtly slid her daughter's phone into her blazer pocket while her back was turned. Just in case.

It was dusk when Sandhya greeted her back at HMRC. 'Is everyone here?' she said the second she was corporeal.

'Everyone on the list came.'

'Good.' She hadn't given them a choice. 'Let's not keep them waiting.'

Helena led the way, striding through the mostly empty offices. Only a skeleton crew worked the night shift for emergency teleportation and the like. They took the elevator to Boil and Bubble, the first floor canteen, where the sun terrace overlooked the rose gardens out back. The HMRC gardens were well-kept, perfectly symmetrical, four quadrants of Crimson Glory hybrids just coming into bloom around a central ornamental fountain. It was a beautiful space, even by lamplight.

While her assistant hung back, Helena gripped the railings and observed those she'd gathered: her strongest allies within HMRC. Each of these women had proven themselves to be loyal. 'Sisters, thank you for coming at such short notice,' she shouted and the politely curious hubbub of conversation stopped at once. She hadn't given Sandhya any indication as to why she needed an emergency session.

Below she saw her response team: statuesque Robyn Jones, Jen Yamato, Clare Carruthers. The Finch sisters – irritating gossips but both powerful elementals – were present. So was Irina Konvalinka and young Amy. They were joined by half a dozen other grey-caped witches who were rising through the ranks. All highly committed individuals, Helena had psychometrically vetted them herself.

Yes, this would do nicely. Just the right mix of skillsets, and not too many bodies to arouse suspicion. The witch equivalent of a SWAT team.

She began, 'I'm sure you're wondering why I summoned you so urgently. Some of you fought alongside me in the war, some of you are too young to remember the horrors of that era. When I became High Priestess, I swore that such bleak times were behind us forever. But it's with great regret that I must confirm that certain rumours are true: a far greater threat to our coven now presents itself.'

She stepped aside and allowed Sandhya to come forward. 'Show them.' Sandhya transmitted into them all Amy's terrible vision. Helena scanned their faces as they received the images, waiting for them to twist into disgust, fear, panic. And they duly did.

'The Sullied Child is real, my sisters. Through him, Leviathan will rise. Right now, in Hebden Bridge, he proclaims he is female; a paltry attempt to infiltrate our coven and destroy us from within. In this instance, we must not let the laws of mundanes divert or delay us. We have always made our own rules, and we must forge ahead as witches now. The Sullied Child is an abomination, and one which must be stopped.'

Her witches talked among themselves, frantically unpacking the oracle's vision *and* her words.

'Sisters, please. I know the premonition is deeply distressing, but I gather you here not for talk, but action. You are a task force, my most trusted and accomplished witches. Tonight, I need you. We have one chance to get this right and we are dealing with two powerful sentients who will know we're coming.'

'Two?' Venice Finch called up from the garden.

Helena nodded sagely. 'Regretfully, our sister Niamh

367

Kelly is harbouring the Sullied Child. It is possible, even, that she is in league with Leviathan himself . . .'

That caused another scandalised ripple in the pond below.

'I know. No one is more concerned than I am. Niamh, as you know, is a dear friend. But what sort of High Priestess would I be if I put my own friendship above the interests of the coven? I will not stand idly by as this child perverts everything I, we, stand for.'

More tittering. Paris Finch raised her hand. She wore her fingernails long, and manicured. Helena imagined peeling each nail off her fingertips, how much it would hurt. 'What if Niamh intervenes? She's a Level 5 adept . . .'

Helena paused a moment, refocusing. Belial craved pain. 'Together we are stronger. Tonight we move on Hebden Bridge. I cannot force you to come, but your coven asks it of you. The primary objective is to apprehend and detain Theo. If he, or anyone, tries to impede our mission, I authorise lethal force.'

This time, there was no commentary. She'd just shown them how serious this was. 'Now. We can prevent that horrific vision from coming to pass, but time is of the essence if we are to exploit an element of surprise . . .'

She felt Belial stir inside her, hungry, a metallic taste on her tongue. She harboured the strangest urge to chew batteries. There was an outside chance it wouldn't come to it, but if Niamh wanted a fight, oh she'd give her one she'd never forget.

Helena hoped Niamh wanted a fight.

Chapter Forty-Seven

AN URGENT LETTER

Niamh

Theo had fallen asleep in the armchair while Niamh inched across the sofa to nuzzle into Luke. This all felt very right. She was only half watching the tawdry crime drama they were binging, more captivated by the closeness, and the promise of even closer closeness to follow perhaps.

Her phone hummed – the email alert. She was on call and felt she probably shouldn't ignore it.

Hmm, that was odd.

'What is it?' Luke asked.

'I've got an *email* from Snow Vance. You know, the young girl I'm teaching.' It was weird because Snow would usually communicate via WhatsApp or even DM.

Hello Auntie Niamh
Mum has stolen my phone?!?! I don't know why, but she's making me go down south with my grandma and granddad. I think something is up with her, she is acting fully mental. Pls can you help her pls?
Love Snow xxx

It was a very bodily reaction. Niamh sprung up off the couch like she'd been stung.

'What? What is it?' Luke said again.

Ignoring him, Niamh instead woke Theo. 'Theo, wake up.'

The girl's eyes pinged open, and she sat up with a jolt.

Niamh's throat felt tight. 'We have to go. Helena's coming.'

Chapter Forty-Eight

DOUBT

Helena

All of the women had agreed to come to Hebden Bridge
without hesitation, and now eleven witches in HMRC
grey gathered in the oratorium, awaiting teleportation.
They'd had to call in emergency healers for such a large
transfer. It was taking far longer than Helena would like
and, to make matters worse, dithering Sandhya had
vanished while rounding up additional uniforms.

Helena didn't even see Irina appear at her side, the
blind woman placing a cold hand on her arm. Helena
recoiled, very nearly blasting her into oblivion. 'Is there
a problem?' she snapped, taking out her irritation on the
oracle.

'There very well might be.'

'Can it wait?' she said through a tight jaw.

'I think not.'

Helena guided the oracle away from the waiting troops,
to the perimeter of the dome. 'What is it, Irina, you tire-
some crone?'

'I have conferred with oracles all over the United

Kingdom, both HMRC and independent, and not one among us can verify Amy Sugden's vision.'

Helena blinked expectantly. 'And . . . ?'

'Oracles work in harmony with good reason, priestess. We are human, fallible. Our omens can be tainted by our personal prejudices, or swayed by the whisperings of demonkind, and some of us simply have overactive imaginations. What I am trying to tell you is don't believe everything you read.'

'Why would some demon send *that* oracle such a portent? What could it possibly hope to achieve?'

Irina clasped her hands at her chest, like she was in prayer. 'The role of demon, historically, was to manipulate man into doing his bidding, although *I* personally haven't experienced their rapture . . .'

Rip her feeble head from her shoulders. Helena pushed the urge aside and instead smiled kindly, often the best way to deflect patronising words. 'Miss Konvalinka, have you told anyone else about the validity of Amy's prophecy?'

'I have not.'

'Wonderful,' Helena said, grasping her face and squeezing hard. The oracle whimpered softly. 'See that you don't. If another oracle dies, people will talk. As you were.'

Helena patted her on her bald head and returned to her task force. It was almost time.

Chapter Forty-Nine

THE INTRUDER

Leonie

It had been a subdued Black Mass that evening. Lovely old Mrs Rashid was very sick indeed – pneumonia – so they'd dedicated the meeting to sending her as much energy as they could. She was very elderly. At this stage it wasn't so much about unnaturally extending her lifespan as it was about making her as blissfully receptive to death as one could hope to be.

Still, she was a popular congregant. Everyone would be sad to see her depart.

As such, Chinara had suggested a stop-off at Kreemy on the way home. Leonie fucking loved this place; lights as bright as an airport terminal until 2 a.m., seven nights a week. That suggested *someone* in South London was sad, high, or pregnant pretty much all day, every day. Why else would you need ice cream at 2 a.m.?

'Can I get two scoops? One cherry, one dark chocolate? With sprinkles!' she asked the super bored-looking Albanian dude behind the counter. Judging from his face, you could probably get weed here if you knew the magic password too.

'Tub or cone?' he droned.

'Cup, please. You want anything?' she asked Chinara. She was lactose intolerant but they did a line in sorbets too. She didn't want anything, so the guy went to get Leonie's order. 'You are an angel,' Leonie told Chinara. 'This is exactly what I needed.'

'Cherry and chocolate though? What? Are you some sort of deviant?'

'It's so good! Like Black Forest gateau!' Leonie cried and Chinara looked baffled. 'You should have some. It's worth getting the shits, trust and believe.'

She got her ice cream and ate it as they walked the last couple of blocks to their flat. London doesn't sleep, ever, but it was subdued for a Wednesday night in May. Even Zone 2 can find a sort of tranquillity. The jerk chicken place on the corner was shut, which was weird, and only one guy was in the launderette, reading a battered copy of *Catch-22* in the window seat as they passed. Leonie sensed foxes too. There were always wily foxes.

How could she ever leave London? Ice cream and laundry at almost eleven o'clock. What more could anyone want? This was her home.

'We should have a baby,' she said.

Chinara stopped dead in her tracks. 'Am I hearing correctly?'

'Yeah. Look, I know I've been dodging the issue, and you know why.'

'I do. But I didn't like to say.'

'You know me well.' They arrived outside the flat and climbed the wide stone steps. 'This kid will belong to you and me. Wherever we go, she or he – or they – will come too. I'm not on my own.'

'Never.' Chinara unlocked their front door for them.

Leonie carried on as they climbed the steep stairs to the top floor. 'It's scary though.'

'Of course it is!' Chinara laughed. 'It would be more weird if we didn't have doubts, right? Creating new life! What could possibly be more daunting?'

'Totally! They should make you sit an exam or something.'

As they reached the door to their attic flat, Leonie froze. 'What?'

She grabbed the top of Chinara's arm. 'There's someone in there . . .' she whispered.

Chinara didn't need telling twice. 'Get behind me.'

Leonie rolled her eyes. She was no fucking damsel in distress. She scanned the flat. It was a woman, and the woman was *scared*.

It's one woman. I don't think she wants to hurt us, she told Chinara. Chinara entered first, conjuring a ball of flame in her palm. *Please don't burn the flat down, we'll never get the deposit back.*

The flat was dark, quiet, as they tiptoed down the hall. 'We know you're in here!' Chinara called. 'Show yourself. I warn you, I'm armed.'

Living room.

Chinara barrelled in, Leonie right behind her.

'Don't hurt me!' the young woman cried and Leonie pulled Chinara back before someone got hurt. Leonie recognised her – a pretty Asian girl. 'I'm from HMRC!'

'Sandhya, right?' Leonie said as Chinara extinguished the flame. She dimly recalled her being one of Niamh's students, and later joining the coven. Leonie had once emailed her about Diaspora and she'd received back a very polite, if – in her opinion – naïve email explaining how she wanted to make HMRC more inclusive from within.

'Being from HMRC doesn't mean much in this house,' Chinara said gravely. 'You broke in.'

'I'm sorry!' the girl said, panicked. 'I got a couple of my friends at the office to teleport me here. She'll kill us all if she finds out.'

Leonie sensed she wasn't kidding. She truly feared for her life. 'It's OK. Calm down. We won't hurt you.' She guided her to their new Ikea sofa. 'Here, sit down.'

'We haven't got time!' Sandhya said, although did as she was told.

'What's wrong?' Chinara asked.

'It's Helena . . .'

'Well of course it fucking is . . . what's she done now?' Leonie scooped up the cat from around her feet and hugged her tight.

Sandhya's eyes were pools in the dim lamplight. 'She's going after Niamh and the Sullied Child.'

'Theo?'

'She's got a dozen witches teleporting into Hebden Bridge tonight. She's put a barrier around the whole town and is going to cloak the mundanes.'

'All of them?' Leonie said.

'She has all of HMRC working on it in Manchester. I can't get through to Niamh . . . I didn't know where else to go.'

The balls on that woman. 'Fucking hell.'

Sandhya wrung an old tissue in her hands. 'I've worked with her for years . . . and she's always been intense, but this is something else. I think something's going on. She had us raid some contraband magicks from this place in Rye, and then her security pass accessed the vaults. I checked – some of the controlled items we seized have gone.'

This Sandhya chick was *good*.

'What does she intend to do with them?' Chinara said.

She didn't have the answer to that. There was not a trace of exaggeration or deception in Sandhya's mind. She laid it wide open for Leonie to read. 'If they resist arrest, the HMRC witches are authorised to kill them both.'

Urgently, Leonie turned to Chinara. They didn't even need to communicate telepathically because they both understood at once they'd made a rookie mistake. They'd underestimated a vindictive white woman.

Chapter Fifty
SOS

Elle

Elle was in the middle of brushing her teeth with her Sonicare when she got the message. It slammed into her mind without warning, clanging like tin cans. She dropped the toothbrush into the sink and crouched by the shower.

It's Leonie. Elle, why is your fucking phone off?

Elle gripped her skull, trying to keep it in one piece. *Leonie, get out of my head!*

No. Get to Niamh's now and warn her. I can't reach her, they've shielded her, even from me. Helena and HMRC are coming for Theo and they'll kill them both if they resist arrest. Go NOW.

Leonie vacated her mind and there was a gorgeous second of silence. 'Shit,' she said aloud.

Jez popped his head around the door and looked quizzically at her toothbrush buzzing away in the basin. 'You all right, love?'

Elle picked herself up. 'No, I'm not.' She pushed past him to get into the bedroom. Her phone wasn't off, but on silent on the bedside table. She saw she indeed had four missed calls from Leonie.

She unplugged it and quickly dialled Niamh's number. *'The number you have dialled is out of service. Please check and try again.'*

Elle glared at her phone as if the handset was to blame. How could Niamh's number possibly be out of service? HMRC, of course. Helena could teleport through space, for crying out loud. Disconnecting someone's phone was child's play. As a last-ditch effort she tried Niamh's landline too, and was met only with a strange tone.

'Elle, love, what's going on?' Jez looked utterly baffled, but poised like an action figure, ready to roll at a moment's notice.

Where to even start? 'There's trouble at Niamh's.'

'What sort of trouble?'

Downstairs, they both heard a door slam and footsteps clattering around. 'Mum! Come on!' Holly cried.

Oh great, Elle thought, *of course* the sentient in the house got the message too. She was reminded of KerPlunk. If you pluck the wrong straw, everything tumbles down. Her lies suddenly looked like a house made of straw. They were a single huff and puff away from disaster. She ignored Jez's question and hurried out of the loft. 'Elle!' he called after her.

Elle found a pyjama-clad Holly putting on her trainers in the hallway. 'What on earth are you doing?'

Holly looked at her, not for the first time, as if she were thick. 'I heard what Leonie said. We have to get to Auntie Niamh's.'

'I don't think so, madame. Get to bed.'

'No! If HMRC are coming for them, they need all the help they can get.'

Jez now appeared at the top of the steps too. Elle's head was spinning. This was *it*. This was going to be the one she couldn't explain. Was Holly able to wipe him yet? No, she couldn't risk that, she could end up severing him. She floundered in the hall, not knowing which way to turn.

'Mum, come on!' Holly shouted.

'Elle, what is going on, babe?'

Elle closed her eyes and willed it all to stop. 'Shut up! Both of you just give me a minute please!'

'They haven't got a minute, Mum! Are you coming or not?'

'Holly, you are not going anywhere near that house if—' Elle went to grab her, drag her up to her room if necessary, but Holly held up a hand to block her. Perhaps harder than she intended to, because Elle felt an invisible wall slam into her. She was winded, tumbling backwards onto the stairs and landing on her butt.

Holly fled for the front door. 'Sorry!' she cried as she darted into the night.

Jez raced down the stairs to help her up. 'What the fuck was that? Did you see that?'

Elle gritted her teeth. 'Yes, Jez, I saw that.'

His face, his lips, went sickly pale. 'She just . . . she just sent you fucking flying.'

Elle shook him free and went for the door. Where the hell Holly thought she was going on foot was anyone's guess. They were about a forty-minute walk away from Niamh's, a ten-minute drive. 'I need to get Holly.'

'No. No way.' Jez reached past her to slam the door shut, trapping her inside. 'You tell me right now what's going on. I mean it, Elle.'

Elle pushed her hair off her face. Tiny hairline cracks

had advanced silently across her life over the years. Sooner or later, the vase was going to shatter. She had known that the whole time, they'd been on a countdown clock since they were nineteen. And now, time was up.

Or was it? If there was a tomorrow, Niamh could just wipe him again.

'Jez, please let me go.'

'No. Not until you tell me. I deserve to know. We don't keep secrets.'

'Jez . . .'

'Elle, I mean it.'

He didn't look angry so much as concerned. Maybe that was something, a shred of hope. Maybe he would be like Conrad had been; curious, intrigued, supportive. Maybe her future life could be exactly like *Bewitched*.

'Jez . . .' She fought to keep her voice even. 'I need to get after Holly because she might get hurt.'

'Then you better tell me fast.'

Elle wanted to open her mouth and scream and scream forever. She'd always imagined this moment would be cinematic: accompanied by horns or sweeping violins, perhaps overlooking the ocean at sunset. Instead, there was a draught sneaking around her ankles in the hallway, and the house still honked of fish curry. Figured, really. 'Can you remember how everyone used to say my grand-mother was a witch?'

'Yeah.' He waited for her to finish. She waited for him to catch up. 'What? You for real?'

Elle nodded. 'I am a witch.' All it took was four words. 'I come from a very long line of famous witches.'

He was still waiting for a punchline. Elle just stared him out. 'No. Fuck off.' She nodded again. 'What? Your mum?'

381

'No. Not my mum. It skipped a generation.'

Jez considered this. 'Oh. That would have made more sense, actually.'

Any other time, Elle might have found that funny. She squeezed Jez's arms gently. 'You once said that there's something special with me and my friends – well this is it. They are more than just friends, they're my sisters. Niamh needs me. I really have to go to her.'

Holly needed her too. Elle understood now; Holly wasn't just her daughter any more and nor was Elle just her mother. They were sisters too, equals in that respect.

He was about to argue but she put a hand to his lips. 'Jez, please! We can talk about this for the rest of our lives but right now, I have to get to our daughter. Will you stay here with Milo? I can't do everything.' Something a mother was never supposed to admit.

Jez nodded, reluctantly, and stepped aside. She was about to open the front door until he stopped her again. 'You going out like that, babe?'

She was in a satin nightie. He had a point.

Elle wasn't sure what she was getting into. Her head was skittering all over the place. Niamh versus Helena? There was a disappointing inevitability to it. *Girls can never get along*, her mother always said. Elle had always thought that was because her mother slept with so many women's husbands, but perhaps there was a grain of truth to it.

She quickly changed and raced to the car in the most *active* outfit she had: stretchy yoga pants from Kate Hudson's Fabletics range, a TK Maxx sports bra and her rarely-used jogging trainers. She tied her hair into a topknot. Whatever happened, Elle Pearson was *ready*. In the rear-view mirror, Jez watched her go from the front doorstep. It hadn't sunk in yet, she could tell. She'd have to be there when it did.

Focus on the task at hand. She bumped off the driveway kerb and only drove about two minutes down the street when she saw Holly marching towards Hebden Bridge in her pyjamas. She felt a swell of pride. A girl who didn't even hesitate to help her friends. Tears stung Elle's eyes but she blinked them back. Annie would be so proud.

She wound down the window. 'Get in loser, we're going shopping!' Elle called.

Holly's head whipped around. It was as if she was surprised to see her for a split second and then, she smiled, running for the passenger seat.

Chapter Fifty-One

FLEE

Niamh

Niamh shoved the final case into the back of the Land Rover and slammed the boot shut. 'Where's Tiger gone? Tiger!' she raced back to the kitchen. 'Tiger? Good boy!'

Luke caught a hold of her. 'Niamh, please stop! You're out of control!'

'Luke, just go! I've asked you a hundred times. The best thing you can do is just be gone.'

Theo hovered at the side of the car, looking every bit as concerned as Luke did. Perhaps she did look a bit wild, but there was no time to worry about *looking* crazy on top of actually being crazy. When they were safe, she'd run a brush through her hair.

'I'm not going to leave you like this, Niamh.'

Niamh caught hold of Tiger's collar and led him to Theo. 'Theo! Get him in the car, I'll be two seconds.' She did as she was told.

'You don't owe me an explanation. You don't owe me anything, but I'm sure there's *something* I can do to help.'

Niamh laughed. She actually laughed because Helena

Vance could squash him like a fly. 'Luke, there isn't a good way to explain this, but if you stay here, there's a chance you'll die.'

He looked half convinced. 'I don't . . .'

'Oh, but I do. Please go home. And lock your doors.' Niamh turned to get in the car.

'Wait! Will I see you again?'

'I don't know,' she admitted.

'So this is goodb—' And then his eyes rolled back into his head and he slumped to the floor like a sack of spuds.

'What the actual fuck?' Niamh cursed the sky.

Theo clambered back out of the car and stood at her side. *What did you do to him?*

Nothing. Did you put him out?

No!

Fuck. 'That means they're here. They must be putting mundanes under to keep them out of the way. We used to do it during the war.' Fuck, fuck, fuck, fuck, fuck. 'Shit the bed. Open the back door.'

Theo did so and Niamh employed telekinesis to lift him into the car. It wasn't easy, like threading a needle, but she steered his considerable shoulders onto the back seats.

Is he coming with us?

Niamh shot her a doubtful glance. 'I'm not sure we're at the eloping stage in our relationship,' she replied. 'OK, new plan. We leave him outside his apartment block. I can't leave him here. It'll be the first place they look.' Theo merely nodded. 'Right, let's hit the road.'

Chapter Fifty-Two

THE HUNT OF HEBDEN BRIDGE I

Helena

Helena materialised first, closely followed by Robyn to her left and Clare to her right. She wore an HMRC cape over her clothes to show solidarity with the women she couldn't help but think of as her 'troops'. She'd dug out the hardwearing combat pants and tank top she used to wear during the war.

They were at war again.

Static crackled in the air and more 'troops' apparated at strategic points around Niamh's home.

The cottage however looked quiet. 'Any signs of life?' she asked Robyn.

'It's empty.'

Helena scanned the lane and Niamh's Land Rover was gone. 'Someone warned them . . .' And she suspected she knew who. Sandhya Kaur was still AWOL. The treacherous little bitch. After everything she'd done for her. 'Are they at least within the exclusion zone?'

'I believe so,' Robyn told her.

Better than nothing. No one was getting in or out of Hebden Bridge without her permission. It would have been lovely if Niamh had unexpectedly surrendered Theo back into the care of HMRC, but not a single part of Helena believed that would happen. There was still a narrow possibility that this night could end peacefully. After all, she only wanted the child in *custody*. No one *had* to be harmed. At that thought, she heard almost a gravelly chuckle from the voice at the back of her skull.

A part of her knew what was going to come, and craved it. How disappointed she'd be with *peaceful*. 'Very well,' she said. 'They can't have gone far. Gather around!'

Her witches came close – a team of ten now that Sandhya had absconded.

She addressed them together. 'Ladies, Hebden Bridge is a very small town but with a lot of nooks and crannies. I will fog the streets. The mundanes are either asleep or cloaked so they aren't a concern. We are not leaving here without that boy, so I suggest you get looking. Teams of two. A sentient in every pair in case you're somehow seen.' The girls paired off.

Helena nodded, satisfied. 'Now, tear this town apart if you have to.'

Chapter Fifty-Three

THE HUNT OF
HEBDEN BRIDGE II

Niamh

Because of the river running through Hardcastle Crags, there was no direct route to Pecket Well unless she flew. As such, Niamh drove downhill into the valley.

'Some breaking news tonight. We have a severe weather warning in place across the Midlands,' the late-night DJ said in her husky bedroom voice. 'Strong winds, reaching gale-force, sweeping north. Expect to see branches coming down and roof tiles coming off, with some people even reporting seeing a torn—' Niamh switched the radio off. She needed to concentrate.

That said, the roads were deserted – even the main road towards Todmorden. A thick, freezing fog was lurking above the road, getting denser as she descended into the valley. 'It's them,' Niamh told Theo. They were making it harder for them to escape.

A single Volkswagen rested at the side of the road on the grass verge. The mundane driver, a woman, had evidently half pulled in as the sleep spell took hold. Lucky too. That could have been nasty.

'What the fuck is she thinking?' Niamh said aloud. 'People could have been killed!' Niamh was approaching the turning point to head back into town when a pair of women materialised in the middle of the road. Both wore the tell-tale grey capes of HMRC.

Theo slapped the dashboard as a warning, but Niamh already saw them. With the road empty, she swung the car into a U-turn, the tyres screeching. Theo clung to Tiger, who squatted between her legs in the footwell. In the rear-view mirror, she saw a tiny blond witch summon a bolt of lightning from the sky. She waited until she lashed it towards the car before veering onto the other side of the road. Blinding light shot past her window.

'Theo, hold on.'

She stamped on the accelerator. The witches would tell other witches. Now all they could do was flee. She chanced a quick look at the big figure tucked up across the back seats. *Luke, it looks like you're coming with us after all.*

The car hopped over the crest of the hill and careened past the Co-op onto Market Street. Another bolt of lightning pocked the road, and Niamh mounted the kerb to get out of the way. What even happens if a car gets struck by lightning?

The blond witch flew in front of the car, blue electric blazing at her fingers. 'Shit!' Niamh cried.

Theo held out a hand and swatted the witch into a coffee shop frontage like a bug. She smashed through the window. Niamh briefly glanced at Theo, who looked apologetic. 'Don't be sorry. Well, not for her. We'll figure out the shopkeeper later, I guess.' Action movies never show the clean-up. Who pays to tidy up after Superman and Batman? Funny though, it hadn't even occurred to her to *fight*. 'You do fight, I'll do flight,' Niamh told her.

Niamh had to slow to navigate a taxi that had come to a stop on the bend by the Old Gate Pub. The road here was narrow, and she had to creep around.

Do you feel that?

The road rumbled, the Land Rover veered out of her control. 'What now?' Creating an earthquake was serious stuff. It would take a powerful witch . . .

Suddenly the concrete erupted in their path as a water main burst. A torrent of water rained down on the windscreen. Niamh frantically steered around the gushing fountain, only for the road ahead to burst in another place. In sequence, one more jet, and then another burst up through the earth, trying to force them off track.

'Can you see where she is?' Niamh asked, navigating the obstacles. Somewhere, an elemental was pulling the water up through the cement.

Theo wound down her window to try to get a better look overhead. *I can't see her.*

A jagged ravine split Market Street, Niamh accelerated to get around it. A streetlight toppled into the crack, exploding with sparks as it fell. The surface was slick and she almost – almost – lost control, sailing into the railings outside the bike shop. 'Fuck!'

She had two choices: uphill past Hardcastle Crags, or out of town towards Mytholmroyd. If she could get out of town, the sleep spell could only possibly stretch so far. Even HMRC couldn't put all of West Yorkshire under. 'Is Luke OK?'

Theo swivelled to check the backseat. *Seems to be.*

'Can you try to . . . buckle him in somehow?'

Theo got to work on that. Niamh drove past the Picture

House and the Baptist church, checking the rear-view mirror. She couldn't see anyone, maybe they'd given them the slip. The way was clear aside from the lingering mist, and she accelerated up the gentle slope out of town.

Suddenly the engine cut out. They rolled back a couple of metres before she could grab the handbrake. 'What the fuck?' She restarted the engine and drove on, but the same thing happened.

What is it?

'There's some sort of barrier.' Of course there was – another tactic from the war. 'We're kettled in. We can try the other way.' This time, Niamh started the engine and tried to reverse. It worked. She sensed someone moving in – at speed. She performed a messy turn in the road, reversing into a parked car with the horrid crunch of metal on metal.

She shot back towards the town centre and the turning towards the forest.

Niamh, stop!

The road directly ahead ruptured, the ground splitting open like a wound. Niamh hit the brakes, but it was too late. The front wheels hit a newly-formed step in the concrete, and all she could do was inhale as the car flipped forwards.

Up and over they went. For a second, Niamh felt weightless. Too shocked to breathe, she tried to find the inner clarity to suspend the vehicle mid-air, keep them safe and still. But she didn't know which way was up or down and couldn't focus, couldn't stabilise any of them. It was too much. She was beaten.

With a deafening crash, they came back down to earth.

Chapter Fifty-Four

THE HUNT OF HEBDEN BRIDGE III

Leonie

A tornado advanced across the Peak District, whipping up dust into a spiralling column. It felled trees and fences, tore bushes up by the roots. Nature is destructive. To pretend it isn't is to be at odds with the world.

The calm at the eye of the storm was Chinara. Perfectly still, perfectly in control, her eyes electric white. She carried the others with her, all calmly suspended in the funnel. Leonie was ready though, she could easily stabilise any of them if they got caught up in Chinara's storm.

At short notice, she'd called on those she trusted the most: Valentina and Kane. Diaspora was not an army, she had not raised fighters, but – like any queer she could name – Val and Kane were inherently warriors. When you have fought to be who you are your whole life, you are used to fighting. Sandhya rode with them too, helping Leonie guide their course.

'We're close!' Sandhya called. 'Can you sense the barrier?'

Leonie nodded, no sentient would be able to miss it. Helena had – she sensed – at least ten sentients beaming a barricade over the whole town, like it was trapped under a massive pint glass. No one would get in or out.

'Chinara, stop!' she cried. The whirlwind slowed down and Leonie again made sure she could catch Kane if they started to fall. They were only a Level 3 – not able to levitate without help.

The five of them came to a gentle halt, suspended high over the lush green landscape below. 'Are you OK?' she asked her girlfriend. A cross-country gale-force flight could not have been easy.

Chinara just nodded, regaining her strength. Leonie held all of them aloft.

Sandhya reached out with a hand. 'It's here. It's strong.'

Valentina backed up and summoned a lightning bolt. It rippled over her body and she channelled it at the blockade. The energy skittered over the surface, briefly making the forcefield visible to the naked eye. It was vast.

'What do we do?' Sandhya said.

'We break in,' Leonie shouted, the wind whipping her hair into her face. 'Find their frequency and just slide your fingers in . . .'

With everything she had, Leonie chipped away at the wall, like forcing her nails into wood. The sentients casting the shield would feel it just as much. It was a battle of wills. 'Sandhya, Kane, help me.'

All three focused on the exact same point. The spot became irritated, throbbing a sore yellow shade before peeling open. They were in. Leonie seized hold of the gap with her mind and tore it asunder, forcing it further apart. It hurt, fuck it really hurt her head. 'Get through!' she hissed.

Valentina slipped through the hole first, followed by Chinara.

'Sandhya, go, I got it.' Sandhya glided in. 'Kane, quick!'

'No! You go,' they said. 'I'll hold it open for you.'

'Can you manage it?'

'Go!' they cried and Leonie propelled herself in. Kane could only hold it a second and the barrier sealed behind her, trapping Kane on the other side. Too late, Leonie saw what would happen. With the barrier between them, there was no one to keep Kane afloat. 'No!' Leonie screamed as Kane plummeted to the ground. She held out her hands. She found she couldn't stop them, but she could slow them.

Leonie rapidly lowered herself to the ground, an ordinary field on the fringes of town. On the other side of the invisible forcefield, Kane lay in a hedgerow, motionless. Chinara landed next to her. 'Are they OK?'

Leonie cast her mind out, difficult through the divide. 'They're alive. They're hurt.' She looked to Chinara. 'What am I doing?'

'Everything you can,' she replied gravely.

Leonie couldn't get to Kane, the wall now between them. 'Fuck.' She saw them stir, thank gods, but still felt powerless.

'Come on, or all this was for nothing. Niamh needs you.'

She reached for her girlfriend's hands. 'Stop! Wait! Chinara, now that we're here I don't know what to do. Where do we start?' Maybe it was the tornado ride over, or maybe it was sheer panic, but she was pretty sure she was going to hurl. Her mouth went wet like it was lubing itself for puke.

Chinara held her cheeks, almost blinkering her from

the world. 'Calm, my love. Where is Niamh? Can you feel her?'

Leonie put out her feelers, letting her senses wash over Hebden Bridge. 'Fuck.'

'What is it?'

She took hold of Chinara's hand and lifted them both into the air. 'She's hurt too . . .'

Chapter Fifty-Five

THE HUNT OF HEBDEN BRIDGE IV

Elle

Elle had never seen a car flip over in real life. It was oddly graceful, like the time she'd forced Jez to take her to the ballet in Leeds. How could something so big travel through the air with such delicacy? Only then it slammed back down to earth with an ugly crunch.

'Oh my god! Mum!' Holly cried, but Elle pulled her back by the arm. They had abandoned the car on the bridge when all the water pipes started bursting up through the road. She'd seen Niamh's car turn back around and head this way.

'Just wait!' Elle screamed. 'It might explode!' That's what always happened on TV.

The ground shook again under their feet and Holly fell to her knees. 'You have to help them.'

She was right. 'Stay behind me, Holly. I mean it.'

Elle ran into the road, hopping over the jagged crevices that now scarred the street. Where were the witches causing the earthquakes? The patter of water raining down drowned out anything else, and Elle could only hope they were some way away.

Before they even reached Niamh's car, Tiger wriggled out through the shattered passenger-side window. He shook his whole body before he limped over to them. Holly hooked her fingers through his collar and checked him over. Elle's trainers crunched over broken glass. She crouched and saw Theo first, held upside-down by her seatbelt. She was alive, wriggling, trying to free herself. 'Theo, are you hurt?'

She shook her head no. Elle saw Luke was face down on the roof of the car, and Niamh was unconscious. This was not good. Theo managed to get her seatbelt off and she landed on the upturned roof with a thud. 'Holly! Help Theo out – carefully.'

Elle squatted down at the driver's side and reached for Niamh's head. She touched it gently, and it was enough to revive her friend. Niamh's eyes popped open and she recoiled in fear. 'It's just me!' Elle said.

'Elle?'

'Yeah, you OK, love?'

'I can't move . . . Luke! Is Luke OK?'

Elle reached for him and put her hand on his. 'He's in a bad way.' What was the point in lying? Niamh would know.

'Can you get my seatbelt off?' Elle tried, but it wouldn't budge. 'OK, stand back . . .' Niamh used her powers to rip the thing clean off and lower herself down. She crawled out of the wreckage.

'Come here . . .' Elle took hold of Niamh's cheeks, fixing up the superficial cuts and scrapes in seconds.

'Thank you.'

'Theo, let me take a look at you . . .' She was forgetting, of course, that Theo could fix herself without assistance.

'Mum, is Luke dead?'

Elle crouched down again. 'No, but I need to help him urgently. Niamh, can you get him out?'

'Everyone stand back . . .' Niamh held out her hands and ripped the top – or rather the undercarriage – off the car and tossed it aside like she was opening a tin of sardines. Staggering slightly from his weight, she then floated Luke out of the wreckage and to the side of the road.

Elle grabbed his jacket and rolled him over, mid-air. Niamh rested him on the pavement. Elle placed her hands on his bloodied forehead again. This poor guy was having a rough summer and it was only May. 'His ribs are broken, they're crushing his lungs.'

'Can you fix it?' Niamh asked.

'Maybe . . . if it's a clean break.' Theo came to her side and placed her hands tentatively too. In no position to refuse assistance, Elle said, 'Can you help?'

Theo nodded and they got to work. She started to direct her energy towards the lungs while Theo tackled the cracked ribs and—

STAY WHERE YOU ARE. A voice boomed through their heads. Elle lost her focus.

'Don't stop,' Niamh told her.

Three HMRC witches floated down Market Street through fog and spray, led by Robyn Jones – a witch she wouldn't want to meet down a dark alley late at night. Which was a shame, given that's exactly where they were.

IF YOU RUN, WE ARE AUTHORISED TO TAKE LETHAL ACTION.

'Niamh, I need more time,' Elle said. Niamh lifted what

was left of her car and hurled it in their direction as if she was bowling. Robyn raised a hand and waved it at the bakery. The pretty display window folded like it were cardboard. 'Theo, run!' Niamh cried.

FREEZE OR WE WILL DISABLE YOU.

The HMRC witches continued to advance. Niamh pushed four parked cars into a barrier between them, but the witches drifted over them, a minor hurdle. 'Theo, just go! I'll hold them off as long as I can!'

Elle pushed Theo away from Luke. 'Theo, love, go. I've got this.'

Theo started to back down the street, not taking her eyes off the Finch sister on Robyn's left – Elle could never tell them apart – as she gathered a ball of lightning between her hands. There was a mean glint in her eye. Elle had never liked that posh bitch.

'Theo, run!' Elle shrieked as a different witch swooped down behind her – an ambush. Only then, the newcomer shot a bolt of lightning *past* them and directly at the Finch sister, who was punched all the way back down the street. Elle's head spun.

'Valentina!' Niamh shouted, recognising her. Elle had no clue who she was, but it looked like she was on their side. This Valentina caught hold of Theo and they embraced as if they were old friends.

'Take cover!' a voice called from above.

Elle looked up and saw Chinara overhead. Oh, thank the goddess. *The cavalry.* Even from a distance, she saw Chinara suck a deep breath in and, her eyes blazing white, she opened her mouth wide, unleashing an inferno from her lungs. A torrent of fire poured down Market Street, driving the HMRC witches back. Elle shielded her face. It was intensely hot.

'She can breathe fire!' Holly exclaimed.

'Yes she fucking can,' Leonie said, landing gracefully alongside her, seemingly out of nowhere. 'Why'd you think they call her *The Dragon?*'

'Literally no one has ever called her that,' Holly muttered.

Elle grabbed onto Leonie, and Niamh got in on the hug action too. 'I have never been so glad to see anyone in my life,' Elle whispered into Leonie's curls.

'You come from Pilates, babe?' said Leonie and Elle told her to fuck off.

'How did you know?' Niamh said.

'You got friends in high places.' Leonie released the hug and nodded towards someone else. Sandhya Kaur coyly hung back.

Niamh went to greet her. 'You have no idea what this means, Sandhya. Thank you.'

The junior witch shrugged. 'It was the right thing to do.'

There wasn't time for this. Elle dropped to her knees at Luke's side once more. 'I need to get him somewhere safe so I can fix him.'

Like a sign from heaven above – the traditional one – the front doors to the Baptist church opened, and Sheila Henry emerged, in her vicar uniform. Who knew what she was doing at the church at this hour – again, thank God – but Elle had known her since she was a little girl *and* she and Annie were old, old friends. Possibly more than friends, but Elle didn't like to think about that.

'What in the name of creation is going on out here?' Sheila watched in horror as Chinara continued to drive HMRC back towards town with fire. 'I didn't have Judgement Day on the calendar, it must be said.'

'Sheila! We need help!' Elle pleaded.

And Sheila was not the sort of person to question the nature of help someone in need needed. 'Quickly, then. Get your bums inside.' Sheila was on the council. This was directly disobeying Helena, and Elle sensed that Sheila knew that.

Elle looked to Leonie. 'Go. We've got you covered. Go on!'

Niamh and Theo lifted Luke between them and started towards the Baptist church gardens. It was an imposing structure, not especially church-like, the entrance flanked by looming stone columns on both sides. It was old, secure. Elle followed the patient. 'Holly, come on.'

'I'll stay with Leonie—'

'Holly, *now*!' Elle's eyes said she was not fucking kidding and Holly meekly followed them into the church. Elle cast one last look at Leonie as she took flight into a brawl, and desperately hoped it wouldn't be the last time she saw her. This was horribly familiar. She couldn't believe they were back here again. How had no one learned *anything* from war? What? It wasn't bad enough last time, let's go another round?

Once inside, Sheila closed the double doors. 'They're hazel and mistletoe,' she said. 'No one's getting through those in a hurry. Now who's going to tell me what's going on?'

Elle ignored her question, instead getting to work on Luke, who now lay by the font at the rear of the church. Wartime mode: trying to heal with chaos all around. She closed her eyes and located the livid scarlet hot spots in his body. If she didn't get this right, he'd never breathe normally again. Bones are a piece of piss, but organs are something else. Honestly, he might be beyond repair.

Niamh, meanwhile, filled Sheila in. 'Helena is after us.'

'Ah, this is our Sullied Child?'

'Sheila, I swear on Gaia, Theo is harmless.'

Sheila huffed. 'Oh, for crying out loud, I know. Helena wants to spend some time at our Rainbow Youth Group.'

Elle smiled, absorbing some of Sheila's positive light and channelling it into Luke. Sheila was Hebden Bridge's lesbian nana. She should have known she'd be unflappable.

'We can't stay here,' Niamh said. 'Those doors won't hold out forever.'

'Can we fight them all?' Holly asked.

'*You* can't!' Elle called over. She was a mum; she multitasked.

'No,' Niamh said. 'But I've had an idea. Is there a back way out?' Sheila said there was. 'OK, Theo and I will head up to Hardcastle Crags and get to Annie's.'

'Why?' said Holly.

The water conduit. Theo answered for her.

'Yes. If we can't go *over* Hebden Bridge, I'm betting we can go *under* it. The conduit will send us to the sister well in Blacko.'

Sheila nodded. 'Go now. Shield yourselves.'

Niamh came to Luke's side. 'Is he OK?'

Elle looked up at her. 'I don't know. I need time. This could take a while, and even then . . .'

'You stay here. Leonie has got the church covered . . . and it's not Luke she's after.'

Elle nodded. Niamh swept away but Holly came to her side. 'Can I help you?'

'No,' Niamh told her. 'Your mother is the only person who can save us if something goes wrong. I need you to protect *her*. And Tiger too. Can you do that?'

402

Holly didn't flinch. 'Of course.' She once again took hold of Tiger's collar so he wouldn't follow his owner out.

'Theo, come on.' Theo hugged Holly and followed after Niamh. Elle couldn't help but think every goodbye felt very final.

Sheila showed Niamh and Theo to an inconspicuous door at the side of the pulpit and they slipped out. Holly returned to Elle's side. 'Is there anything I can do?'

Elle tried to focus on Luke. 'Not really, just be careful. I can't worry about you and fix him.'

Sheila returned – presumably having shown them the exit. 'There was no one out back . . .'

Glass shattered overhead. Elle's eyes pinged open just in time to see a trash can sail in over the gallery level and crash land near the altar. A solid shape filled the now empty window frame and the bulk of Robyn Jones levitated into the church. 'Shit,' Elle said.

Sheila, a sentient herself, held up her hands. 'Stay where you are!' she commanded, but Robyn was the more powerful witch by far. With a snarl, she flung Sheila down the aisle, and the rotund vicar clattered into the wooden pews with a cry.

Holly charged. 'No!' Elle screamed, but she ignored her. Her daughter, her only girl. Elle had never known fear like this. It felt suffocating. In the moment, her whole body froze and she could only look on as her child took on the witch singlehandedly.

Robyn landed and laughed as Holly sprinted towards her. 'What are you gonna do?' she said, a sneer curling her mouth. 'Float a feather at me?'

Holly stopped mid-aisle. 'Not a feather, *glass*.' There were dozens of shards of glass all over the floor. Holly raised them up and whipped them at the Amazon. Like a swarm of flies, the fragments tore at Robyn's face. She staggered back, holding her hands to her eyes. 'Bitch!'

Elle breathed again, and felt a swell of pride. The crimson waves pouring off Luke were now a dull orange. It was working, he would live. Elle left his side and crawled down the left-hand aisle, keeping her chest low to the ground. Hopefully, Robyn wouldn't see her coming.

The tiny glass blades continued to swirl around Robyn, whose face was now covered in nicks and cuts, blood trickling down her face. 'Nice try, little girl.' Robyn grimaced and held out a big hand.

Holly choked like that same hand was around her throat. The glass rained back to the church floor as Robyn lifted her daughter off the ground. Elle crawled faster, seeing only snippets as she passed each pew.

'You'll fucking pay for that, you little shit,' Robyn snarled, her teeth red. Holly's legs kicked and thrashed at thin air. Her eyes bulged out of the sockets.

Now behind her, Elle stood and dove over the prayer rail. She clamped both hands on either side of Robyn's skull. 'Why don't you pick on someone your own size?' she hissed in her ear.

The role of the healer is to absorb the pain from a patient, but that stream can flow in either direction. Elle's body was still full of the agony she'd cleansed from Luke, and now she turned it all back around, pouring the vicious, vivid reds into Robyn Jones's head.

The big witch howled in abject agony. It was a sickening, pitiful noise, and it went against every instinct in Elle. Holly fell into an untidy heap but scrambled back to her feet as Robyn folded to her knees. She screamed and screamed as Elle continued to twist her bones and fire her pain synapses. A second more, and the torment was too much for her. Robyn blacked out, slumping forward. Elle released her, her body tingling all over.

'Wow,' Holly said. 'Go Mum.'

Elle said nothing. She had work to do.

Chapter Fifty-Six

THE HUNT OF HEBDEN BRIDGE V

Niamh

She had to land before she dropped Theo off her back. She brought them to an unsteady and ungraceful stop on the edge of the mill walk, deep in the heart of Hardcastle Crags. She let Theo go and fell onto her bottom at the side of the stream. It was flowing fast after the recent rain, gushing over the rocks in foamy rapids. 'Sorry, I need a rest,' she said.

Are you OK? Theo summoned a discreet ball of fire in the palm of her hand so she could see her face.

'Yeah, just give me a second.' She'd grabbed Theo and levitated, piggybacking her up the steep, steep hill to save time, but staying low to avoid being seen. The dense, dark forest now provided some cover and she dared to regain her strength.

She took a deep breath and crawled to the water's edge. Her limbs felt hollow, airy, like she might faint. She made a cup out of her hand and took a couple of mouthfuls.

The water was safe enough to drink for a witch. Theo came closer and wrapped her fingers around Niamh's wrist. She transferred some radiance into her and Niamh felt it flow through her veins like honey. That was better.

She sat herself on a smooth boulder, still absorbing as much energy as she could from nature. The crash and flight had drained her. Who was she kidding? The last three months had drained her. 'We'll follow the beck,' she told Theo. 'Water is powerful and noisy, it'll hide us from the sentients.'

I'm so sorry about this. It's all my fault.

'Fuck that jazz. All she had to do was leave you well alone. You've done nothing wrong.' She took hold of Theo's hands and steered her to sit next to her on the rock. 'You hear me? What happened in your past – at your old school – is on us. The coven should have found you *years* ago and taught you about your gifts. The system failed you, not the other way around.'

That doesn't help us now.

'No, it doesn't, but I'll tell you what will: your powers. I need you to fight now. When the time comes, give it all you got.'

What if I hurt you?

'I'm a big girl. Theo, you are so strong. Don't hold back.' She didn't look at all happy about that. Niamh rose once more to her feet. 'Let's get going. We should get to Annie's in no time at all if we follow the beck.'

Hand in hand, they started down the haphazard forest path. For the first time, Niamh thought they might just succeed.

Chapter Fifty-Seven

THE HUNT OF HEBDEN BRIDGE VI

Leonie

Where did the big bitch go? Leonie flew around the perimeter of the church. One of the windows was broken. She looked through the gap and saw Elle deal with Robyn Jones all by herself. The giant went down like *TIMBER!*

Remind me not to fuck with you, she told Elle and refocused on what was happening outside the chapel.

Chinara and Valentina were doing most of the heavy lifting, beating back the HMRC capes with fire and lightning and wind, back towards Market Square. Leonie took another peek inside the church and couldn't see Niamh or Theo anywhere.

Niamh? You there?

There was no response. Leonie glided back down to street level and to Sandhya's position. 'Do you know where Niamh is? She's not in the church any more.'

Sandhya winced. 'I can sense her, but it's weak.'

'Me too. Maybe she's near water.'

Leonie saw the other Finch sister soaring down, diving like a bird of prey. She was moving too fast to stop her. She unleashed a bolt of lightning, knocking Chinara out of the air. She tumbled to street level, rolling arse over tit.

Leonie braced herself against Sandhya and they both seized hold of Finch mid-flight and slammed her into the side of a parked van so hard she left a dent. She went down and stayed down.

Leonie ran to Chinara's side. 'You OK?'

'I felt that one.'

Leonie helped her up. They were in the town centre now, on the cobbled street alongside the river. On the other side of the bridge, a witch materialised in a grey cape, then another, and then another three. 'Fuck, she's called for backup.'

'Where's Helena?' Sandhya yelled.

'I don't know.'

Valentina landed alongside them, her face pasty and dotted with sweat beads. 'I can't hold them any more. I'm getting weak.'

The grey capes flanked towards them. 'I'm bored of this shit now,' Leonie said. She marched towards the bridge. 'Stop!' she shouted, almost insouciantly.

All five witches froze. Five was a lot. She'd done three-somes, but never fivesomes. Still, Leonie felt *strong*. Stronger than she'd felt in years.

She knew the one up front – Jen Yamato. She'd once been salty about Diaspora, saying Leonie favoured Black witches. Well someone fucking ought to. This seemed appropriate payback. 'Forward,' she commanded. The witches, fighting her hex, dragged their feet forwards, walking like something out of the 'Thriller' video. They tried to resist her control, but she held on with everything she had. Leonie steered them all onto the Old Packhorse Bridge.

She turned to Chinara, telling her what she wanted. Chinara came to her side. 'Ready,' she said simply.

'Sorry about this, ladies,' Leonie said. '*Following orders*, though. Seriously?'

Sandhya, help me hold them. The other sentient joined them.

Leonie held out both hands and twisted her fists. The sandstone bridge was old, sturdy. The mighty blocks didn't want to budge. She squeezed harder, her nails digging into her palms. Blood trickled from her clenched fists. She dug and dug and twisted. With a cry, she snapped it in two. The famous bridge that gave Hebden Bridge its name crumbled like sand.

The witches screamed as she released her hold on them, and they plummeted into the river below.

Chinara raised her hand and a mighty torrent of water surged down from the hills. The tsunami broke the banks, spilling across Market Square and washing all the witches downstream. Taken by surprise, they flailed helplessly as the surge tide carried them out of town.

'Incy wincy spider,' Leonie said.

'What?' Chinara replied.

'Never mind. Babe, I just fucked Hebden Bridge.'

Chinara didn't flinch. 'Nothing lasts forever.'

Leonie scanned the streets. The Finch sister was still in a heap, unconscious in the road. They seemed to be alone. Market Square was flooded again, brown murky water streaming up against the shops and pub, but the damage wasn't *too* bad. 'I don't like this,' Leonie said. 'Where the fuck is Helena?'

Chapter Fifty-Eight

THE HUNT OF HEBDEN BRIDGE VII

Niamh

Moonlight rippled on the stream as they made their way through the forest. The air had a bite. Niamh felt strong, nocturnal, like the creatures around her. She felt bats, badgers, foxes. She borrowed from them, sharpening her vision, heightening her sense of smell.

She ducked past branches and leaves, flitting between the trees. She was a wild animal. Humans *are* wild animals under the bras and perfumes and mascara. We're beasts. And she would fight to protect the cub.

Behind her, Theo stopped. 'What's wrong? We're almost there.' With her new night vision, she could just about make out the dark shape of the water mill. Another five minutes and they'd be out of Hebden Bridge. Then what? Well, they'd cross that bridge when they came to it.

Even in the darkness, Niamh saw panic all over Theo's face. *Can you feel that?*

'What?' She expanded her senses across the woods.

Something's coming . . .

'The Big Bad Wolf,' a voice from above called.

Lightning shook the whole sky, forks licking the earth. Niamh pulled Theo close and they both staggered into the fast-flowing stream. She stumbled over backwards, landing in the freezing water. It snatched her breath away.

Helena hovered over the beck, electricity dancing over her body. Her eyes were as black as the sky. 'It was a good plan,' she called down. 'I'd forgotten about the old water conduit at Annie's until you reminded me.'

'How?' Niamh shrieked, aware that probably wasn't the most pressing question.

'You're not the only adept in town any more.'

Helena held out a pale hand and lifted Theo out of the stream without touching her. How was she doing this? Impossible! Theo's wet hand slipped through Niamh's fingers. 'Theo!'

Theo wriggled mid-air, trying to get free, but Helena held fast. She looked Theo over quizzically as though she was seeing her for the first time. '*This* is what she's so scared of?' There was something amiss with Helena's voice. It was too deep, too husky. 'Pathetic.' With a swipe of her hand, she tossed Theo into the trees like a ragdoll.

Niamh stood. She flexed her fingers and lifted the largest boulder from the bed of the stream. She fired it at Helena, only for it to shatter around her like it was nothing more than a lump of dry soil. Niamh almost laughed, some hysterical reflex.

'Can you remember when we were kids?' Helena growled. 'We always used to argue about who'd win in a fight? I'm gonna go out on a limb and say it would be me . . .'

Niamh's eyes widened. Downstream, the water turned

into fire, pulsing in her direction. She blinked, praying it was merely a glamour . . . and yet it continued to blaze towards her. Niamh ducked, shielding her face from the burning tide. She braced for pain, but it never came. She glanced up and saw the river of flames diverting around her. She had a small island of water left, but could still feel flames licking at the hairs on her arm.

'Stick around.' Helena stated the obvious and lowered herself to the riverbank.

Niamh tried to push the flames back with her mind. Fire is made of matter, like everything else. It needs gas to burn. But the more she pushed, the closer the fire got, her safe circle constricting around her.

She was trapped. She watched as Helena stalked through the trees to where Theo had fallen. She was hurt, a nasty gash on her forehead. *Get up*, Niamh told her. *Theo, get up. She's coming.*

Theo came to and – terrified – scrambled into the undergrowth. *Run!*

Niamh looked on in horror as the forest seemed to come alive. Flexing her fingers, Helena manipulated the trees and roots around her, entangling Theo in a web of branches and shoots. She hoisted her aloft, the poor girl stuck like a fly. Niamh saw the vines tighten around Theo like serpents. She was going to strangle the life out of her.

Theo was terrified, too scared to put up anything like a fight. Her thoughts screamed through the forest, raw and feral.

Niamh wept. She felt weak, useless. There was only one thing left, only one card left to play, although it wasn't her strongest suit. She was an adept. Part sentient, part healer. Niamh knelt down in the water. She closed her eyes. She let go. She opened herself like a flower in bloom, offering as much of herself to Theo as she humanly could, releasing what energy she had left over the water and into Theo's body. It flowed. It shimmered: silver and gold, and indigo and sapphire. Niamh felt it ebb away from her.

Take it.

Take it all.

Use it.

She'd give her every last drop if she had to.

Chapter Fifty-Nine

METAMORPHOSIS

Helena

They stood over the child. 'Now what are we going to do with you?'

Theo woke up and, in shock, started to back away, scrabbling through the undergrowth.

'Where are you going?'

Helena cast a brief glance at the trees and a host of vines and branches reached down for Theo like tentacles. The forest obeyed, seizing his wrists and torso, hoisting him off the ground. A fly tangled in a web. He made a tragic whimpering sound. She curled a vine around his face to silence him.

'Not so scary now are you . . .' Helena said now that she had a captive audience. 'You understand I can't let you live, Theo? Despite anything Niamh may have told you, it's really nothing personal. I couldn't care less whether you call yourself a boy or a girl or a helicopter. The problem is that you're a *time bomb*, whether you know it or not. I swore an oath twenty-five years ago that I would put the coven above all else.'

Helena felt tears sting her eyes. Belial held it all back.

'The things I have done to stop you. The lengths I have gone to. It has to matter. It has to mean something.'

Theo's eyes – frantic, like a cornered animal – became suddenly tranquil. Helena frowned. Perhaps her creepers were too tight. His eyes closed a moment and, when they reopened, they seemed to glow in the night. They gleamed like gold or amber. His expression changed too. *Resolve.*

Helena looked back to where she'd imprisoned Niamh. She too was glowing, luminescent, as if she was being healed. She no longer needed to summon lightning from the atmosphere, she generated it within. She struck Niamh down with a bolt.

Theo, however, continued to shine. His skin shimmered with the most incredible pearlescent sheen, a radiance beaming from inside. Helena backed off, ready to strike him down dead. It was so bright though, too bright, like staring at the sun. She held her arm in front of her face. 'Stop this!' she cried. 'Stop this now.'

The light reached a crescendo and died down. Helena squinted and saw a girl hovering amid the trees. The vines and branches elegantly released her, retreating back from where they came.

Oh, the clever little witch. It was and wasn't Theo. Recognisably the same human, in the same jeans and t-shirt, but also different. She was quite beautiful really, long raven hair swimming about her delicate face as though she were submerged. She gracefully lowered herself to the forest floor.

'An effective glamour,' she conceded.

'It's not a glamour,' she said, and it took Helena a second to realise she'd spoken aloud for the first time. 'Niamh healed me, and this is who I am, who I always was. I'm Theodora. The way I should have been. The way I choose to be.'

She had a new poise, a new strength. Pompous little twat. She wasn't going to tolerate a lecture at this stage in the game. 'You are still the Sullied Child.'

'I'm *a* child. I'm just a girl, Ms Vance, and I mean you no harm. I don't want to hurt anyone.'

Helena felt her teeth grind together. 'What you *want* doesn't matter. You'll destroy us all.'

Helena conjured balls of fire in both hands and hurled them at him. It didn't matter how pretty she looked, how much fucking hair she had, whether it had a penis or not, that thing was a boy *inside*. She wanted it dead.

A cold front blew in around Theo, extinguishing her fireballs. The wind lifted her – him – off the floor and a flurry of ice and snow pummelled Helena. She stumbled back, almost going down, but soon found her footing. Did he really think he could better her? 'You'll have to do better than that,' she growled.

Lightning split the sky, bolts pouring into Theo. That forced him back down to earth. The hailstorm subsided and Helena held out a hand. *Help me, Master Belial, make me strong.*

The scrawny kid shot towards her. It screamed as it was catapulted through the clearing and into her waiting palm. She wrapped her fingers around his bony neck, holding him aloft. Belial had kept his promise. She was strong, none stronger.

Theo gasped, trying to prise her fingers off his throat. He looked like a girl, but he was not. *He is not.* Yes, yes this was right. She wanted to squeeze the life out of him with her bare hands. She wanted to feel his last breath. She wanted to feel the body go soft and limp.

Annie. Losing her friends. This *thing* inside her body. This was all because of *him*.

None of this would have happened if he hadn't arrived. She squeezed harder and harder, her – *his* – face went blue.

Stefan. Her mother. Hale. Tammy Girl.

You were glad when he died.

What? No. Helena's breath trembled. Tears burned her eyes.

They don't like you.

No!

It was *him*.

For all this pain he has caused.

For all he had done.

Chapter Sixty

HUMAN WEAKNESS

Niamh

She was weak. Transferring almost all her radiance into Theo had left her drained, flat on her back in the shallow waters. She felt the stream ripple against her cheek, through her hair, like it was nuzzling her back to consciousness.

She had felt it, though – Theo's transformation. The final piece of a puzzle, snapping into place. A sense of rightness. The satisfaction of completion.

But only for a moment. And then terror.

Absorbing energy from the water, from the silt, Niamh forced herself up. She sat up and saw, through the flames, Helena throttling Theo. A remodelled Theo. She lurched forwards to help, but the flames leapt at her face again, burning her. She smelled singed flesh. 'Theo!' she screamed. She saw her look her way, tears running down her face, but she could only kick and wriggle.

'Theo, focus! You're stronger than she is!' If she panicked, she wouldn't be able to control her magic. Niamh reached out through the fire again, but the flames snapped at her fingers.

419

Niamh wasn't an elemental. She didn't know how to use the water to douse the flames.

Oh.

That wise old Obi-Wan Kenobi Yoda bitch.

Annie's words came to her: *You can't fight fire. Water extinguishes fire just by merit of being water.* What did that mean? She was surrounded by water, but Helena had turned water into fire. All bets were off.

Helena, a fire witch. Niamh, a water witch.

You can't fight fire. Water extinguishes fire just by merit of being water.

Did it mean she could beat her? Niamh climbed to her feet, her legs uncertain, and held out a hand. With everything she had left, she tried to throw Helena down. Helena's head whipped to face her and punched her back, just with a blink. She fell back painfully onto her bottom. She slapped the water in frustration.

You can't fight fire. So just be water? What did that even mean? Niamh couldn't focus. The fire, Theo's screams, her sodden icy clothes. Too much noise.

Niamh dunked herself under the water. She needed silence. It was a myth that witches could breathe underwater – as had been discovered during many a witch trial – but Niamh had always found a certain quietude in her element.

It all went out. Blissful solace. With everything silent, she could hear *everything*. All of nature's symphony, all perfectly tuned. She could pretend, under here, that everything was fine. Every part of the orchestra was exactly where it should be: percussion from the croaking toad; a violinist spider in her web; the barn owl on woodwind in the old mill; the adder under his rock and the beehive, dormant until morning, inside the hollow trunk of a rotten tree stump.

Sometimes, you soar so far out of yourself you see the whole picture as Gaia herself must see it. Above and below and from all sides. How things happened, and when and why. The beginning and end of things.

Ten years ago, Ciara used a glamour to incapacitate Helena in the Hotel Carnoustie. Twenty-five years ago, a thirteen-year-old Elle had saved Helena's life when they were far from home among the bluebells.

Something only a friend would know.

Niamh surfaced, letting the water run off her face. She got to her feet. The punchline was it wasn't even difficult. *Birds and insects are easy.*

She cast her mind out, over the water, through the fire, past Helena and Theo, into the reeds and grasses, and inside the rotten stump. The hive was full of life, just waiting for a wake-up call.

Niamh kicked the nest.

Helena didn't even notice the first bee. It orbited around her face, but she was much too focused on Theo. Theo herself was slipping out of consciousness, her skin a sickly blue. Niamh didn't have long. Two or three honeybees can make a compelling buzz and Helena realised what was happening.

She dropped Theo with a thud.

Five, six, seven bees. They danced around Helena in a figure-eight formation. Helena turned to Niamh, her black eyes blazed with rage. 'Copying your sister's party piece?'

The distraction worked. The flames died down on the water and Niamh waded to the riverbank, every step that bit worse. She shook her head sadly. With great regret, she said simply, 'No.'

Ten, fifteen, twenty bees.

Not happy at being awakened. The buzz became a humming chorus, an almost physical wall of sound.

Helena looked into Niamh's eyes and saw she was telling the truth. She panicked, swatting at the bees. 'Ni—' A bee flew in her mouth.

Thirty, forty bees.

They started to sting. Helena screamed, toppling backwards into the undergrowth. Nature is brutal and, once one bee has stung, it sends a pheromone telling other bees to attack the threat too. The insects swarmed her, crawling over her face, in her ears and hair. Helena clutched now at her own throat, her windpipe closing up. Niamh had seen this once before, and it wasn't pretty. Her lips swelled up like plums, her face turning red.

Helena's puffy eyes closed, and when they opened, they were hazel again. Helena reached out to Niamh, wordlessly begging for help. Bees crawled over her hand.

Niamh first ran to Theo's side. There were nasty welts on her neck, but she seemed otherwise fine. 'Are you OK?'

'Yes,' she said aloud, and it was quite the song hearing her voice at long last. It was unexpectedly, well, mundane.

Niamh focused and shooed the bees away, dismissing them. She forced them into retreat. The throbbing hum subsided.

Helena's body convulsed, her spine arching. Niamh and Theo recoiled as a viscous green smog erupted from Helena's swollen mouth. Niamh's hand flew to her nose. The odour was putrid, sulfuric.

'What *is* that?' Theo asked.

Niamh had seen something similar once before, after she attacked Ciara, when the entity left her body. 'It's a demon,' Niamh said, understanding now how Helena had been so strong.

The green cloud started to take shape in the air above Helena. Niamh and Theo stood together ready to repel it. The outline was perhaps that of a bull, something with two curved horns at any rate. The form seemed inquisitive, considering them, sizing them up, before retreating. The foul fog seeped into the roots and leaves of the trees closest to them, off to lick its wounds.

The forest was the forest again. The stream babbled, the night air got its crunch back, and everything smelled of wild garlic and damp moss. Only Helena's desperate choking was out of place. Her eyes had closed up, her whole face pillowy and deformed.

Niamh went to her side, and burst into tears.

This was so fucking unnecessary.

She knelt beside her. How on earth had they got here? Her friend was disfigured, fighting to breathe. And she'd done it. Niamh buried her face in her hands and cried. She wasn't even sure if she could heal her, she was so far gone.

There was one more thing she had to do, and she could only do it while Helena was weakened. She touched the side of Helena's temple with her index finger and read her. She could have felt the vinegar of guilt a mile away. *Annie.* Niamh witnessed her final moments: the cottage turning bitterly cold, sub-zero. Annie's heart gave out first. That was what killed her. She saw her slump down in her armchair, saw her wig slip off.

Niamh let go and pulled her knees up under her chin. She had so badly wanted to be wrong on that one. Helena had killed her, and Niamh wondered the exact point, the fork in the road, where they'd lost her.

Sobs shook her body. At first she felt Theo tentatively embrace her, her slight shoulders awkward. Although she'd now found her voice, she said nothing. She *smelled* Leonie – lavender, patchouli and cigarette smoke – before she heard her voice or felt her curls brush against her cheek. 'Babe, don't cry,' she whispered. 'We're here, now. We're here.'

Niamh collapsed against her and heard another voice. 'I can save her.' It was Elle, gently, in her other ear. 'It'll all be fine.' Elle's arms wrapped around them all.

Niamh peeked out from behind her hands and saw Chinara land effortlessly on the riverbank, Holly clinging on to her back for dear life. She pressed her head against Elle's and felt the healer absorb some of her guilt, her anguish. 'You did what you had to,' Elle said before turning her attention to Helena.

'Oh my goddess,' Holly said, racing to Theo. 'Behold the glow up!'

Leonie was similarly enthusiastic, pulling Theo into a bear hug.

Niamh watched as Elle worked on Helena. 'Luke . . . ?'

Elle looked over her shoulder. 'He'll be fine. Probably. He was coming to when we came to find you. He's with Sandhya and Valentina . . . they'll call an ambulance now that the spell is broken.' She concentrated on Helena, whose injuries started to improve; the swelling going down and the hives fading.

Niamh let herself go deaf, focusing on the chatter of the beck. She wanted the silence back a moment.

She watched Holly giddily admire Theo's new features; Leonie and Chinara kiss tenderly; Elle work diligently on Helena, and, somewhere, Luke was OK. Niamh's shoulders unclenched, and she wiped away her tears. She was safe. She'd be *fine*.

She was with her coven.

Chapter Sixty-One

AFTERMATH

Niamh

They got back into town the old-fashioned way: on foot. Just as tiring as flying probably, but no one had the mental capacity to even consider it. At least it was all downhill. By the time they reached Hebden Bridge village, the mundanes were all over the 'earthquake' that had befallen their town.

The huddle of bedraggled women emerging from the woods probably didn't seem too out of place. Reverend Sheila Henry had alerted HMRC Scotland who had sent a unit to Hardcastle Crags. Helena, still unconscious, would be taken to the infirmary at Grierlings until they established what the appropriate next step was.

What a fucking mess, honestly. Blue lights swooped across the sandstone buildings and the faces in the crowd.

How did we sleep through it?

What magnitude was it?

It's a miracle no one was hurt!

News crews and police vans and ambulances clogged Market Street, townsfolk especially keen to get a look at where the Old Packhorse Bridge had 'collapsed'.

'I can't believe you took out the bridge,' Holly told Leonie. 'Do we just live in Hebden now? Hebden Hole? Hebden Gap?'

Elle said her goodbyes, explaining how she had to get home to face the music with Jez. She told them she'd left on a bit of a bombshell. She took Holly, and they went to find their car, hopefully still in one piece after the fight.

Niamh scanned the crowds. He had to be here somewhere. It wasn't hard to see Luke amidst the chaos outside the White Swan. He towered over most of the heads. He was dirty, and bloodied, a paramedic trying to get him into the back of an ambulance, but he seemed to be looking for someone.

Their eyes met across the river. He was looking for her.

Niamh ran forward and lifted herself over the river, cloaked of course, from everyone except him. He ducked around the paramedic to get to her and she fell into his arms. 'You're OK!' she said, pressing her face into his chest. 'Thank the gods for that.'

'Did you just . . . ?' he told the crown of her head.

'Yep. That's something I can do,' she admitted, looking up at him. Sometimes the right time is that time. 'I can do other stuff too.'

He cupped her face in his big hands. 'It's OK, Niamh. I kinda figured there was something going on. I'm not daft.' He shrugged. 'I didn't think you were, like Supergirl, but we can work with it.'

'I'm not Supergirl,' she said, clutching his hands. 'I'm a witch.'

He considered this a moment and then nodded. 'That makes sense.'

'It does, doesn't it? You know that thing in between us? The thing that was stopping me and you from being me and you? It wasn't just Conrad. I used Conrad as an excuse. Well, this is what it is. I'm a witch and if we're going to go somewhere, you need to know that.'

'A witch? Like magic?'

'Yes.'

'Are you going to get in trouble for telling me?'

'Probably not.'

'Good. Are you . . . a good witch?'

Oh, that hit hard. She swore she felt her brain twist, like wringing out a sponge. 'No,' she said holding back a sob. 'There are no good witches or bad witches, there are just witches and the choices we make.'

'That's true of humans too.'

Niamh smiled. 'I'm still human. Just a witchy one.'

Luke smiled back. 'Well that's probably for the best. Can I kiss you?'

'You absolutely can.' He kissed her tenderly, dipping a toe, before they had a proper one. This time she wasn't even worried about what it meant. It was just lovely.

As she made him swear he wasn't physically hurt, and as she filled him in on what he'd actually slept through, Niamh became aware of a commotion behind them. She turned and saw Radley and a bunch of guys in cabal green capes sweep down Market Street towards them. Mundanes paid them no mind, which led Niamh to think they were shielding.

'Rad?' Leonie went to greet him, Niamh close behind. 'What are you doing here?'

He surveyed the destruction with grave concern. 'I could well ask the same of you. Is this your handiwork?'

'No. That's crazy talk,' Leonie said. Radley did not look convinced.

'What happened here?'

'Helena went mental and tried to kill the kid,' she jutted a thumb in Theo's direction.

If Radley was surprised at Theo's physical transformation, his face didn't register it. 'I see . . .'

Chinara was more forthcoming. 'She authorised a small unit from HMRC. She had no permits or court orders to remove Theo from Niamh's care. There were no grounds for immediate arrest. She also invoked a demoniac entity and we believe she assassinated Annie Device.'

Even ice-cold Radley flinched. 'I see . . .'

'That all you gonna say?' Leonie said. 'You see what? Cos I see fuck all.'

If possible, her brother became even more fraught. 'I wasn't aware you were here,' he said, carefully selecting his words.

'Then why are *you* here?' Niamh asked.

'We are investigating a serious cabal matter. There's been a . . . situation.'

'What's the cabal?' Luke whispered.

'Later,' she told him.

'A situation that isn't this situation? Well spit it out,' Leonie said.

'Earlier tonight, Dabney Hale was released from Grierlings,' Radley said gravely.

'What the fuck?' Leonie exploded.

'What? Why?' Niamh added.

Radley shook his head. 'We don't know! As best we can tell, Helena Vance went to Grierlings and let him go.'

'He just walked out of a high security prison?' Chinara said archly.

And now he blushed deeply. 'It would seem that way, yes. No one has any memory of it, however.'

They looked to one another. Theo looked somewhat

confused, Luke looked entirely confused. 'Helena invoked a demon,' Niamh said. 'It must have wanted Hale to be free.'

'Why?' Theo asked innocently.

Niamh had no answers for her. She'd been awake for almost twenty-four hours. Her brain was only just ticking on. Up on the hill, she'd felt more clarity than she had in a while but now everything was muddied again. How did Hale fit into all this? And what demon did Helena invoke?

'So Hale is at large?' Chinara asked.

'We believe so. We have him on CCTV leaving the compound, and that's the last we've seen of him. But rest assured this is a cabal matter and justice *will* be served.'

He was so resolute she could almost believe him. Niamh was so numb, so exhausted, in the moment, but when the morning came, she'd process what this information meant. It meant that the war was far from over.

Chapter Sixty-Two

THE PIPES

Helena

With hindsight she should have had this block torn down. There was a horrible irony that her only real professional foot-dragging would bring about her demise.

With hooded, faceless guards on each side, Helena was led through the narrow Grierlings corridors. It smelled chemical, petrolic, or whatever accelerant it was they used in the Pipes. One of the lights was bust and it buzzed and skittered. It reminded her of the bees in the forest and she squirmed. The guards pulled her along.

Oh, what was the point in delaying it further? They had her. Elle, the treacherous bitch, had healed her past the brink, but left her unconscious, undefended. Every sentient in HMRC had taken a voyeuristic peek inside her sleeping brain. They'd seen it all. Helena wished she'd died in the fight, in the forest. This pageant was mortifying.

It had always been a risk, of course, one that would have paid off had she succeeded on that miserable night four weeks ago. With hindsight – again – she saw her mistake very clearly: men.

Everything would have worked had she not listened to Hale, trusted Belial. She cared not about her friends, or Theo. Her greatest betrayal was to women. Men had made her reckless, tainted her cup with careless masculine bravado. She had no memory of going to Grierlings, of freeing Hale from his cell. On the day of the raid, she'd taken a power nap in the afternoon to prepare for the long night ahead. She saw now she hadn't been tired, she'd been *tricked*.

And now she would pay.

They reached the stairs that led up to the cavernous hall which housed the Pipes. One of the guards rang a discordant klaxon and someone on the other side opened up. Helena kept her eyes down, but felt the stares of those who were congregated. Ghouls all. She was frogmarched towards the middle chamber.

The Pipes – as Helena knew all too well – were built in 1899. After HMRC was formed they needed a deterrent against any witch harbouring thoughts of rebellion after the coven cosied up to the government and crown. The first part of the twentieth century saw a number of separatists organise, and if they attacked the coven, they ended up here.

It was known initially as Automated Execution by Fire, but that's not very catchy, is it? So the tall cylindrical chambers quickly became known as the Pipes. There were five of them, not that all five had ever been used at once. In 1909, self-proclaimed 'Covragettes' Enid Poole, Ava Crabtree and Phyllis Lyndon faced the fire simultaneously for their attempt to hex the king at the grand opening of the V&A Museum.

The Pipes had not been used since the 1960s. It was funny. Somewhere deep inside, Helena understood why her predecessors hadn't dismantled these monstrosities. Yes, they were a deterrent, but she'd always known that one day they'd have to fire these chambers up once more. Maybe there's a little bit of an oracle in all of us.

Helena was steered into the vast chain-link tube. She'd never stepped inside one. It was narrower than it looked from the outside, hardly room to stretch out her arms. The steel was blackened, charred. One of the guards swung the inner door shut and the lock slid in place with a metallic clank. She felt acutely nauseous, it reminded her of morning sickness. *Sisters' Malady* drifted down through the air vents and filled her nostrils. She couldn't light a match in here, far less get herself free.

'Helena Jane Vance,' a familiar Scottish voice said. Helena looked up finally. Oh, for fuck's sake, this really was adding insult to injury. Moira Roberts wore her ceremonial black robe. She, and the audience, were stood at a safe distance, behind a guard rail on a viewing platform.

The viewing platform was particularly morbid. The Victorians had a lot to answer for.

Helena ensured they hadn't brought Snow as she'd requested. She couldn't see Snow's distinctive hair. Good. That was something at least.

It was hard to see who everyone was with the hooded capes, but she assumed the figure in the wheelchair to be her mother, her father alongside. She inhaled. They shouldn't have to see this. To the left of Moira was the rest of the council, to her right was Niamh, Elle and Leonie. Elle wept openly.

That fucking Judas. And the gall of Leonie Jackman getting Chinara to attempt to overturn her sentence on humanitarian grounds. Was that supposed to be ironic?

She wouldn't be here if it weren't for them. This was their fault. Let them fucking weep.

A wave of hot air pulsed up through the grille she stood on. She wore simple, cheap black shoes and a matching shapeless smock. There would be no Balenciaga at this pyre.

Moira read from an iPad. 'As set out in the constitution of 1869, and recognised as witch law since the fifteenth century, you have been found guilty at fair trial of the following counts: Betraying your Coven; the Unlawful Killing of a Sister Witch, and the lesser charges of Consorting with Demons and Gross Misconduct in Public Office. The punishment is death by burning.'

Of all people, it was Niamh who spoke out. 'Please, Moira. We don't have to do this.' *Bit late for that, Niamh sweetheart.*

Moira winced, and Helena could only speculate at the hours they'd toiled in backrooms, deliberating her fate. Still, at least this was quick. They hadn't even detained her in Hale's swanky cell. One way or another, she wasn't getting out of Grierlings alive.

'We are better than this!' Niamh went on.

'This is the way it has always been.' There was a hint of sadness in Moira's voice.

'Then maybe it's time for a change,' Leonie put in.

Helena actually laughed. Hypocrites. How *moral* of them. What was it Snow called the mewling handwringers on Twitter? *Social justice warriors.* Make them fucking watch. Let their hearts bleed dry.

'Let's not prolong this sad day with debate,' Moira said. 'Helena Jane Vance. Do you have any final words?'

She would have loved nothing more than to perform her martyr's speech. She longed to tell them how history would prove her right, how *they* had betrayed the coven by allowing Theo to live. She only wished she would live to see them tremble as Leviathan manifests. But she did not say those things. She actually said, 'Please, show mercy. I have a teenage daughter. I want to see her become a woman.'

Why had she risked that? And under it all, this is why she was furious. She had, in a strange way, chosen Theo over her family. *What is wrong with me?*

'There will be no appeal,' Moira decreed. 'Guards . . .'

To the side of the room, one of the hooded witches – or warlock possibly – lifted a cover and pressed the red button concealed beneath. Another klaxon sounded.

With a mechanical creak, the thick thermal shield began to winch down over the inner pipe. It was made of brick; red on the outside, black on the inside. She was under no pretences. This wasn't to stop the spectators getting inadvertently burned, it was to spare them seeing what was about to happen.

They vanished from view as the shield clunked past her face. Helena closed her eyes and threaded her fingers around the chain link. She heard the furnace grumble to life in the guts of the prison below. With a thud, the shield hit the ground. Her eyes blinked uselessly in pitch darkness.

The next light she saw would be her last.

Chapter Sixty-Three

SOLSTICE

Niamh

Despite everything, Niamh felt a certain pride inside watching her young acolyte step up to the Great Sleeper, that big flat stone altar. Tonight Moira Roberts wore the scarlet cape and the coronet: a wreath of ivy leaves rendered in silver. 'Who here knocks upon the night?' she said theatrically.

'Holly Pearson.'

'Snow Vance-Morrill.'

'Theo Wells.'

Niamh's heart box was fit to burst.

Moira handed the goblet first to Holly, then Snow, and then Theo. There were only three witches ready to say the magic words this summer. Each took their sip from the cup, and mere seconds later, their eyes turned jet black. At her side, Leonie whispered in her ear. 'Can you remember how scared we were?'

'Like yesterday.' On her other side, Elle blubbed like she was at a wedding. 'Oh, reel it in, Waterworks.' Niamh handed her a fresh tissue.

'It's a big day!' Elle said, and it was, for Jez was there to hold her hand, looking very uncertain about the cape he'd had to borrow. *I look like Dracula*, he'd helpfully said. And anyway, he looked nothing like Dracula, Annie had met him once.

'Understand the oath is not one to be taken lightly,' Moira told the initiates, careful not to direct her words directly at Snow. Lilian and Geoff Vance had brought their granddaughter and Niamh honestly wasn't sure if she ought to say something or not. 'You are pledging your life to the sisterhood; to the coven of the world. Wherever you are, from this night forth, you are a witch first and foremost. This is your last chance to turn away from your birthright. Speak now, fledglings, yes or no?'

'I wish to take the oath,' Holly said.

'I wish to take the oath,' Snow said, her voice icy.

'I wish to take the oath,' Theo said finally.

'Very well,' Moira smiled. 'All together.'

To the mother I swear
To solemnly uphold the sacred sisterhood
Her power is mine to wield
The secret ours to keep
The earth ours to protect
The enemy of my sister is mine
The strength is divine
Our bond everlasting
Let no man tear us asunder
The coven is sovereign
Until my dying breath.

The kids then added a drop of their own blood to the goblet. 'Welcome, witches . . .' Moira said at last, a broad smile lighting up her face.

There was rapturous applause and Elle ran forward to hug Holly. 'Mum! SO embarrassing!'

'Jez! Jez! Take a picture!' Elle demanded.

Niamh more casually went to collect Theo and the two embraced. 'See, that wasn't so bad now was it?'

'My vision is weird,' Theo said, blinking her big black eyes.

'Your eyes will stay like that for an hour or so. Enjoy the night vision while you can.' Theo nodded bashfully as some elders came to wish her well. With Helena's swift trial and execution there had been serious talks about cancelling the solstice festivities this year, but HMRC were keen to have business as usual, and sweep the events of last month under the carpet.

Niamh wished it were so easily swept. Every time she thought of Helena, it truthfully felt like she was being stabbed in her gut. She'd never known guilt like it, not even after what she did to Ciara. Well, that wasn't quite accurate, but what HMRC had done to Helena reminded her, more than ever, that she was a witch. They didn't follow mundane laws because they were not mundanes. And that was scary.

'Glad you did it?' Niamh asked.

'Yes,' Theo said, clearly glad her moment in the spotlight was done. 'This is who I am.'

Niamh gave her another squeeze. 'Yes it is. You look stunning by the way.'

'Elle did my makeup.'

'She had a great canvas to paint.' There was a cheer in the meadow below as someone lit the bonfire and the drumming started. They had a long night ahead. 'Go on, then, this is your party . . .'

Holly grabbed Theo's hand and the two ran down the path towards the fire. Niamh scanned the clearing for Leonie and Chinara, failing to see Moira approach. 'Niamh, a word?'

'Of course,' Niamh said, when what she really meant to say was *get to fuck, you executed the last High Priestess.*

'I brought you a glass of mead. It's traditional.'

It was also rank, but Niamh accepted the glass out of politeness.

'Walk with me a while.' Niamh obliged and they strolled in the direction of the party. It was all shielded from mundane view, of course. 'Now, I'm well aware that some people think I'm really enjoying this fortuitous turn of events given my history with Helena . . .'

'Is that what they're saying?' It absolutely was. Everyone was.

The Cailleach said, 'Niamh, did you know Iain's been ill of late?'

Iain McCormack was Moira's husband. 'No, I didn't,' Niamh said. 'Is he OK?'

'He'll be fine. Well, we hope so, but contrary to popular opinion, I have no desire whatsoever to uproot us to Manchester. I'm very happy with my lot up in Fife to tell you the truth. With Iain on the mend . . . well, I want to spend more time with him, not less. I have no intention of running for High Priestess. And that's where you come in.'

'Me!' Niamh's cry woke the pigeons in the canopy above. 'I'm not even English!'

'Your grandmother was. It's fine, I checked.'

'It has been foreseen,' a new voice said, slithering out

of the shadows. Irina Konvalinka's pale face glowed out from under her cowl like a crescent moon.

'Foreseen by who?' Niamh said, suddenly feeling spannered after a single sip of mead.

'The future is in flux,' Irina said. 'An intriguing, if unsettling, era dawns.'

Niamh asked a question she'd been haunted by late at night. 'What of Leviathan?'

Irina looked to Moira, who said nothing. 'Leviathan will rise.'

Well that sealed the deal. 'In that case, you'll understand my misgivings about coming back to HMRC. Now, if you'll excuse me, I'll be dancing with my sisters.'

'We have seen you in the crown,' Irina said, halting her in her tracks.

Niamh ignored them both and stormed down the path. With the bonfire now well alight, the woods were well-lit enough for her to see where she was going. She was so intent on reaching her friends at the party that she failed to notice Snow as she emerged from the parallel footpath.

'Snow!' she said, 'I didn't see you there.'

Snow said nothing. She was thin before, but now she looked gaunt.

Niamh understood she would have to be the adult in this stalemate. Stupid adulthood. 'Snow, look—'

'No,' Snow said cutting her off. 'Don't say it. I don't want to hear anything you have to say.'

She hadn't expected it to be easy. 'You have to know that I didn't want things to end that way, I—'

'Save it. I'm not listening,' Snow said. 'I'm going back to Boscastle with Grandma and Granddad for the summer. Maybe longer. They can't handle all the nosy bitches asking questions about Mum.'

Niamh nodded. 'I can imagine . . .'

'Yeah, imagining it must be really tough,' Snow snapped before regaining her composure. 'You know what? Don't say anything else, because I'm getting stronger and stronger every day. Grandma thinks I could be Level 5 soon. And when I come back to Hebden Bridge, and I will, I'm going to fucking destroy you and that tranny freak down there.'

Snow looked her dead in the eye as she cut past Niamh to reach the party. Hatred, both ice cold and red hot burned behind her stare. Niamh said nothing. She took it, because – if the tables had been turned – she'd have felt the same.

And on the fateful day Snow Vance-Morrill returned to this town, Niamh would be ready for her.

Chapter Sixty-Four

A WITCH'S WORK

Leonie

He was supposed to be here. He'd told her he was going to be here. Warlocks actually induct their newbies at Samhain, not Litha, but Radley should be here tonight. But he wasn't. Why?

Some of the elder witches didn't get out much, so they were already getting their groove on around the fire. Dancing was as much a part of their culture as were spells or potions. To revel in the body, to move it with joyful abandon was spiritual. Ecstatic movement was trancelike, a pathway to a higher state of consciousness.

Raving is most witchy.

'What's up?' Chinara asked her, returning with two beers. You could keep mead.

'Where the fuck is Rad, seriously?'

'Maybe he didn't fancy it? He's not exactly a party person, is he?'

'He has to be here in an official capacity. Have you ever known my brother to skip his duties?'

She had not. 'Relax. Maybe he was here for the

441

ceremony and slipped away right after. He is dealing with the most spectacular fuck-up since Brexit.'

'Maybe . . .' Chinara looked so beautiful tonight, the flames dancing on her skin. She wore gold makeup on her eyes and cheekbones, and she shone like a bronze statue. Leonie was compelled to kiss her and did so.

'What was that for?'

'Thank you.'

'For what?'

'You always know what I need. How do you do that? You're not secretly an adept are you?'

Chinara smiled. 'Hardly.'

'I hope I can pay you back someday. I owe you so much.' It was true, Leonie was the metaphorical bull, and Chinara was the one who followed her around with a dustpan and brush.

'You owe me nothing. You give as much love as you take.'

'I promise I will always do that. Always.' They kissed again.

'I'm going to say something now,' Chinara said. 'And I want you to say nothing, but just place the words in your head to let them marinate. OK?'

Leonie frowned. 'Sure?'

'I think this would be a very lovely place to raise a child. All this space. All this sky, with all these stars. I don't know if I have many years of the city left in me.' Leonie was about to argue, but Chinara placed a finger on her lips. 'Marinate.'

Leonie de-escalated internally. She saw Nicholas Bibby, Radley's deputy getting some food from the barbecue stall. 'Oh, just wait here. I'll be right back, I promise.'

She left Chinara's side and made a beeline for Nicholas.

On the way, she sauntered past Jez Pearson, who looked entirely out of place, bobbing his head uncertainly to the beat of the drums. He nodded her way.

'Hiya, Jez mate!' Leonie swerved his way. 'Having fun?'

'Oh aye! Bit different isn't it?'

She leaned in very close. 'So now you know, right? Elle can heal people, me and Niamh can read minds, and so can Holly. How long do you think it's going to be before Holly finds out what you've been up to with her from that hotel, eh?'

Jez's face went a sickly, ashen shade of white.

The fake chumminess evaporated from her voice. 'End it, or tell her, Jeremy. You know what we are now. You don't wanna fuck with us.' She gave him a big kiss on the cheek as Elle appeared at their side.

'You all right?' she said cheerfully. 'What did I miss?'

Leonie gave her a dazzling smile. 'Nothing at all, babes. Just making sure Jez is having a nice time at his first ever solstice.'

He looked like he was going to vomit at any moment. 'Aye, it's grand.'

'I'm the luckiest witch in the whole world,' Elle said, kissing his hand. She beamed, so beautiful, so content. Leonie wasn't gonna be the bitch who shat on that.

'I'll be back in a sec,' Leonie said, desperate to nab Bibby. She lost him briefly in the crowd, but warlocks tend to stick together like tween boys at the school disco, and she found him with a trio of emerald capes. She scanned them to ensure none of them were her brother. 'Nicholas? Nick?'

He turned to face her. *If* Leonie was in any way attracted to men, Nicky might get a look in. Tall, angular, pleasingly nerdy. 'Leonie! How are you?'

'I'm good. Look, do you know where my brother is?'

He looked shifty for a moment before steering her away from his cabal colleagues. 'Officially, I know nothing at all.'

'Nick, I pray to Gaia you're never held for interrogation.'

He rolled his eyes. 'I swore I wouldn't say anything. I'm *meant* to say he's working on a research grant in Salem.'

'Is that where he is?'

'I honestly have no idea.'

Fuck this. She launched herself inside his head. '*Hale.*' Nick flinched, embarrassed at giving it up so quickly. 'He's gone looking for Hale?'

'I didn't say anything.'

Leonie gripped his arm. 'HMRC have a team of oracles and sentients searching for him. What is he doing?'

She already knew the answer. Her brother had worked so hard to reform the reputation of the cabal after Hale and now everything was in tatters. Nick sighed deeply. 'He thinks Hale is trying to recruit warlocks, reignite the troubles. He wants to stop him.'

'Be the hero . . .' Leonie finished for him, her thoughts drifting. 'If he finds Hale, he'll be killed.'

Nicholas Bibby said nothing. Nothing needed to be said. Her brother had embarked on a suicide mission. Leonie looked across the fire at Chinara, throwing her head back in laughter as she danced with Elle and Niamh.

Tears made her vision fuzzy. Life, babies and rural idylls would have to wait a minute more. She had to save her little brother.

Chapter Sixty-Five

SEPTEMBER

Niamh

Niamh accidentally overslept and woke to the sound of crockery being loaded into the dishwasher. She threw on a kimono over her nightie and hurried downstairs. She didn't want to miss Theo's first day. 'Gosh, look at you.'

Theo straightened up and Niamh admired her box fresh uniform. 'Do I look OK?'

'You look adorable, who doesn't love a kilt?' Niamh picked a stray hair off her jumper. 'Have you got your lunch and bus pass?'

'Yes and yes,' Theo sighed.

'What's up?' Niamh flicked the switch on the kettle and leaned over to get Tiger's bowl. The dog stirred, knowing it was breakfast time.

Theo shifted uncomfortably. She muttered, 'What if they know I'm not a normal girl?'

Niamh made a face. 'Who the fuck is *they*? And anyway, you're not a normal girl, you're an adept of Her Majesty's Royal Coven.' That didn't seem to offer much comfort. 'Hey now. There's no such thing as a *normal girl*. There's as many ways to be a girl as there are girls. How's that?'

Theo smiled. 'Better. Thanks.'

'Are you meeting Holly?'

'Yep, on the bus.'

'Grand.'

Perhaps Theo picked up on Niamh's nervousness because she said after a moment, 'Are you going to Manchester?'

'I am. Today's the day.' *Ciara.*

Theo gave her a brief hug. 'You'll be fine. It's the right thing to do.'

'I know. I'll be back here when you've finished. Go knock 'em dead. Not literally.'

'Got it!' Theo swung her rucksack onto her shoulder and left via the back door of the cottage.

Niamh heard her footsteps crunch down the lane and then heavier ones thud down the cottage stairs. Luke padded across the cold stone floor in bare feet, wearing only his Calvins. 'Do you think she knew I was here?' he said.

Niamh laughed ruefully. 'For so many reasons, yes, she did. But she's not a kid, and I'm not her mam.'

Luke slid his arms around her as she spooned the coffee into the cafetière. 'As good as.'

Niamh leaned back against his hairy chest and looked out of the kitchen window over the valley below. The leaves were just starting to yellow, matching the buttery sunshine. She inhaled deeply.

Her life was happening again, and it felt good to belong to the world.

Mildred, the kindly old witch who worked the day shift at the Manchester townhouse showed Niamh up to Ciara's room. 'Any change?' Niamh asked.

'Afraid not, Niamh, my love. Same as ever.' She stood aside to let Niamh enter, and she saw Ciara was in the same peaceful slumber as always. 'I'll leave you to it.'

'Thank you.'

It had been . . . two years since she'd been last. It was selfish but she just found it too sad. The room wasn't hospital-like in nature. It was decorated with draped wall hangings and lit with candles. There was nothing medically wrong with Ciara, it was simply that Niamh had severed her spirit from its vessel.

Her sister looked very small in the big bed. She lay flat on her back, hands folded across her torso. Her red hair spilled across the creamy pillow like some Renaissance painting. The room smelled thickly of *Virgo Vitalis*, a pungent restorative resin of frankincense and sage. The nightstand was dotted with an array of crystals, calibrated to foster good dreams.

Niamh always felt like she should wait for her sister's permission before entering. She reached out psychically, but there was only that cold blackness, like staring down a deep well. Instead, Niamh took her usual spot in the guest armchair to the left of the bed. This had been Annie's last request – that she make amends with Ciara. It was the least she could do to honour Annie's memory.

'Hello, Ciara,' she said. 'Sorry it's been a while.'

She scanned her for any sort of recognition. Nothing.

Niamh began. 'Sister, I am sorry. Truly. What I did to you was out of spite and vengeance. I wanted to hurt you the way you had hurt me. I . . . I know now that that never helps. It only makes you worse. All those years ago, you needed my help and I . . .'

Niamh . . .

It was so distant. The voice at the *bottom* of that same well.

'Ciara?' She'd been waiting for this for so long, it could well be a hallucination. Hope can do some funny turns on you.

Niamh . . .

'I'm here!' Niamh turned to the door and was about to call for Mildred when Ciara's pale hand flinched, just a fraction across the blankets.

She was reaching for her. 'I'm here,' Niamh said again and took Ciara's hand in hers.

Ciara was weak, desperately so, but Niamh felt her softly squeeze her hand. Only then she felt something small, sharp and hard press into her skin and—

Chapter Sixty-Six

Ciara

There was an intense, azure-white flash – lightning behind her eyes – and she was on her feet for the first time in almost a decade. Oh, it was strange, oddly sordid, like sitting on a warm toilet seat. Ciara flexed her sister's limbs, wiggled the fingers and toes, rolled her jaw.

'Oh that's so weird.' She tested Niamh's tongue. It felt swollen, sluggish. Everything felt ever-so-slightly off-kilter, like stepping into ill-fitting hand-me-downs.

And wasn't she just.

As she adjusted to the outrageous abundance of light in the room – it's fucking dark behind eyelids for ten years – she looked down at her old body. They'd let her hair grow too long. She looked a proper fucking hippie. Ciara wrenched her old hand open and retrieved the tiny ruby she'd been clinging to since the demon wearing Helena Vance's skin had placed it in her palm all those weeks ago.

Small gemstone, big power. As soon as it had touched her skin, Ciara knew exactly how it was all gonna play out. What a fucking twist. She loved it.

She stowed the ruby in Niamh's jacket pocket. She leaned down and whispered in her old left ear. 'Poor, sweet Niamh. Never saw that one coming, did you? Oh, girl, I know you can hear me because I heard you well enough. All those sorrys. I'll fuckin' give you *sorry*.'

Ciara found her old powers were still intact. She might even be more powerful in Niamh's body now that she thought about it. Her sister had always had that edge. Always. She scanned her body and, indeed, Niamh now resided in her old shell. A straight-up, *Freaky Friday*, Lindsay Lohan body swap.

She arched her back and stretched, fully rested and raring to go after her ten-year snooze. This skin felt good. She'd forgotten – honestly – what it felt like to not share your body with demons. Felt good. Felt *strong*.

But, alas, nothing could be left to chance. Her worn and torn cage of flesh and bone wouldn't hold a witch like Niamh for long. With them both around, nature would try to right itself. She always does.

And so Ciara slipped the pillow out from under her body and, checking no one was watching, placed it silently over her face. Definitely one for the therapist, she thought to herself. Freudian. Talk about death of ego.

Niamh didn't, couldn't, struggle. She pressed the pillow down harder.

'And *that's* what you get for always making me be Sporty Spice, you cunt,' Ciara said.

THE COVEN WILL RETURN IN
HMRC: THE SHADOW CABINET

ACKNOWLEDGMENTS

Truly, it takes a coven.

I'd like to thank my agents Sallyanne Sweeney, Marc Simonsson and Ivan Mulcahy for keeping my lights on for all these years. Sallyanne believed in *HMRC* even when I didn't. *We* did it. To Paradigm in the US – especially Alyssa Reuben and Katelyn Doherty – it means the world to finally have a home in the States. It was one of my last hurdles and I finally cleared it! I was entirely consumed by the world of this novel. I became the sixth member of the coven. I was possessed and often thought I'd gone insane. It meant the absolute world that two other women felt the same way. Natasha Bardon and Margaux Weisman – your enthusiasm meant the world. I feel wholly vindicated in my mania.

To everyone at Harper*Voyager* and Penguin Books, thank you so much. Every publicist, every intern, every marketing person, every editor (thanks Jack Renninson, Vicky Leech Mateos and Mayada Ibrahim) for working so tirelessly to make the book as good as it can be. Thank you especially Helen Gould for your insightful sensitivity reading. Thank you Holly Macdonald and Lisa Marie Pompilio for your cover design.

A name regular readers of mine will recognise is Samantha Powick, who always reads my novels before anyone else. When you were as excited as I was about *HMRC*, I knew I was on to something special. Thank you so much. Thank you to Darren Garrett, Kerry Turner and Max Gallant for letting me use them as a sounding board throughout, too. Thanks also to Samantha Shannon and James Smythe for their fantasy trilogy pep talks!

Finally, YOU, dear reader. *Coven* is derived from the Latin for *Convention* and that's what we are: a delegation of readers, fans, witches, women and queer people. If this book spoke to you like it did to me, you are my people, and I am yours.